Taming Him

USA TODAY BESTSELLING AUTHOR

KENNEDY FOX

Each book in the Bishop Brothers World can read as standalones but if you wish to read the others, here's our suggested reading order.

BISHOP BROTHERS SERIES
Original Bishop Family
Taming Him
Needing Him
Chasing Him
Keeping Him

SPIN-OFF'S
Friends of the Bishops
Make Me Stay
Roping the Cowboy

CIRCLE B RANCH SERIES
Bishop Family Second Generation
Hitching the Cowboy
Catching the Cowboy
Wrangling the Cowboy
Bossing the Cowboy
Kissing the Cowboy
Winning the Cowboy
Claiming the Cowboy
Tempting the Cowboy
Seducing the Cowboy

It's not a silly little moment
It's not the storm before the calm
This is the deep and dyin' breath of
This love we've been workin' on

"Slow Dancing in a Burning Room"
-John Mayer

PROLOGUE
RIVER

TWELVE YEARS AGO

ROUNDING the corner into the hospital room, I see Rylie lying in bed and immediately rush to her side. She's hooked up to machines and oxygen, and though it's common for her, it still feels like a stab to the gut when I see her like this.

"Riles," I whisper, holding her hand in mine and squeezing three times. "Can you hear me?"

With a nod, she squeezes my hand back three times. She slowly tilts her head down and tries to open her eyes. The medication makes her sleepy, and she can't always stay awake even when she tries.

"Love you, baby sis," I tell her like I always do. She'd normally reply with, "Love you too, big sis," and we'd both smile.

My father catches up to me and stands on the other side of her bed. "River," he says in a deep scolding tone. "What'd I say about running?"

"Well, had I known she was in here earlier, I wouldn't have ran to get up here as soon as I could," I tell him, returning the tone. My father had just picked me up from school and told me Rylie was back in the hospital.

"I already told you there was no need to take you out of school. She's just running a fever," he says so casually as if having a fever while being treated for cancer was no big deal.

Rolling my eyes, I hide my disapproval and focus on Rylie. "What's the doctor saying?" I read the monitors, too familiar with what the numbers represent.

"He's running more tests," my mother answers, walking into the room with a Styrofoam cup of coffee. She's wearing big sunglasses, most likely to hide the bags under her eyes. Mom stresses more than she sleeps, and Dad works nonstop. It's Mom, Rylie, and me most of the time, and even though I love my dad, I wish he was around more for our sakes during times like these.

Dad walks toward Mom and gives her a quick peck on the cheek before he starts digging around in his pockets for his keys. "I have to get back to the office; call me when there's news, okay?"

"You're leaving?" I glare.

"I left work early today, River. I have to finish some things up."

"But Rylie's sick." I say the obvious, furious that he'd leave us at a time like this.

"I know, sweetie." He steps toward me and presses a kiss to the top of my head as if I'm a baby, but I'm not. I don't need his coddling anymore. I'm a freshman in high school who's watched her nine-year-old sister battle leukemia for the past two years. "I'll work as fast as I can," he says before rushing out of the room.

I recognize the disappointment on my mother's face immediately. It's always the same thing. Rylie spends more time in the hospital than she does at home, and having him here would give us comfort, but he leaves that role to Mom instead. She always plasters on a fake smile and pretends to be strong for Rylie and me.

The doctor comes in not long after with Rylie's chart and tells us they'd like to keep her overnight for observation. She more than likely has an infection, which triggered the fever.

"Until we locate the source of infection, we'll keep her on oxygen and monitor her stats," he tells us. "The nurse will move her to another floor in a bit."

"Thanks, Dr. Potter," my mother murmurs.

The bare hospital walls, the cold air, the cream-colored floors—they're all I've seen the last three years. Rylie got sick over two years ago, and we were in the ER at least once a week until she was officially diagnosed and they started chemo treatment.

"I'm going to call your dad," she tells me before standing up and leaving. I can see the distress and exhaustion all over her features. Mom quit her job and has been Rylie's caretaker since the beginning. She and Dad never go out anymore—at least not with each other—and if they aren't fighting about bills, they're fighting about his long hours at the office. I've overheard some of their conversations and sometimes wonder if Dad wishes he could leave us and find another family. Mom's accused him of cheating, and though he never denies it, he just tells her she's crazy.

The tension is thick when things are rough like this. Before Rylie's diagnosis, they both worked full-time but always made sure to be home in time for dinner so we could eat as a family. We'd talk to Mom about our day, and Dad would ask about homework. It was predictable, but it was nice.

How easy it is to take life for granted until it throws a curve ball and changes the entire course of it.

I hate seeing Rylie like this. She doesn't deserve this, and I'm often angry that she's the one having to go through it and not me. I'd take her place in a heartbeat. She was only seven, and though she annoyed me on a daily basis, I loved her so much. Mom used to tell me stories of how I'd beg them for a baby sister, and when they got pregnant, I was so excited. Growing up together wasn't always rainbows and sunshine, but I knew I was lucky to have her in my life.

I press the back of my hand to her cheek and feel how cold it is, even with a low-grade fever. These hospitals are always cold, and I hate it. Doing what I always do when Mom isn't around, I crawl onto the bed next to her. I'm always careful of her lines, but then, at least, I can give her some of my body heat and comfort her.

"Let me know if I'm hurting you, okay, Riles?" Even though my voice is just above a whisper, when she squeezes my hand back again, I know she heard me.

I rest my chin on top of her head and hold her close to me before closing my eyes and sending another prayer up. "Love you, baby sis."

A nurse comes in an hour later to move her to another floor.

Once she's settled, Mom tells me Dad is coming to pick me up soon.

"Why can't I stay here?"

"You need to eat some dinner and finish your homework," she says with little emotion.

"'I'm not leaving!" I shout. "I'm staying with Rylie."

Dad arrives twenty minutes later, ordering me to come home with him for the night.

"I'll bring you back tomorrow. Let's go. *Now.*"

I kiss Rylie's cheek and squeeze her hand three times. When she squeezes mine back, I smile and promise her I'll be back as soon as I can. When Rylie is kept overnight, Mom always stays, but Dad never does.

The next morning, I call Mom before school, and she says she doesn't have any updates yet. I make her promise to call the school if anything changes so I can know right away, and even though she agrees, something in my gut tells me otherwise.

After not hearing any word from Mom all day, Dad picks me up and drives us straight to the hospital. He's eerily quiet during the ride over. That could mean anything since he's not much of a talker anyway, but something isn't settling right in the air.

"What is it, Dad?" I finally ask as he searches for a parking spot in the hospital garage.

"Nothing, River."

I narrow my eyes at him, wondering why he's lying. As soon as he parks, I jump out of the car and run the entire way up to Rylie's room. Doctors and nurses swarm in and out, all holding charts and double checking her monitors.

"Mom, what's wrong?" I pant, catching my breath.

She's wearing her sunglasses again, but I know she's choking up before she even speaks. "She's septic." Her words barely leave her mouth before one of the monitor alarms starts going off. It's her heart monitor. The doctors have talked about sepsis previously during other visits, so I know it's a life-threatening complication of an infection.

"She's flatlining!" a nurse calls out, and they all rush around.

I've never felt this kind of panic in my life, and I've had many reasons to up to this point but watching her heartbeat flatline on the monitor has me gasping for air. I can't seem to catch my breath between the tears and screaming.

Dad's arms wrap around me from behind, holding me tight to his body as I scream for Rylie. Hysterically, I watch as they use the defibrillator and shock her chest.

I still remember the way her hair smelled. She was obsessed with everything pink and strawberries, so anytime I smell something fruity, I immediately think of her.

Watching Rylie battle for her life was painful. During her good days, she'd smile up at me, and I swear she was stronger than me through it all. She always made sure I was okay, which was crazy because I wouldn't be okay until she was cured. Even then, I'd always fear the worst anytime she'd get a fever or a cold.

Memories flash through my mind of everything we went through for all those years, and when it was time to choose my career, I knew without a doubt what I wanted to study. Hell, I'd been experiencing it for years. The rest was just textbook stuff that I knew I could learn, but being at someone's side while they were in their most delicate state was something I knew I could and wanted to do.

I went to nursing school, more determined than ever to soak up any and all information. Mom and Dad fought and grew apart and eventually divorced. Our family was broken, but I wouldn't let it take me down. Even when I failed to stay strong, thoughts of Rylie always kept me focused. What she endured proved she was always the strongest of us all.

PART I

CHAPTER ONE

ALEX

I WATCH the early morning fog roll over the hills as I walk across the pasture toward the barn. There's something about waking up before the roosters crow or the sun rises that gets me going. Maybe it's because ranch life is ingrained in me, but I wouldn't have it any other way.

"What the hell?" Dylan shouts, carrying grain in buckets for the horses. I glance down at his boots and can't help but laugh as he stands smack dab in the middle of a steaming pile of fresh shit. He groans as he slides his boot across the wet, dew-soaked grass, but there's not much hope for his boot.

Dylan's mom and mine have been best friends since they were both kids, so we met when we were in diapers and have been inseparable ever since. Every summer since high school, he's worked for my father until it became a full-time gig. He's become my partner and sidekick around the ranch, though he's definitely not the greatest influence. He's always up for anything regardless of the consequences, which has gotten us into plenty of trouble over the years.

"You should be happy you didn't trip and fall face first in it," I tell him, chuckling. "It makes for a pretty shitty day."

"Sounds like you've fallen a time or two." He snorts, knowing damn well I have. Dylan struggles with smearing the crap off the sides of his boots because his hands are full.

"One time, after tripping and being covered in cow shit, Jackson refused to let me go change. Basically, had to stay like that for the entire day. Eventually, it dried, but I swore I could taste it in my mouth for days."

"Jackson can be such an asshole," Dylan says with a laugh.

"It must be a Bishop thing." I chuckle.

Once we're inside the barn, we dump the feed into tubs for the horses in each stall, then head down to feed the pigs, chickens, and cows. By the time we finish, the sun is barely peeking over the horizon, and I know we need to get a move on if we're going to finish our tasks on time. Though feeding the animals happens every day, what we do afterward that changes on a weekly basis and is usually discussed over breakfast with my father every Sunday morning.

Dylan and I make our way to the east side of the land where we'll be replacing fences along the property line. It's physically laboring work, but I don't complain. I enjoy the hard tasks even when it feels like it's going to kill me. I was born and bred to be a Bishop, and I've been helping my parents around the ranch since I could walk. One day it'll be my and my three brothers' responsibility to manage, but for now, we all have our own tasks to focus on to keep everything running smoothly.

We drive down the old county road along the pasture, and from a distance I can already see a group of workers pulling metal pipes from the back of a lowboy and laying them on the ground. As soon as we park and walk up, I can tell Evan, my oldest brother, is in an agitated mood just by the attitude and stink face he's wearing. His hair is a blond mess as pieces stick to his forehead and cheeks from the sweat.

Evan spends most of his time working at the hospital, but on his days off, Dad drags him out to help on the ranch. *You're still a Bishop*, Dad likes to remind him, so Evan puts in his time when he can. He's nothing more than a pain in my ass anytime he's around. He's years older than me, so we didn't grow up together and bond like my older brothers did, but I still enjoy giving him hell when he serves it to me.

"Who smells like shit?" Evan asks over his shoulder as he carries the post hole digger across the way so we can get started.

Dylan glares at me. "Do you think he can really smell it?"

Bursting out into hearty laughter, I shake my head at him and throw him his work gloves. "I have ever since you stepped in it."

I stand by and watch Evan crank the driver. When he rams it into the ground, Dylan and I begin mixing cement. After each hole is dug, we slam the six-foot pipes in the ground and make sure they're level before adding cement to set them in place.

"So I got some good news," Dylan tells me as he fills the hole with the rock mix.

"Yeah? Mallory wants you back?" I like to give him shit about his ex every chance I get because I warned him about her. Several times, in fact.

"Hell no. I wouldn't take her back again."

I glare at him in denial and snort. "That's what you said last time," I remind him.

"Shut up," he fires back. "Honestly, after I found out how many times she cheated on me, I wouldn't even fuck her with *your* dick," Dylan states, laughing in disgust.

"Fuck you. My dick takes offense to that. I don't make village bicycles a habit," I say matter-of-factly, slamming a pipe into the ground.

"That's 'cause you *are* the village bicycle." He chuckles at my expense, and I groan. He's damn lucky my hands aren't free at the moment to slap that shit-eating grin off his face. He clears his throat and tips his chin up. "Everyone with a tight pussy and big rack step right up!" he hollers, raising his arms up for emphasis. "Come and get a ride on the Wild Stallion, Alex Bishop! Six-foot something, dirty blond hair, and a smart mouth to boot! He may be a cocky son of a bitch, but don't worry, his mama taught him right. He'll wine and dine you before fucking you till you forget your own name! Now ladies, who's first?"

I snort at his pathetic performance, shaking my head but not entirely disagreeing with his words. "Yeah, well, everyone knows a stallion can't be tamed." I smirk, lifting my cowboy hat and repositioning it on my head while Dylan rolls his eyes.

We get back to work, and that's when I remember his announcement earlier.

"So, asshole, what's your news?" I ask as we continue to work.

"Oh so, remember that big giveaway contest at the fall carnival last month?" he asks with a knowing grin on his face.

Narrowing my eyes, I think back on it. "Yeah, the romantic Key West getaway?"

Dylan continues to nod. "That's the one! Guess which lucky bastard won?" He gloats.

"Don't tell me that bastard is you?" I mock.

"Fuck yeah, it is! Two weeks all expenses paid! As long as the boss lets me take off, I'll be packing my bags to set out into the sunset with all the beer I can drink."

"That sounds like the most pathetic country song I've ever heard."

"Sorry I don't have a line of women waiting to jump my saddle, so I'd rather go alone than miss out on a free vacation."

"Ya sure you don't want to call Mallory?" I tease him again.

Dylan drops his shovel, and as soon I glance over at him and realize he's charging at me, I start running in the opposite direction. He has the same look on his face like the time he tried to kick my ass in seventh grade when he caught me kissing his longtime crush, Summer Sanders. *What can I say?* She came onto me first.

Luckily, the only thing he has on me is speed. As he tackles me to the ground, I'm quick to put him in a headlock before he can throw the first punch. Struggling to get out of my grip, we both freeze when the motor of the pole digger stops. Seconds later, Evan pulls me up by my collar and glares at me.

"Dylan might not be able to take you in a fight, but if you don't get to work, I'm going to kick your ass from here to San Antonio and back," Evan threatens before I push him out of my way. Considering we live in Eldorado, that's a three-hour ass kickin', and I don't fuckin' think so.

"Just because I'm your little brother doesn't mean you're my boss. So, pull out the stick that's wedged in your ass and worry about yourself," I snap at him, walking back over to the metal pipes and cement mix.

Looking over my shoulder, I see Dylan is curled over laughing his ass off.

"Shut up, asshole!" I yell back at him.

He quickly runs and catches up with me. "You started it by bringing up Mallory." He slams his shoulder into mine.

I smile, not denying it. I live to give him shit about her. Mallory's the epitome of a snobby, rich girl who thinks she's a Southern belle who's above being nice to anyone who works for a living. Yeah, I didn't exactly like her, so I bust his balls about her every chance I can. Getting tackled and caught by Evan? Totally worth it.

"Well, you know how cranky Evan can get sometimes. He's probably gonna tell Dad we were fucking around again. Asshole," I say. "Maybe if he got laid every once in a while, he wouldn't be such a prick," I mutter under my breath, shaking my head.

"Mr. Bishop doesn't care as long as we get our work done. You know that," Dylan reminds me, and although he's right, Dad won't think twice about putting me in my place if he thinks I'm not doing my fair share around here.

"So anyway, before I was rudely interrupted." Dylan snickers, glancing back at Evan as we pick up another bundle of pipes. We carry them across the way before dropping them on the ground, causing a loud clang.

"Since the trip is for two, I thought you could come with me," he says, shaking out his arms from carrying the heavy iron.

"Wait, hold up," I say, stopping him from continuing and

furrowing my brows. "You want me to go on a romantic two-week getaway with *you*?" I ask, glancing over at Evan who's painfully holding back a smirk. I narrow my eyes at him, then turn my attention back to Dylan.

"Well, it won't be a damn date, cowboy hotshot, because honestly, you ain't my type. However, considering the trip is free and bound to be crowded with single girls, I thought we could go together. Plus, I ain't got nobody else to take, so if anything, come be my wingman. Help me find a woman." The corner of his lips curls up, and I know exactly what he's thinking. "*Partaaaay,*" Dylan adds, confirming my thoughts as he waves his cowboy hat above his head and dances in place.

Shaking my head, I laugh at his antics, but before I can give him my answer, Evan clears his throat.

"You two ain't going nowhere till this fence is built. I can promise you that," he snaps, adding himself to our conversation.

"Worry about yourself. Dig your holes and mind your business," I snap. "Shouldn't you be at the hospital saving some lives or somethin'? You're slowin' us down anyway."

Evan huffs, knowing he hates when I bring up his job at the hospital. It's a reputable career, and I know he's worked hard to become a doctor, but he's the first male Bishop in decades to pursue something outside of the ranch life. I wouldn't be doing my Bishop duties if I didn't feed him shit about it every chance I got.

"Keep runnin' your mouth, I'm going to be takin' a life today." He directs his eyes toward Dylan. "Maybe two."

The rest of the afternoon passes by quickly. As I drive us back to the main house, my shoulders tighten from driving poles into the ground and dumping cement nonstop for hours. Dylan and I are exhausted, but we'll be working on that damn fence for the rest of the week. Quite honestly, I'm still salty that I have to work on it in the first place, and it's all because of Jackson.

A few months ago, he threw a huge party, which quickly got out of hand when he started driving around in his Jeep. He'd been drinking and being more of a dumbass than usual when he decided to go off-roading and lost control, slamming straight into the barbwire fence. The next day, we spent the whole damn morning rounding up the cattle that escaped. Jackson was the only one amused by the whole situation, said it was the best one-eighty turn he'd ever done in his mud-covered Jeep.

Dumbass. Although according to Mama's gossip, he got plastered because of a girl. I highly doubted it because Jackson Bishop didn't do serious relationships—or relationships at all—but then she mentioned Kiera's name. It all made sense once I heard that, and I forgave him just a little.

Kiera Young and Jackson have known each other since they were babies. Her parents and ours were friends, and we've spent a lot of time on their ranch just as much as she has on ours. She was like an older, annoying sister to me, but not to Jackson. He's always had a thing for her but never grew the balls to admit it or even tell her. We all know she feels the same, but she continues to date other guys, pissing Jackson off and causing him to drink and act a damn fool. They're both too stubborn and continue this vicious cycle of denying their feelings.

After months of planning, Dad decided to replace the barbwire fence along the county road. If someone crashed into it again, only their vehicle would get damaged, and we wouldn't risk losing our cattle again.

Dylan's excitement brings me back to our conversation. "I've never been to Key West before, so as soon as I won, I did some browsing online. If it's half as fun as it looks, I might never come back! The nightlife, the beaches, the views," he rambles on. "You're gonna thank me that I dragged your ass along." Dylan beams as we head back to the main house.

"I haven't agreed to go yet," I remind him. "Depends if we can get off work or not. Might need to smooth talk Dad a little first," I say, knowing that if we don't get ahead of schedule, we'll never get approval to both take off for two weeks. "Or maybe a lot. Duties have to be done rain or shine, and if I'm not there, that means someone else has to do it."

"I'm gonna go buy him a bottle of Crown Royal Reserve." Dylan chuckles.

"To butter him up or get him wasted?" I laugh.

"Both," Dylan tells me.

I park the truck in the driveway and see Mama unloading groceries from the back of her car. Dylan and I rush out to help her.

"Mama, you shoulda called me," I scold. "I would've come sooner." I reach into the trunk, trying to grab as many bags as possible. Dylan stands next to me, doing the same, so we don't have to make a second trip.

"I knew you were busy. It's no big deal," she says sweetly, walking ahead of us to hold the front door open.

As soon as I enter, I see Jackson sleeping on the couch with his boots on, snoring loudly. After I set the bags down on the kitchen table, I walk quietly into the living room, and Dylan follows behind silently.

I get real close to his face, watching his chest rise and fall and wait for just the right moment before yelling, "FIRE!"

His body jolts up, his feet kicking in the air. With beet red cheeks, his eyes gaze over the living room. "What the fuck, Alex?" he barks, scrubbing his hands over his face.

In no time, Mama comes storming from the kitchen with a wooden spoon in one hand and glares down at Jackson.

"I've got a bar of soap with your name on it if you keep using that language in my house, young man," she scolds, fearlessly.

I cross my arms over my chest and smirk.

"Mama," he begins, but she's quick to shut him up.

"Hush. Get your boots off the furniture, too." She walks away before Jackson can argue some more.

"Wakey, wakey, asshole," I whisper, just loud enough for him to hear.

As soon as Mama is out of sight, he brushes his fingers through his hair, trying to process what just happened. "You bastard," he mutters to me. "You nearly made me shit myself."

I scoff. "Good. That's payback for me having to work on replacing that damn fence today. You should be out there fixing your own damn mess," I tell him.

"Oh sure, then you can be the one to train the horses and do all the guided tours for the guests at the B&B."

I grimace at the mention of the Circle B Bed and Breakfast that he helps manage on the ranch.

"That's what I thought," Jackson mocks. "Be glad you were building fences, little brother." He says the words with venom laced in his tone. I know Jackson loves working on the ranch, but there's working with horses, and then there's working with people. In Jackson's case, he's better off working with the horses.

As soon as he stands up from the couch, Evan comes bursting through the front door with a scowl on his face. "I owe you," Evan hisses with a finger pointed directly in Jackson's face. "Do you have any idea how much work replacing that damn fence is?"

I clear my throat, satisfied to see Jackson getting what he deserves. I glare at him, but all he does is smirk.

"Both of you need to chill out," Jackson says with a laugh, not taking either of us seriously.

"Boys!" Mama yells from the kitchen, breaking the tension in the room. It's like she has a sixth sense about us and tends to break up fights before they can truly begin.

Evan rolls his eyes before walking toward the kitchen. Dylan and I follow closely behind him, leaving Jackson in the living room, unharmed—*this time*.

As soon as we round the corner, I see Mama throwing the breaded chicken into a pan, then placing homemade cornbread into the oven. Before speaking, she rinses her hands, dries them off, and then wipes her blonde hair from her eyes with the back of her hand.

Looking directly at us, she puts both hands on her hips as she always does when giving an order. "Now listen, I don't want to hear no bickering tonight, ya hear?"

"But—" Evan tries to interrupt.

"No!" She's quick to cut him off. "I don't want to hear it. Your father will be home any minute, and I want us to have a nice dinner together," she states sternly, then turns back around to give the chicken in the hot sizzling pan her attention.

Quietly, the three of us help unpack the grocery bags. We set everything on the table before Mama directs us where to stock it all. After growing up in this house, I know where most things belong, but she has a "system" that she makes us abide by.

Just as she's mixing the homemade mashed potatoes, John—Jackson's twin—and Dad walk through the back door. I hear the clomping of his boots against the wood floor before I see him. Once they're in the kitchen and see us all, he places his hat on the table before glancing over at Evan. "Y'all finish placing the poles?"

"All are set with cement. Just need to paint tomorrow," Evan tells him.

"Good," Dad says, walking to the fridge and filling a cup with ice and water.

As Mama tells us to set the table, Dylan tells everyone bye.

"You sure you don't want to stay? I got plenty for you too," Mama tells him.

"I'd better get home. If I miss dinner again this week, my mother may disown me," Dylan explains, shrugging.

"Yeah, we know how mamas can be." I look over at Mom with an overly sweet smile on my face.

"Yeah, you'd better get going then." Mama gives him a side

hug, and he leaves.

Mama finishes up dinner while John and I set the table. We carry in the dishes of chicken, potatoes, and cornbread and set them on the long wood dining table that's a family keepsake.

Once everything is ready, we all take our seats and sit around the table like a big, happy family. Dad says grace as per tradition, then Mama plates his food. Once everyone has what they need, John makes small talk about the B&B and how booked it is for the next eight weeks. Dad then informs us about the hay bales that need to be picked up from the fields on the east side of the property and stored in the barn. This is how most dinner conversations go when I stay. The Bishops are workaholics and talk shop all day and night.

I'm nervous about asking Dad for time off, but I know that if I'm going on that trip in a couple weeks, I need to tell him in advance. That's the only bad thing about working for your parents. They aren't afraid to say no.

"Dad," I mumble over all the voices. As the table quiets, I continue. "You think it'd be possible for me to take a few of my vacation days soon?" I ask. It's so still in the room, all I can hear is Jackson's loud ass chewing.

"Hmm," he says, barely looking up at me. "When're ya thinkin'?"

I glance at Mama for a moment, wondering if she'll back me up or not. "About two weeks from now."

He nods as he continues shoveling food onto his fork. "For how long?"

I clear my throat, swallowing hard. "Um, well. I'd need two weeks."

"For what?" John asks, but his question gets ignored.

Dad shakes his head without even taking a second to think it over. "You know we still have things to do before the holidays and—"

"Scott," Mama interrupts Dad by using his first name, which always means business. "I think it would be perfectly fine for you to take off, son." My brows shoot up into my hairline, shocked at her words. "Alex works hard and deserves a break. Besides, Jackson can rearrange his schedule so he and Dylan can take care of your daily chores till you get back."

"Seriously?" Jackson groans, glaring at me.

"Well, actually…" I swallow hard before continuing. "Dylan needs off, too. There's a trip we'd like to go on."

"Absolutely not," Dad snaps, taking a sip of sweet tea. "That's far too much to rearrange. I can't have two men out at the same time." His words are final, and I know there's no point in arguing.

Mama clears her throat, an obvious signal for Dad. He looks over at her, and they hold a silent conversation as Mama purses her lips and raises an eyebrow. When she gets that look on her face, we all know it's her way or the highway, even when it comes to Dad.

He clears his throat before taking another sip of his drink. "We'll handle it," he finally mumbles, but I can tell he isn't happy about it.

Jackson mouths a, "You suck," to me when I look at him, and all I can do is smile because I'm going to Key-motherfucking-West for two weeks, and there's nothing that asshole can do about it.

Can't remember the last time I even had a vacation, and at this moment, I make a vow to myself that this trip will be one to remember.

After we help Mama clean up the table, I pull out my phone and see Dylan's already sent me a text.

Dylan: Well? Any news yet?

Alex: Hope you're ready to be my ride-or-die!

Dylan: Seriously?! We can go?

Alex: Yep! Pack your bags because we're about to give Key West some Southern cowboy hell!

CHAPTER TWO

RIVER

"River!" My name is called as I rush down the hallway toward the blaring sound of the beeping alarm. As I round the corner, I realize it's coming from room 448. McKenna Black's room. Mrs. Black is screaming my name, urging me to hurry. My aide, Jenny, is already inside the room waiting for me.

I memorize all my patient' files word for word. I know their personal information and their medical history. It's part of my job at Milwaukee Children's Hospital where I treat sick kids in the PICU—pediatric intensive care unit. No matter how long they've been here or how short their stay is, my photographic memory allows me to remember every detail of their conditions and treatment plans.

"What's her O2 level?" I ask Jenny as I silence the alarm. She rambles off the baby girl's stats, and I immediately unwrap my stethoscope from my neck so I can listen to her heart.

"She's seizing," I say aloud before rolling her little body to the side. McKenna is only five weeks old and in a fragile state after being diagnosed with bacterial meningitis. She's been here for a week and is on a twenty-eight-day antibiotic treatment, but side effects like this from the medication or illness are common with these types of infectious diseases.

"*What*? She's seizing?" Mrs. Black cries from the end of the metal crib.

"Call Dr. Weasley," I order Jenny. "She's going to need anti-seizure medicine before it happens again."

"River, what's going on?" Mrs. Black cries out again, her voice filled with panic.

Before I can explain, Jenny speaks up. "Dr. Weasley isn't here."

I wave my hand in the air. "Whoever's on call then. She needs something before it gets worse."

"Worse? Why? What's wrong?" Mrs. Black is frantic, concern evident in her voice. She's in constant fear of her daughter's life, and it breaks my heart. It's something I see here every day.

I watch as her stats start to level out and breathe out a sigh of relief.

"She's okay, Mrs. Black," I face her and say softly. I try to get to know my patient's family as best as I can because it helps put their minds at ease and builds trust as we give the best treatment possible. I know all too well what it feels like to be in their place and feel alone. "It was a tonic seizure. I'm going to have the doctor prescribe some medication to prevent it from happening again."

"Wh-what's that?"

"It's where her body stiffens and muscles spasm. It's most likely caused by the infection, and although not uncommon, we want to control it and make sure it doesn't happen again. Otherwise, it could make things worse."

"Worse?" She gasps. Shit, I should've left out that part. I always try to be honest and up-front with the family, but I know sometimes I have to leave out things that will only cause more concern.

"The infection that's in the spinal fluid leading to her brain can cause seizures depending where the infection is, but the seizure subsided, and her stats are already normalizing, but the meds will help stop it from happening again. Okay?" I place a hand on her shaky fingers that are gripping the crib rail.

She nods, keeping her eyes locked on McKenna. Her tiny little body is covered in PICC lines, an oxygen line, a feeding tube, and artery lines in both of her cute, chubby thighs. Her face is swollen from the fluids, and her tiny arms are in casts so the lines stay in.

It's a sight no parent should ever have to see, but in the PICU, it's an everyday occurrence.

Hours later after McKenna gets her medication, I finally take my break. I work twelve-hour shifts on rotation and have been on my feet for ten hours straight. As I'm sitting in the cafeteria about to stuff my face, Natalie plops down across from me.

"You look like hell." She bites into a carrot stick, and it makes a loud cracking noise.

"Should've seen me before I fixed my hair and makeup." I reach for my coffee and take a long sip. "I can't feel my feet, and I'm pretty sure my ankles have swelled to twice their normal size."

"Isn't your shift almost over?" She looks down at the time on her phone. "You're taking a late break."

I nod, agreeing. "Had to wait for the on-call doctor to prescribe some medication for my patient and then once I administered it, I wanted to wait to make sure she was stable. Her mom was upset, and I didn't feel right leaving."

"You know your aide could've stayed with the patient's mom so you could leave for twenty minutes," she reminds me. Natalie works in radiology and is constantly telling me to take care of myself, or I'll burn out, but I can't help it. I love my job and my patients.

"I'm fine, *Mom*," I tease.

"You need a vacation," she says matter-of-factly. "Get some sun on your pasty ass."

I snort. "Sure. Vacation for one!" I roll my eyes. "And your ass is probably as pasty as mine."

"I sunbathed nude on the rooftop all summer, so joke's on you." She smirks.

"Thanks for that." I wrinkle my nose. "Didn't need that visual."

She rolls her eyes, and I laugh.

"But seriously. You could use a vacation. Or a distraction. Find a hot guy and bang his brains out." She waggles her brows with a sultry smirk.

Still chewing my food, I burst out laughing and shake my head at her. "Banging random men isn't going to change the fact I gave the last six months of my life to a man who 'forgot' to tell me he was married." I suck in a deep breath and exhale the anger that's been weighing on my chest for the past three weeks since finding his wedding ring hiding deep in his dress pants pocket.

"Oh, screw—what's his face anyway…" She scrunches up her face in disgust. She never liked him much anyway based on the few times they met. "*Asshole.*"

"Andrew," I fill in for her, feeling bile rise in my throat at saying his name aloud.

"Andrew. Asshole. Same thing, really." She curls the corner of her lip. "Screw him. Go on a single's cruise and find yourself some hot man meat!" The tone of her voice is serious, which terrifies me. Once Natalie gets an idea in her head, she pushes it until I cave in. We've been friends since elementary school and attended the same college, so we know everything about each other. The good, bad, and ugly.

"Hot man meat?" I arch a brow. "We graduated from middle school over a decade ago," I inform her with a teasing grin. "The only hot meat I want near me is a big fat turkey." I smile, getting excited about spending Thanksgiving with my family next month up in Eagle River where I'm originally from. I moved down here for college, and once I got hired at the hospital, I made it my permanent residence.

"Okay, so no singles cruise." She frowns.

I give her an eye roll, then reach for my purse. I dig around inside until I find my prescription bottle. Once I open it and grab a pill, I toss it down my throat and swallow it with a big gulp of water.

"What's that?" she asks, tilting her head to read the bottle as she takes another bite of her carrot stick.

"It's my STD medication. A parting gift from Andrew," I deadpan. She starts choking on her carrot, and I nearly die of laughter.

"River! That isn't funny." She smacks her chest as tears form in the corner of my eyes.

"Oh my God. The look on your face was priceless," I say, wiping tears from my cheeks.

"You're seriously a bitch. You deserve an STD after that." She scowls.

Once I've controlled my laughter, I shove the bottle back in my purse. "Don't be so dramatic. My doctor prescribed it for my sinus infection; thankfully, it's almost gone now."

"Oh my God!" She slams her palm down on the table, the loud bang echoing through space. I jump at her unnecessary spasm.

"Jesus, Natalie," I scold. "Nearly made me pee myself."

She points a finger in my face. "You deserved it." She smirks. "Anyway. I just got the best idea. Adam and I are going to Key West soon for two weeks. You should totally come!"

I furrow my brows at her like she's crazy. "I'm not going on a couples' vacation with you and your boyfriend, Nat. That'd be weird."

"No way. We'd have a blast," she insists.

"I'd be the third wheel," I correct.

"Hardly. Adam plans to go fishing like every morning. You can keep me company on the beach drinking margaritas and checking out the local eye candy. Then when he's back, the three of us can find fun stuff to do like snorkeling or sailing."

"That sounds fun, it really does, but I can't just tag along on your couples' trip. I'd feel like such a burden."

"Girl, stop it. Adam and I are basically an old married couple. Truth be told, I'd have more fun with you hanging around anyway. Once Adam starts talking about fish and worms, and God knows what else, I start to fall asleep."

"Oh, so now you want me to be your buffer. This is sounding better and better," I muse.

"What's it matter?" She grins. "Just come and enjoy the sun and the beach and the water and forget about the STD married asshole man."

"For the record, I don't have an STD, Natalie!" I whisper-shout.

She waves me off as if it's irrelevant.

"Just think about it, okay? You can book a separate room at the same resort. We can head down to the pool and have breakfast together and read books by the beach, and then when you get yourself drunk enough and find a hot, *single* man, you'll have a room all to yourself for slutty banging time."

I groan at her words but laugh at the eagerness in her tone. She's nearly begging at this point.

"I don't know. Two weeks? I doubt I'll be able to get off work in such a short amount of time." I pick at the remaining food on my tray, thinking it over.

"You work nonstop, River. You deserve a vacation." She stands up and grabs her baggie of carrot sticks. "Just think about it." She winks before walking away.

As I finish the rest of my shift, the thought of spending two weeks on the beach and how nice it'd be to get away for a bit invades my mind. Once I finish charting and clock out, I walk to the bus stop near the hospital and wait.

Digging my cell out of my purse, I turn it on and see I have a few new voice messages. As soon as I hear Andrew's voice, my body tenses.

Hey, baby. I miss you. I know you hate me right now, but I promise I can explain—

I delete the message before he can continue his lies. I click on the next one.

I can't stop thinking about you, River. Please come back to me. I'll—

Delete.

Any guesses who voicemail number three is from? *Asshole.*

Shoving my cell back into my purse, I stand as the bus comes into view from down the road. Within moments, another bus passes and drives through a puddle only to splash muddy water on my shoes and uniform. The gentleman standing next to me steps to the side, glaring at me as he takes in what a mess I am.

Oh my God!

I'm completely drenched, except my hair. Not that it matters because it looks like a bird set up home there anyway. It's early October in southern Wisconsin, which means the temps have dropped into the forties and fifties. Stupidly, I wasn't wearing my winter jacket, and now I'll sit on the bus freezing my ass off.

Once I'm home, I strip off everything before I enter the kitchen. The ride across town was complete hell, and I'm cold to the bone. My shoes, scrubs, and bra find their way to the floor. My roommate is a girl I went to college with years ago, but she's never home. Sasha spends most nights at her boyfriend's place, which makes being her roommate easy. As long as she pays her half of the rent, I don't care if she's home or not. The only complaint I have is how she leaves her cat, and I'm constantly feeding and watering him since she seems to forget that responsibility.

"Hey, Leo," I coo as he jumps on my bed, begging for some kind of attention. I pet him briefly before grabbing my towels and heading to the bathroom for a shower.

The hot water feels amazing and soothes my tense muscles. My legs and feet are sore from walking so much today, and I can't wait to climb into bed with my Kindle. But as soon as I turn off the water and wrap a towel around my body, I hear noises coming from the hallway.

First, pictures are falling off the wall. Next, I hear giggling. Then more smacking against the wall.

What the fuck?

Tightening the grip on my towel, I open the door and peek out. Long brown hair falls loosely down Sasha's back, and her legs are wrapped around a man's waist as she dry humps him against the wall.

Blinking, I'm shocked to see her home at this hour on a Tuesday night, considering I know she works early in the morning. But then I look over at the guy she's sucking face with, and that's when I realize it's not her boyfriend.

It's Asshole.

By the time I get to work the next day, I'm still in shock. Suffice it to say, I had a shitty night's sleep. Not because I found my roommate with my ex, but because Andrew is loud in bed. Once I started thinking about it, I understood why he was that way. He was overcompensating for his teeny weenie by insisting he loved eating pussy more than making love.

I roll my eyes so hard at the revelation.

No guy needs to make that much noise while feasting between your legs. The woman should be the loud one; if he's doing it right, anyway.

After texting Natalie on the way to work to tell her what

happened, she insisted it was a sign. A sign I needed to go to Florida with them, and after hearing his voice and seeing his nasty face, I could use a vacation more than ever.

During my break, Natalie and I meet up again.

"I can't believe he left you a voice message and then hours later ended up in your apartment with Sasha," she says for the third time, just as shocked as I was.

Well, there's a club she can join because I can hardly believe it either.

"Yeah, he probably thought I was her, considering I have bleach blonde hair and she has dark brown hair. It'd be easy to get us confused." I snort.

"God, I'm so glad you broke up with his nasty ass. I should send Adam over there to kick his butt." She starts to get all worked up.

"Natalie," I say, covering her hand with mine. "I appreciate the sentiment, but Adam would hurt himself before hurting Andrew."

She scowls. "Hey, he's muscular."

I chuckle. "I know he is. I wasn't saying he isn't, but Andrew ate steroids for breakfast, so no one stands a chance. He's a fake, liar, and cheater, and not worth anyone's time or energy."

She frowns. "I'm sorry you had to find that out the hard way."

I shrug, lowering my eyes to the floor. "Live and learn, right?" I blink and meet her gaze. "Besides, he left his six-thousand dollar watch in my room." I grin.

"Holy shit!" She gasps. "What kind of watch costs that much? It better come with fifty-five hundred dollars and a male stripper on the side."

Bursting out laughing, I'm easily reminded why Natalie and I are friends. She always finds a way to make me smile in the worst of times.

"Some hoity-toity designer, but it was a gift from his job when he got promoted last year."

"Oh, boo for him." She wiggles a finger down her cheek to

mimic a tear. "You should pawn it instead."

I snap her a look. "That's a little vindictive."

"Or…" She snaps her fingers. "It's being resourceful and now paying for your *well-deserved* vacation. Think of that as a *real* parting gift." She starts to hold up her fingers. "He cheated, lied, and now screwed your roommate in the same apartment as you. That dirtbag deserves a lot worse."

I can't argue with her, but I don't feel right pawning it. Though, he doesn't exactly deserve to have the watch returned to him either.

Or does he?

After my shift, I head home and sit on the edge of the bed. Deciding to take the high road, I grab the watch from my nightstand and stare at it. It really is a nice-looking watch. Too bad he doesn't know a good thing when he has it. He should know better than to leave valuables lying around.

Thankfully, he and Sasha were gone this morning before I left for work because I'm not sure what I would've done. Thinking back to the night before and hearing them in the room next door boils my blood even more. I'm so pissed I wasted my time on him. I replay moments of us together and realize all the signs pointed to this. I should've known from his sketchy behavior and random phone calls. I shouldn't have been so naïve, and I almost can't believe how vengeful he is. Fucking my roommate and knowing I'd be home was just a low blow. That bastard.

I take his watch and place it on the kitchen counter. A moment passes, and I stare at the shiny gold band and diamonds on the face. Searching through the drawers, I find a meat tenderizer—well suited name, too—and grip it firmly in my hand. Raising it above my head, I lower it and slam it against the watch. I do this over and over, groaning and grunting until only tiny pieces are left.

Whew! That felt fucking great.

Next, I find an envelope, shove all the remaining pieces inside, and before sealing it, write him a little note.

Hope you think twice before wasting someone's TIME again.
Love, River

P.S. Fuck you.

Feeling satisfied, I write his business address on the front and shove the envelope into my purse, so I can mail it first thing in the morning before work.

Looking around my apartment, I realize all the anger and resentment I've been harboring, and it makes me really consider Natalie's offer.

I grab my phone from the nightstand and type out a text to her.

River: Okay, you win. Send me the info for the resort. I'm going.

CHAPTER THREE

ALEX

DYLAN and I finally finish up for the day and double-check that we've completed everything Dad's given us to do over the past two weeks. Ever since I asked for two weeks' vacation, he's overworked us, but we've not complained once. The fence is finished, hay is baled and stacked, and we even dug out a ditch on top of our regular morning duties. We've started work before sunrise and stayed out past sunset, but it's been worth it because I plan to take full advantage of this trip.

"Jackson was volun-told to drive us to the airport in the mornin'," I remind Dylan as I drive him back to his truck parked near the cattle barn.

"Good. Don't wanna leave my pickup in the parking lot that long," he says. "I'll be here around five, so we've got plenty of time to make it to the airport."

"Just be prepared for Jackson to bitch the entire drive." I smile, knowing how irritated he is that he has to do our work on top of his own, but that's payback for the fence incident, so I don't feel bad about it.

After dropping Dylan off at his truck, I head home, knowing I still need to finish my laundry and pack. I've been putting it off because I have no clue what to bring to Florida. My closet is full of

Wranglers and work shirts. I have some Oxfords for when I go out, but I'm sure those will stick out like a sore thumb on the beaches of Key West.

For the last few years, Jackson and I have lived together in an old ranch hand house we remodeled. Since then, Friday nights have been known as Whiskey Fridays. He and a bunch of his friends listen to country music, shoot off their rifles into the fields, and drink like it's the last few bottles of whiskey left on Earth.

As soon as I walk through the door, Jackson strolls over to me and places his arm on my shoulder with a wide, drunken smile.

"Now the fun has arrived," he shouts to a room full of people who then lift their glasses in the air with a loud round of hollering.

He pours me a glass and hands it to me. "I have to pack," I tell him with a smug smile on my face, realizing he's already drunk his limit, and the night is still young.

"Come on, little brother, you can do it later," he reassures, clinking his glass against mine. "After the shit show of a day we've had, drinks are in order!"

I look down at my clothes and hands that are stained with oil. For most of the day, Dylan and I worked on a damn truck that decided to break down while we were in the middle of hauling hay from one barn to another. Oil was everywhere and made a big fucking mess. We did nothing but fix shit all day. Not one task was completed without a mini disaster, which meant we were out way after the sun set to finish everything, but that's common 'round here.

One thing leads to another, and soon, Jackson and I are sharing a bottle of Jack Daniels. A few of the guys who live in the ranch hand quarters are singing with the radio at the top of their lungs. By the time I drink the last bit of whiskey, I realize I've totally screwed myself.

"I gotta go to bed," I tell Jackson. "Don't forget you're driving us to the airport tomorrow, too."

Alcohol and exhaustion swim through my veins, which isn't a good combination.

"It'll be fine," Jackson says with a wave of his hand, stumbling over his words and not concerned about anything. The words of a true drunk.

I smile, pat him on his shoulder, and tell everyone good night. Even though the music is blaring and everyone in the house is loud as hell, I manage to remember to set the alarm and fall asleep in no time.

The morning comes early, and my head is killing me from drinking way too much. I already know today will be rough. Looking over at the clock, I realize Dylan will be here in about ten minutes. I grab my suitcase from the closet and shove clothes into it along with my toothbrush and deodorant. Procrastination mixed with Jackson's peer pressure got the best of me again. I'll just buy whatever I forget at the resort because I don't have time to overthink it.

Just as I'm slipping on my blue jeans and boots, I hear a knock on the door and know it's Dylan. I walk through the house and see Jackson asleep in the recliner in the corner of the room. After I rub my hands over my face to try to wake myself up, I open the door. Dylan steps in and laughs.

"Whiskey Fridays." He knows the aftereffects all too well.

"Unfortunately," I say with a groan. I walk back toward Jackson and shake him, but all he does is groan and slap my hand away.

"You're supposed to drive us to the airport," I remind him.

"He's probably still drunk," Dylan says, looking at Jackson who's still wearing his clothes from yesterday, including his boots.

"Without a doubt," I mumble, walking to the kitchen to make some strong coffee. I lean against the counter and wait for the coffee to drip into the pot as I grab a few ibuprofen from the medicine cabinet.

"I assume Jackson isn't bringing us to the airport." Dylan stares at Jackson who's snoring loudly.

The coffeemaker beeps as I grab a travel mug. "Mama's gonna kill him today if she finds out he didn't drive us down there," I say, pouring the coffee.

"I wouldn't mind seeing that." Dylan chuckles. "Mrs. B on a rampage isn't a force to be reckoned with."

I nod. "She's the scariest when she's pissed. Even Dad won't mess with her when she gets that way. It's fine. I'll drive my truck since Jackson has the extra key. I'll have him and John drive there and pick it up later, so it's not sitting down there for two weeks."

Jackson snores himself awake, and he sits up, forcing his eyes open. "Shiiiiiiiiiiit."

"What?" I ask, feeling a little more like myself after the coffee warms my veins.

"That's what I feel like." Jackson tries to stand but stumbles and trips over his feet.

Dylan and I nearly fall over laughing. That's what he gets for making me drink with him. Misery loves company, my ass.

"You're not driving us anywhere." I chuckle as we watch him struggle to pick himself up off the floor. "Sit back down before you hurt yourself."

"If the room would stop spinning, I'd be just fine," he groans, finally sitting his ass back down.

"We've got to get going or we're gonna miss our flight." Dylan checks the time on his phone. "Ready?" He gives me a big cheesy grin because we both know I'm not.

I double-check my suitcase really quick, refill my travel mug, then holler, "Goodbye," to Jackson before stepping out the front door and walking toward the truck.

Dylan grabs his suitcase from his truck and throws it in the back before we both get in and head to the airport. Our drive isn't too far—a little over an hour—but we have to get on one of those little planes I hate before connecting in San Antonio. Once we're at the airport and parked, I can see the sun rising in the distance. We check our bags and sit at the gate while we wait for our departure to be announced.

"Nervous?" I look over at Dylan.

"Nah, just ready to get there and relax," he says, but I can see he's sweating beads.

I hate the small planes, too, but luckily, we'll only be on it for about an hour.

After we board and the plane takes off, I feel a little more relaxed. By the time I get used to feeling every little bump, we land in San Antonio and head to our next gate. My head is killing me again, so before we board the next plane, I buy a pack of ibuprofen and a bottle of water then say a little prayer and hope it goes away before we land in Key West.

It's confirmed—Jackson is a bad influence.

The next plane is bigger, giving us more room to stretch out our long legs. My head isn't throbbing as badly anymore, and I can actually take in the view from the small window next to me.

"So yesterday after work, Mama had me run to the grocery store, and guess who I ran into?" He gives me less than a second to guess before continuing. "Gretchen Garcia. Dude, she's still so pissed at you." He starts cracking up. "I wonder how many women have you on their hate list right now. I can count about six without even thinking about it too hard." Dylan chuckles again.

"Hey, it's not my fault they don't understand the concept of casual sex. It's not like they didn't know that up front when I said I wasn't looking for anything serious. I'm always honest. I use my manners and am polite, so if that's not good enough for them, then that's on them. They know what I have to offer before anything happens. Every one of them says they're okay with it, and then afterward decide they aren't. They always think they can change my mind or that they'll be the 'one' to change me, but nothing's going to change the fact that I don't want or have time for a relationship. I ain't lookin' for anything other than a little fun. But I guess that's what being honest gets me," I tell him with resentment in my tone. Gretchen knew all of that, too, before we ever hooked up. Not my fault my words fell on deaf ears. And considering we hooked up over a year ago, she needs to get over it.

"Well, either way, she said she wanted to cut off your balls and feed them to the pigs," Dylan says with a teasing grin.

I adjust myself. "I knew she was crazy but damn. I need my balls."

"I promised her I'd relay the message if she promised not to cut mine off."

I burst out into laughter. "Smart."

After a while, I close my eyes and end up falling asleep until the plane lands. Relieved to be back on the ground, I look out the window again. Besides all the water surrounding us, I also notice how bright and sunny it is. We're definitely not in Texas anymore. Even though I have no idea what to expect, I'm more psyched than ever to be here.

We deplane and retrieve our suitcases before taking the shuttle to the resort we'll be staying at. I actually feel a lot better since sucking down those ibuprofen and getting in a short nap, so now I can't wait to get settled and explore the city and beaches.

As we get closer to the resort, I'm completely taken aback by the view. Palm trees and tourist shops line both sides of the street. People walk with smiles on their faces as they shop and take photos. They all look so damn happy to be here. I catch glimpses of the clear-blue water behind it all, and as we get closer to the resort, I notice beach chairs and cabanas along the beach. This is just the kind of vacation I need.

The shuttle parks outside of the hotel, and we grab our luggage and step out. As we're standing in front of the hotel, I look over at the people walking in and out of the hotel, and then over at Dylan and I realize we stick out like a sore thumb. Cowboy hats, boots, and plaid shirts—we're Texas twins right now in the same getup, and I'm sure our accents aren't going to do us any favors.

Walking in, we chat about what we want to do tonight and wait in line for reception. Once we're waved up, we walk up to the woman and greet her with a loud *howdy*. The corner of her lips tilts up as she eyes our Stetson hats before asking for our information. Dylan gives her his name and slides his ID across the counter. She continues to type on her keyboard, only briefly glancing at the two of us before going back to the screen. As soon as she makes eye contact and hands over Dylan's ID, I give her a smile and a wink. She tries to hide the blush that hits her cheeks behind the computer screen, but it doesn't work.

"Mr. Hart, how many room keys would you like?" she asks, chewing on her bottom lip.

I look over at Dylan and whisper, "Wait, did we get separate rooms?"

"About that…" He laughs, then looks back at her. "Two, please."

The woman clears her throat and slides our room keys across the counter. "All meals and beverages are included with your stay, along with nonmotorized water sports. You do have a couple's massage that you'll need to schedule by using this number here," she says, pointing down at the brochure before placing the keys inside.

Since Dylan thinks this is so damn funny, I decide to play along by wrapping my arm around him and pulling him to my side. "Honey, when would ya like to schedule those? In the morning perhaps?"

Dylan elbows me hard in the side, and I can't help but laugh. The woman smiles at us sweetly.

"The elevators to your suite are right down the hall to the left. In the morning, breakfast is served from six to ten. If you have questions or need anything, just dial zero."

"Thank you, ma'am," Dylan and I both say in unison before walking toward the elevator, dragging our luggage behind us.

"This is going to be interesting," I mumble as we pass guests in their shorts and swimsuit tops.

"You embarrassed that poor girl," Dylan tells me as we step into the elevator, and I hit the button for our floor.

I shrug, holding the rail as we shoot upward. "She was looking at us like we were real-life cowboy lovers. Thought I'd help her fantasy a little."

"This is why girls like Mallory threaten your balls," he teases as we get off the elevator and walk to our room. As soon as we slide our keycard and step inside, I'm shocked to see how large the place is. It's as big as one of the cabins the ranch hands live in at home. There's a giant bathroom, TV room with chairs and couches, and a separate room that leads to the bed. The windows lining the wall overlook the ocean, giving us an amazing view of the beach.

I can't help but laugh when I see a champagne bottle in an ice bucket and red rose petals spread across the bed. There are even towels at the end of the bed folded in a heart shape. "This is a perfect touch; don't you think, sweetheart?"

Dylan looks at the flower petals and laughs so hard that he nearly chokes.

I pull my phone from my pocket and snap a quick picture.

"Gonna show Jackson what he's missing out on." I laugh as I send him a text.

"Yeah, I'm sure that'll make him jealous." He snorts.

Checking the time on my phone and seeing it's already nearing late afternoon, I ask, "So what if I find a chick I want to bring back to the room?"

Dylan removes his boots and sets his hat on the dresser. "I thought about that, too," he admits, brushing his fingers through his messy dark hair. "Maybe we come up with a code phrase or something, so we know not to walk in on each other? I've decided I'm going to be more like you on this trip."

"Gonna get your dick wet finally?"

He scoffs. "I meant a no-strings-attached kind of thing. Just having fun. Be completely up front with women without the pressure of what it means."

"About time you let loose. You've been single way too long. So if and when we decide we want to bring someone back, we just text each other the phrase."

"Okay, so what's the code word?" Dylan asks.

I contemplate for a moment before thinking of the perfect one.

"I've got it: Cowgirl—after my favorite position." I flash him a smug grin as he thinks it over.

"Reverse cowgirl." He shakes his head, laughing at me, but reluctantly agrees anyway. "You're such a dirty bastard."

I pop the cork on the champagne bottle and pour us both a glass before handing him one. "C'mon, you know you're dying to find a girl to ride you bareback like a stallion!" I slap a hand on his shoulder just as he tips the flute back, and he nearly chokes on the liquid.

"Well, if someone catches a glimpse of our phones, at least they'd have no idea what the hell we're talking about." Dylan takes another swig from his glass.

"And that's why we're friends," I tell him, clinking the edge of my glass against his. "Now, let's go have some damn fun and show Florida how cowboys really party."

"Okay, but first…" He tilts his head back and finishes off his champagne. "…let's go shopping and find some different clothes," Dylan suggests.

I look at my Levi's and boots. "Yeah, good idea." I smile then take the final sip of my drink. "Then we show them how to party!"

CHAPTER FOUR

_____

RIVER

I CAN'T BELIEVE I'm really doing this.

After begging my supervisor, she put in the request for my time off and made sure our boss approved it. She knows I'm a hard worker and work nonstop, and after giving her the sob story of Asshole, she sympathized, having had her own experience with a married man. God, the men here just suck.

Not that I'm expecting the men in Florida to be any different because let's face it, downtown Key West is party city. But at least now, I have zero expectations. Don't get too close. Have fun. No rules.

Yep. That's going to be my life for the next two weeks.

And I couldn't be more excited and nervous about it. The last time I ever did anything spontaneous was back in my sophomore year in college when I ran through the commons area topless in the middle of January. My nipples nearly froze off, but it was for some club I was in. We were protesting something, but I can't even remember what it was now. So obviously, I lived it up during my college years.

Actually, I studied nonstop. Nursing school is no joke and definitely not for the weak. I almost quit five times, but I wouldn't let it defeat me. More determined than ever, I graduated with honors with a 3.8 GPA.

I smiled as I boarded the plane, feeling brave for taking this step. Thankfully, it was a direct flight from Milwaukee to the Key West International Airport. Natalie and Adam left yesterday, but all the airlines were booked, so I had to fly out the next day. I didn't mind though, because I planned to read during the flight anyway.

"Going for business or pleasure?" a deep male voice asks next to me.

Blinking, I look up and see a man sitting next to me who I hadn't even realized was there. I had taken my seat by the window first and buried myself in my book right away. He was dressed in a sharp, black suit and looked to be a tad older than me.

"Um, I'm going for a vacation. So pleasure, I guess." I flash a small smile. "You?"

He brushes his fingers over his black tie. "Business." He confirms my thoughts, his attire giving it away.

"Well, maybe you'll get a few moments to enjoy the beaches. I hear they're amazing," I say, making small talk because I'm not really sure what else to say. I spend my days with children and hard-ass doctors, so I almost feel rusty when it comes to communicating with people outside of my job.

"Yeah, not a lot of time for beaches on work trips." He smiles wide, showing off his perfectly white teeth.

"Oh, that's a bummer."

"Well, I might be able to squeeze in some extracurricular activities…if you're interested." His voice goes silky smooth, yet his tone makes me shudder. Then he winks, sealing his offer.

Is he seriously hitting on me right now?

"No thanks," I blurt out, uncomfortably. "I'm meeting a couple friends there, and we'll be busy." I flash a weak smile that I hope gives him a hint.

He digs into his pocket, making me wonder what the hell he's up to next. Pulling out a business card, he flicks it at me and smiles. "Well, if you change your mind and have some extra time, hit me up."

Reluctantly, I grab it and crumple it in my fist.

"Sure," I mutter, nearly hugging the window to keep my distance. Just as he shifts in his seat, my eyes gaze down to his hand, and that's when I see it. That rat bastard. "How sweet of your wife to share you. Too bad she doesn't realize what a skeez you are." The words come out harsher than I intended, but even so, I don't even feel bad about it.

Without saying a word, he turns his body away from me. Coward.

If this is what being out in the dating world is like, then count me out. I'd only met Andrew on a rare evening out with a friend for her birthday. She'd gotten so wasted, I had to help her walk outside and hail a cab. I nearly slipped on my heels—that I hardly wore—and both of us were about to face-plant when Andrew grabbed my waist to keep me steady on my feet. He'd just so happened to be walking out of another bar when he saw us stumbling and ran to help.

It was one of those damsel-in-distress moments, and if I'd been thinking clearly, I maybe wouldn't have wasted the last six months on him. However, he saved us both, helped me get my friend in the cab, and before I followed behind, he asked if he could have my number. I figured he'd never call anyway, so I gave it to him. He surprised me when he called the following day and asked me out.

Completely smitten, I'd fallen for him hard and fast. I kept pushing away any signs that I was being paranoid and kept telling myself that I was lucky to even have a guy like him interested in me. I wasn't naturally an insecure person, but after a few failed online dating attempts, I decided there was no way decent men exist anymore. Up until three weeks ago, I thought Andrew was the exception.

But it seems married men can't seem to keep it in their damn pants no matter what state I'm in.

Relieved when we finally land, I grab my luggage after deplaning and stop for a coffee before hailing a taxi. By the time I'm in the cab, I already have Natalie on the line to let her know I'm here, and she nearly popped my eardrum with her excitement.

"Oh my God, River! It's gorgeous here, isn't it?" She releases a dreamy sigh into the phone. I can already picture her lying out poolside with a drink in hand. "Adam decided to go looking for some good fishing spots for tomorrow morning, so it's just me, the sun, and my Bahama Mama."

I chuckle, loving how relaxed she sounds. This is just what I needed right now.

"Well, I can't wait to join you. Once I check in and settle into my room, I'll change and meet you down there," I tell her, looking out the window at the touristy views.

"Perfect! I'll have a drink waiting for you!"

The warmth is the first thing I notice when I get out of the cab. The wind brings a nice breeze my way as I walk through the doors of the hotel, reminding me I'm no longer in Wisconsin. It was cold and gloomy this past week, so this weather is definitely a welcome change.

As soon as I walk in, I take in everything from the bright blue color palette to the ocean views all along the back through the windows. It's something straight up from a magazine. People walk around with their oversized beach bags, sunglasses, and flip-flops. It instantly brightens my mood.

"Hello, welcome to the Hyatt. Can I help you?" the receptionist greets me, and I'm more than happy to say, "Yes, yes, you can!"

Once I'm all checked in, she directs me to the elevators, and soon I'm scanning my keycard into my room. I ended up with a corner room, which at first, I was hesitant about because I wanted all ocean views, but as soon as I walk in, I see I'm not the least bit disappointed.

With the wraparound balcony and two sets of sliding glass doors, it looks like the ocean is *in* my room. The entire half of my wall is taken over by the sliding doors and the perfect beach views.

"This is heaven," I mutter to myself with the biggest smile I've had in weeks.

Once I give myself the tour, I unpack my luggage and dig around for my swimsuit. I'm never been more eager to wear the damn thing, which considering all the winter weight I put on last year, says a lot. When I'm at work, I wear scrubs and clogs, so this is a change I don't mind.

I change, find my swimsuit wrap and pull it over my body. Grabbing a towel, my key, and bag, I head out ready to find Natalie and one of those umbrella drinks.

"Oh my God!" Natalie screams, jumping out of the chair as soon as she sees me rounding the pool. "I can't believe you're actually here!" She wraps her arms around my neck and squeezes. "Perfect timing, too! I just ordered another drink and got one for you."

"Great, thanks! It feels a little unreal that I'm actually here," I say, squeezing her back. "Thank you for inviting me," I continue as she releases me. "Or rather, thank you for forcing me to come." I grin.

"What are friends for if not to give you a little push when you need it?" She smirks, grabbing my bag in one hand and leading me over to her spot.

"I can't believe how beautiful it is, and I've only seen the airport and lobby so far." I pull my cover off and start digging into my bag.

"Well, look at you," she teases, eyeing my body. "I haven't seen that much skin on you since that time I walked in on you changing."

"That's because you have no boundaries," I remind her, chuckling.

"No doubt you'll definitely find a Florida hottie during this trip." She waggles her brows. "Big ta-tas, curvy hips, slim waistline."

"I'm starting to feel a little violated now," I mock, adjusting my swimsuit top to make sure it's covering all appropriate boobage and nipples.

"Okay, well, I'm just saying. You have nothing to be embarrassed about." She takes a long sip of her drink, and I give her a look that says otherwise.

"I can't wait to go down Front and Duval Streets. I looked them up on YouTube, and they look like a lot of fun," I say, kicking off my shoes.

"We have lots of time to explore, but today is the perfect pool day." She sighs, getting comfortable in her chair. She leans back with her large sunglasses on her face and tilts her head up to the sun.

"I hope you put sunscreen on," I tell her, pulling some out of my bag.

"I came to Florida for a tan," she says matter-of-factly, adjusting herself deeper into the chair.

"And melanoma?" I raise a brow even though she's not looking at me.

She groans.

"C'mon, sit up," I order. It'll take me five seconds."

"Yes, Nurse River." She winks. "That sounded way dirtier coming out than it did in my head."

I roll my eyes and laugh. She does as I say, and when I finish, she motions for me to turn around so she can spray my back and arms. When she's done, I spray my face, chest, stomach, and legs. This Northern girl is as white as they come, but that doesn't mean I want to risk it either.

Once I'm settled, I sprawl out on the chair with my own pair of oversized sunglasses and a topknot on my head. I grab my phone and turn on some tunes just as a gentleman comes over with a tray of drinks.

"Your drinks, ma'am," he greets, handing the first one to Natalie, who hands it to me and then takes the other for herself. She smiles at him before handing him a tip, and we both thank him.

"This is the life." I chuckle before taking a large sip. "Drinks just taste better when they get delivered to you by the pool."

"You said it, sister," she quips. "Especially when the cabana boys aren't that bad to look at." She tilts her sunglasses off her nose and eyes him as he walks away.

I laugh. "I'm sure Adam wouldn't think so."

"Are you kidding?" She chuckles. "He basically dragged me down here and told me to have a 'good time,' if you know what I mean." She smirks.

"You two have the weirdest relationship I know."

"Nah, it works just fine. Looking at other people is what we use to keep things hot in the bedroom." The playful tone of her voice lets me know there's more to the story, but I have no desire to dig for further information.

"Good to know." I smile even though she's not paying attention to me. Natalie and Adam have been together for as long as I can remember, so it doesn't surprise me that their relationship is the way it is. As long as he takes good care of her and treats her right, I keep my nose out of it.

Sipping my drink till it's halfway gone, I set it down before adjusting myself on the lounge chair and lie back. The sun heats my body in no time, and I almost fall asleep when the cabana boy arrives with another round of drinks.

"When did we order those?" I ask, taking the glass off the tray.

"I have them on a schedule for every hour." Natalie beams.

Smiling, I shrug and take a sip. "Ooh, this one tastes different."

"I ordered Bermuda Triangles. It sounded more tropical."

I laugh at how serious her tone is and take another sip. "These taste like trouble."

"Oh, trust me, they are. These got me in so much trouble during Frat week my sophomore year, I swore to stay away from them forever."

"That lasted long." I grin.

"Vacation is an exception," she states matter-of-factly. "And bonus, I don't have to get up tomorrow and give an oral presentation for a psychology exam."

My head falls back as I burst out laughing. Natalie was always known for being the life of the party, whereas I always had my face buried in a book. Nursing school nearly killed me. There was no time for ludicrous parties or getting so drunk I couldn't function the next day. Even though nursing school certainly made me want to.

The following morning, I wake up stretched out in my king-sized bed with a slight headache. Though I only drank two of those Bermuda Triangles, we didn't stop there. After we soaked up the sun, Natalie dragged me to the hotel bar until Adam came and tore us away. He walked me to my room before leading Natalie back to theirs.

Rolling over, I check my phone on the nightstand and see a text waiting for me.

Natalie: Continental breakfast in the lobby! Meet us there at 9!

Natalie: AND MIMOSAS!

Natalie: To cure that hangover you probably have, you lightweight ;)

I smile and laugh at her messages. Natalie has always known how to keep things entertaining.

Once I've showered and dressed, I make it down for breakfast just on time. Natalie and Adam are already at a table waving me over.

"Good morning, sunshine," she says with a bright smile.

"Does she always wake up this perky?" I direct my eyes toward Adam as I take a seat.

"Only on days I don't have to work or when I wake up in paradise," she answers for him with a dreamy sigh.

"I thought you'd be out fishing already?" I reach for the mimosa already set in front of me and take a drink.

"I was."

"He was."

They both speak in unison like a lovesick couple who finishes each other's thoughts and sentences.

"I was on the water by five. Came back to check on Nat and have breakfast with her before I head back out."

"I expect you to catch us enough fish to last all winter, okay?" Natalie teases.

"Don't forget the lobster and crawfish, too," I add.

"Yeah, I'm on it." He winks.

"Well, I'd better grab something to eat to soak up this alcohol before I end up like Nat during Frat week." I wink in her direction as Adam tilts his head to give her a side-eye.

I eye the buffet like it's the best thing I've seen all year. It's full of pastries, fruit, and yogurts on one end, and hot items on the other. I grab a few pieces of sausage and a spoonful of scrambled eggs before heading over to the other side.

As I'm walking toward the fruit platters, I notice a couple guys with full plates making their rounds from the hot and cold sections. They're acting like they haven't eaten in days. I smile internally at the thought of these two bulky guys eating enough for four. They definitely aren't from around here. Though they're both good looking, I find myself eyeing the blond guy. He's got the palest blue eyes, and his shirt is stretched across his muscular and wide chest. Not half bad actually.

The guy speaks in a very noticeable Southern accent, and suddenly I'm finding myself a little flushed at the thought of him saying my name with that accent.

"Dude, these ain't nothing like Mama's pancakes, but they sure smell good."

"Yeah, I can tell the maple syrup isn't homemade either, but I can't complain when we're in the Keys." They both chuckle as they continue piling food on top of food.

And they live with their mama. Great. I always know how to pick 'em.

I've dated a man, or rather *boy,* who was highly dependent on his mother, and as much as I like a guy to be respectful to his mom, being a mama's boy isn't the quality some think it is. In fact, it became borderline annoying.

Just thinking about how my ex would have to text his mother goodnight after we had sex sends shivers down my spine. Maybe that makes me the weird one, but there needs to be a healthy balance.

I take my seat with Natalie and Adam a few tables away from

where the Southern men are sitting while trying to shake the images of my ex from my head. Natalie's discussing how she swore she saw a Kardashian sister in the bar last night, and Adam's pretending to add to the conversation by throwing in some 'uh-huhs' and 'mm-hmms.'

Just as I stab a sausage link and shove it into my mouth, I feel a shift. Natalie looks up over my shoulder with wide, dreamy eyes, and I know somebody is standing at my side.

"'Scuse me, ma'am?" I hear the Southern accent and immediately feel the hairs on my neck rise.

I chew as quickly as I can and swallow it down, nearly choking when I try to speak. "Uh, yes?"

Up close, he's even bigger looking. Well over six feet tall, and I can almost see his ab muscles through his shirt.

"I was wonderin' if you could help settle an argument between my friend and me?"

I blink up at him, mouth gaping open. "Sure." I clear my throat, realizing what he's doing. I've heard dozens of pickup lines start just like this. It usually ends up being something super cheesy. By the smirk on his face, I'm almost willing to bet him and his friend are arguing about how pretty I am and want me to say which one I'd go on a date with.

"Well, my friend over there said there was no way you'd find me good-lookin'. I told him there's no way you'd be able to resist my Southern charm and undeniably sexy abs, so since we can't seem to agree, I figured I'd come right to the source and ask myself." He stares intently at me for a moment, licking his lower lip before he sucks it in briefly as I remain dumbfounded. "So whaddaya think? Is he right?" He gives me one of those smug, I-think-I'm-God's-gift-to-women winks before showing a slight preview of the abs he felt so inclined to mention.

Natalie snorts in the background, laughing while covering her mouth with her hand. Adam's grinning and shaking his head as if he's thinking, *poor bastard*.

"Hm…" I decide to play along, tilting my body around him to

get a look at his friend. Dark hair, light eyes, and I can tell he's muscular too. When our eyes meet, he tips his head at me with a wide grin. Then I direct my eyes to the guy in front of me and act like I'm giving it serious thought. Clearing my throat, I gaze my eyes back up to his with a confidence smile. "Tell him I've seen better."

Natalie can't contain herself anymore and totally loses it. His friend overhears my response and starts laughing.

"Damn. That hurts," he teases, placing a hand on his chest. The corner of his lips tilts up into a small grin.

"Sorry, but I'm sure there's plenty of ladies around here that'd be happy to mend those wounds." I wrinkle my nose at him to soften the blow. He bows his head down, slouches his shoulders, and begins to slowly walk away back to his friend.

"You think *I'm* attractive, though, right?" the friend shouts from his table, and the blond guy punches him in the arm to silence him.

"Jesus, they're relentless," I mutter so only Natalie and Adam can hear.

"Oh, c'mon! Give 'em a bone," she quips.

I roll my eyes at her in response and pop a piece of fruit in my mouth.

"You know the only way to get over a guy is to get under another one," she teases, her voice carrying throughout the entire room.

I nearly choke on a grape and almost have to give myself the Heimlich.

"Natalie!" I whisper-shout. "Swear to God, I can't take you anywhere."

Adam's smiling and trying to hide his laughter behind a forkful of food.

"This is *your* fault." I point my finger at him. "You just let her roam around free without any kind of restrictions or *muzzle.*"

"Don't look at me," he defends. "You knew her before I did, which means you let her be this way long before I came around."

I chuckle in defeat.

"What happened to having fun on this vacation?" Natalie ignores us and changes the subject. "Those were some cute Southern guys who wanted to show you how to ride their mechanical bull. I bet you can last all eight seconds even."

Choking again, I give up and put my fork down. "I've gotta stop eating around you. I never know what will come out of your unfiltered mouth."

"I bet he's hung like a horse, too," she states dreamily, looking past us toward their table.

"And I bet if you asked nicely, they'd even let you ride them bareback." Adam adds fuel to the fire, getting another laugh out of Natalie.

"You two suck," I say, pointing my fork at them.

My eyes land on a woman walking in our direction. She's all legs, long dark hair, and tan. She's a dark-haired Barbie, wearing one of those teeny bikini tops as a shirt with a pair of booty shorts, though the word "shorts" is questionable since I'm pretty certain her ass cheeks are hanging out. She rounds our table and heads directly for the two Southern men.

"Howdy," the blond says, looking up at her with bright eyes.

"So last night was fun," she tells him, her voice all high-pitched and annoying. The guy nods in agreement as his eyes scan up and down her body. "Call me if you want to do it again." She reaches into her back pocket to grab a piece of paper and hands it over to him.

The guy takes it and unfolds it. "Sure thing, darlin'." His accent is even more noticeable when he says that. Damn, it's kinda hot too. Before the woman walks off, he winks at her with a smile that can only mean he'll be calling her soon for another hookup.

The dark-haired guy is smirking and shaking his head.

"Nice." I mutter my annoyance at the fact that he was literally just hitting on me, and five seconds later he's drooling over this chick.

Better yet, why do I care?

"What's that?" the blond guy asks, startling me when he raises his voice loud enough for me to hear. "You jealous already? I didn't even sleep with that one…" He smirks, then winks as if that's his seductive trademark.

"Wow, I'm shocked by your willpower. Better catch her and remedy that then." I hold back rolling my eyes, which is my own trademark when I'm annoyed.

"Nah. I'm not impressed with the local cuisine. I'd rather try something…new and interesting. Any suggestions?" He arches a brow, giving me every opportunity to mock him.

Natalie's about to burst a vein with how hard she's trying to hold back her laughter.

Swallowing, I hold my stance and play his little game. "I'd suggest you stick to what you know, so you don't get bitten. Or worse."

"Damn," the dark-haired guy blurts. "She's my new favorite person." He chuckles, and the blond elbow jabs him. "She shot you down and put you in your place. You'd better marry her, or I will."

I snort. "I'm leaving now." I stand, taking my plate, and push in my chair.

"Okay, but don't forget we have a couple's massage at ten!" Natalie shouts. "Unless you'd prefer Mr. Southern 'n Dirty accompany you?"

I wave a hand up in the air and salute with my middle finger.

CHAPTER FIVE

ALEX

THE SUN FEELS like it's burning my skin straight through the window as I roll over in bed. Last night, we stumbled back to our suite, and since we drank and sang karaoke all night, I forgot to close the curtains—hell, I'm lucky I even made it to the bed at that point.

Just as I sit up, my head pounds hard and loud like the beat of the music at the club. Drinking so early after we traveled all day was a bad decision on my part, but Dylan was all for it, as usual. We aren't letting any part of this vacation go to waste.

I stand and walk to the bathroom only to catch a glimpse of myself in the mirror.

You look like shit, I think to myself, needing to clear my throat that's sore from all my loud singing. Favorite song of the night: "*All My Exes Live in Texas.*" I chuckle because they do.

The world's spinning, and I place my hand against the wall to steady myself before I face-plant on the floor. I stumble to the mini fridge to grab a bottle of water and realize I don't see Dylan anywhere in the room. Opening the door that leads to the sitting area, I find him sleeping on the couch with his legs and arms hanging off the side. He's too tall for that small couch, and it makes me laugh, even though it hurts my head when I do. He's trying so hard to be comfortable, it's comical. We might be a hungover shitshow, but we showed Florida how to really party—Texan style.

Last night, after we bought some swim trunks and flip-flops, we changed clothes, grabbed a quick dinner, then went down to the cabana bar by the water where country music was blasting loud and proud. Five shots of tequila and a few beers later, we were dancing and singing, and now today I'm paying for it.

Just as my stomach growls, Dylan rolls over off the couch and lands flat on his ass. He rubs his hand over his face, and I can tell he feels as bad as I do.

"Ugh," he moans, trying to get up but fails miserably. Walking over to him, I hold out my hand to pull him off the floor. As he stands in front of me, I see bright red lip prints all over his face.

"Last night must've been good." I chuckle, plopping down on the couch and leaning my head back.

Dylan looks at me confused before walking to the bathroom. Once he flicks on the lights, I hear him mutter, "What the hell?" I know he's referring to the lipstick on his face and neck. "All that and I slept on that damn miniature couch alone!"

My stomach growls again, and I know the only way to fix this hangover is to eat something.

"I'm hungry," I tell him as I force myself to stand and go to my suitcase. I slip on a T-shirt and a pair of jeans.

"Me too," Dylan agrees.

Just as I walk toward the door and slip on my flip-flops, Dylan falls in line behind me. He's still wearing his clothes from yesterday but doesn't seem to care.

We take the elevator to the ground level, walk through the lobby, and head straight to the room where the continental breakfast is served. The smell of sausage and bacon fills the room, and my mouth instantly waters. Not wasting any time, Dylan and I stack food on our plates like we always do, yet with the selection in front of us, we keep adding as if we haven't eaten in a week. Pancakes, sausage, bacon, fruit—hell, we got a little of everything.

Before we sit, I notice a pretty blonde at the buffet. As soon as I make eye contact with her, she looks the other way, pretending as if I don't exist. Dylan and I end up sitting a few tables away from where she and her friends are.

"You should go talk to her. You're eyeing her more than the eggs on your plate," Dylan encourages with a smirk.

"Nah," I say, pouring syrup over my pancakes and cutting into them.

"Dare you," he whispers with a mouthful of food.

Now there's one thing a person shouldn't ever do, and that's dare a Bishop.

I eye him, knowing there's no going back on it now.

"Unless you're chicken," he teases before he begins clucking at me.

After I finish chewing my food, I try to listen to their conversation because if it sounds important, I'll have to take a rain check. Dare or not, Mama always taught us boys not to interrupt important discussions. Once I realize her friend is chatting about a celebrity, and everyone at the table looks tuned out of the conversation, I take it as my cue to walk over.

Standing behind her, I catch the slight hint of her strawberry-scented shampoo. Her friend peers up at me and smiles, and I throw out some cheesy pickup line that always works when hitting on girls in trashy bars.

She looks over at Dylan then back at me, and that's when I see a hint of blush hit her cheeks. I'm talking loud enough so he can hear our conversation, and I quickly look over my shoulder at him. All he does is shake his head and laugh.

Once I'm completely rejected by her, I pretend to be hurt and walk back over to Dylan who's laughing so loud other people in the dining area are staring at us.

"Damn. She's a savage. I like her," he says with a shit-eating grin. Moments later, I see Miranda or Mazie—whatever her name is—bounce up to our table with a devilish look in her eye. I take full advantage knowing the blonde girl is watching even though she rejected me just moments ago.

Miranda or Mazie hands me a piece of paper, and once I see it's her phone number, I look up and wink, knowing I have no intentions of actually calling her. But I'm a gentleman after all, so of course, I smile in return. We had a good time last night at the bar drinking and dancing, but that's as far as things will go.

I watch her walk away, and when I look up, I see the blonde girl glaring in my direction. The opportunity to taunt her is too good to pass up when I see her muttering under her breath.

Just as I take a huge bite of my pancakes, the redhead that was sitting with the blonde girl who just rejected me walks over to our table with a beaming smile on her face.

"Hey, I'm Natalie, and this is my boyfriend, Adam," she says, waving her hand to the guy standing next to her. "And that girl at my table you were talking to is my friend River."

Smiling, I quickly swallow down the rest of my food. "Nice to meet y'all. This is Dylan, and I'm Alex."

"River likes to play hard to get, but she's totally single." She flashes a wink. "Just in case you were wondering," she adds, then continues, "and she'd probably murder me if she knew I told you that."

Now I'm the one laughing. "Probably, but I can keep a secret."

"Okay, good. Thanks." She grins. "Well, I hope we'll see you around the resort."

"I'm sure you will. We're here for two weeks," I add, giving her a smile.

"Us too!" Natalie squeals. "Wait, are you single?" She furrows her brows at me. "Want to make sure there isn't a wife, girlfriend, or fiancée waiting for you at home."

Dylan snorts. "Ma'am, his middle name is single."

I glance at Dylan, but Natalie doesn't seem to notice.

"Well, that's great news." Her eyes light up, and I can tell she's already trying to play matchmaker. It's not the first time I've seen that look on a woman's face, and I'm sure it won't be the last.

"Babe, we gotta go. The boat leaves in twenty minutes," Adam reminds her.

She nods at him with a smile then looks back at me. "We'll totally see you around."

Once she walks away, Dylan scoffs. "Seriously? I swear, it's so easy for you. She's already trying to hook you up. What a nice friend." He grins.

I continue to stuff my face. "Basically, but she's just trying to play matchmaker. I already know what type she is—overly flirty and sweet, but a loyal friend. And I sincerely appreciate her giving me the scoop on her pretty friend. The info might come in handy."

After Dylan rolls his eyes then basically licks his plate clean, he sits back in his chair and pats his stomach. "Might need a wheelbarrow to get me out of here."

"Wasn't like Mama's cooking, but it hit the spot," I admit, overly full too. Dylan and I finish our juice before we stand and stretch. Thankfully my head stopped pounding, and I feel like a new man after eating.

"Whatcha wanna do today?" Dylan asks just as a man with a stack of bright yellow flyers walks through the hotel lobby and hands us both one.

"Stand up paddleboarding, windsurfing, jet skis, kayaks, snorkeling, and an all-day pass is *only* $149. But wait, for just $59.99 more, we can add a sunset cruise with a romantic dinner."

"You've got the creepy infomercial voice down," I tell him with a chuckle. "I saw some people on those board things yesterday. It looked like fun."

"Yeah and the weather outside is perfect. We should do it. The rental place is right around the corner." Dylan folds the paper and shoves it into his pocket.

"Let's get ready and head over there."

After we go to our room and change into swim clothes, we walk down to the water sports shop, just like the flyer says. Before we leave the hotel lobby, I glance around for River but don't see her anywhere. That woman is officially on my radar. Her smart mouth and the way she responds to me is intriguing, and I'd be lying if I didn't admit I was curious. After I shake the image of her round ass walking away from breakfast this morning, I realize Dylan is talking to me.

"What do you want to do first?" he repeats himself, annoyed.

"Let's start at the beginning of the list and work our way down."

As we walk a few blocks, we see the big yellow signs pointing to the shop.

"Hey, welcome!" a high-energy woman says from behind the counter when we enter.

"Howdy, ma'am," Dylan and I both respond in unison. It's easy to blend in with the tourists in our board shorts and flip-flops, but the moment we open our mouths, people know we're not from around these parts. Though we've been here less than twenty-four hours, Key West is a culture shock to us. It's much different from the rolling hills, cactus, cows, and ranch. Reggae music plays in the background, and seashell wind chimes rattle in the breeze.

"Have you ever been on a paddleboard before?" The cute woman walks around the counter as we look at the different boards and paddles lined up against the wall.

"No, ma'am," Dylan says, putting the Southern accent on real thick, and I'm pretty sure she's about to melt in his palm.

"Please don't call me ma'am. I'm twenty-two years old, not eighty," she tells him with her eyebrow raised. "I'm Trish."

"Nice to meet you, *Trish*," Dylan says in a low raspy voice. Right about now, if he was wearing his cowboy hat, he would've tipped it.

She blushes. "I have a class in ten minutes to teach beginners if you'd like to sign up," she tells him with a flirty smile playing on her lips. "We'll meet right over there by the flags." She points to the bright blue flags out by the kayaks on the shore. The shop is walking distance from the water, which'll make carrying everything convenient, considering the boards are so bulky.

Dylan looks over his shoulder at me for approval, and I nod my head at him with a smirk.

"Yeah, we'll sign up." He pulls out his credit card and pays.

We happily walk to the beach with our boards and paddles while the sun beams down on us. A slight breeze wisps through the palm trees, and it feels as if we're in actual paradise on Earth. I take off my shirt and throw it on the beach, trying to enjoy the warmth while I can. In a month, the temperatures in Texas will drop below forty before lunchtime, so warm days like this will be few and far between.

"She was cute, don't you think?" he asks, removing his T-shirt too.

As soon as I get ready to open my mouth and give him some shit, Trish comes bopping toward us in a small bikini. After a quick explanation of how to mount the board, she starts giving extra attention to Dylan, allowing her eyes to linger a little too long on his chest and abs. I encourage him with every innuendo she throws his way.

"Get on your knees." She points at the board that sits on top of the sand. "This is a very important *position* especially when you need a break from…" She licks her lips, and Dylan waits on edge for her to finish the sentence.

"…standing," she says with a wink.

Considering we're the only two in the class, I'm starting to feel like the third wheel.

"I agree," he says with a smirk, eating up everything she's saying. I'm trying really hard to keep my scoffs and eye rolls to myself.

Once we've practiced a few times on the sand, she tells us to take our boards to the water, which is as calm as can be. We mount our boards how she taught us, and at first, we both look like baby cows learning to walk for the first time—all wobbly and trying not to fall on our asses.

But before too long, we're both standing and paddling around.

After an hour, Trish lets us know the beginner's lesson is over and releases us to the ocean alone but tells Dylan now that if he wants another lesson, she'd be happy to give him a one-on-one. Knowing Dylan, he'd be more than happy to take her up on that offer, but he wouldn't leave me alone, so he tells her maybe another time.

Without further hesitation, we head back into the water, but paddle farther than before. From a distance, the people lying out on the beach look tiny, and I know it's time we turn around.

"Race you back?" I ask Dylan, and he happily agrees to the challenge.

"Loser buys drinks tonight," Dylan calls out, confidently.

"Deal." We line our boards up and then count down before we both take off.

We're laughing and talking shit, and just as I start to pass Dylan, he takes his paddle and swings it at me, but misses and falls off his board.

"Cheater!" I yell back at him, waiting for a rebuttal. I'm halfway to the shore when I turn around and realize he's not on his board or floating in the water. Panic rushes through me, and I start yelling his name before diving from my board back toward him. I swim as hard as I can, searching for any sign of life when I finally find him sinking lower into the water.

Seconds feel like minutes as I wrap my arm around Dylan's chest and pull us up above the surface. I swim as fast as I can back to shore with one arm. Before I make it to the shore, a few people take notice and run into the water to help me carry him. I'm freaking the fuck out as Dylan lies on the sand on his back, blue in the face and completely unresponsive.

Like an angel, River comes running from out of nowhere and immediately goes to work on Dylan. Without hesitation, she checks his pulse and begins chest compressions as hard and fast as she can. It all happens so quickly that I can barely think, and I feel so helpless as River directs her ear to his mouth to check if he's breathing. Someone behind me cries out on the phone, and I realize the woman is on the phone with 911. I'm completely speechless watching River work like a pro. She tilts his head back and pushes air into his mouth twice before going back to chest compressions. A moment later, Dylan begins to move.

"He's breathing!" River exclaims, rolling him over onto his side, and I watch as he coughs up water. The crowd that gathered around us breathes a collective sigh of relief as Dylan blinks up at us.

Just as he comes to, the paramedics arrive, and once River explains what happened, they begin the process of inserting an IV with fluids into his arm and ask Dylan how he's feeling. He responds while they place an EKG monitor on his chest and clip a thing onto his finger.

"What's that for?" I ask, nodding my head at it

"A pulse oximeter so we can see how much oxygen is in his blood and make sure he's getting enough air," one of the paramedics answer.

"The normal range is between ninety-five to ninety-nine percent, so he's a little low right now, but that's common given the circumstances," the other paramedic adds.

More questions are asked as to what happened, how long was he underwater, how long it took for him to start breathing on his own, and River and I answer the best we can as they load him onto a gurney and recommend he see a doctor for follow-up tests.

"I don't need to go," Dylan says softly, trying to sit up. "I'm just fine," he insists.

"You should," I hear River tell him. "They need to make sure you're okay, and that I didn't fracture a rib or anything." She smirks at him, and he actually decides to listen to her.

As Dylan's pushed into the ambulance, I climb in behind and sit on the bench next to the gurney. The paramedics strap in and we take off to the hospital. On the way, all I can think of is how his mama is going to kill me as I replay every moment in my head.

One minute, he was being an asshole trying to cheat by

knocking me off my board, and the next I'm dragging his unconscious body to the beach because he nearly drowns. It seems surreal, actually. I couldn't find him, and when I did, adrenaline pumped through me so hard I rushed back to shore as fast as possible.

Once we arrive and Dylan is unloaded, they immediately move him to a private triage room as we wait for a doctor to evaluate him.

"What the fuck happened?" I ask when we're finally alone, emotion thick in my voice.

"I don't know," Dylan tells me, making eye contact. "I was never a strong swimmer."

I run my fingers through my hair. "How have we been friends for forever, and I never knew that? Why'd you agreed to get in the water then? And why the hell did you go out that far?" I'm throwing question after question at him because I don't know what else to do. I've never felt fear like that in my entire life. "You could've died, Dylan. Do you know what your mama would've done to me if that had happened? I would've blamed myself forever," I scold a little too sternly. My face softens, and I let out a long breath. "I'm glad you're okay. You scared the shit out of me."

Dylan smiles. "Not getting soft on me, are you?"

"You're a dick," I spit out just as a female nurse walks in, holding a file in her hand.

"Mr. Hart," she addresses sweetly. "How are you feeling?"

Dylan sits up in bed. "Better. I'm breathing," he jokes.

"That's great to hear. Just to be completely transparent, the doctor wants to do chest X-rays to double-check there's no fluid in your lungs or anything. Otherwise, you could get pneumonia, and that can be very serious," she continues to explain. "The X-ray technician will be here in the next few minutes with their portable machine to do testing. But before then, do you have any questions for me?"

Dylan glances over at me, then back at the nurse. "How long do I have to stay here?"

"The doctor will follow up with you on that after the results come in, but normally it's recommended you stay overnight so we can monitor your oxygen levels and make sure everything stays normal."

Dylan huffs, and I can tell he's unhappy with that answer. After the nurse exits the room, he starts his bitching.

"I'm a walking party foul! All I wanted to do was a have a good time and now look at me. Being pumped full of shit and having to get X-rays of my lungs…" Before he can finish his rant, the technician walks in, and I'm asked to wait in the hallway.

I sit in the waiting area and find myself becoming more antsy with each tick of the second hand on the clock. Standing, I walk to the window and stare out at the blue sky and thank my lucky stars that Dylan is alive. It was such a close call and frightening as fuck. Sure, I've had to deal with some shit on the ranch, like cuts and bruises, dying animals, and snake bites, but there's nothing like watching my best friend lie unconscious. Before I'm allowed to fall too deeply into my thoughts, I'm told I can go back into the room.

I enter, and we sit there for at least an hour listening to the beeps of the machines before a doctor finally enters with a file in her hand and a smile on her face.

"Hi, Mr. Hart. I'm Dr. Jacobs. I've had a chance to review your X-rays," she states sweetly.

"Howdy," Dylan greets in return.

She opens the file and grabs the films before placing them onto a screen, and the X-rays light up when she clicks a button. "Your lungs look clear for the most part. This cloudy area down here…" She outlines the area with the end of her pen. "…somewhat concerns me, so just to be on the safe side, we're going to keep you overnight for observation. I'd like to continue monitoring your heart rate and oxygen levels and keep you hydrated with the IV. I'll order another X-ray in the morning just to be sure, and if everything looks clear, you'll be discharged." She flashes a hopeful smile, though Dylan looks displeased.

Dylan forces out a smile so as not to be rude.

Dr. Jacobs smiles back at him. "Do you have any questions for me?"

"No, ma'am. Thank you," he tells her.

"If you need anything till then, you can press the call button, and the nurses will be happy to help. Don't hesitate to reach out, especially if you start feeling any differently," she says before leaving the room.

We sit in silence for a few moments, and that's when Dylan groans.

"Suppose that means you won't be texting the code word tonight." I chuckle, breaking the tension, but he rolls his eyes instead.

"On a serious note, after I'm moved to my room, you should go back to the hotel where you can actually sleep comfortably. I don't want you to be a prisoner in the hospital, too."

I stare at him. "Are you sure? I'll stay here with you. I don't mind."

"Yes, I'll be fine," he insists. "I'm gonna try to get some sleep so I can live it up the rest of the time we're here. I don't think what happened has completely set in yet, but I feel exhausted, and it's barely five."

I nod, not wanting to argue with him because I can only imagine how he feels. Though I don't feel right about leaving him here, I don't argue with him. An hour passes and Dylan is finally moved to his room. I go with him, and when we enter, I'm almost grateful he doesn't want me to stay. It's small and stuffy, and there's a chair in the corner with a blanket draped over the arm. A nurse closes the blinds and tells Dylan the kitchen will close pretty soon. He smiles and nods, but I can tell he's too tired to eat.

"If you need me before tomorrow, don't hesitate to call me. Also, text me when you get discharged, okay? And don't be too damn stubborn while you're here."

"I'll let you know," he says.

As I walk toward the door to leave, Dylan calls my name. "Alex."

I turn around and look at him. "Yeah?"

"Thanks for saving my life."

I smile. "Really glad you weren't a statistic, man. Next time, no fucking water sports." I point a finger at him as if I'm scolding him. "Honestly though, without River, I don't know what would've happened." I shrug, hating to admit that and terrified of the what-ifs.

"Well, from the sounds of it, both of you saved my life. I owe you one," he says sincerely, pulling the blanket up to his chest and releasing a yawn. "You better not tell my mama."

"I won't. I'll see you tomorrow," I say as I exit.

After a taxi ride across the island, I arrive at the hotel and head up to the room. As soon as I get in the room, I jump in the shower and wash the day away before changing into some jeans and a button-up shirt. I grab one of the miniature whiskey bottles from the wet bar and slide the balcony door open. I plan to soak up the late evening breeze and forget about what happened. From a distance, I can see the calmness of the water and hear the wind blowing through the palm trees.

Glancing around outside, I scan the bar outside near the pool, and that's when I see her.

River.

She's smiling and chatting with Natalie, and I find myself watching her play with her long locks. I notice a few little things, like how she throws her head back when she's truly laughing. One can only imagine the conversation they're having after all the excitement today, and Natalie seems like the kind of friend who constantly gives her shit regardless if she saved a man's life or not. There's no telling what they're discussing.

I let out a small chuckle and realize I never properly thanked her for stepping in without hesitation and saving Dylan.

That changes *now.*

CHAPTER SIX

RIVER

After the day's excitement, I need a drink. Or ten.

I've saved many lives before; hell, I've worked on a child's chest, pumping and giving him CPR while the mother screamed and cried and called me every curse word in the book. I've also had many experiences with life-threatening emergencies, even before I was in nursing school, but the Dylan situation definitely made me nervous.

"Look at the hero walking in," Natalie teases as soon as I take the seat next to her at the bar.

"Stop," I groan. "I can't escape it."

"Of course not! You're the town hero!" she mocks, lifting her shot glass up victoriously before tilting her head back and shooting it down her throat.

I give her a look that tells her to tone it down a notch.

No one could've anticipated what happened with Dylan today. Over the years, I've found when emergencies arise, I don't give myself time to even think before rushing into action. As soon as I saw that blond guy pull Dylan out of the water, I knew something was wrong. I hurried over and immediately saw how pale he was as he lay motionless on the sand.

The entire scene has been running on repeat through my mind

nonstop. Relief flooded through me when he finally came to, and I assume he's going to be okay now, or at least I hope. I'm thankful he agreed to go to the hospital because you never know what other issues can arise from situations like that. That alone eased my mind because there have been many instances of others not being so lucky after nearly drowning.

"Hey, you're that girl who saved that guy on the beach today!" the bartender shouts loud enough for everyone in the pool area to hear.

Natalie responds before I can. "She sure fucking did!"

I glance at her and scowl, not wanting the extra attention.

"Drinks on me, pretty lady," he says with a wide grin. "What you did was amazing."

I force out a smile. "Thanks. I'm a nurse, so it's just instinct," I respond, trying to brush it off so he stops talking about it.

"So what can I get you? You deserve one!" he insists.

"She needs sex on the beach!" Natalie hollers before I can speak, *again*.

"Nat!" I scold.

"Oh, sorry. I meant, she'll take a Sex on the Beach." She looks over at me and winks. All I can manage is to shake my head at her and laugh.

"You got it," the bartender responds, reaching for a clean glass.

"Fruity drinks get me drunk way too fast," I complain, just loud enough for Natalie to hear me.

"That's the point," she states matter-of-factly. "Unless you plan on staying sober this trip?" She grins.

"Not if you're going to be this way the entire time." I chuckle, and she's too drunk to even realize that was a burn directed at her.

Moments later, the bartender serves me my drink and winks before walking to the other end of the bar to help another customer.

Natalie holds up her drink before I can even take a sip of mine.

"To River!" she shouts, making Adam and me hold our drinks up, too. "For being a kick-ass nurse!"

Okay, I can drink to that, I think to myself before clanking my glass with theirs and taking my first sip. It's strong as fuck, but luckily, my room isn't far.

Adam knows how Natalie gets when she's in party mode, so he knows she'll need some assistance getting back to their room tonight, which is why he takes it easy and only drinks a couple. I haven't seen her this way in a really long time, but I know she works hard and doesn't let loose that much anymore. At least not since our early college days.

"River," I hear a rough and deep voice say behind me. It's one I recognize.

"Alex!" Natalie squeals before I even have a chance to turn around. "How's your friend?"

"He's doing fine. They kept him overnight for observation."

Inhaling a deep breath, hoping I don't look too tipsy right now, I straighten my posture and turn around to face him.

"That's good," I sincerely say in response to Dylan's condition.

I don't know why, but things feel awkward between us. We barely spoke on the beach today mainly because there was no time. I didn't even know his name until just now, yet he knows mine.

"Can I sit?" he asks, nodding his head toward the empty seat next to me.

"Of course, you can!" Natalie answers.

"I think we should take a walk," Adam says, sensing the awkward tension between Alex and me and grabs Natalie's hand.

"Ooh, I've always wanted to take a walk on the beach. It sounds so romantic," she slurs against his chest after he steadies her.

I chuckle, while silently thanking Adam because no telling what embarrassing things Natalie would say in her current condition.

After Alex takes the seat next to me, he gets the bartender's attention and orders himself a beer then places money on the counter.

"So you didn't stay with him?" I ask, facing the bar again.

"I offered, but us Southern men are stubborn when it comes to our pride," he explains with a smirk on his face. "I told him to call me when he's discharged so I can bring him back. I'm sure he'll be itching to party."

"As long as he stays far away from the water," I add, smiling.

The bartender takes his money off the bar while shooting me a wink.

"So I don't think we've formally met," he states, holding out his hand. "I'm Alex Bishop."

Swallowing, I place my hand in his. "River Lancaster."

"That's a beautiful name," he tells me, moving my knuckles up to his lips and placing a soft kiss on them.

"Thank you," I whisper.

We stare into each other's eyes, and he keeps my hand in his. Somehow, I'm stuck in his trance, and I don't know how to get out. He's a beefy guy, solid and muscular, and I've never seen a man like him before. Most of the guys I've dated were gym rats, but I can tell he's not. His body was built from hard labor.

"Here you go, bud," the bartender interrupts with a sneaky grin on his face as he sets the beer down. The intense moment fades, and he gently releases my hand.

"Thanks." He tips his head to the guy and brings the glass to his lips. I find myself watching his every move before blinking and tearing away my gaze.

He sucks down half his drink before setting it down. Turning toward me, his eyes lock on mine and pin me to him. "So I actually never thanked you for today. I was scared shitless and you doing CPR ultimately saved his life. I don't know what I would've done without you."

A blush surfaces at his compliment, which is insane since I do this type of stuff every day at work. I tell myself it's what I do, it's in my nature, but to hear those words from him has my heart racing.

"So thank you, River. Sincerely. Those words hardly do justice to how thankful we both are that you were there today."

His words are so soft and tender, his accent making the words even sweeter.

I release a small smile and lower my eyes before blinking and meeting his again. "You're welcome. I didn't think twice about it and would do it over again if I had to."

"That's what makes you so amazing." He winks.

"I'm actually a nurse," I admit. "I've had lots of training." I shrug as if it's not significant.

"That makes a lot of sense actually," he says, nodding. "You were so calm, and when you spoke to the paramedics, you used all the technical terms."

"Yeah, they kind of beat those into you during nursing school."

He laughs, reaching for his beer again. I grab my own drink and take another sip.

"Where you from?" he asks as we easily fall into conversation.

"Wisconsin," I answer. "Milwaukee, actually."

"Oh, wow." His eyes widen. "Aren't you known for being the beer state?"

"Dairy, actually, but beer is basically its own food group up there." I shrug and smile.

Laughing, he nods as if he agrees.

"Or I guess you could say the frozen state considering we have some of the coldest winters."

"Is that why you're here? To escape the cold weather?"

"Oh, it's not even that cold yet. Still had highs in the forties when we left."

"Fuck." He shakes his head. "That's too damn cold for this born-and-raised Texan."

"I guessed Texas."

"That obvious, huh?" He smirks, and I playfully shrug.

"Actually, the coldest times are between January and March. It's usually in the negatives with the wind chill, but that's when the ice freezes on the water and becomes thick enough for people to go ice fishing. They build these ice shanties and carve a hole in the ice, so they can sit around and fish for hours."

"And y'all do that for fun?" He raises a brow, skeptical.

"Yup." I laugh, nodding. "Snowmobiling, snowboarding, skiing. All that stuff. But that's not until January usually, sometimes even February. Right now, it's just cold and gloomy, not yet ready to give up fall even though winter is right around the corner."

"I bet that brings lots of dumbasses into the hospitals up there."

"Well, yes it does, but I actually work at the children's hospital in the PICU."

His eyes narrow as if he's not sure what that entails.

"I work with sick kids who need around-the-clock care and treatment."

"Wow…" His voice is soft. "That has to be a tough job."

I nod, agreeing. "It is. But I love it. As bad as it can be, it's also very rewarding. Many of the kids have been there a while as they await transplants or getting treatments for life-threatening illnesses. I get to know them and their families quite well. It's always disheartening when a child isn't getting better, but it's part of the job." I shrug, taking a gulp of my drink to get ahold of my emotions.

"I can tell how passionate you are just by the way you talk about it. And especially how you ran to Dylan's rescue without a second thought."

"I am. I've wanted to be a nurse since I was a teen." I basically already was to my baby sister by the time I was twelve.

My drink is completely gone, but I keep sucking on the straw, and Alex has already ordered his third beer when Adam and Natalie come strolling back by.

"We just wanted to let you know we're heading to our room,"

Adam tells me, holding Natalie's hand tightly as if to keep her from roaming away.

"Are you two getting along?" Natalie speaks up, making things awkward again. "He's single, River. Don't worry, I checked for ya," she says nice and loud, flashing a very obvious wink my way.

"Thanks," I mutter, sliding off my stool and tossing my purse over my shoulder. "Let me help Adam get you back to your room before you tell everyone here I have daddy issues and a broken heart, m'kay?"

"I would never say that," she whisper-shouts in a very serious drunken tone, forcing a laugh out of me. "Don't worry, Alex. River's totally normal and is a goddess in and out of the sheets." She winks at him, and she doesn't know how to wink with alcohol in her system, so she's basically just blinking harshly at him like a witch trying to put a spell on someone.

"Okay, time to go." I grab Natalie's other hand and start to follow Adam.

"Bye, River!" Alex calls out, grabbing my attention.

I blush for some unknown reason and wave back. "See ya!"

The first five days in Key West have certainly been interesting. After meeting Alex and Dylan on Monday, we haven't seen much of them since then. We've run into them during breakfast, but then Natalie and I have kept busy shopping and exploring the streets as well as tanning and drinking by the pool. I'm sure

TAMING HIM

they've been busy themselves, but Alex has still been on my mind for some reason.

I can't deny that he's good looking, and his accent definitely alerts my senses, but there's something else I can't quite put my finger on. However, knowing my history with men, it's probably not a good thing. Even if he is single, we're from two different worlds. What would be the point of getting involved with someone who lives hundreds of miles away?

The fact that I'm even thinking about this makes me want to slap myself.

It's gotta be from all the sun, I tell myself. *Or the abundance of alcohol.*

Either way, I'm quick to push those types of thoughts from my head. There's no time for men in my life right now, especially after Asshole wasted half a year of it.

"Tonight, we're going to a pub on Duval Street!" Natalie tells me as we sit for lunch.

"I think I need to detox for a night," I whimper, waking up with a headache for the fourth morning in a row.

"No, tonight's different!" she insists, and I resist rolling my eyes because she says that every time. "It's ladies' night, which means we drink for dirt cheap! Plus, there's a local live band, and I really, really want to hear them play. Please!" she begs pathetically, yet it works.

"Being the third wheel was cute the first time, but now I'm just looking pathetic as fuck," I tell her, groaning at the thought. I stab a piece of chicken with my fork and stuff it into my mouth. Considering the drinks have been nonstop, I need all the food I can get to absorb the alcohol.

"Oh, I'm sorry. Did you come to have fun and drink, or did you come to wallow like an old lady?" she scolds in a motherly tone. When she catches me roll my eyes that time, she continues. "That's what I thought. You can be responsible and shit when we get back home. Until then, we live it up!" She raises both arms above her head like we're on a roller coaster.

"Okay, I'll go, just put your damn arms back down." I chuckle around my forkful of food.

"Invite Alex and Dylan," she tells me again, as she has for the last three nights. I've already told her my concerns and reasons for not wanting to get too close, but she waves it off and reminds me I'm here to have fun.

I head back to my room and get ready for the night. Natalie ordered me to wear my best dress, which isn't hard considering I only own one. Working nonstop doesn't give me a lot of time for going out or dancing, but this little black number has paid for itself in drinks time and time again.

Once I've showered and finished my hair and makeup, I slip it on and pull out my heels. I'm not sure exactly what kind of bar this is, but if there's dancing and a band, I can only assume I'll need to dress up.

I'm used to throwing my blonde hair up into a ponytail or bun while working, but tonight, I decide to leave it down and curl it in loose waves. I take a look in the mirror and barely recognize myself but smile at the reflection anyway.

A knock on the door grabs my attention, and as I walk toward it, I grab my purse and phone off the table before opening it.

"Girl!" Natalie squeals, barging her way in. "Hot damn."

She gives me a once-over, and I do the same to her. She's wearing an emerald cocktail dress that complements her fiery hair and pale complexion. She looks damn good, but Natalie always does. Walking over to the full-length mirror attached to the closet door, she reaches into her purse and digs out her lipstick.

"This color would look amazing on you. Come here," she orders, opening the lid and twisting the bottom till a bright red color appears.

"Holy shit, that's bright," I tell her, wary of putting it on. "What color is that?"

"It's called Hooker Red, but don't let the name scare you. It's actually really pretty on."

My eyes widen, and my brows rise. "Why don't I trust you?"

She chuckles, then pulls me to her till we're both in the mirror's view. "Just shush and trust me, all right?"

"But I don't trust you." I laugh, pulling away, but she grabs my wrist and pulls me back again.

Giving in, I let her put the Hooker Red color on my lips, and when she turns me around to face the mirror, I actually don't hate it.

"Told you," she gushes.

I playfully scoff in defeat and smile. "You got lucky." I point at my black dress that would match any color anyway.

"Okay, let's go! Adam's waiting for us in the lobby."

Even though the bar isn't that far, we take a taxi because I'll be damned if I'm walking in these heels. I don't need to go back to work with a sprained ankle, or worse.

"Oh my God!" Natalie squeals as we exit the backseat. "How cool is this?"

People are piling out of the bar, hanging out on the streets, and the music is so loud it could probably be heard from the beach. This is definitely going to be a wild night.

CHAPTER SEVEN

ALEX

HANGING out with River and talking to her really opened my eyes to the kind of person she is—kind, caring, sweet. She didn't hesitate for a second to come to Dylan's rescue, and I find myself so intrigued by her that I want to know even more—if she'll let me.

"Did you harass the nurses all night?" I tease Dylan while we're in the back of the taxi.

"More like, they harassed *me* all damn night. When I'd finally fall asleep, they'd barge in, flick on the light, and say they needed to check my vitals. The first time, I was like okay, no big deal. But by the fourth time, I told her to get the hell out of my room."

I snort, shaking my head at him. "You did not."

"I sure as fuck did. Couldn't get no more than fifty minutes of sleep before they were waking me up, and when four a.m. rolled around, I was over it."

"Damn. Now, I'm glad you made me go back to the hotel last night. Otherwise, I'd be a cranky asshole like you." I grin, adjusting my ball cap.

He wrinkles his nose and doesn't respond. Once we're back to our room, it's just past noon, and I'm starving.

"Should we find someplace to eat?"

"Sounds good to me. Let me grab a quick shower first to get this hospital stank off me."

I grab the remote and flick on the TV while he showers. The first few days in Key West have definitely been interesting ones, and even though it got off to a rough start with Dylan's near-drowning, I know we aren't going to let that ruin our time here. In fact, Dylan's ready to party more now than ever.

Over the next few days, we continue exploring the island and even take one of those bus tours. I keep a lookout for River but don't see her at the pool, bar, or beach. I'm partially worried she left, but then I remember Natalie saying they were here for two weeks too.

"Stop," Dylan groans as we walk around the historical parts of the Keys.

"What?" I ask, not bothering to look at him.

"You keep looking for River."

That grabs my attention. "What are you talking about? I'm looking at all the…" It's then I realize I have no idea what I'm looking at. "This historical building."

He scoffs. "You idiot. This is the Hemingway House."

Blinking, I look around and realize he's right when I see the sign. We've been walking around and taking buses to different areas, but I've also been so lost in my head I hadn't realized where we were.

"I knew that."

Looking up at him, he rolls his eyes and keeps walking as I follow behind.

"Okay, I was looking for her," I finally admit, catching up. "I haven't seen her since the bar on Monday night, and I kind of want to see her again. Is that so bad?"

"See her or bang her?" he teases, knowing my reputation.

It takes me a minute to really think about it. "Well, I wouldn't say *no* if she offered, but I really liked talking with River and just being around her. I don't know, she has this vibe I'm gravitating toward. It's hard to explain," I confess, feeling more confused than before. I don't typically hang out with girls unless it's to get her into my bed.

"I should've known," he says as I fall into step with him, and we make our way back to the hotel.

"Known what?"

"That you'd get hung up on the first hot girl you saw—who's way out of your league, by the way—even though there are probably hundreds for you to pick from, and now I'm gonna hear about it for the next ten days."

"Okay, asshole." I punch him in the shoulder. "I do not get hung up on girls. Wanting to chat up a girl is no different than when I meet a girl in a bar back home," I lie, mostly to convince myself, but Dylan knows me way too well to know I'm bullshittin' through my teeth.

"Fine, then prove it. Let's go out tonight, hit up a busy bar or somethin' and find a girl to hook up with."

"You're telling me to go sleep with someone to prove to you I'm not hung up on River?" I confirm, realizing how insane it sounds. But what's crazier is how much she intrigues me, and we've only just met. If I'm going to hook up with a chick during this trip, I want it to be her.

Any other time, I'd be all over a dare like this. I'm not about to admit that to him, though.

"Pff, easy." I swallow, not wanting him to see through my lies.

After grabbing a quick bite, we go back to the hotel and get ready for the night. I'm more determined to prove to myself that I *can't* be hung up on River than to prove Dylan wrong. I can do this. I can find a chick and bring her back and fuck her brains out. Hell, it should be second nature by now.

"You ready?" Dylan calls out an hour later.

"Almost," I tell him.

I finish up and step out of the bathroom, dressed and ready to head out. Deciding to leave my ball cap off, I comb my fingers through my hair until it's tousled, then I decide to wear my black cowboy boots with my relaxed fit jeans.

"'Kay, I'm good to go."

Dylan and I walk down Duval Street, knowing it has the best nightlife near the hotel. We've learned a cab ride back is cheap since most of the bars are within walking distance, but when you're tipsy and can't walk straight, it feels like miles.

"Don't forget our deal," Dylan reminds me as if I need reminding.

"Yeah, yeah. I know."

He slaps a hand on my shoulder. "Good. Don't forget the code word either." He flashes a shit-eating smirk.

We head into the bar we've visited the last couple of nights and order our first round of beers. The streets are packed with tourists, and my hope for seeing River again diminishes.

"Hey, mates!" Liam, a guy we met the other night, greets us just as we order our second round. He has a girl hanging off his arm tonight, though. He's from Sydney, which was pretty obvious once we heard him speak.

"Hey!" Dylan and I both say. "How's it goin'?"

Before Liam can respond, the girl speaks up. "Oh my God! I love your accents!" she squeals.

"They sound like you," he tells the girl, but she dismisses him with a wave.

"Texas, right?" she asks in an overly flirty tone.

"Yes, ma'am," Dylan answers. "Where you from?"

"Ontario," she replies with a wide smile. "I'm Jessica, by the way. I just love the south. I'm completely infatuated with it."

The girl's hand loosens out of Liam's arm, and soon he's shrugging her off and ordering himself another drink.

"Did you find your girl yet?" he asks me while Dylan chats with Jessica, or, rather, Jessica chats up Dylan.

I frown. "No. I'm starting to think it's hopeless." I shrug, pretending it's no big deal.

"Oh, for fuck's sake," Dylan interrupts with a groan. "You told Liam about her, too?"

Liam grins and nods.

"Not really," I start to explain. "He asked why I wasn't out on the dance floor, and I said I was trying to find a girl I met the other night. That's all."

"River," Liam adds. "Guess we'll need to put together a search party soon." He chuckles.

Dylan shakes his head disapprovingly. "Well, he's been given a new mission tonight," he tells Liam and Jessica. "Find a girl to bring back to the room to prove he's *not* hung up on her." He jabs his elbow into my side.

Liam's eyes widen as he takes a pull from his beer. "Really, mate?" He turns and looks at me for confirmation.

I shrug and purse my lips.

"If he brings a girl home tonight, where does that leave you?" Jessica asks slyly, directing all her attention back to Dylan.

Tuning them out, I turn toward the bar to order another beer. If I have to go through with this dare, fuck if I can do it sober.

"What if you end up finding her, after all?" Liam asks, sitting on the stool next to me without concern that Jessica is now all over Dylan. Apparently, he's not bothered by it.

I shrug, not really wanting to answer that. "What if I don't?"

"You won't know, but I bet if you do, you'll regret sleeping with someone else." His words go straight to my gut.

"I've only regretted sleeping with two women in my entire life," I tell him matter-of-factly. "One was because she *forgot* to tell me she was engaged—and I don't sleep with women who are spoken for—and the other because she turned out to be bat-shit crazy. She left me thirty-four voicemails within twenty-four hours, and because that wasn't enough of a hint to leave me the hell alone, she showed up at my door."

Liam starts cracking up laughing. "No!"

"Not only that, she shows up wearing an oversized trench coat with a bottle of whiskey."

"A trench coat?" He looks confused.

"Yep, and when I told her I wasn't interested, she opened her coat and was completely naked." I take a pull from my beer, shaking my head at the memory.

"Holy fuck. Naked?" Liam continues to laugh. "How'd you talk your way out of that one?"

I hang my head and shake it.

"No…" he slowly says. "No, mate. Don't tell me…"

I close my eyes and reluctantly shake my head. "Yep. I blame the whiskey, though."

"So then what happened? How'd you get rid of her?"

I pinch my lips together, realizing it probably wasn't the best story to share with a person I barely know, but what the hell. It's not like I'll see him ever again once we leave.

"Walked her to the door the next morning, told her I'd call her, and then changed my number."

Liam is dying with laughter, completely losing control.

"Then when I saw her at the diner in town two months later, she walked up to me with an entire pie and smashed it in my face in front of everyone."

"Oh, fuck." Liam continues his fit of laughter.

"Then to top it off, she grabbed my hot cup of coffee and poured it in my lap."

Dylan finally breaks away from Jessica long enough to show his interest in our conversation. "You talkin' 'bout Crazy Carly?" He grins, and when I confirm it, he starts laughing along with Liam.

"Crazy Carly?" Liam asks. "Sounds fitting."

"Way, way too fitting," I agree, grabbing my beer and finishing it.

We hang out with Liam and Jessica for another hour before we decide to take off and find another bar. Loud music comes from both directions, but we head toward the bar where a live band is playing.

"You're going to run out of time," Dylan teases. "However, some girls are probably desperate enough to go back to the room with you tonight." He chuckles.

"Fuck off." I push him slightly as we enter the bar. "I don't need a babysitter, so why don't you find your own girl for the night."

"I was trying to get Jessica, but I felt like I'd be stealing her away from Liam."

"Nah, I don't think he cared. Seemed like they'd just met anyway."

"Really?" His brows raise. "Well, then I'm going to go back and find her. You sure you don't mind if I leave?"

I shoot him an irritated look. "No. Go. Just make sure to check your phone or text me if you head back to the room. I don't need to see your white ass again."

"You got it." And with that, he turns around and heads out.

Relieved I finally have him off my back, I step inside. The live music is loud as fuck, but within a few minutes, my ears adjust, and it's not so bad. I can't help it, but I glance around with hopes that my luck changes.

I head up to the bar and order another drink, and just as I turn around to face the band again, I see *her*. Blinking several times to make sure I'm not imagining it, I take a few steps closer to confirm.

She's in a short, tight black dress and her beautiful blonde hair is down around her shoulders in loose waves. I only got a glimpse of her side profile, but I'm damn certain it's her. After a minute, I realize she's not alone. Natalie and Adam are next to her, and a guy I don't recognize has his arms around her waist. My heart races and my feet gravitate toward her before I can stop myself.

"River," I lean down and shout, hoping she can hear me over the music.

Startled, she quickly turns and when she realizes it's me, her eyes and smile widen.

"Alex!" she shouts back. "Hey!"

Natalie, Adam, and the other guy all turn around at the same time.

"Alex! Yay!" Natalie shouts. She attacks me and wraps her arms around my neck. "Where have you been?"

"We've been out exploring and partying," I respond. "Haven't seen you guys around in a few days," I say, hoping I sound casual, but I can feel the energy buzzing between River and me. Lowering my eyes, I keep them locked on her. "What have you guys been doin'?"

"Beachin'!" Natalie offers in her tipsy voice.

I grin and nod. "Can I buy you a drink?" I ask River, keeping my attention on her. The guy's grip tightens as he pulls her to his side, and my teeth clench.

"She's with me," the guy speaks up, his voice weak and pathetic.

Blinking, I take one look at the dweeb before bringing my eyes back to River. She lowers her head as if she's not sure what to say or do.

"River," I drawl, grabbing her attention. "Is that right?"

She pulls her lower lip between her teeth and bites down.

"Dude, what's your problem? I said she's with me, so back the fuck off." The guy's voice gets louder, and River visibly cringes.

Taking that as a sign, I grab River's hand and pull her out of his grip. "Not anymore. Get lost, asshole."

I lead her the other direction before the guy can even respond. She clings to me as if her life depends on it and when we reach the bar, I swing her around until she's facing me.

"Who was that?"

"Brant...*something*," she answers with little confidence. "We met earlier, a few hours ago, I guess."

My brows raise. "And he already held his claim on you?"

She sighs. "I guess, I mean...I was dancing, and he just started getting closer and closer, and because Natalie demanded I have fun tonight, I was trying to let loose." She shrugs almost as if she's embarrassed about it, and I feel bad for asking.

"Well, we can still have fun tonight." I grin, and she flashes a wide, genuine smile up at me.

"Sounds good to me."

I order us a round of drinks, a beer for me and a cocktail for her. We sit at the bar and chat for at least thirty minutes before Natalie and Adam find us. River is tipsy from already having a few drinks tonight, but Natalie is past the point of tipsy.

"You two are so damn cute together!" she squeals, wrapping her arm around River and squeezing. "Seriously!"

"Okay, Nat." River laughs. "Time for you to be cut off," she says, eyeing Adam.

"Guys, I mean it!" Her tone is so serious, it's hard not to laugh. "River's been talking about you nonstop," she directs toward me, and River's face immediately turns red. "Alex this and Alex that. It was getting to the point where I was about to send her to rehab."

"Oh my God." River's eyes squeeze tight before she opens them.

"Is that so?" I grin.

"I *maybe* mentioned you a couple of times," she admits, the red deepening on her cheeks.

Leaning down to her ear so only she can hear me, I whisper, "It's really fuckin' adorable when you blush."

She sucks in her lower lip, shaking her head up at me. "Don't be getting a big head now," she teases.

Thank God Dylan isn't with me because I know he'd be telling her the same damn thing right now.

"I'm going to take Natalie home," Adam interrupts. "River, do you want to ride with us in the cab?"

"Um…" she contemplates while Adam looks up at me, giving me a warning look.

"If you want to stay, I'll make sure she gets back safely," I promise, making sure Adam can hear my sincerity.

"That okay with you?" Adam directs the question to River, making sure she's comfortable with staying.

"Yeah, I'll be fine." She smiles.

"You two would make the most beautiful babies." Natalie

hums, wrapping her arms around River's neck and lazily dropping her head on her shoulders. "Just don't have babies before I do, okay?"

"No worries," River says, confidently. "You two can make all the babies you want."

Natalie giggles, and Adam carefully wraps his arms around her and leads her away.

I chuckle as we both turn back around. "That girl knows the definition of having a good time, doesn't she?"

River laughs, nodding. "She's drunk so much, she'll still be drunk when we get home."

We continue chatting, and I order us another round because I don't want this time with her to end. The live band is still jamming, and the crowd fills in even more.

Just as the band starts singing a John Mayer song, I notice River's eyes light up.

"Oh my God, I *love* this song!" she gushes, and it takes me less than five seconds to decide to pull her out on the dance floor.

"Come on," I say, grabbing her hand and helping her off the stool.

She lets me lead her to the middle of the room, and soon our bodies are fused together as our hands wrap around each other.

"'Slow Dancing in a Burning Room' is my absolute favorite," she tells me as we rock back and forth.

"I can't say I'm familiar with it, but I can see why you like it."

"He gets a bad rap in the tabloids, but he's talented as hell," she says, her chest moving more rapidly against mine. She looks up at me with bright green eyes filled with lust, and I know she's thinking the same thing I am.

"Maybe he's just one of those misunderstood types." I grin.

She smirks. "Aren't all musicians?"

The longer I listen, the more I understand the meaning behind the lyrics. The guitar acoustics are rad as fuck, but it only adds to the melancholy of the song. The steadiness of the beat really gives me that visual of two people being together, yet they know their relationship is coming to an end, and it's only a matter of time before it burns out.

"The lyrics are kind of depressing," I say, moving her closer to me.

"They really are," she agrees. "You can hear the heartbreak in his voice."

"It's tragic," I add.

She blinks, giving me those sultry eyes again, and I can no longer hold back. I cup her face in my hand and watch her for a moment, just staring into her eyes before I lean down and press my mouth to hers.

Her lips move against mine, parting so I can slip my tongue through and kiss her the way I've been dying to since the first time I saw her. My other arm tightens around her waist, holding her possessively as I inhale her scent and taste her.

River moans against my lips, encouraging me even more. My hand slips around to the back of her neck, and when her head tilts up, I deepen the kiss further. She tastes sweet and fruity, like the drinks she's been ordering, but that's not all. She has a fresh and clean scent that I inhale as my tongue twists with hers.

She grips my shirt in her fists, pulling me against her as close as we possibly can be. Taking control, she runs her hand up my body until it reaches my hair and tugs, eager to feel and taste me with the same fervor I have.

The song is ending, and I know people will soon notice us making out hardcore on the dance floor. It's not that I really care about people seeing us, but I want to do so much more than kiss her. *So* much more.

"River…" I whisper against her lips. "We should…"

"Yeah," she interrupts before I can finish. "Want to come back to my room?" she asks, and I don't know why, but I'm a bit shocked. I was going to say we should stop so we don't give the entire bar a show, but she has something much better on her mind.

"Uh, yeah." I step back slightly just as the song ends and

notice how red and swollen her lips are. Yeah, I like that look on her. "I'll close out our tab if you want to grab us an Uber?"

"Sure, I'll schedule one right now."

Taking her hand, I lead us off the dance floor and get the bartender's attention and pay. Once it's settled, I grab my phone to let Dylan know I won't be coming back to the room tonight. As soon as I unlock my phone, I see he's already texted me.

Dylan: REVERSE COWGIRL, BITCH!! Don't even think about coming back here, asshole!

Shaking my head, I laugh at his message. Guess going back for Jessica paid off.

Poor Liam.

Alex: I'm not even surprised, you fucker! I'll be at River's for the night anyway.

Alex: P.S. You're paying housekeeping to do an extra thorough cleaning tomorrow.

"Ready?" River asks, grabbing my hand. "The Uber is here."

Shit, if she only knew. I was fucking ready days ago.

CHAPTER EIGHT

RIVER

I'VE BARELY SCANNED my keycard and opened the door before Alex's mouth and hands are on me. The moment I saw him tonight, something inside me ignited, a deep desire I'd been fighting to acknowledge. Perhaps getting some of that liquid courage helped me realize I wanted him as much as he wanted me.

I cling to him as he kicks the door shut and pushes us deeper into the room. He's pulling at my dress while I undo his belt buckle and tug at the button of his jeans. Soon I'm standing in just my bra and panties while he kicks off his boots. As he cups my breast, our mouths crash together. Strong arms wrap around my waist as he pulls me up and my legs instinctively wrap around him.

"Alex!" I squeal with laughter as he walks us closer to the bed.

He plants my ass on the mattress, and I lean back just as he stands and wraps his hands around my knees. Flashing me a mischievous smirk, he pulls my body toward him until my ass is on the edge of the bed, nearly hanging off.

Leaning over me, he closes in and presses another kiss to my lips. "I hope you don't mind, but tasting you earlier has me dying to taste another part of you." He winks, making me melt at his words.

His large hand slides down my stomach and cups my pussy over my lace panties. Just the sensation of him touching me has my back arching, and I'm already desperate for more. I want anything this man is willing to give me, but I have a feeling I won't have to beg. He wants this just as much as I do.

"I can feel how wet you are already." He teases my clit with the pad of his thumb. "You want it, don't you?"

I bite my lip and nod—wanting him is an understatement at this point.

"Say it, River," he demands, his eyes locked on mine. "I won't do anything without your permission."

"Yes," I whisper, my hand reaching out to wrap around his forearm. *"Yes."* I dig my nails into him, showing him just how badly I do.

The corner of his lips tilts up, satisfied with my answer. He kneels, spreading my legs wider until they wrap around his neck. Kissing along my inner thigh, he continues rubbing circles on my clit as his mouth moves closer to where I need him. His moans are turning me on so fucking badly, I'm ready to combust.

"You liked me that day we first met, didn't you?" he asks, my mind spinning and unable to concentrate. "You pretended not to."

"No," I disagree. "I thought you were an egotistical ass."

He smiles against my leg, and I know he's amused.

"I seriously doubt that," he mocks, reaching closer to my clit. His tongue replaces his thumb, and soon, he's sucking on it through the thin fabric of my panties.

My hand fists the sheets as my eyes roll to the back of my head. I feel the strokes of his tongue along my slit and back up to suck my clit, then he repeats it several times over. The fabric just adds to the intensity, but I want to feel him against me.

I reach down with one hand and pull my panties to the side, letting him know exactly what I want. He takes my cue and wraps his hands around my ass and squeezes before sinking his tongue deep inside me.

Moaning, I use my free hand to fist his hair and keep his head anchored.

The last time I had a guy pay me this kind of attention was… hell, I don't even know how long. That's how long it's been. Most guys don't believe in foreplay, or maybe they just don't care to put in the effort. Not Alex. He's already devouring me, and I'm seconds away from exploding.

"Oh my God," I moan, the muscles tightening around his tongue. "Yes, right there!"

He flicks his tongue, swirls it around my clit, and inserts two fingers inside. *Oh God*. This guy is too fucking good. There's no way I'm going to survive him. No fucking way.

I'm on the edge when he increases his pace and pushes in deeper, his lips flicking and sucking and when he curls his finger and reaches that spot, everything tightens, and I scream.

My entire body rocks and shakes, and I've never felt anything like it from a guy going down on me. He keeps up his pace as I ride out my release, and once my body relaxes, he presses a quick kiss to my thigh. When I finally peel my eyes open, he's sucking on his fingers. *Those two fingers*. Holy fuck, that's hot.

"I knew you'd taste good, but goddamn. That should be the flavor of the fucking day." He winks, and it's hard to hold back my laughter.

As he stands looking like a Greek God, I watch him lower his jeans and kick them off along with his shirt. He's just in his boxer shorts, and my eyes lower to the very noticeable tent he's sporting. I'm staring at it so hard that I'm completely taken aback when he grabs my waist and flips me over on the bed. My legs are still hanging off the edge, so I crawl forward until I'm centered and on my elbows. He waits until I'm situated but then slaps a hand across my ass cheek.

"These aren't needed," he tells me, pulling my panties down my legs and tossing them aside. "And I think you'd be more comfortable without this." He reaches for my bra, and I chuckle a little when he starts cussing. "The fuck?"

I laugh again at how puzzled he sounds.

"The hook's in the front," I finally explain.

"Ahh, I was just about to find some scissors and cut the damn thing off."

"Figured you'd be a pro at ripping off bras," I tease as he leans down and wraps his arms around my chest.

"You're kind of damaging my ego here." I can tell he's smiling as he struggles to find the hook. Moments later, he finally unlatches it.

"Good. It could go down a few notches," I quip as I help him slide it off my arms.

"Ooh, you're even sassier when you've been drinking." I turn my head just in time to see him smirk. "Or have you just been holding back on me?"

"Get off your high horse, cowboy."

"Really? A cowboy joke?" He arches a brow as he cups my bare breast and squeezes. He begins to massage and flicks the nipple, getting it hard. My eyes close, and before I can stop myself, a moan releases. "That's what I thought, city girl."

He slaps my ass again, making it tingle. Lowering his body, he brings his mouth down to the small of my back and presses light kisses up my spine. I moan at the contact and the way his erection presses against my ass. He rocks his body against mine, letting me feel how hard he is, and it's pure torture because I want him. *All of him*.

"Alex..." I plead, his mouth sucking on my earlobe. He brushes my hair to the side and devours my neck.

"Yes?" he whispers.

"Fuck me. *Please*," I beg. I *fucking* beg because that's how worked up he has me.

Pathetic. But I can't help it. Between the alcohol buzzing through my veins and the heartbreak I'm trying to get over, I'm desperate to feel him inside me.

KENNEDY FOX

Desperate for him. Desperate to forget.

He smiles against the flesh of my neck. "How do you like it, baby?"

I hadn't expected him to ask me that, but if I was honest, it was nice to actually be asked. Lord knows, Asshole never did or put my needs and wants first.

"Hard," I answer, hoping I don't sound pathetic in my plea. "And rough."

"Fuck, River…" he growls in my ear. "That's the hottest damn thing I've ever heard. You sure you're up for that?"

I turn my head and grin. "You sure *you* are?"

He presses his lips to mine briefly before pushing off the bed and reaching for his jeans. I hear him digging for a condom in his wallet, and thank God he came prepared. I'm on the pill, but I'd rather be safe than sorry and bring an STD back home.

Looking over my shoulder, I wait in anticipation as he slides his shorts down and sheaths himself. Placing a knee on the bed, he spreads my legs before grabbing my hips and pulling me up slightly until our bodies meet. Once I feel the tip at my entrance, I arch my back and rest up on my elbows as he rocks his hips and thrusts inside. I inhale sharply as I feel him inch by inch.

"Goddammit, River," he growls, gripping my hips with both hands.

We've barely moved yet, and I can already tell he's thick. His size is impressive, not that I'm really surprised. It's not until he pulls out and thrusts back in again that I can really feel the length and girth of him, stretching me every time he enters inside me.

"Oh my God," I whimper, my head falling down between my shoulders. He increases the pace, digging his fingers into my hips deeper as he thrusts harder and faster. "*Yesyesyes*…" I mutter.

One hand slaps my ass again as he continues fucking me from behind. God, it feels so good at this angle, and he fucks so damn good, too. His body towers over me, and his lips press against my neck as he moans and cusses in my ear.

94

"Fuck, River, fuck," he growls before biting down on my shoulder.

We continue that pace until he pounds so hard into me, the buildup becomes too much, and I moan out his name. The way my body tightens, I'm shocked he holds back his own release.

"Hell if I'm done with you yet," he tells me, flipping me over onto my back. He hitches my knee up as he slides back inside, thrusting harder and harder.

I dig my nails into the flesh of his arms, biting down on my lip until I can no longer hold it in. Moaning, I tell him how close I am and beg him not to stop. I'm so close, which seems impossible since I rarely orgasm even once during sex, but three times? That had to be some kind of record.

"C'mon, baby," he encourages, bringing his mouth back to mine. "Come on my cock again. It's fuckin' hot."

Oh my God…the thought barely comes when I feel it ripping through me. My pussy tightens more than before, and I feel his body jerk above me.

"God. That's so perfect," he tells me, wrapping my hair in his fist. "You're so perfect."

I can tell he's close now too.

"Let me ride you," I say, wanting to watch him come like he's watched me.

"Fuck, yes." He grins.

I straddle his legs and press my palms to his chest as I slide over his length and feel him harden the deeper he goes. His lips tilt up when I start moving my hips, and even though he's already worked my body into a blissful state, I give him everything I can. First, his hands are on my thighs, moving my hips faster, and then he rests them behind his head as I rock my body against his, desperate to feel him come undone.

"Christ, River…" he growls, his eyes closing as his head tilts back. "Fuck. Fuck. *Fuck*." He moans, grabbing the back of my legs again and squeezing them with all his strength as I feel him release inside me. The look on his face is pure fucking bliss, and I can't believe how hot he looks right now. He groans and curses, arching his hips deeper inside me as he continues chasing the high.

"Holy shit," I mutter, feeling an orgasm hit me unexpectedly. We ride the wave together as he pushes himself up and wraps his arms around my waist so he can press our mouths together. I welcome his lips on mine as we slowly come down. All that can be heard is our rapid breathing.

His hand on my cheek keeps us still, and we're both relaxed and completely sated. I feel his breaths against my lips while he presses our foreheads together. That was the most intense night of my life, and even though I know we're both only here on vacation to have fun, I can't help but think that's how sex is meant to be, and I've been missing out.

If that's the case, my expectations just doubled.

"You're really beautiful, you know that?" Alex whispers, breaking the silence.

"Thank you." I smile lightly as a blush surfaces. I don't know why him giving me a compliment after what we just did embarrasses me, but luckily, it's too dark for him to notice.

"I'm going to clean us up and get some water before one of us passes out from dehydration." He smirks, pressing his lips to mine before moving off the bed.

"Considering how much we drank tonight, it's actually possible considering seventy-five percent of Americans suffer from chronic dehydration and don't even know it." I lean back as he walks toward the bathroom, and I smack myself in the head. I am so lame.

His chuckles echo from the bathroom, and I want to die from embarrassment. Grabbing an oversized T-shirt, I slip it on and start fussing with my hair. It's a complete mess, but considering it's sex hair, I kind of don't mind.

When he returns, he's holding a cup of water and a towel for me. I thank him and gulp down the water before climbing into bed next to him. He eyes the old T-shirt and tells me to remove it because sleeping naked is the "best thing ever," and I'm too satisfied to argue, so I shrug it off and climb into bed next to him. Way too exhausted to analyze the fact that Alex is sleeping in bed next to me, I let him wrap me up in his arms and hold me until I fall asleep.

Oh. My. God.

It's the only words my brain forms as my eyes flutter open and my head begins to pound. I'm thirsty and desperate for a glass of water. The sun blares through the windows and patio door and announces it's morning. Groaning, I roll over, and the first thing I see is a bare muscular chest and that sexy V that leads to one of the happiest places on earth.

Oh. My. Fucking. God.

I blink hard to confirm I'm not dreaming, and when he rustles, I know I'm not.

The images of our drunken night together come in quick flashes, and that's when my mini freak-out happens because hooking up on vacation wasn't really on my things-to-do list. Even if Natalie was very persistent on it being the *only* thing on my list.

All my insecurities about men and dating come rushing through me, and I think *what the hell did I just do*?

Thinking back, I try to remember how this happened. He had me the moment our eyes met, and somehow, he's now asleep in my bed. The only things I can blame is the tequila, loneliness, and that deep Southern accent that's sexy as sin. What a dangerous combo. However, if I'm pointing fingers, then Natalie gets her fair share of the blame too, just for encouraging this.

I can't remember the last time I had a one-night stand but can definitely see why I haven't made it a habit. It's awkward as fuck. Do I continue lying with him and assume everything is fine or do I get the hell away before he can reject me first? As I'm contemplating my options, I realize we're in my hotel room, so escaping before he wakes isn't even a choice. Trying to stay calm, I close my eyes tight, hoping he'll disappear, and I won't have to make any decisions, but when I peel them back open, no such luck.

Knowing I can't lie here any longer while my mind races, I decide to jump in the shower with hopes that when I get out, he'll be gone. Surely, he's done the one-night stand thing before and he'll know that is his cue to leave.

However, as soon as I move, a large arm wraps around my bare waist and pulls me close. My eyes widen when his length presses hard on my back. When he smiles against my ear, I nearly melt into him, forgetting all the warning alarms that are going off in my head.

I'm not doing this. I can't do the pretend couple thing. Not after everything I've gone through in the past six months. I'd be stupid to let myself get attached again, even for only a week. All I can think is, *he has to go*. I need time to process my thoughts, process what happened, and where we go from here. Maybe I'm making this more complicated than it needs to be, but one-night stands are not in my repertoire. Somehow, I can hear Natalie's voice tell me that they are now, and I should just have unadulterated fun for the last week we're here.

"Good morning, beautiful," he whispers in a deep, rough drawl. All the little hairs on my neck stick up, and a shiver rushes through me. One night and my body responds to him like it's found its other half. Last night was good. No, it was fucking *amazing*, but that doesn't change anything. It can't.

Regardless, my body is heating up again just by the way he feels pressed against me. Stupid, traitorous body—betraying me again, like it did with Asshole.

His strong hand trails across my hip and stops on my stomach. I still and pretend I'm asleep, but he knows I'm not when my breath hitches at his contact. Soft lips kiss my neck, trailing across my shoulder and up toward my jawline. *Fuck*. My eyes flutter closed, but then I blink them open and realize I have to stop before his hand or mouth trails any lower. I turn my body and look up at him. Deep blue eyes stare seductively into mine, and I swallow hard, knowing what I have to do so I don't lead him on or give the wrong idea. Last night was fun, but that's all it can be now—a memory.

"I'm sorry, Alex." I sit up, pulling the sheet up to cover my bare breasts.

He smiles. "For what, darlin'? You have nothing to be sorry for. Not even for the way you screamed my name and buried your head in the pillow."

My eyes widen, a blush creeping up my neck and cheeks. "I think you should go," I tell him, keeping my composure, trying to make it less awkward than it already is.

Placing his hands behind his head, he takes me by surprise when he lets out a big hearty laugh. "Before breakfast? I could grab us some plates from the continental breakfast downstairs and bring it back up, so we can refuel." He flashes a wink as if to indicate refuel for round two, *or three*.

I purse my lips. "Umm, I don't think that's a good idea." I use a gentle voice to lessen the blow.

Alex sits up, and he's basically face-to-face with me. Smiling, he tucks loose strands of hairs behind my ear and rubs his thumb across my cheek before standing. "I'm in room 5513 if you change your mind, sweetheart." The confidence in his tone makes me think he doesn't really think I'm going to let him leave or he's pretending that being kicked out doesn't bother him.

My heart flutters, but I ignore it. Why does he have to be such a gentleman? Pushing him away and getting this reaction is making me feel guilty, but I'm not sure why.

As hard as it is, I can't take my eyes off his sexy ass as he walks across the room, buck naked. Confidence oozes from him as he grabs his clothes and puts them on.

Looking over his shoulder at me, he smiles. "Last chance to stop me." He winks, and it almost has me second-guessing my decision. I'm half-tempted to say the hell with it and pull him back into my bed, but I stay silent instead.

It's better this way. At least that's what I tell myself as he flashes another smile before leaving. As soon as the door closes, I lie back in bed and let out a long sigh. I lie there for a few moments, thinking over the events of last night and how Alex—basically a stranger—worked my body and made me feel so damn good. After a while, I peel myself out of bed, not wanting to waste the day. Refusing to let my thoughts get the best of me, I get up and walk to the shower. I turn on the hot water and step inside. My body is sore, and each time I move, I can feel exactly where Alex had been. He marked his territory, and as much as I don't want to admit it, it was some fucking good sex—okay, admittedly, it was the best sex I'd ever had. It's no secret the man knows his way around the bedroom.

As I'm washing my hair, I can feel how sore my arms and legs are. Jesus. The man was a savage.

The glass door of the shower fogs up, and I take that as my cue to get out. I grab a towel and wrap it around my body and take another one for my hair. As I walk toward my suitcase, I hear my phone vibrating on the nightstand. Picking it up, I see several texts from Natalie.

Natalie: Seriously, you're not awake yet? It's 9am!

Natalie: Is someone having Texas sausage for breakfast?

Natalie: I'm dying over here. I need the deets!

Natalie: I swear this is the last text I send, but I have to make sure you're alive. Adam is leaving to go fishing, and I need to drink away this hangover.

Her messages make me smile, even if telling her is going to be a whole debacle, and she's going to want intimate details. I check the time and realize it's been over an hour since she sent them.

As I finish towel drying my hair, I think back to the last time we got rid of our hangovers by drinking more. We were freshmen in college and went to our first frat party. The next morning, we woke up and drank shitty Bloody Marys until we couldn't taste the cheap vodka anymore. As I sit here with a pounding headache, it actually doesn't seem like such a bad idea.

River: I'm alive. I think. Where are you?

Her text bubble instantly pops up.

Natalie: Finally! I'm having brunch at the hotel restaurant. Best eggs beni I've ever had. Come meet me!

River: Order me the same. I'll be down in a sex.

River: I mean *sec.

Natalie: I know what you've got on the brain. ;)

Rolling my eyes at her last text, I lock my phone and grab my keycard before heading to the elevator. I'm halfway hoping I don't run into Alex, not after I all but pushed him out the door this morning. The guilt of how I acted is starting to build, but I have a good reason.

Once I step off the elevator and walk into the restaurant that overlooks the beach, I see Natalie. Her fiery red hair gleams in the sun, and as soon as she makes eye contact with me, she smirks.

"I think you're actually glowing—and *not* because of the sun," she says before taking a bite of her eggs.

"I don't want to talk about it," I tell her just as the waitress arrives with my plate of food.

She rolls her eyes at me. "You're no fun. When did you become such a prude?"

"Apparently, I'm *not* fun. I'm beginning to think there's something wrong with me."

"By the smug-ass look on your face, it seems like it. Did someone piss in your Cheerios this morning? Was it something he did? Was he an asshole toward you?" Her face is full of concern. "Do I need to kick his tight Texan ass to Kentucky?"

Her protective words make me grin, but I shake my head. "No, no. Nothing like that. The opposite actually. He was an absolute gentleman this morning, and I'm sure if he would've gone home with anyone other than myself last night, it would've continued on this morning. But instead, I asked him to leave."

Natalie's mouth falls open. "What?" she shrieks loudly, not realizing how loud she's being when I shush her. "Why? Don't you know how vacation flings work? Did I forget to teach you that?"

I glare at her, not responding to that comment. I turn to my plate and take a few bites of my Eggs Benedict and the hollandaise sauce basically melts in my mouth. "Oh my God, Nat. You were right. This is to die for."

"Nope. No, I'm not going to let you change the subject on me like that. Not this time. I'm not falling for it," she states matter-of-factly.

Groaning, I knew I wouldn't be able to distract her for long. "Apparently not. Why don't you enlighten me?" My tone is laced with sarcasm that isn't lost on her.

"You're supposed to lock yourself in your room with Mr. Southern 'n Dirty, and you don't leave until your vagina falls off or your plane flies out. And sometimes the sex is so mind-blowing it's worth missing a flight. Trust me." She wiggles her eyebrows, making me smile. Being around Natalie helps me relax a bit, and I'm so grateful she's my best friend who knows what to say to help me out of my funk.

"I'll keep that in mind the next time I see my vag lying on the floor." I can barely get the words out before I burst into laughter.

"Seriously, though, Riv. Let loose for once. Let your hair down and give yourself permission to enjoy yourself. You've been taking care of people for almost your entire life. It's time for you to finally take care of River and just have fun. When we get back to the tundra, then you can go back to being guarded and uptight in your fancy scrubs." She flashes a teasing smile, but her tone softens at my reluctant facial expression before continuing. "Just promise me you'll try to have a good time the rest of the week." Natalie gives me a small smile, and I can't deny her when she's being this sincere.

"Okay, fine. I promise to *try*. Just for you," I tell her between bites of toast, hoping I can push away my reservations because I know she's right. I've put people first for as long as I can remember without really thinking about what I wanted.

"Good. Just remember, though, what happens in Key West stays in Key West." She winks.

And I honestly hope she's right.

CHAPTER NINE

ALEX

WAKING up with soft skin pressed against my chest and legs tangled with mine immediately makes me smile. Inhaling her scent, I press my lips to the flesh of her neck and whisper in her ear. Just as she turns over and I look at the beautiful woman lying next to me, her eyes flutter open.

At first, River smiles with almost drunken happiness, then as reality sets in, her brows furrow. Sitting up in bed with wide eyes, she pulls the sheet to cover her breasts. When I look at her, I think she might actually be in shock that I'm here. She glances at my chest, then looks up at me. "I think you should go."

Tilting my head, I search her face, waiting for some sort of smile or anything that gives her away, but nothing does. We both know she enjoyed last night just as much as I did, but when she keeps her serious stance, I take that as my cue to leave. The dream of her quickly turns into a nightmare as she acts confused by me. This is the same woman who nearly begged me to come back to her room last night, isn't it?

Standing, not giving a fuck that I'm naked, I search around for my clothes that are not-so-conveniently scattered around the room. I feel her watching me, and when I look over my shoulder to meet her eyes, blush hits her cheeks. Knowing I'm getting to her, even if it's just the slightest bit, is cute. It makes me want to kiss the fuck out of her, but if she wants to play hard to get, I'm game. A Bishop always gets what he wants, and I want—no—*need* more of her, especially after our night of pure ecstasy. And I know she secretly wants me too, even if she's not ready to admit it just yet.

Being together was more emotional than I could've ever expected, so I understand why she's pushing me away. While we were together, I found something I'd been missing with other hookups. Deeper feelings surfaced than I'd ever experienced before. From seeing her that first time at breakfast, to her coming to Dylan's rescue on the beach, to spending hours chatting and drinking together—it's already felt like more than any of my previous flings. In that short amount of time, we've built a connection that even I don't understand. It's frightening, but exhilarating all at the same time, and I'm ready to dive in head first to see where it goes. We have a week to experience each other to the fullest, and I'll be damned if I allow precious time to be wasted. Sometimes a person has to put their cards on the table, call the bluff, and make a bet, even if the odds are stacked against them. I have to know if this is just a stupid vacation fling or if there's potential for more between us. Our story could already be the lyrics to a stupid country song.

After I'm dressed, I give her a wink, taking one last long look at her—knowing deep down it won't be the last time we're together—before leaving. The connection we shared was almost too much. It's intoxicating and feels like it will completely swallow me whole or break me—I'm not sure which one it is yet. We may barely know each other, but something about her pulls me to her, like an invisible lasso. She's holding the rope and calling the shots.

Hunger takes over as soon as I leave her room, so I take the elevator down to the coffee shop in the hotel lobby and grab a few muffins and a giant coffee to take back to my room.

To know I've actually been snubbed is a strange sensation. Not often has that happened to me; actually, I don't think it ever has. I'm usually the one pushing girls out of my bed in the morning, and oddly enough, it makes me want her that much more. The chase makes it that much more interesting and fun, as crazy as that sounds. For a moment, I slightly understand Crazy Carly then try to forget the stupid thought as I ride the elevator to my floor.

Before I slide my keycard, I pound on the door like I'm the police and wait for some sort of noise on the other side. Since there's no answer, I assume the coast is clear and enter.

"Fuck!" I shout. "It stinks like nasty sex in here." Just as the words leave my mouth, I see rustling in the bed, then Jessica's head pops up like a prairie dog.

"Howdy," I tell her, taking a bite of my blueberry muffin, feeling slightly bad for being an asshole. As I chew the dry ass muffin, all I can think is how much better Mama's are. Even my sister, Courtney, could put these nasty bricks to shame. In Key West, the biggest disappointment is the cooking.

Dylan groans and pulls the blanket from over his head, giving me a death glare. "Go away!"

"No, sir. The night's over. Time to get up. It's nearly ten in the morning. Going back to work is gonna be a bitch if you keep sleepin' in late," I tell him matter-of-factly, turning my back as Jessica tries to slyly slip on her clothes without revealing too much. Poor girl has to take the walk of shame, and the look of it is all over her face. It's always easier to sneak out before the other person wakes, that's one-night stand basics, but even I didn't follow the basics this morning. As I take the last bite of the first muffin, I hear lips sucking and smacking each other and groan.

"Get a room," I say with a laugh.

"I've got one!" Dylan throws a pillow my way.

"Get *another* room," I correct myself, just as Jessica walks around the bed to grab her purse.

"Bye, Alex," she says as she sashays toward the door, blowing Dylan a final kiss before she leaves.

Just as she walks out, I turn and look at Dylan. "You're dirty as fuck."

He sits up in bed, rubbing his face. "I know. What was I thinking?"

"You weren't. I don't remember her looking quite like that last night." I try to think back, but honestly, the only thing on my mind right now is River. Her body against mine. The way she tastes. She's like a poisoned apple and has already made her way through my veins. I can't stop thinking about her, and it's been less than an hour since I left. Goddammit.

"Beer goggles. Those sneaky bastards will make a two a ten. You'd think I'd learn my lesson by now," Dylan says with a grunt. "No wonder Liam was so willing to push her off on me."

"No regrets, though. Right? I'm sure she's a nice girl." I bite into the last muffin, and when my stomach gurgles, I regret eating them, but finish it anyway because this hangover isn't going to cure itself.

"I swear, if you wouldn't have shown up, she may have never left. Which is okay, I guess. But to me, she seems like a psycho. You know the phrase: a freak in the sheets? Well, that's her times ten. I'm not gonna go into detail, but if for some reason I go missing and don't make it back to Texas, she's suspect one."

"Damn, dude," I say with a laugh, but he looks at me a little too seriously for my liking.

"I need a shower." He doesn't even wait for me to reply as he walks into the bathroom—bare ass and all—and shuts the door.

After he's showered, Dylan decides he needs to eat. I'm so full of sugar the thought grosses me out, but I go anyway, secretly hoping I run into River.

"Gonna tell me what happened last night?" Dylan asks with a shit-eating grin on his face as we leave the hotel and walk down the sidewalk.

"Nah. I'm good."

He punches me in the arm, and I'm half-tempted to punch his ass back.

"So you found your girl, and she turned out to be a psycho, too?" Dylan leads us into a burger joint a few blocks away. Every blonde I see in the distance makes my heart race, but it's never her.

"No. She's not a psycho. She's actually pretty fucking perfect. Maybe a bit guarded, but perfect nonetheless. And that's where the problem lies."

Dylan orders himself a double cheeseburger, and we sit at a huge window that overlooks the beach. I stare out, watching people walk up and down the white sand having a good time.

"Because Cowboy Prince Charming found his Princess Cowgirl and all she left was her boot on the stairs at midnight?"

"No wonder you're single," I tell him, stealing a fry from his plate, hoping to change the subject.

"I have little sisters. Give me a break. Disney and princess shit is something I've had to deal with for years. So I guess things didn't go as planned, then?"

I give him a look that tells him he's right.

"This just keeps gettin' better and better." He continues eating, not taking his eyes from me, waiting for me to spill the beans.

"Or worse," I correct. "After one of the best nights of my life, I was kicked to the curb like a stray dog," I finally tell him.

Dylan laughs so hard I'm concerned I might have to give him the Heimlich. I'm beginning to think he's a serious liability on the island. After he catches his breath, he shakes his head.

"I've always heard that *Karma's a Bitch*, but now I might actually believe it. Alex Bishop has finally met his match. Perfect. Can't wait to watch how this plays out."

"You're a dick," I mutter as he cleans his plate. "A nasty dick at that."

"I learned everything I know from you," he says as he stands to dump his tray in the trash.

I let out a laugh. "So what you're saying is I've created a monster. *Great*."

Most of the day passes, and we spend it exploring other parts of the island. I'm no fun because all I want to do is go back to the hotel, pound on River's door, and ask her if we can talk. The more I think about this morning, the more bothered I become. Call me a hypocrite because of my track record, but it all feels wrong.

Once we've basically explored every inch of the west side of the Keys, and I grabbed some tacos from a food truck, we decide to Uber back to the hotel. Just as I see the hotel in sight, my palms become sweaty and my heart races. I have to figure out exactly what I'm going to say to her because I *will* see her again.

"Apparently, there's a volleyball tournament on the beach tonight at six. Wanna go play?" Dylan asks.

"Do you think it's a good idea? I'm afraid you'll break something or hurt yourself." I joke with him, though I'm halfway serious.

"You only live once, right?" Dylan smirks as he thanks the driver and gets out of the car. We enter the hotel lobby and round the corner only to find Jessica waiting impatiently by the elevators with a big smile on her face. Dylan turns and looks at me with wide eyes, and all I can do is laugh.

"You chose it." I smirk, patting him on the back and giving an encouraging push toward her. I should be a good friend and save him, but I don't because it's funnier this way. He deserves it for all the shit talking he's done today, and at least, he'll have a good story to bring home.

"We actually have plans tonight." Dylan turns and looks at me.

"Nah, we don't." I give her a wink as his face turns blood red.

"See, that means we *can* do the boat tour and watch the sunset!" She shrieks in excitement.

When I make eye contact with Dylan, he whispers, "*I'm going to kill you,*" before he's whisked away to the beach for a romantic afternoon. He's too much of a gentleman to tell her no, and if he's learned everything from me, then I'll take that one as a compliment.

Considering I'm alone and the night is still young, I make my way through the lobby, past the pool, toward the cabana bar that overlooks the beach. I order a beer and stare out at the water as the sun begins to set in the distance. Chatter echoes from the pool, and I'm lost in my thoughts before I realize my name is being called in the distance.

Just as I turn, I recognize the voice.

Natalie.

"I'm really sorry my friend is such a sour puss," she says with a smile. She's alone, and her mouth is the color of the blue drink she's sipping. Drunk Natalie just might be my ticket to finding River.

I smile and pretend like I don't know what she's talking about, but I'm sure she already knows everything. I'm not the kinda guy who kisses and tells because some secrets are better left buried, and Mama raised a gentleman.

"I'm going to fix this, I promise," Natalie says before flashing me a wink as she stuffs her phone into her pocket and waves bye before I can ask any questions. Curiosity gets the best of me as I watch her walk away.

I don't know what she's up to, but I kinda like her style.

She's fierce with a side of no fucks given.

CHAPTER TEN

RIVER

I FEEL COMPLETELY RELAXED after Natalie and I had massages this afternoon. The masseuse really worked out the kinks of having rough sex last night. Afterward, we parted ways, and I went up to my room where all I did for the next few hours was lounge around. I decided to read one of my romance books because someone should get a happily ever after on this vacation even if it's living vicariously through fictional characters.

About halfway through my book, I decide to take a nap, and it felt good to actually do nothing for a change. Instead of meeting Natalie and Adam for dinner, I decided to order room service and stay in, hoping to detox my mind and body of everything Mr. Southern 'n Dirty. Reading a steamy romance was probably not the smartest choice to help me forget about last night, but I don't think I could ever forget…even if I tried.

Once my food arrives, I sit up against the headboard and flick through the TV channels, inhaling my food in the process. I stop once I come across an old black-and-white western. Just the sound of the man's deep, gravelly voice has my mind back on that damn cowboy. I turn it off and finish my dinner in silence, but everything in my head goes back to him and the way he cherished my body. Gah! It's ridiculous.

The sound of a text has me shaking him out of my head, and after I grab it, I see it's from Natalie.

Natalie: Meet me at the cabana bar past the pool ASAP. It's really important!

River: On my way. Is everything okay?

My instincts take control as I slip on a sundress and flip-flops. I quickly pull my hair up into a messy ponytail before grabbing my keycard and phone. I can't help but wonder if there's something wrong. When she doesn't respond to my message, I grow more concerned. Did she and Adam get into a fight? Or worse, *did they break up*? Different scenarios flood my mind, and without another thought, I rush toward the cabana.

When I step outside, the warm breeze brushes across my skin, and I can't help but glance at the plum-colored sky as the dark orange sun falls below the horizon. Everything about this island is incredible, and I'm definitely going to miss seeing its beauty once I'm back home and surrounded by the cold and snow.

Music flows lightly through the crowd, and I immediately search for Natalie's red hair once I reach the pool area. People surround the bar, so I move closer to see if I can spot her on one of the stools. Worry consumes me when she's nowhere to be found. I glance over the nameless faces, and though I'm in a crowd of people, it doesn't stop me from seeing *him*. And when I do, he's looking directly at me.

For a moment, I contemplate turning around and pretending I didn't see him but find it hard once our eyes and bodies are locked together in a trance. It's as if we're the only people on this whole fucking island. My phone vibrates in my hand, breaking the tension, and when I glance down, I see it's another text from Natalie. I quickly unlock my phone, hoping everything is all right.

Natalie: Don't hate me, but you needed a little push. Love you!

I let out a hard sigh when I realize this was all a sham so I'd jump out of my comfy bed and come down here where she must've known Alex was waiting. I grind my teeth, already planning to give Natalie an earful when I see her tomorrow.

By the time I look up from my phone, Alex is gone. The glass he was drinking from now sits empty along with the vacant barstool. For a split second, I'm slightly disappointed that he left, but I know I shouldn't be. I'm half-tempted to text Natalie back and rub it in her face that her stupid plan didn't work after all.

Annoyed, I turn around and immediately bump into Alex who's now standing directly in front of me. The smell of him suffocates my senses—pure man mixed with the ocean breeze. My body remembers every single touch and kiss. Swallowing hard, it takes everything I have to look into his baby blue eyes and keep a straight face.

"Looking for someone?" he asks nonchalantly with a smirk on his face.

Inhaling a deep breath, I keep my composure. "Actually, I was meeting Natalie," I tell him, unable to move as if I'm glued to the ground. He actually laughs, which confirms my suspicions about this all being a setup. I narrow my eyes at him, and he shrugs unapologetically.

"Hmm. Doesn't look like she's here." He pretends to look around, then his eyes fall back on me.

Being this close to him forces heat to permeate through my body, and it feels as if hot flames are licking my skin from head to toe. Blinking and clearing my vision, I finally get a good look at him, and he smiles before taking my hand and leading me to the beach.

"Wait, what are you doing?" I ask, but I don't pull away.

He chuckles, not answering my question, and we walk pass

the cabana until we're standing in white sand staring out at the water.

"We need to talk." He finally turns to me, and when I face him, he glides his hand along my cheekbone before brushing a loose strand of hair behind my ear.

Knowing this isn't a conversation I should have, I shake my head, dismissing him. My messy ponytail is loose and starts to fall out, and I quickly try to adjust it.

"Yes, ma'am," he drawls, adjusting his ball cap. "Don't be stubborn." He notices me fussing with my hair and pulls the band out of my fingers, causing it to fall around my face.

Opening my mouth to give him a piece of my mind, I barely get a word out before he palms my cheeks and his lips crash into mine. Soon, his fingers are threading through my hair, and I can't help the small moan that escapes. I feel as if I'm falling into a bottomless pit as our tongues twist together. The beach and sand and everything surrounding us melt away, and it's just us. By the time we break our embrace, we're both gasping for air, for some sort of relief. The intensity of the emotions behind his kiss is almost too much—too soon—and it makes me want to run and push him away. It's what I *should* do anyway. It's the smart thing to do, but when I meet his eyes again, I'm incapable.

"You were saying?" he asks against my mouth.

"Don't be a smartass." I can't help but smile and chuckle against his lips.

"Just felt like you needed a reminder of last night, ya know, in case you'd forgotten." He releases his hold on me but slides one hand down the length of my arm and threads my fingers with his.

"Uh, no. I actually have a *great* memory, so I don't forget much at all," I retort, remembering every inch of his hard, sweaty body against mine.

"Good to know. Well, I'll just come out and say it then. I had a real fucking good time last night, and I'm pretty sure you did, too. In fact, I know you did, several times. I'd hate for us to stop hanging out, because like I said, last night was a fuckin' good time. So if you plan to spend the rest of the week playing hard to get, I'd just like to know so I can make sure we're on the same page. Otherwise, we can go ahead and continue where we left off last night." He winks, brushing his fingers across my bare arms, causing goose bumps to cover my skin.

Swallowing hard, I try to steady my racing heartbeat. I should've known a guy like Alex Bishop wasn't going to let me off easy, especially with the way I kicked him out this morning.

"Trust me when I say I'm not the girl you want." I'm trying to convince him, or maybe myself, but either way, he doesn't let me continue. His finger reaches up and softly covers my mouth, stopping me.

"You don't know what I want, River." His voice is low and sincere, but his demeanor is serious as he searches my face. "And you're wrong."

All the words I wanted to say to him disappear with a single breath, and I'm left speechless. I'm insanely attracted to him, there's no doubting that, but the last time I allowed myself to get caught up in a guy is the very reason I'm here on this vacation—to escape the drama men seem to bring into my life.

"You can't deny there's something between us—a connection. I can't quite put my finger on it, but I felt it the first time I saw you, and if my instincts are right, you did too."

I nod in agreement but don't offer him anything else just yet.

"But if I go back to Texas knowing I didn't try my hardest with one of the prettiest and most stubborn women I've ever met, I'll live to regret it. And I'm sorry, darlin', but I don't like to regret anything in my life. So, as I said, we can go about this the hard way or the fun and easy way. I'm even willing to play all the games you want, but we're runnin' out of time here. So I'm going out on a limb and cutting to the chase." He tilts my chin, so our eyes are locked. "I haven't stopped thinking about you since that first time we met, so while we're both here, why don't we explore this connection we have?"

My heart beats rapidly in my chest, and I feel like I'm

dreaming because his words are perfect—a tad *too* perfect. I'm tempted to pinch myself just to make sure I'm not. Being my typical logical and cynical self, I can't help but have questions and concerns. But just as I get ready to voice them, I dig deep and ask myself, *what do I have to lose?*

Nothing.

"Please say something, River," he demands.

"I'm sorry. It's just… I need a little bit of time to think about this. I've been burned before, and I can't just jump into your bed because you're good-looking and say all the right things at the right time with that damn accent. It's all confusing to me," I blurt out, needing to catch my breath. "It's like there needs to be rules or something, but how can there be rules when we only have days left of our vacation? Oh God. Now I'm rambling. I'm making this more difficult than it needs to be, aren't I? Like always. Spoiler alert?"

Alex cracks up, a sound I could actually get used to hearing.

"I like rules, sweetheart. How about this? I'll promise to always make sure you come first. When you beg to be fucked harder, I won't hesitate for a minute. But I'll also take you out because I'm not a complete asshole. I'd love to go out and explore the city together. No strings attached, just fun."

"Just fun?" I confirm, my brows rising.

He nods. "And to be fair, you haven't jumped into my bed… yet. But I can check my schedule for tonight." The smile on his face grows as the heat hits my cheeks.

Instinctively, I bite my bottom lip while last night replays in my mind. I could do *just fun*, right? I mean, I've never done casual before, but Alex sure makes it sound really good.

"I'm not asking for marriage here. Just a week together. Then we can go our separate ways and continue living our lives with only the memories we made. I can guarantee you'd enjoy making memories with me, darlin'. This sizzling tension between us is electric, and if we don't get each other out of our systems, we're both going to explode," he adds, just as a couple of drunk people stumble close to us on to the beach, invading our privacy.

"This fucking sand is so hard to walk in," the whiny girl complains as the guy she's with falls down laughing.

"Babe! Babe! Help me up. Dammit. I think there's sand in my underwear." The guy holds out his hand, but she's not strong enough to lift him and tumbles onto his chest. I hear lips smacking together and clothes rustling, and I turn my head away from them. I'm somewhat thankful for the interruption because my head is in overdrive right now.

"I think that's our cue to go," I tell him, stepping farther away from the couple.

"I'll walk you to your room." He wraps his arm around my waist, holding me close as we head toward the hotel. Just as we walk into the lobby, I see a brown-haired girl hanging off Dylan's arm, but he doesn't look happy about it.

"There you are." Dylan huffs. "I've been texting you because I forgot my keycard," he says to Alex.

"Sorry. I've been busy," Alex tells him, nodding toward me.

"Hey, River." Dylan acknowledges me with a smile and a head nod.

The woman looks me up and down, but then she smiles wide when she notices how close Alex and I are standing to each other. "Hi, I'm Jessica."

"River," I reply.

Alex hands Dylan the card, and we all ride the elevator together. I have to hold my laughter back when Dylan tells Jessica his head hurts and he's going to call it an early night. The elevator stops at their floor, and the two of them exit together, but I have a feeling she won't be staying long.

"Did he really just use the headache line?" I ask, laughing.

"Totally did, but she's persistent, so I wouldn't be surprised if she pulls some extra-strength Tylenol out of her purse then tries to ride him like a bull."

The elevator stops on my floor, and Alex walks me to my door.

Before leaving, he places a soft kiss on my lips. "Think about it, okay?"

I smile and nod.

"Have a good night, River. Sweet dreams." He winks, leaving me breathless.

"Night." I scan my keycard, and once I'm inside, I lean against the door, my legs feeling like jelly as I slide down.

What the actual hell just happened?

My mind is racing, and I need to talk my thoughts out with someone. Pulling my phone from my pocket, I text Natalie and make sure to give her a dose of her own medicine.

River: Nat. I'm back at my room. Can you meet me here? It's really important.

Natalie: I'll be right there. Give me a few minutes.

I change back into my comfy clothes and sit on the edge of the bed. The room service menu is still open from when I ordered dinner earlier, and if I'm going to really think about Alex's offer, I'm going to need reinforcements. I decide to get the double chocolate cake I passed on before. After calling in my order, I lie flat on the bed and stare up at the ceiling, letting my mind wander to all kinds of places. Twenty minutes pass, and when I hear a knock on the door, I fly off the bed to answer it. However, I'm shocked when I see it's room service with my dessert instead of Natalie.

Sitting on the couch, I cross my legs, and before I can take a bite of the most heavenly chocolate cake I've ever seen, there's another knock on the door. Dammit, it better be Natalie this time. I open it, and she's standing there with a giant red drink, and I swear a whole pineapple is stuffed inside.

"What the hell? Did you have to crawl here or something? What took you so long?" I scold her before realizing how tipsy she is already.

"Sorry," she slurs, stepping inside the room. "Adam distracted me, and then I had to wait forever for my refill."

Shutting the door behind her, she follows me to the bed.

"I was about to send the search team out for you," I tease, deciding to let her off the hook.

"Is everything okay?" she asks, knowing damn well what she did to me earlier.

I give her a smile. "I'm fine. But you deserve a mouthful right now after setting me up like that."

Laughing, she sets down her drink on the nightstand, then grabs my plate and proceeds to eat my chocolate cake.

"A mouthful of what?" She wiggles her eyebrows and smirks.

"Ew, no!"

"What?" She swallows the bite of cake down. "I was talking about this delicious cake."

"Right." I roll my eyes.

"Okay, I'm sorry I set you up, but I saw Alex in the lobby earlier and could tell he was looking for you before he went to the cabana. Whatever you two have is so obvious, and I knew if he could get one more opportunity to talk to you, he could help you see it, too." She flashes a smile that tells me her plan was sincere, albeit manipulative. "Chemistry like that means the sex is bound to be out of this world," she adds.

"Well…you're right. I can't deny there's something there," I say honestly. "He laid it all out for me and said we should have fun and basically get each other out of our systems because we enjoyed being with each other," I explain to her, and the smile on her face grows wider.

"I like where this is going." She nods her approval.

"That's crazy though, right?" I ask, knowing I'm asking the wrong damn person right now. She's totally Team Alex. "I just keep second-guessing it and thinking how wrong it'll go."

"Oh, honey. Casual sex is healthy," she schools me. "In fact, you're a nurse. You should know that." She chuckles.

I roll my eyes but smile. "It's the emotional stuff I'm struggling with, especially after Asshole. How do I just turn that off?"

"You do it like you do everything. You've gathered all the facts, and you know the expectations and outcome, which means there'll be no surprises." Her words are convincing, even though I don't really need it. Being with Alex even for the week would be an experience of a lifetime. A very *fun* experience at that. "Hell, if I were single, and he was offering me no-strings-attached sex, I'd be naked the entire time and order room service between the sex marathon and sleep. In fact, the only time I'd see that beach is when my body was pressed up against that balcony window."

I burst out laughing, my head falling back as I take in her words. I can't deny how fucking great that all sounds.

"Let your inhibitions go, River. It's just sex. That's it. Fuck him out of *your* system, then go home and add the memories of it all to your rub club."

I think about her words and really let them sink in. "See, that's why I keep you around. You're blunt with no filter."

"I know! What would you do without me?" she asks, reaching for her drink and taking a sip.

"Have a full piece of cake left," I tease.

"You love me! So you know what you've got to do, right?"

I nod with a smile. "I think I do."

CHAPTER ELEVEN

ALEX

Dylan: We're going out to find a bar and go dancing. Wanna join?

I SHAKE my head at his dumb ass.

Alex: Guess that headache went away quickly.

Taking the elevator back down to the lobby, I decide to grab a drink from the cabana until they're out of the room.

Dylan: Fuck you. Beer will solve that.

Alex: Beer Goggles. Good idea, man.

Dylan: Yeah, whatever. You comin' or not?

Alex: Nah. Gonna grab a drink by the pool. Go have fun with the future Mrs. Hart.

Dylan: That's not even funny! Damn, I thought you gettin' laid would soften you up.

I blow out a breath of frustration.

Alex: Text me if you're not coming back tonight so I don't worry she's kidnapped you.

Dylan: Yeah, I will.

Finding a seat at the bar, I order my usual and watch the people around me. Looking out at the water, I think about all the stuff I still want to do on this trip—jet skiing, snorkeling, parasailing. Lord knows I'm not risking Dylan in the water again. I'd love to do them with River, but now I'm overanalyzing everything I said to her and wondering if I pushed too hard.

I've never had to convince a girl to be with me, but maybe that's why I'm so damn intrigued by her. She's more than just a chase, and I know it would only be for the week, but fuck if she hasn't consumed my mind since day one. But why wouldn't she? Beautiful, intelligent, compassionate about her work. She's the whole damn package.

And as long as I take my own advice and keep to the rules, what could possibly go wrong?

The sun has long set, but I walk down to the beach anyway. Lights from the hotel illuminate the beach just enough so I can see where I'm going. These views are stunning—something I'll sure miss. Sitting on the white sand, I find it so peaceful out here. Most of the tourists are barhopping by now, but some of the hotel guests are still partying by the pool.

I stare out at the water for almost an hour before finally getting up to head back to my room. Adjusting my cap, I spin around and gasp when I see River standing there.

"Hi," she says softly, tucking her hair behind her ears. She's not wearing the sundress she was earlier but seeing her in leggings and the oversized sweater is pretty freaking adorable.

"Hey." I take a step toward her. "What are you doing here?"

She blinks and lowers her eyes before looking up at me. She's nervous.

"I was looking for you."

Smiling wide, I reply, "Well, you found me."

She swallows before inhaling a deep breath. "I was thinking you could maybe help me out with something."

Confused, I furrow my brows and nod. "Sure."

My eyes are drawn to her lips as she licks them. "What you said has me thinking that this trip is really a once-in-a-lifetime vacation for me, mostly because I work a lot and don't travel much, but it's made me realize I should take full advantage of it while I can."

So far, I'm liking where this is going. "Okay?"

"So maybe you could help me accomplish a vacation bucket list?"

I tilt my head, encouraging her to continue.

"I've never had a one-night stand with a stranger I met on vacation, so I can mark that off."

"Glad to have helped." I chuckle.

"But maybe we could add more. Sex in a public place, skinny-dipping, sex on the beach, a threesome."

"A threesome?" My eyes widen, shocked.

"Kidding!" She laughs, her smile reaching her eyes. "Well, just about the threesome. Not about the other stuff."

Taking another step, I close the gap between us and cup her

cheeks. "I'd be honored to help you fulfill a vacation bucket list, but on one condition."

"What's that?" Her big green eyes look up into mine, making me smile at how beautiful they are.

"I get to take you out. Sex with you is great, no doubt, but let's make the most of this bucket list. Let's go on adventures and experience as much as we can with each other. What do you think?"

"I think you have yourself a deal, cowboy."

Grinning, I pull her lips to mine and devour her mouth. I slip my tongue inside and kiss her the way I've wanted to all damn day.

I reach down and grab her hand, leading her off the beach.

"Where are we going?"

"About to mark an item off that list." I look over my shoulder and wink.

Luckily, there's a little convenience store near the hotel, and when we step inside, I lead us directly down the aisle where the condoms are stored.

"A twenty-four pack, really?" She chuckles when I grab the largest box.

I press her against my chest and lean my mouth down to her ear. "Darlin', I plan to fuck you against every possible surface, which means I need to stock up." I wink, and she blushes. After I pay, I lead her back toward the beach.

Since it's dark out and the hotel lights only hit certain areas on the sand, I look for a shady spot and walk us down to one of the empty lifeguard huts.

"Turn around," I order, unbuttoning my jeans. She wraps her hands around a post and looks over her shoulder at me.

Fingering her leggings and panties, I pull them down to her ankles. "From now on, dresses or skirts only."

She nods, grinning.

I grab a condom from the box and slide it over my erection that's been hard since the moment she agreed to this arrangement of ours. Aligning our bodies, I grip her hips and pull them toward me. Dipping my head down, I taste her neck and kiss along her jawline.

"Spread your legs, River," I growl, and she immediately obliges.

Grabbing my cock, I position it against her and thrust inside. Her head falls back against my shoulder as I pull out and push back inside deeper.

"Oh my God," she whimpers, her eyes sealing shut. I remind her to hold the post and keep her legs spread wide.

I wrap my hand around her throat, keeping her head tilted back so I can watch the pleasure on her face. It turns me the fuck on as I keep up the pace and fuck her hard.

"Christ, River," I growl in her ear. "You're so tight from this angle."

She moans, and I tighten my grip on her. The beach is empty, but the cabana bar isn't that far away. Luckily, the music will drown us out, but knowing anyone could see or hear us has me pounding into her deeper and faster.

"Shit, Alex," she groans, struggling to catch her breath. I can tell she's close, so I slide my hand down and rub circles on her clit.

"Come on my cock, baby. I wanna feel how tight that pussy gets," I encourage.

Within moments, her entire body is shaking as she rides out her climax. She tightens around my throbbing cock, making it impossible to hold back my own release.

"Fuck," I mutter against the flesh of her neck. "River."

We're both panting as we come down from the high, my cock still deep inside her.

"That was really fucking hot." She breaks the silence with a satisfied smile on her face.

"You have *no* idea," I tell her, pulling out to dispose of the condom.

I kiss her shoulder before spinning her around and taking her mouth.

"You feel way too good. At this rate, I'm not sure I'll ever get enough," I tell her honestly, which also scares the shit out of me. I've never felt like that before, but I don't allow myself to dwell on it now.

"You have seven days to give me your best, cowboy," she teases, licking her swollen lips. "Let's not put them to waste."

I all but haul River up to my room and text Dylan to stay the fuck out tonight before I'm slamming back into her sweet body. This time, she's bent over the chair that overlooks the beach. My hand is wrapped in her hair while I pound into her over and over again until she screams out my name. I know I'll have dreams of her voice when I'm back home, but for now, I'm bottling it all up.

We fall asleep a tangle of arms and legs and wake the next morning when a loud knock disrupts us.

"I think Dylan wants his bed back," River says in a sleepy voice, laughing.

"Yeah, he's gonna be pissed knowing we fucked on it." I chuckle, tilting her chin up so I can give her a quick kiss before I look for my clothes.

"Hold the fuck on," I shout at his persistent knocking. I slip on my jeans before opening the door for him. "Are you on fire or something?"

He barges in within seconds, looking like he's just escaped prison.

"Jessica," he offers as I close the door. "She's like a vulture, yet I can't stop sleeping with her." He turns toward me, his face all flushed. "What the fuck is wrong with me?"

He starts undressing, but I clear my throat and nod my head over to River.

"Oh, shit." He pulls his jeans back up. "Hey, River."

She tightens her grip on the sheets pulled against her chest. "Hey, Dylan."

He turns toward me with a wicked grin plastered on his face. "Guess you had a good night after all."

"Sure the hell did." I slap a hand on his shoulder, giving him an obvious signal to get the hell out. "Go back to Jessica's room."

He shrugs my hand off and winces. "I swear to God, that girl has no off button."

"You like her," I tell him, knowing it's obvious. Dylan wouldn't screw around with a chick he didn't at least like a little. He's just not willing to admit it.

"I'm getting in the shower," he says, walking to the bathroom, dismissing my statement. He looks over his shoulder and adds, "And get the hell out of my bed, you motherfucker."

Grabbing some clothes, River and I head out and walk to her room where we can shower and get ready. Since we were so rudely awakened, we take advantage and mark another bucket item off her list—morning shower sex.

"Want to go parasailing today?" I ask over breakfast. Her friend, Natalie, is spending the day with her boyfriend, so I finally get River all to myself.

Her eyes light up as she talks around a mouthful of food. "Yes! I've been wanting to try it!"

Over the weekend, River and I do a handful of water activities as well as lounge on the beach and find new and fun places to have sex.

I can't deny how happy I am being around her and being able

to experience all this new stuff with her. Not only is she willing to be spontaneous and adventurous with me, but she's also fun as hell. I love hearing her laugh and squeal with excitement when we try something different. She's also in great shape and keeps up with everything I throw at her.

By Tuesday morning, the strong realization that we only have days left haunts me. I push those thoughts away, not wanting to ruin the time we do have. We spent all morning in my bed, ordered room service and showered, then spent all afternoon in her bed. Dylan's still pretending he can't stand Jessica, yet we still switch rooms so they can have their privacy.

"We've successfully checked eleven things off the vacation bucket list," River tells me over dessert. We finally left her room and went to dinner.

"Oh yeah? What's left?" I ask, taking a bite of our strawberry cheesecake.

She looks up at me and grins mischievously. "Skinny-dipping."

Taking the final bite, I leave some cash on the table and grab her hand.

"What are you doing?" she whisper-shouts as I lead her through the restaurant and out the door.

"Condoms," I say, smiling at her over my shoulder.

Once we've restocked, I lead us to the beach. The sun has just set, and there's only a handful of people left lounging on the sand.

"Take off your clothes," I order.

She looks around, a blush rising to her cheeks. "Are you sure we won't get caught?"

I kick off my shoes, pull off my shirt then my shorts. "No." I smirk. "Hurry."

Quickly, she removes her sandals and sundress, standing in only her panties and bra.

"I'm nervous." She bites her lip, contemplating on removing the rest.

"It looks like you're wearing a swimsuit," I tell her,

appreciating the way her undergarments hug the curves of her body. "But it's called skinny-dipping, not swimsuit-dipping."

She chuckles, looking over her shoulder once more.

"Want me to help?" I arch a brow.

I'm on my knees before she can respond and slide my fingers into her lacy panties. Luckily, we're near a palm tree and can use it as a shield for now.

"What are you doing?" she squeals when I slide a finger inside her.

"Helping you relax." Once her panties are removed, I spread her legs and press a flat tongue along her slit. She whimpers, fisting her hands in my hair as I coax an orgasm out of her. She doesn't disappoint and gives me exactly what I want. "That's it, baby."

I stand, wrapping an arm around her waist and pressing her to my chest. My hand cups her cheek, and I kiss her. "Ready now?"

Sated, she nods. I step back, giving her room to remove her bra. I remove the last of my clothing, my hat and boxers, and soon we're both standing naked.

"On three," I say, grabbing her hand and facing her. I start counting, and on three, we run from the edge of the beach all the way into the cool water. Hearing her laugh as we make our way is music to my ears. I love hearing her sweet laugh.

I wrap my arms around her waist, so we're chest to chest. Pressing my lips down to hers, I hold her face as I kiss the fuck out of her. My tongue slides inside, and when we walk deeper into the water, she wraps her legs around my waist making it easy to carry her.

"I'm going to miss this," she admits as our lips part briefly.

"What's that?" I coax, hoping she'll say what I'm thinking.

"The ocean and beach." She smiles looking up at me. "And you."

My lips twist up into a smirk, happy that she's enjoying our time together as much as I am. I bend down and kiss her once more. "Me too."

We swim farther into the water until it's to our chests and no one can tell we're naked.

"So how was your first skinny-dipping experience?"

"I'd give it an eight out of ten," she teases. After every new adventure we've done, I've asked her, and she'd rank it.

"What'd make it a ten?" I ask, moving us closer together.

She purses her lips as if she's thinking about it. I watch as she looks around, eyeing the beach to see if we're still alone.

I feel her hand slide down my stomach until she firmly grips my length in her palm. "River," I warn, knowing we don't have a condom way out here. She's going to get me all worked up without being able to do anything about it.

"Shh…" She shushes me with a devil grin. She steps closer before giving me a wink and sinking down into the water.

"What the hell?" I ask, though she can't hear me now. But it doesn't matter because the moment I feel her mouth wrapped around my cock, I know exactly what she's doing. The water is usually clear, but without the sunlight, I can only see the top of her head.

"Oh my God," I groan, arching my back and hips. "Fuck, River." I fist her hair in the water and help control her movements. She bobs her head up and down, sliding her tongue along the vein of my shaft. Who knew a blow job could feel this fucking good under water?

She stands up, slicking her hair back and catches her breath. Before I can say anything, she sinks back into the water, and I feel her stroke my dick between her breasts. *Oh, fucking hell*. The girl has great fucking tits, too. I only wish I could see the way she looks right now.

Switching between her mouth and breasts, she works me up so goddamn good, I know I can't hold back much longer. When she stands up to take another deep breath, I stop her and plant her back on her feet.

"We have to go. Right now." I grab her hand and lead us to our clothes.

"Why?"

I look at her over my shoulder, and she laughs as soon as she sees my pained expression.

"Got it," she says.

Once we're dressed, we waste no time and head straight to her room. Within seconds of entering, I have her flat on her back on the bed. I devour her pussy as she wraps her thighs around my neck. Fuck, I love the way she tastes. So damn sweet.

"Alex," she pleads, kneading her fingers into my arms as I insert two fingers inside her tight body. "More."

I love the way she begs for me. It encourages me to increase the pace until I feel her climax on my tongue, and when she does —I fucking lose it. Ripping off my jeans, I grab her ankles and place them on top of my shoulders as I slam into her. She cries out as I thrust deeper and harder, and when I feel my own release building, I quickly pull out and stroke my cock till I come on her stomach.

"Shit," I mutter, as I collapse on the bed next to her.

"What?" She's panting, trying to catch her breath.

"I forgot to put on a condom." I face her, brushing my hand along her cheek. "I lose all control around you, River." Which is the damn truth. I know the deal we made and how this isn't anything more than a vacation fling, but that doesn't stop the swelling in my chest anytime I think about her.

She gives me a small smile, completely sated and relaxed. "Well, I'm on the pill and take it religiously," she tells me, easing my nerves "And after my last boyfriend cheated on me, I got myself checked out and was clean."

"I've always used a condom," I tell her. "I'm clean."

"Good, then we don't have anything to worry about." She smiles, looking up at the ceiling as her eyes flutter closed.

Once we're cleaned up and dressed, we lie in bed. "So what kind of dumbass would cheat on you?" We talked about some personal stuff, but mostly, we've treaded carefully. I think both knowing this is only a short-term thing, we've been trying to prevent getting too close. However, I can't imagine any guy stupid enough to cheat on a girl like River.

She groans, biting her lip. "Technically, I was the mistress."

My brows shoot up. "Wow."

"Yeah, I know. Then once I left him, he banged my roommate."

"You're kidding." I couldn't believe the audacity.

"I wish. He completely blindsided me. Split personalities or something, because I didn't see it coming."

"Which I bet made it that much harder when you found out, huh?" I hold her tighter, pissed that any guy would put her through that much pain.

"Oh, yeah. Hence this trip." She sighs.

"I'm sorry."

"Don't be. It's not your fault." Shrugging, she snuggles closer to my chest and wraps her arm around me.

"Well, I'm sorry it happened to you. Send him my way, and I'll give him a genuine Texas ass kicking." I grin, though I'm serious. Assholes like him deserve it.

"He's not worth it," she says, confidently. Her strength is admirable, but I hate to think how he made her feel.

"I'm going to think of it as a blessing," I tell her, matter-of-factly. She looks up at me puzzled. "His stupidity led you to me." I tuck a piece of wild hair behind her ear. "You wouldn't be here if it weren't for him."

She nods. "You're right." Smiling, she holds her fist up as if she's making a pretend toast. "To Asshole: for being a cheating dirtbag and putting me in the arms of the sweetest and sexiest cowboy I've ever laid eyes on!" I hold a fist up to hers, and we bump them together.

"Good riddance, Asshole!" I wrap my arm around her body and press my weight on top of her.

Giggling, she gazes up into my eyes. "I couldn't think of a better way to celebrate."

CHAPTER TWELVE

RIVER

NATALIE and I are having mimosas at the hotel restaurant Friday morning when Alex approaches our table. He presses a kiss to my cheek before taking the chair next to me.

"Good mornin', ladies," he says, taking off his ball cap and setting it down. I have a feeling he does that a lot back home with his cowboy hats. He's always a proper gentleman, making sure my needs are met before his, and being super polite—yet not too polite in the bedroom.

Too bad there's none of that Southern charm in Wisconsin.

"Morning!" Natalie beams, the smile on her face gives away what she's thinking. We've barely seen each other since the weekend, but as she's said over and over, she more than understands.

"Where's Dylan?" I ask when he doesn't take the other chair like I expected.

"Buried in Jessica probably."

I laugh, knowing he's more than likely right. We've hardly seen Dylan either, not that Alex seems to even mind.

The waitress comes over and takes our orders. Adam left early for one last fishing trip since he and Natalie fly out tomorrow night. My flight isn't until Sunday, giving me only one more night with Alex since he and Dylan leave Saturday afternoon.

The past few days, we've explored more of Key West, checking more items off my vacation bucket list—or rather adding items so we could check them off—and the more time we spend together, the harder it's going to be to leave him.

"I can't believe I have to go back to work on Monday," Natalie whines. "Maybe I could convince Adam to move down here instead. I'm sure they could use a radiologist at the hospital or something." Her tone is serious, though I know she'd never leave her family.

"Doubtful." I chuckle. "He's too much a country boy. He'd miss his ice fishing and snowboarding."

Her shoulders fall. "Damn. A girl could get used to this beach lifestyle."

I grin, agreeing. "It's definitely going to be hard going back to twelve-hour shifts after this."

"Damn, you work long hours," Alex states. "I'm usually up around four or five a.m. to feed the animals before starting on the day's chores, but Dylan and I fuck around most of the time." He chuckles, and I have a feeling he's being humble about how hard he actually works.

"Twelve hours minimum," I add. "Then sometimes I don't even get a break until the end of my shift, which means my feet are swollen and I look like I've just ran a marathon."

"That's intense," he says, studying my features.

"I'm sure you're used to those long hours, too," I say. "Don't ranchers work till the late afternoon or something?"

"Oh, yeah. It just depends. Every week can be different, especially at the Bishop ranch. My older brothers, Jackson and John, live on the ranch, too, so we're supposed to split up the duties."

"I can't even imagine living on a ranch," Natalie blurts out. "Being constantly dirty and smelly and oh my God, the heat. That's a double hell no from me."

Alex chuckles. "You city girls."

I grin, not denying he's right. I love my job, and at least I get to work indoors.

Moments later, our food arrives, and we dig in. Alex talks more about the family ranch and his brothers. It's very family-oriented, which actually sounds nice. But there's no denying we're from two completely different worlds.

"So you've talked about different aspects of your job, but I don't think you told me what made you want to become a nurse in the first place," Alex says, curiously, and though his question isn't out of line, it does come a little unexpected.

Natalie lifts her face right away to watch my expression and waits to see if I need an out. I don't let her give me one, and even though talking about Rylie never gets easier, I don't avoid it either. Hiding what happened to my baby sister won't change the past.

"I ended up spending a lot of time in hospitals when I was eleven or twelve. As sad as it sounds, it became my second home for a few years. I met a lot of nurses and doctors and started learning more and more about it as I got older," I begin.

"Were you sick?" His brows squeeze together.

"No, I wasn't." I swallow, lowering my eyes before looking back up. "My baby sister, Rylie, had leukemia, and after she was diagnosed, I didn't leave her side. Every doctor appointment, ER visit, or chemo treatment—I stood next to her because I didn't want her to be alone."

"Oh my God, River. I'm so sorry." He reaches over and squeezes my hand. The tears surface, but I blink them away.

"It was horrible," I admit. "I watched her deteriorate and become a lifeless version of herself."

"Is she okay now?" he asks, and even though I anticipated that question, it does nothing to my aching heart.

I try to find the right words as I respond. "No. When I was fourteen, she ended up in the ER for the millionth time and contracted an infection that took a turn for the worst. She became septic, and her organs rapidly shut down."

"She didn't make it," he says softly, his voice somber. He closes his eyes.

I cover his hand and squeeze three times. He couldn't have known, and I know he feels bad now for bringing it up.

"Alex," I whisper, and he opens his eyes.

"I'm sorry."

"It's okay," I tell him. "I like talking about Rylie, even when it's sad."

He wraps his arms around my shoulders and pulls me close. "You became a pediatric nurse because of her."

"Yeah. I knew I wanted to be around children, and as weird as it sounds, it makes me feel closer to her. I want to do good by her, make her proud."

"By the sounds of it, I'd say she'd be very proud." His smile is genuine.

We turn our heads, putting our attention on Natalie who's staring dreamily at us with tear-filled eyes. "I'm not crying." She wipes her cheeks.

I laugh through my own tears. "Me either."

"Me either," Alex says in a thick voice, making Natalie and I both laugh.

We finish our breakfast and part ways with Natalie so she can start packing.

"So…" Alex begins as we walk hand in hand along the beach. "Yeah?"

"What do you want to do for our last night here?"

I was hoping he wouldn't bring it up actually and that we would just continue the way we've been without saying it aloud that he leaves tomorrow.

"I'm not sure. Do you have any ideas?"

"I do, but I'm not sure if you'll approve or not."

I give him a side glance. "Why? Is it some weird kinky shit that's going to have me tied up with a gag?"

He narrows his eyes at me, almost scared. "What kind of romance books are you into?"

I chuckle.

"I guess it's a little more than just our casual sex agreement. But I figure I'd risk it anyway because what's the worst that can happen? Not like you can call it off now." He smirks when I look up at him and winks.

"So what you're saying is it's a romantic gesture?"

"Yeah, I would say so, but I saw the ad for it and think you'd really enjoy it. One last vacation bucket list item to check off." He stops and turns so we're face to face now. "Whaddya say?"

Smiling up at his hopeful face, I couldn't deny him even if I tried. "Lay it on me, cowboy."

Alex and I spent the afternoon in my bed, both of us wanting to memorize every inch of each other. I love his rough and bossy side, but I also really like his sweet and passionate side too. Alex makes love as good as he fucks.

Later that night, he tells me to get dressed because he's taking me out for dinner. We end up at a nice steakhouse where he orders us wine, and we talk about anything and everything.

Once dinner is over, we travel to another part of the island, and in the distance, I can see exactly where he's taking me.

"A hot air balloon?" I exclaim, my smile widening from ear to ear.

"Yeah, you ever been on one?"

"Hell, no! Oh my God! This is so exciting!" I wrap my arms around his shoulder and tightly hug him. "It's perfect," I tell him. *The perfect way to say goodbye*, I think to myself.

"I was hoping you'd say that." He grins against my lips.

As soon as we're inside the bucket, the instructor talks a little about what to expect. I'm so giddy, I mostly tune him out. Before long, we're floating toward the clouds.

The view is incredible as I look out with Alex's arms wrapped around my waist. His chest is pressed against my back as he holds me, and it's the most romantic thing I've ever experienced.

"The sunset is amazing," I say when he rests his chin on my head. "No view will ever be able to compare now."

He dips his face and buries it in my hair, inhaling the scent of my shampoo. His lips linger down to my ear where he presses kisses along my neck. "Agreed," he says, though he's not looking at the sky.

He's looking at me.

The hour ride is over too soon. I'm dreading the descent because we'll be back on land where time exists. Up in the balloon, we floated above the horizon, over the beaches and water, and it was as if time stood still.

"Thank you," I tell him as he holds my hand and leads me back to the hotel. "Definitely my favorite on the list."

"Even more than patio sex?" His brows rise, teasingly. A couple nights ago, Alex turned into a caveman and pressed my body up against the patio glass door and took me from behind. And if that wasn't the hottest damn thing ever, he then opened the door and bent me over the railing. I could see people down at the pool below us, and the fact that any of them could look up and see us had me hot all over.

I chuckle and shrug. "Okay, I guess it's a tie then."

He brings our hands up to his mouth and kisses my knuckles. "I can deal with that." He winks.

When we're finally in my room, the mood is somber, both of us knowing what's to come tomorrow. Neither of us want to bring it up again, and the tension is thick in the air. It's obvious this week together turned into much more than just a fling, but that doesn't mean anything can change once we leave. We aren't from the same worlds, and another broken heart would be inevitable at that point.

Nerves take over my body, and Alex can sense my apprehension.

"River." His voice is deep and thick with emotion. I look up at him and see it in his eyes. He's sad, too.

"Yes?"

Wrapping his hand possessively around my neck, he brings his mouth down to mine and slowly kisses me. He takes the time to really explore my mouth and savor the taste. I cling to him, gripping my fingers in his shirt and holding him to my body. We mold together effortlessly.

"I'm going to miss you," he says, breaking the kiss. He rests his forehead against mine, and the deep breathing between us is all that can be heard as he waits for my response.

Swallowing, I do my best to keep my emotions at bay. "You're supposed to be the strong one," I tease, choking back tears.

He flashes a small, gentle smile. "Let's not waste our last night together being sad, okay?"

I nod against his forehead. "Okay."

Slowly, he strips me of my clothes. His movements are calculated but not rushed. Taking his time, he studies everything about me, placing it all into his memory. He kisses my neck before moving down to my shoulder and collarbone. My head falls back as I welcome his mouth on me, burning his touch into my skin.

Alex roams his hands around my waist and pulls me close. I grab his shirt, needing to feel his skin on mine. Pulling it over his head, he doesn't waste a second before crushing his mouth back down. Our bodies mold together, hunger and desperation taking over our senses.

I wrestle with his belt and undo his jeans. A throaty moan escapes his lips when I pull his boxer shorts down and palm his cock. I want to memorize everything about him—the feel of his skin, the length of his hardness, the way his lips burn into my neck. It's perfection.

Alex makes me feel like the only girl in the entire world, and I've never felt like that before. I know what we have is based on variables—being on vacation with limited time, meeting a sexy stranger, and knowing that whatever happens can only happen *here*—but that doesn't mean I haven't let thoughts of *what-if* escape me.

We were, in fact, slow dancing in a burning room.

It's only a matter of hours before we leave everything we shared behind.

I push all those thoughts away, not wanting to think about it. Not tonight, anyway.

Moaning at the way his mouth devours mine, I absolutely love it when he palms my cheeks as if I'm the most precious and important thing to him—at this moment, at least. After he removes the rest of his clothes, he pushes us to the bed, and I adjust my body till we're lying in the middle of the mattress and his body towers over mine. Though I've seen his naked body all week, I'll never get tired of looking at him. He's rock solid all over, has one small tattoo on his chest, and a small happy trail that leads all the way down to his glorious cock. Both of his ears are pierced, and with his blond hair and blue eyes, he's the very definition of a Southern playboy. Always the smooth talker with his dirty words, yet he's charming and polite. Everything about Alex Bishop screams perfection, and I've been the fortunate one to have his complete and undivided attention during this trip—something I sense many other women don't get from him.

Even though it feels like it's been a real-life fantasy, no one can ever take this week from me. It's one I'll hold in my heart forever, and once we leave this place, that's where it'll stay stored.

"River…" his deep voice murmurs against my lips.

"Mm?"

"You're so beautiful," he tells me—something he's told me often, but not always believed.

I peel open my eyes and see him looking down at me with a small, crooked smile.

"You are too."

His fingers brush over my lips softly, and when my breath hitches, he paints my mouth with his. Alex continues to devour me all night long, taking his time and building me up over and over again.

I've left scratch marks all over his back and arms, no doubt. His teeth and lips have left bruises—the good kind—over my neck, shoulders, and chest. I love feeling the scrape of his teeth along my back when he takes me from behind as if he can't get enough of my skin against his.

He takes me slow, pushing inside me with firm thrusts, but doesn't rush. Building me up ever so slowly yet pounding into me deeper as I ride out my orgasm. His fingers lace with mine as he brings my arms over my head and chases his release. As my thighs wrap around his waist, I dig my heels into his ass and push him inside deeper. His face twists as he howls out a guttural moan, his entire body tightening as he comes. It's the most beautiful thing I've ever seen, and now that I have the vision of Alex coming permanently etched into my memory, I don't know that anything could ever come close to topping it.

Afterward, he always rubs his palm along my chest and stomach. He massages my breasts, flicking and sucking on my nipples, and runs his fingers along my hipbones. Tonight, he doesn't disappoint, but rather, he holds me tight to his chest and rests his palm on my racing heart as if he's storing the beats of it to his mind.

Later, we take a shower together, and he pins me to the wall and kisses every inch of my body. The way he cherishes me is something I know I'll miss.

Once we're fully satisfied and back in bed, he keeps me wrapped in his arms and legs and holds me there until morning.

"Alex?" I whisper, wondering if he's awake or not. His breathing has picked up, but he hasn't moved.

"Hm?" he finally groans.

"What time does your plane leave?" I cringe at the words, but I know if he doesn't get up, he'll more than likely miss it.

"Whenever I get there."

I chuckle at his arrogance. "Oh, you must be a personal friend of the pilot."

"Yep." He rolls me over, and I see a cocky grin on his face.

"Have you packed yet?"

"Nope." His eyes aren't fully open, but he doesn't seem to be worried about it.

"Has Dylan?" I furrow my brows, wondering how the hell these two guys even made it here in the first place.

He yawns, stretching his arms over his head. "No idea."

I purse my lips together, narrowing my eyes. "Okay, well do we have time for breakfast? Or do you want help packing?"

"Oh, there's always time for breakfast." The corner of his lips curls up into a mischievous grin, and it takes me a second to realize what he's doing when he pulls the covers back and kneels between my legs.

"What are—"

He wraps my thighs around his neck as he digs his fingers into my ass and presses his mouth between my legs.

"Alex!" I squeal and laugh, then moan and scream because he licks and sucks, circling my clit with his tongue, and then presses a finger inside as the orgasm builds and releases around him.

"Sorry, darlin'." He winks, licking his lower lip. "They do say breakfast is the most important meal of the day."

Once I convince him to get up and dressed, I walk with him down to his room. As soon as we walk in, it looks like a bomb went off. Clothes, bedsheets, shoes, towels, food, and room service trays are spread out all over the floor.

"Dylan, you sick fucker."

I chuckle when I see girl's clothes spread all over the floor, and the air reeks of sweaty sex.

"Go away." We hear his mumbles from the patio.

"Ah, shit," Alex groans, rubbing a hand along his scruffy jawline.

"Hey, Dylan," I call out, making sure he knows I'm in here, too.

"He looks in rough shape," I whisper, making sure only Alex can hear me.

"Yeah, he doesn't do goodbye very well."

I pull in my lips. *That makes two of us.*

"You want me to leave you guys alone to pack and...maybe throw him in the shower?"

He wraps a hand around my waist and pulls me into his side, kissing the top of my head. "We have to leave at three to make our flight." He checks the time on his phone. "Come back at one?"

"Sure, that'll give me time to start packing my own shit." I tilt my head up and kiss him.

When I shut his door behind me, realization hits that it's the final time I'll be in there.

I text Natalie and tell her I'm heading over. She also leaves this afternoon, so I figure I'll keep myself busy for the next couple of hours by helping her pack.

"Oh, River." She frowns the second she sees me. I step inside and wipe my eyes.

"What?"

"I hate that we're leaving, but I hate even more knowing you and Alex are going your separate ways."

I hear the shower running and know we have a few moments of privacy till Adam is done.

Shrugging, I sit on the edge of the bed. "We both knew what we were getting into. One week, no strings or attachments, no expectations."

"Even I know that's a bunch of bullshit," she blurts out.

"This was your idea, Nat," I remind her, eyeing her.

"I know, but I didn't know he'd turn around and be Mr. Perfect."

"It's because we're on an island, sipping margaritas, and living on the beach. That's not real life," I say, trying to convince myself more than her. "Even if we lived on the same planet, you know the moment we'd get back home, shit would hit the fan. It always does."

"You sound so cynical," she spats.

I arch a brow, knowing I have every right to be. Shrugging, I play it off because I don't want to talk about it anymore.

"Did you two have a nice night together at least?"

I smile, thinking about it. "Yeah, we really did. It was a great way to say goodbye." I look up at the ceiling, knowing if I see her face right now, it's going to make me an emotional wreck.

"Are you going to exchange numbers?" she asks, drawing my eyes back to her.

"No, that's part of the 'no strings and casual sex' agreement. Why draw something out that's only doomed to fail? I'd rather take all these great memories and hold onto them than taint them with trying to make it work. Because let's be honest, we live hundreds of miles apart, and I doubt we could 'just be friends' after a week like this."

"That just makes me so sad, River. I wanted you to come here and have no-attachments sex, but I hadn't expected the guy to be…well, Alex."

"Yeah, damn those Southern cowboys," I mock. "All charming, sweet, and polite."

"And in bed?" She wiggles her brows.

"Definitely not polite." I smirk. "Always the gentleman, though."

After I help Natalie and Adam pack, we say our goodbyes. They're going to grab lunch before heading to the airport, so once they're off, I head back to Alex's room.

When I walk down the hall of his floor, I see his door is propped open, and when I get closer, I see it's housekeeping.

I look around for him or Dylan, but when I step in, a woman is stripping the beds.

"Hello," I say, shyly. "Are the two guys who stayed in here around, do you know?" I feel silly for asking, but I have no idea where else they'd be.

"No, ma'am."

"Okay, thank you."

Where the hell would he be? He knew I was coming back.

Swallowing, I walk out and head up to my floor. Once I'm at my room, I see a piece of paper taped to my door with my name written on it. I open it up and see it's the scratch paper we used to write out my vacation bucket list. After deciding that we were going to follow one, Alex and I had handwritten one out. He must've had it in his pocket.

River,
We got a notification that our flight was canceled, and the only flight available back to San Angelo was right now or we'd have to wait till Monday. We had no choice but to take this one, and I'm so sorry I have to leave like this. I looked in the lobby and around the bar, before coming back to your room to double-check if you were here. But we have to go now.

I don't want this to be the way we say goodbye, so please call me. (325-555-2539).
Love, Alex

P.S. For what it's worth, you were much more than a no-strings-attached-vacation-hookup. You made these last two weeks memorable in every sense of the word, and I'll never forget it.

Oh my God.

My feet feel frozen to the floor as I scan the note again. *He's gone.*

I feel my heart racing, and I blink out of my trance before

running back to the elevator. Maybe he's still down there. I have to at least look.

Searching the lobby, pool, and bar area, it's confirmed. He's gone.

Go to the airport, a thought pops into my head. And for a second, I consider it, but then push it away. Calling him and hearing his voice or seeing him one last time isn't going to change anything. In fact, it'll only make things worse. Saying goodbye wasn't going to be easy in the first place, so maybe this is the way it had to be.

As I walk back to my room, thoughts of last night surface and how wonderful and magical it all was. Those are the memories I want to remember. Like I told Natalie, *that* was the perfect way to say goodbye. Anything else would only deepen the wound.

PART II

CHAPTER THIRTEEN

ALEX

THREE MONTHS LATER

THE RAIN WON'T STOP COMING, and by the looks of the forecast, the rest of the week will be exactly like today. I'm cold, wet, and miserable, and no amount of rain gear helps me stay dry. By the time Dylan and I break for lunch, we're soaked from head to toe.

"This fucking sucks," Dylan complains as we slosh through the mud toward the truck. Once we're inside, the rain pounds so hard against the windshield, I can't see shit. I put the truck in reverse, and the wheels do nothing but spin. No amount of pressing the gas pedal is getting us unstuck at this point. I look over at Dylan, and he's pinching the bridge of his nose.

"Guess we're walking back to the house. Dammit," I hiss between gritted teeth.

I keep the truck running and try to warm up my frozen hands.

"Let's call Jackson to come get us in the Jeep. It has 4-wheel drive at least, and we won't have to walk over a mile in this crap. It's cold as hell out there."

"Good idea," I say, grabbing my phone from my pocket. Jackson's probably doing nothing right now anyway, so I don't even feel guilty bothering him. During the day, he usually trains

horses and takes guests trail riding, among other things. When the
weather is shit like this, he doesn't really have much to do.

**Alex: Hey, the truck is stuck and we need a ride back. Can
you give us a lift?**

Jackson: Busy.

**Alex: Don't be an asshole. We're stuck at the barn in mud
to our fucking knees.**

Just as I'm about ready to call John, he texts me back to let me
know he's on the way. Bastard just likes to make me sweat.

"He's coming. Thought he was gonna let us deal with this shit
on our own," I tell Dylan, shoving my phone back into my pocket.

"If he did that to us, I'd kick his ass. Or tell your mama. I think
the latter would be worse, though. Mrs. Bishop's wrath is
frightening as fuck!"

Chuckling while agreeing, I lean my head against the seat and
watch the rain slide down the windshield. It's a nice distraction
but doesn't keep my mind from wandering.

It's been three months since Key West, and I haven't been able
to forget the time I spent with River. At the oddest moments, I'll
think about her and wonder what she's doing. I'll relive our last
day together over and over, wondering why she never called me. I
knew the deal and that it was just supposed to be a vacation
hookup, but I hadn't expected her to bulldoze into my heart the
way she did. It hadn't been like anything I'd ever experienced
before and knowing she chose to end things the way she did has
me obsessing over every little detail.

If I dig deep, I can almost smell her shampoo or hear her
laugh. My heart aches when I think about how she really left
everything we shared back on that island. I could've sworn there
was something more between us than just the physical stuff. I felt
it and know she did too, whether or not she wants to admit it.

Hands down, I would've taken a million-dollar bet that she would've called me as soon as she read my note. To her, we were nothing but two lonely strangers and a vacation bucket list.

"You're thinking about her again, aren't you?" Dylan smirks, giving me shit like he has almost every day since the plane landed in Texas.

"Something like that," I groan. When I talk about her, it makes all the memories I've buried over the last few months rise to the surface. How the hell did I end up in this state of mind? Women don't usually affect me like this. But River was different. She was a bad girl pretending to be good, a thief who stole my heart without warning. The intentions of giving it back never existed, and what makes it worse is I never saw it coming. I never saw *her* coming. Being completely blindsided by the memory of her soft kiss, warm touch, and everything we experienced is no stranger to me. Now that's all that remains. *The memories of us.*

"You're doing it again. You get this look on your face every time you have River on your mind. It's kinda disgustin'. Like a love sickness or something." He pretends to throw up in his mouth.

"I don't wanna hear about it, considerin' you're still talking to Jessica—who lives in New York, by the way—every single night. So disgustin' is your middle name."

Dylan takes a deep breath, getting ready to tell me where to go, but before he does, a fist bangs against the passenger window. We both jump, and Jackson's on the other side laughing his ass off as the rain pours around him in buckets. Once we're out of the truck and in the Jeep, that's when the shit talkin' really begins.

"The truck was all fogged up like you two were makin' love in there," Jackson teases, putting the Jeep in reverse, slinging mud everywhere. "Only thing missing was that palm print on the window like in *Titanic*."

"Fuck off," I tell him. "Dylan's not really my type anyway."

"I'll never let go, Jack. I mean, Dylan," Jackson continues.

"More like, I'll never let go, *River*," Dylan adds.

I turn around and shoot daggers at him. If looks could kill, his ass would be dead in the back seat.

"Good one. I'm almost certain that Alex has cried himself a roaring river over the last three months because at this point, I'm not sure she's actually real." Jackson has been antagonizing me about her, too.

"You motherfuckers can drop dead."

The biggest mistake I made when I got home was telling Jackson about River, but I couldn't help it. I needed someone to chat with other than Dylan, and I wanted another opinion to make sure I wasn't losing my fucking mind. Unfortunately, Jackson's unsolicited advice was to fuck a different woman every night for two weeks, and he guaranteed that'd get her out of my system and off my mind. Knowing that would never work—that no woman could replace River, nor would I want to do that—I swore I'd never ask him for female advice again. And I shoulda known better, considering he's hung up on Kiera, even though he'd never admit it.

Jackson drives fast down the dirt road that's turned to mud as if he has somewhere to be. I hold on to the oh-shit handle and can hear Dylan being knocked around in the back as Jackson creates his own path to Mama's house. Jackson can't stop laughing as Dylan and I huff at his horrible driving. By the time he drops us off close to the porch, we're ready to fall out of the Jeep.

"Thanks, man," I tell him as I get out, and he gives me a head nod before spinning out, slinging mud all over us. I flip him off, hoping he'll see me in the rearview mirror, though I doubt he cares.

"I kinda wish we would've walked now. I thought I was gonna die," Dylan admits. I pat his shoulder and nod.

"Or next time we call John. He doesn't have a death wish."

Jackson and John may be twins, but they're as opposite as they come. Aside from their identical looks, their personalities are what set them apart. Jackson lives every day as if he's turning twenty-one for the first time while John is the more sensible and responsible one. Though if you asked anyone who knew the Bishop brothers, they'd say I was more like Jackson, whereas John and Evan were similar in personality traits.

Before walking inside, we remove our boots and dirty jackets and leave them on the porch. No need to set Mama off by wearing filthy clothes inside her immaculate house.

As soon as we walk in, I can hear Dad and Mama chatting in the kitchen. Smells of cornbread fill the house, and it makes me hungry.

"Hey, Mama," I say, leaning over and giving her a kiss on the cheek as soon as Dylan and I enter the kitchen. "Got the truck stuck again."

"Son, why don't you call it a day?" Mama asks.

"Because there's work to be done," I tell her politely with a smile.

Dad drinks a glass of milk, and when he finishes, he wipes his mouth and makes eye contact with me. "That's enough for today, son. Not too much more can be done in this weather. Waste of my damn time, if you ask me. If it's a mess outside tomorrow, then we'll pick up on Wednesday."

"Yes, sir." I glance at Dylan, knowing we're going to have time to do whatever we want after we feed the animals tomorrow morning.

"You boys be back here around six. Chili should be ready by then. It's perfect for this cold weather." Mama pats me on the back with a grin. "Tell your brothers, too."

"Yes, ma'am. We'll be back."

Just as we head out of the kitchen, Mama calls me back. "Will you bring these treats over to John before you head home? Tell them to set them out for the B&B guests since they'll be stuck inside the next few days."

Though it's a little out of the way, I agree with a smile knowing I'm not on anyone else's schedule today. Instead of getting my truck dirty, I grab the keys to the old Jeep parked in the barn beside the house. It's not the fanciest vehicle on the ranch, but it's better than the work truck we drive around, and it has 4-wheel drive, so no chance of getting stuck again.

"I'm not heading home in this bullshit. Hopefully, a few hours from now it'll let up," Dylan says after we put on our boots and run to the Jeep. We try not to get any wetter but fail miserably. We drive slowly to the bed and breakfast, and when we finally get there, I see the parking lot is full of vehicles.

After I park on the side of the building, I grab the sack of treats, and we bolt to the side door. Guests fill every empty chair available while others huddle around the fireplace though it feels like it's a hundred degrees inside. Glancing around, I spot John who's standing behind the counter reading a hunting magazine.

"Mama told me to deliver these to you. She made them for the guests and all that."

"Again?" John asks, grabbing the bag and peeking inside.

"You know how she gets. When she's bored, she bakes. By the weight of it, probably a hundred cookies in there."

"Well, she sure knows how to butter 'em up," John says, walking behind the bar and looking for something to put them in.

"Butter them up or fatten them up? I'm not sure which one anymore," I say with a laugh. John nods in agreement as he places the cookies in a basket and sets it on top of the counter.

"So what y'all doing today in this lovely weather?" A tinge of sarcasm hits John's tone as he glances outside the bay windows.

"Day drinking," Dylan responds with a smirk.

"Hell no. We can't be showing up for dinner completely wasted. Mama will murder us." I shake my head at Dylan, and all he does is nod. I narrow my eyes at him. "Seriously, no."

"We'll see," he teases.

Guests spot the cookies, and they take them by the handfuls. Everyone is all smiles, and I wonder if Mama made special cookies by how happy they are eating them.

"I'm going home, I guess. Oh, Mama's making chili. Be there at six. Let Jackson know too," I tell John. He gives me a nod before

Dylan and I head out. We ride in silence across the property. Once we get to my house, we run inside and kick off our boots.

I walk to the kitchen and make myself and Dylan a turkey sandwich because we didn't get a chance to eat. "You can borrow some of my clothes if you want so you don't have to sit around in those nasty wet ones. I'm going to shower," I tell Dylan once I finish eating.

As I walk away, I catch him grabbing a beer from the fridge and realize he wasn't kidding about day drinking. He tips it and opens it with a shit-eating grin. Shaking my head, I continue down the hallway to the bathroom.

While I'm in the shower, thoughts of River flood my mind again. Why didn't I ever ask her for her number? Why didn't I insist that we keep in touch? The more I think about it, the more I want to kick my own ass. Once I dry off and get dressed, I head into the living room where Dylan is chatting it up with Jackson, who's wearing shorts and cowboy boots, looking more ridiculous than normal as he drinks a beer.

"You know Mama is expecting us at six, right?" I tell him, glancing at the bottle.

"Yeah, John told me…so?"

I don't dare argue with him while he digs his own grave. Instead, I plop on the couch and watch TV. I'm so lost in my own head I couldn't tell you what's going on.

"I'm going to look her up on Facebook," I tell Dylan, loud enough for only him to hear.

"No, it's not a good idea. Like I've told you before, if she wanted to talk to you, she'd call you. Simple as that. You're just setting yourself up to be let down. So why even go there?" Dylan hounds me much like he has before, but I don't give in this time. "Don't. Give me your phone." Dylan holds out his hand.

I flash him a look and refuse to give it to him. "But what if she lost my number? Or what if she lost her phone? There are a million different scenarios that could've happened. I know what we had was more than just a fling. I know it was," I tell Dylan.

"A hundred days later and you're still hung up on her. That pussy must've been good. That's all I'm saying," Jackson adds from the kitchen.

"Shut the fuck up, Jackson!" I yell back at him, not needing his side comments.

He stalks into the living room and sits on the couch next to me, grabs the remote and flicks through the channels. Pulling up my Facebook app, I look at the ridiculous picture I have on my profile of Dylan and fishing. It's been way too long since I've been on my profile, so I decide to check my friend requests first to see if maybe she looked me up and friended me. There are women in there, but not the one I want.

My mind drifts to the first time we had a real conversation. Dylan was still in the hospital, and I knew I had to speak to her. After formally introducing ourselves, I was lost in her trance as she grabbed my hand and we sat there together, frozen in time. That was the first time I felt the electricity soaring between us. Her touch was like fire and set my body ablaze.

Sucking in a deep breath, I type her name into the search bar and wait for her profile to load. I scroll through several River Lancasters until I find her. As soon as I see her sweet smile, I'm frozen in place. I click on the profile picture of her and Natalie and can't help but swallow down my heart as I see the tight black dress she's wearing. They're both smiling big, and by the decorations that fill the background, I can tell they were celebrating New Years. *Damn.* I wish I would've been there to kiss her as the clock struck midnight.

My finger hovers over the friend button. I suck in a deep breath, and it takes everything I have to close out of the app instead. As hard as it is, I force myself to leave our relationship exactly where it started and ended—in Key West.

A week passes and the rain does too, but the pastures hold water in some places, so it's still a sloppy mess. After work, I go home and shower before driving into town and to the Main Street Diner. I'm in the mood for breakfast for dinner, and the diner has the best bacon and eggs in town. I might even splurge on a big slice of pie. Mama is busy baking for the ladies at church, and we've learned not to even ask about food when she's baking for a purpose. So, instead, I decide to do my own thing.

As I drive across town, a stupid thought crosses my mind to message Natalie instead of River. She was tagged in River's profile picture on Facebook, and I know if I messaged her, she'd at least be supportive, I think. She was always so eager for River and me to hang out, so I can't imagine much had changed. However, the more I think about it, the more I realize how insane that sounds, even in my head. I don't want to seem desperate or like a stalker, but ever since I found her online, it's bothered the shit out of me.

Walking into the diner, I glance around and see Mrs. Betty shuffling behind the counter, so I take a seat in her section because I know she's always been good at giving advice. The woman has been working here since I was a kid, and she's good friends with Mama, plus she always has the latest town gossip to distract me with. Sometimes, when I've got a lot on my mind, I'll come down to the diner and drink coffee for hours. I always leave full and with a grin on my face.

Mrs. Betty instantly greets me with a smile and a steaming cup of coffee.

"So, did you talk to your lady, yet?" is the first thing she asks me. After hearing Dylan and me talking about River one night over dinner, she stuck her nose right in and told me to stop being a foolish man and track my woman down. I left out the part about River and my no-strings-attached sex-only deal, so of course, she thinks I should go to the ends of the earth to find her.

"No ma'am," I say, taking off my baseball cap and setting it on the bar. "I'm not going to contact her. I've decided that if she doesn't want to talk to me, then I don't want to talk to her either." My mood is sour, but I can't help it. It's been controlling my life these past three months, and it's driving me crazy. I can't keep on living like this.

"That's too bad, honey. Personally, I still think you should just go for it. What if she's having the same conversation with herself at this moment? You don't want to look back on your life when you're old like me and realize you didn't fight for love—real love—none of that made up stuff. I don't care about distance; love always finds a way. Trust me on that, sweetie." She flashes me a wink.

I give her a smile but don't speak.

"What do you have to lose?" she adds.

"Apparently nothing but my mind." I sigh as she hands me a menu even though I always order the same thing. I don't bother opening it but give her my order instead.

"Good for you," she says with a sweet smile when I add a slice of pecan pie to my order. She doesn't press me on River again, which I'm grateful for.

Time passes and before long Mrs. Betty is sliding my food across the bar top toward me and refilling my coffee. The eggs practically melt in my mouth, and the bacon is cooked crunchy just like I like it. As Mrs. Betty refills my coffee again, she's smiling, and there's something telling about that smile of hers.

"So tell me again what your dream girl looks like," she says, her smile still lingering.

I finish chewing, not talking with my mouth open, and tell her as I have before.

"She's tall. Blonde. Has a cute button nose and a smile that's so contagious, she could make a whole room smile along with her. She's kind and passionate, and you can tell she really cares about others' well-being just by hearing her speak about her job. When she laughs really hard, her eyes light up like emeralds. Mrs. Betty, she's the most beautiful woman in the world. But don't let her fool you, she's as stubborn as a mule too," I say, chuckling on the surface, but anger is burning through my veins. Angry that I let myself fall for her, something I never do with *anyone*, and angry that I was so duped into thinking the connection we had was mutual. And mostly, angry that I can't seem to get over it.

I look up at Mrs. Betty and catch her glancing around, a mischievous grin plastered on her face. "Well, I have a good feeling things are going to change for you, sweetie." She pats my hand before walking away.

Once I've finished, she gives me my pie in a to-go box and the check. I tell her thanks and that I'll be seeing her soon before putting a twenty down on the counter. As I stand, I grab my coffee cup and finish the rest before placing my cap back on my head. I feel good about my decision. Fuck her for leaving things the way she did. I wasn't ready to say goodbye, but she made that choice for me, so it's time to let go. I need to move on.

"Bye, Mrs. Betty," I call out, walking toward the exit.

"Bye, Alex." She winks.

Pushing the door open, I barely get one foot out before I hear my name being called behind me.

"Alex." I'd recognize that voice anywhere. My eyes widen, not willing to believe it's actually *her*. Not after all this time. Not after I'd just convinced myself to let go.

All the hair on my neck stands up, and when I turn around and see River's face, mixed feelings from lust to rage surface.

She's only standing a couple of feet from me, her scent intoxicating my senses as soon as I step back into the diner.

Looking up at me with her bright green eyes and blonde hair pulled into a side braid, she sways on her feet nervously.

Swallowing hard, I pin my eyes to her as my jaw clenches.

"What the fuck are you doing here?" are the first words to spew out of my mouth. They come out harsher than I intended, but considering everything I've been through, it's not entirely unmerited.

In fact, I think it's more than deserving.

CHAPTER FOURTEEN

RIVER

"WHAT THE FUCK are you doing here?"

His words sting, but I'm not exactly sure what I expected. After not calling him for three months, now here I am in Texas looking directly at a man who seems heartbroken and pained to see me again.

Not that I could blame him entirely. I can only hope he'll forgive me, but I wouldn't exactly blame him if he didn't.

Seeing him after all this time has so many mixed feelings and old memories surfacing. The moment I saw him walk into the diner, I knew it was my chance to approach him. I had planned on calling him once I was settled into my room to ask if we could meet up, but him being here brought us face-to-face much sooner than I'd anticipated.

I'd been sitting here for the last two hours thinking of what I'd say when I finally saw him again, thinking about how I'd explain why I didn't call or why I was here now. The more I thought about it, the more I lost the courage to reach out to him.

I had needed more time. Guess fate had other plans. It was now or never.

"I came to see you," I finally respond, my bottom lip trembling at the way he's looking at me. He's angry, *so* angry. I can see it. Hell, I can feel it steaming off his skin.

He pulls his cap off his head and brushes a hand roughly through his hair. The same locks I used to fist my own fingers through not too long ago.

"Can we go somewhere to talk?" I ask once he doesn't say anything. He's just standing and staring, and I can tell his mind is running a thousand miles an hour.

Before he can respond, someone walks in through the door, bumping Alex and pushing him forward right into me. The guy mutters a weak, "Sorry," and keeps walking. Meanwhile, my heart beats faster and harder now that Alex's arms are wrapped around my waist to steady me.

"Sorry." His voice is just above a whisper, and as he stands only inches away from me, it feels like we're the only two people in here.

I watch his throat as he swallows hard. This isn't how I wanted us to reunite, but regardless, I came here on a mission and am going to tell him what I came all this way for.

"Yeah, let's talk." He nudges his head toward the door, and I follow him out, so we're not in the doorway of the diner anymore. "Where are you staying?" He faces me and asks when we're several feet away from the entrance.

"Uh, this countryside bed and breakfast. I rented a car and was just about to head over there before I saw this diner and decided to stop and eat first." I don't admit that I stopped to grab a snack just twenty minutes before that.

The corner of his lips tilts up in a mock grin. "Of course." He fidgets with his hat and hair some more. "That's my family's B&B," he tells me, and when I lower my eyes, covering the guilt over my face, he snorts. "I'm betting you knew that though."

I nod before slowly looking back up at him. "I wasn't sure if you'd give me a chance to explain, so I figured the closer I was to you, the better chance I had."

"What?" he growls, whipping his head. He pulls his brows

together, looking more pissed off than before. "You honestly thought I'd turn you away? You think that little of me?"

I shrug, feeling worse. "No, I just wasn't sure what state of mind you were in since—"

"Since you chose to end things without giving me a damn chance to say goodbye?" he interrupts, his voice deep and rough. "Or since you neglected to call me to at least say that you didn't want to keep in contact? Or since you left things up in the air without giving me *any* kind of explanation? Do you know what I've been through these last three months wonderin'? Is that really what Key West meant to you? Because then I guess I read the entire situation wrong."

He's mad, obviously, but this is why I wanted us to meet somewhere private. Maybe I shouldn't have stopped him and let him walk out so I could mentally prepare better. God, I'm such a fool for coming here. I blow out a breath of frustration, reminding myself I came all this way for a reason and wasn't leaving until I laid out all my cards on the table.

"Okay, I fucked up!" I shout, taking him by surprise. My hormones have been uncontrollable these past few weeks, but instead of apologizing for my outburst, I continue. "I know I should've called to say goodbye the right way, but I was *scared*. Our time together meant more to me than I wanted to admit at the time, and I was scared I'd get hurt again if I let you in. But then I started to fall for you anyway. The only way to get over you was to try and forget it all happened, but I never could. I'm sorry, but—"

He steps toward me, closing the gap between us, and cups my face with his large hands as he tilts his head to the side and presses his lips over mine. His mouth cuts through my unspoken words, but I welcome it because the moment I feel his body close, electricity radiates from me.

Gripping his shirt in my hands, I pull his chest to mine and inhale his fresh, manly scent. I can tell he just took a shower, yet there's something so rugged about him. God, he kisses so passionately and with purpose. He holds my face like I'm the most precious thing in the world, and when a moan escapes his lips, I know we've lost ourselves in each other. I can't deny that this is the reaction I'd been hoping for, even if we did have a lot to discuss still.

"Alex…" I sigh against his mouth. Our lips part and he rests his forehead on mine, my heart pounding.

"Let's go. I'll take you to the B&B, and then we can talk."

I nod as he grabs my hand. "Oh wait. Should I grab my luggage?"

"Yeah, I can bring you back into town tomorrow to get your rental."

"Is that safe? What if someone tries breaking into it or steals it?" My question puts a wide small on his face before he bursts into a fit of laughter. "What's so funny?"

"Darlin', you're in small town Texas. No one wants to break into your Prius."

"Oh," I mutter, feeling stupid. "You can take the girl out of the city, but you can't take the city out of the girl, I guess." I shrug, lowering my face to hide the blush that's rising over my cheeks.

He chuckles, holding out a hand as I dig for my keys. Once he pops the trunk and grabs my suitcase, he slams it shut and leads me to his truck. My eyes widen when I see he drives a nice black Ford F-150.

"I'm slightly relieved to see you don't drive one of those decked out and lifted trucks with orange and yellow flames on the side," I tease when he opens the door for me.

He gives me a puzzled look.

"What? You Texans are obsessed with your trucks." I slide into the seat and reach for the buckle.

"Damn right we're obsessed," he jokes, adjusting his hat. "This one is even the Texas Edition." He smiles, proudly.

"Texas Edition?" My brows lift. "I'm definitely not in Wisconsin anymore."

Grinning, he shuts the door and walks around to the driver's side. The tension is still thick in the air, yet I'm so relieved even though we have a lot to talk about.

"So, how'd you end up finding me anyway?" he asks once we're on the road.

"Bishop, ranch, Texas. Not hard to Google." I shrug. "The property is huge, and I had no idea if you lived on the ranch or not, so I took a chance staying at the B&B, hoping I'd be able to find you."

He licks his lips as he focuses on the road ahead of us. "Well, guess you didn't need to look hard. Small town perks."

"Yeah. Guess so." I slouch into my seat, my nerves feeling shot already.

He glances over at me before speaking up again. "I looked you up on Facebook but didn't have the courage to friend request you. Figured I'd look needy or some shit since the ball was in your court and you didn't take it." He shrugs, the guilt crawling up my skin. "Saw your profile picture, though. You looked real pretty and happy."

I blush, both sad and pleased he thought to look me up. "Thank you. Natalie and Adam threw a huge New Year's Eve party."

"I figured it was. Natalie looked pretty smashed." He laughs.

I laugh with him and nod in agreement. "Yeah, after she threw up on my shoes, Adam proposed. Then she drank some more to *celebrate*." I don't tell him I hadn't been drinking that night at all and had been thinking of him nonstop.

"They got engaged?"

"Yep. Finally. They've been together since college."

"Wow, tell her I said congrats."

"I will."

The silence fills the air, and when I look out my window, all I see is country. Miles and miles of rolling hills and crispy brown grass. The sun is setting, painting the sky a pretty yellow and orange canvas. Texas is glowing, and I take a moment to take in the scene of the afterglows on the horizon.

"This is so different from city life," I murmur as he drives through the winding roads that are starting to make me nauseous. "So weird to me."

"I'm sure. It's the only life I know, though. I couldn't live anywhere else," he admits, and my heart aches.

After a fifteen-minute drive, we turn down a gravel road until I see a giant house set in the distance with every light on inside. As we slow to a crawl, a large black post with a sign that reads CIRCLE B RANCH BED & BREAKFAST embellished with a bird on top comes into view. It's surrounded by a bed of wild flowers and adds to the rustic feel of the whole ranch. Once I found this place online, I did as much research as I could and discovered that everything about the ranch life fascinates me. It's obvious the whole community is very family-oriented, considering a majority of the ranches and land are passed down from generation to generation. You don't see that much where I'm from.

"It looks even better in person," I say as he parks right in the front.

"Wait till you see it in the early morning. The sun shines and brightens up everything. Mama's worked obsessively on all the flowers, and John and Jackson take turns with the horses and trail riding. John manages more of the business aspect of it, too."

"I can definitely see the appeal." I smile, taking it all in. Alex jumps out and walks to my side to open the door. "If you're interested in riding, we could set something up."

I tuck my lips into my mouth and stop the words that so desperately need to come out.

"Sorry, I didn't mean to rush anything. Just figured while you're in Texas, might as well enjoy some of it."

"No, it's fine." I shake my head. "I mean, maybe. I'm only here for a few days."

The smile drops from his face, and I feel bad for disappointing him once again.

After he grabs my suitcase, Alex reaches for my hand and walks us up the large staircase that leads to a gorgeous house with tall colonial columns and a wraparound porch. Planters and rocking chairs line the porch, and I make a mental note to come out here and sit later. It looks so cozy, and I haven't even stepped inside yet.

"I'll get you checked in. My brother is probably still here, so just a warning." His tone hardens, and I wonder if he's mentioned me to him.

"Okay."

"John," Alex says to a tall, brooding man. He's Alex's opposite with dark blond hair that's longer on one side. Scruff covers his chiseled jawline, but his eyes are the same—soft and kind. He's taller and leaner where Alex is beefy and muscular, probably since he does more laborious work.

"Mama send you again?" he asks with annoyance in his tone. "I already told her—"

"No, she didn't." Alex cuts him off before he can rant. "I have a friend checking in."

His eyes noticeably shift from Alex to me, lowering down my body then back up to my face.

"What'd you do?" he accuses with a strong Southern drawl, crossing his arms over his chest. "Is your house too full of the Delta Gamma Sorority sisters again?"

I arch a brow, pinching my lips together as John gives him shit. I look back and forth between the two and can tell they must do this often.

"Fuck off," Alex spits back, then clears his throat when he realizes his voice was a tad too loud in a house filled with guests. "Just check her in," he demands. "River Lancaster."

Something flashes over John's face, recognition maybe, but his shoulders relax, and he smiles. "River, yes. We've been expecting you."

"What room is she in? I'll take her." Alex's deep voice is possessive, and I can't deny how much it turns me on to hear it again. How much I hope to keep hearing it from now on.

"She's in the Violet room," John tells him, reaching for the key.

"Make sure to show her everything. And how to call down if she needs anything."

"Yeah, I got this. Thanks."

Alex takes my hand and leads us to a staircase. I look at everything as we walk down the hall toward my room. It's all so stunning. Definitely has that country charm with a modern flair.

"The Violet room? Does that mean everything's going to be purple?" I tease.

Alex unlocks the door and opens it for me to walk through first. "No, Mama named all the rooms after dead family members."

"Oh, well that's not morbid at all."

Alex sets my suitcase down and shuts the door behind him. I look around, appreciating all the little touches of flowers, candles, and décor pillows.

"Okay, so before John murders me, here's the booklet on the property. They serve breakfast between six and nine and come hungry because you'll want to try everything. And I mean *everything*. This is homestyle country eatin' down here, none of that city processed pumped-with-steroids food shit."

I chuckle, grabbing the book out of his hand. "Okay, I will, but I draw the line at grits." I don't dare tell him that just about anything can set off my nausea so there's no guarantee I can keep anything down.

"Oh God. Don't let anyone hear you say that." He chuckles. "We're serious about our grits down here. Sugar grits, cheesy grits, salt and pepper grits; there's a grit for every meal, trust me."

"Duly noted." I flip through the book and browse over the details about the ranch, the horses and trail riding, the side by sides and everything their little town has to offer. It's perfect for what I need right now.

"I love it," I say, setting the book down and glancing around the room. "Pretty sure it's bigger than my entire apartment."

"No, thanks," Alex grumbles, shaking his head at the thought.

The silence between us is awkward, but I don't even know how to begin this conversation.

"Do you need anything right away? John's your bitch, so just let me know."

I smile and laugh. "No, I'm okay. Thinking I should shower off the travel smell and change."

"I can wait if you want," he says sincerely, appreciating how he's not rushing me to talk.

"You don't mind?"

He closes the gap between us and cups my face, making circles with his thumb across my cheek. "I've been waiting three months, River. I think I can wait another twenty minutes."

I lean into his touch, loving the way it makes me feel when he does that. Smiling, I step away to grab my suitcase and head into the bathroom. Even though I'm wearing a sweater and it's covering my stomach, I'm still feeling overly self-conscious. Nerves are taking over, and the courage I felt earlier is long gone. I know I need to tell Alex the truth, but knowing I'm about to change his entire life has my heart thumping right out of my chest.

As I shower, I think of how I'm going to tell him. I could just rip it off like a Band-Aid and blurt it all out. That sounds the easiest. I'd rather gradually ease into everything I need to say. Then there's the fear that his reaction is going to burst the bubble I've been so content hiding in.

I can do this, I remind myself. It's a familiar chant I've had to tell myself a lot over the past several weeks.

Once I'm out of the shower, I wrap a towel around my body while I dig for my heartburn pills. It comes out of nowhere and is usually strong enough to make me sick.

"Hey, Alex," I call from inside the bathroom, peeking my head around the door.

"Yeah?"

"Would you mind grabbing a white bottle from my purse? I'm

not dressed yet." I clench my eyes the second the words come out, knowing he's already seen me naked.

"Sure." I hear him chuckling, probably thinking the same thing. His mouth and hands have been all over my naked body.

I step back inside, digging out my hairbrush and deodorant. Next, I look for something comfortable to wear, which consists of leggings and loose shirts because that's all that fits me now.

After a solid minute of waiting, I peek back out. "Alex?"

No response.

What the heck?

Once I finish getting dressed, I throw my hair up into a wet, messy bun and walk out to where I set my purse.

"Alex?" I call again. When I round the corner, I see him standing frozen facing away from me. Finally, he turns around. His eyes are wide, and his face has gone pale. "What's wrong?"

I step closer, finally seeing the stick he's holding.

"Is this yours?"

Planting my feet, I lick my lips and release a deep breath. "Alex…" I breathe out, hating that none of this has gone as planned. I totally forgot I put it in there. I don't know if it's common for pregnant women to keep their tests, but I'd been in such shock and denial the first couple of weeks, I stuffed it in there as a reminder. "Is this yours?" His voice is louder with anger in his tone as he stares me down.

I blink when he steps closer, invading my space. He holds the stick firmly between his fingers, demanding answers.

"Yes. It's mine." I swallow hard.

"You're pregnant." His words are soft, defeated almost.

"Yes."

He stays silent for a moment, and I can tell he's putting all the pieces of the puzzle together. "That's why you're here."

"Yes," I say with a breath. "I didn't think it was something to tell you over the phone," I add honestly, though I'd definitely thought about it at first. Just thinking about coming here and seeing him again had me nauseous for days.

"It's mine?" A pleased grin forms on his lips.

Relieved at his smile, I laugh. "Yes, you dummy."

He falls to his knees and wraps his arms around my waist, pressing his cheek to my stomach. My head bows while I wrap my arms around his neck, tears forming in my eyes.

This man. He never ceases to amaze me.

"Thank you," he says against my shirt.

"For what?"

Looking up at me, I can see the emotion written all over his face. "For coming here. Telling me. Letting me be a part of this."

"Trust me when I say it wasn't an easy decision."

He stands up and wraps a hand around my neck, pulling me closer. "Whatever it was, I'm just happy you're here now. I wanted to be really pissed at you the second I saw you, but I couldn't. Not for long at least. I don't know what it is about you, River, but you just make me want to be a better person. You were all I thought about, and once I finally saw you, I couldn't resist kissing you again. Knowing you could very well walk away with my heart, it was worth the risk."

I feel so guilty, knowing I should've contacted him sooner, and I regret pushing him out of my life like I did. These last three months have been a whirlwind while deciding what to do. I went back and forth with my options, wondering if Alex would even want to be involved or if I'd be better off raising the baby on my own. The conflict consumed me for weeks, battling between my emotions of being able to have Alex back in my life and be a family or learning the hard reality of him rejecting us both. Ultimately, Natalie helped me realize I had to tell him face to face because it was the right thing to do—regardless of the outcome. I'd been sick for weeks, so I wasn't even sure I'd make it on a plane, but I knew I'd regret not telling him if I didn't.

It wasn't just about him and me anymore.

We now had a baby to consider.

CHAPTER FIFTEEN

ALEX

I'VE BARELY PROCESSED ALL this information, but I don't care. The girl of my dreams is right here, in my arms, telling me we're having a baby.

And that changes *everything*.

"There's more," she tells me.

I just want to hold her again, lie in bed with her, and hear her tell me she's staying.

"There's a lot we need to discuss," she clarifies.

I nod in agreement.

Locking my fingers with hers, I lead her over to the bed and sit.

"Do you know when the baby is due?" I ask.

"End of July."

It's mid-February, so that means we still had time to figure everything out, which, if I had it my way, that'd be moving her ass here to be with me permanently.

"Do you know the gender?"

"Not yet. It's too early."

"Okay. Well—" I think of how to proceed, but River is quick to interrupt.

"I had this whole speech planned out, but everything I've been trying to plan has basically backfired, so I'm just going to come out and say it. I found out I was pregnant when I was eight weeks, so right before New Year's. I didn't drink that night, by the way. I was Natalie's personal assistant in making sure she didn't vomit in her sleep and choke to death. Since then, I've had a doctor appointment and ultrasound. I heard the heartbeat and even got an ultrasound picture."

"Really?" My eyes widen. "Can I see?"

She smiles, proudly. "Of course."

Retrieving her purse, she digs out an envelope where she's stashed the pictures. She hands them over to me, and my heart beats wildly.

"I've never seen an ultrasound photo before, but I already know it's the most perfect blob I've ever seen. She already looks so much like you." I grin, studying the pictures.

She bursts out laughing, her head falling back between her shoulders as she releases a sweet, throaty sound. "It's the sac, you fool. It's too soon to see details. However…" She points her finger down at the photo. "You can see the tiny arm and leg buds."

"Wow." I sigh. "I can't believe it."

"Are you panicking?"

"No, the opposite actually. I always imagined I would if a girl told me she was pregnant, but with you—not one bit."

She sucks in her bottom lip, gazing up at me with her stunning emerald eyes. "Honestly, it took me a couple weeks to really grasp that I was pregnant. I was shocked, to say the least, since I was on the pill and we used condoms. However, I'd been taking an antibiotic for my sinus infection, and apparently, it canceled out my birth control."

"It can do that?" I gasp.

"Oh yeah, and I feel really stupid because I should've thought of that, but then we were using condoms, almost every time, but there's still a small chance they're not effective."

"Jesus."

"Yeah, I know." She sighs, and I can tell her mind is racing. "So that brings me to why I'm here, aside from telling you the news of course. Once I found out, I contemplated on what my next step should be. I thought about just raising the baby on my own and being a single mom because I thought dropping this huge bomb on you would be too crazy for you to handle. Not that you can't handle it, just that people don't typically expect to start a life with someone they were just randomly hooking up with on vacation…"

My eyes burn into her as she continues to nervously ramble on, and as much as I want to tell her to stop—that this isn't too much for me to handle—I allow her to continue. "Anyway, once I finally came to terms with it, I decided I'm definitely keeping the baby. I wanted to come and inform you out of respect, but basically, tell you I don't expect anything from you. We live completely different lives, so you can be as involved or not as you want, no pressure."

What? Was she seriously thinking I'd walk away from her? From our baby?

"What?" I blurt out. Was being delusional a symptom of pregnancy? It had to be if she thought I'd let her get away again.

"Well, it's just I live in Wisconsin, and you live here, and like you said, you never want to leave Texas, so the only thing I can think of is to—"

"Move here," I blurt out, interrupting her words.

She blinks, looking up at me. "What?" Her voice is soft, almost a whisper.

"Move here, River," I plead. "I want you. I never stopped. Let me take care of you. Let me provide for our baby."

Her breath hitches, and I can tell she wasn't expecting that kind of a reaction from me. "I have a life back home, and what if—"

"*We* can have a life here. Why not?"

"I'd be lying if I said the thought hadn't crossed my mind, knowing that'd be the most logical and smart choice, but how?

174

We're basically strangers. How are we going to raise a baby together?"

"Well, I wouldn't say we're *strangers* exactly." I grin, and she flashes me a mock smile. "Okay, listen." I take her hand and hold it gently in mine. "I've thought of nothing except you for the past three months. I've been angry, sad, furious, heartbroken…and I had just talked myself into moving on and getting over you. I couldn't continue to live with the fact that things ended the way they did." She visibly cringes, and I feel bad for bringing it up at a time like this. "However, that same day you walked back into my life and told me I'm going to be a father. If that's not fate, River, then I don't know what is."

Her lips part but no words come out. She closes her eyes, and I know she's trying not to cry.

"River…" I whisper, tilting her chin up so she'll look at me. "We can do this together. Let me do this *with* you."

Her chest moves as she inhales a deep breath, and I know she's already been considering it. "I don't want to be a relationship out of convenience, Alex. I wish I could say I have enough confidence to just let us be together, but it'll always be in the back of my mind. Then what if we try, and it doesn't work out? How are we going to raise a baby together then? And how would this even work, given our history? Do we date? Do we start over? Do we pretend we didn't spend any time apart and continue where we left off? What if—"

"River!" I press my finger to her lips, needing her to stop rambling because it's all nonsense. Her insecurities are nothing she needs to worry about, and I honestly can't even believe she'd have them.

"I. Want. You." I pluck her bottom lip with the pad of my thumb. "I wasn't lying when I said I haven't thought of anyone except you, which you should know, never happens to me. Trust me when I say I've been driving my brothers and Dylan insane talking about you nonstop." I chuckle, and she flashes me a small smile. "So, to answer your questions, *what if* everything works out? What if I show you and prove that we can make this work, however you want to do it, but I'm not letting you go this time. Do you hear me? I stupidly left last time without telling you my honest feelings, but I'm not going anywhere now. We're having a *baby*."

She leaps off the bed and wraps her arms around my neck, sniffling in my hair as I hold her tight to my body. I feel the tiny bump of her belly press against me and smile.

"River," I whisper into her hair before pushing her back, so I can see her face. "Stay. *Please*."

She wipes her fingers under her eyes and clears her throat before sitting back down. I don't rush her, but I can see she's thinking hard, probably contemplating every outcome, the way she always does. Her eyes meet mine, and my heart pounds so hard that I feel as if it may beat right out of my chest. Putting everything out there and asking her to stay is a big and risky move on my part. I know that, but as long as we're together, I have no doubt we can make this work. As our breaths mix with silence, it feels as if all time is standing still as I wait for her answer. But that's what I do. I wait patiently.

"Okay," she finally says above a whisper, her eyes bright and glowing. "I will."

"Okay." The permanent smile on my face doesn't falter. She's just made me so fucking happy.

"But I'll need to go back and pack up my apartment. I'll have to let my job know and put in my notice." I smile wider when she tells me that. "This isn't going to be easy, Alex. Everything about this is a huge adjustment and moving will just add to it. In fact, now that I'm saying it aloud, it actually sounds really crazy. Like we should both probably be evaluated for jumping into this." She half-laughs to herself.

"River, baby. I don't need easy. Hell, I want crazy and everything that it entails. As long as it's with you."

She smiles, adjusting her top. "Okay. Well, prepare yourself."

I grin, ready to do whatever it takes. "I can fly back to

Milwaukee with you and help pack or move if you want. Maybe over a weekend?"

"Nah, it's fine. I can hire movers for all of that. I just need to grab the essentials before they pack it into the truck."

I lean in and cup her cheeks, needing to taste her lips, but right before I can, she presses a hand to chest and stops me. I blink, trying to read her face.

"What? Is this where you tell me you want to see other people?" I tease.

"Shut up!" She laughs, smiling. "I think we need to set some ground rules first."

My brows raise. "More rules? Didn't those rules get us into our current situation?"

She narrows her eyes at me, hiding a smirk. "I just don't think we should jump right back into bed together." Before I can comment, she hurries and continues. "And yes, I know that's how we got into our current situation, but nevertheless, if we want a chance at having a real relationship, we need to give it a fresh start."

I crease my brows, twisting my lips up. "A fresh start as in what? You want me to court you?"

She bites her tongue and shakes her head. "Just because I'm pregnant doesn't mean I don't want a genuine relationship. What we had in Key West was a vacation fling based on sex. If this is going to work, we need to start over."

"You expect me to just start over as if everything we shared never happened?" I ask, perplexed.

"Well no, I mean, the feelings and our connection can't be altered. But I want us to really get to know each other, and we can't do that while our hormones are hyperactive on sex. We need to set some boundaries."

"Boundaries, okay. Like what?"

"Sex is off the table."

"Yeah, I got that." I roll my eyes, smirking. "What else?"

"We take things slow. Go out and talk. I'd love to meet your family and learn about the ranch and just get to know you as you."

I can't even be mad about her no-sex rule because honestly, that sounds like fucking heaven. I've never wanted a girl to stick around longer than a night, and knowing that River wants this to work as much as I do makes every grueling day we were apart worth it.

"Okay." I smile. "I think I can work with that." I press my lips to her cheek and groan as I inhale her fresh, clean scent.

This might be harder than I anticipated.

I suck in a deep breath and let it out slowly through my nose. River watches me, and I turn my head to meet her eyes that seem to see straight through me.

"What are your plans tomorrow?" I ask, my nerves getting the best of me.

She laughs. "I'm having breakfast between six and nine. Other than that, my day is free."

"Great. We're having lunch with my parents."

After I kiss River good night and tuck her into bed, I walk downstairs. As my foot hits the bottom step, I see John is getting ready to leave for the night. Christopher was actually on time to relieve him from staying too late, for once. We walk out together, and I'm in a weird state of mind. Noticing, he pats me hard on the back.

"Want to talk about it?" he asks as we stand on the front porch. His breath comes out as smoke because the temperature is dropping again. I've chatted with John about River over the past few months. He knows our history and how infatuated I've been with her ever since. There's no telling what he's thinking, especially with her showing up on a whim and staying at the B&B. "I'm so fucking happy she's here," I tell him. As we watch the late fog roll in over the ground, I try to find the right words to explain what's going on.

"I didn't piece together it was her, or I would've given you a warning when I saw the booking. But I'm happy if you're happy. I just can't help but wonder why she's here exactly." John is as smart as a whip, and I know I won't be able to end this conversation without telling him the truth.

"River came to tell me she's having a baby. *My* baby. So, I guess you're gonna be an uncle to another little one." I glance over at him and watch his eyes widen.

"I'm. Well. Damn, I'm shocked," he finally spits out. "Out of us all, I swore Jackson would be the one to knock up someone." It comes out as a laugh.

"Yeah, I did too, honestly." I chuckle. "But you know, I'm actually over the moon about it. Maybe it's not the traditional way, but I think everything is going to work out just fine."

He pulls me into a brotherly hug. "I'm happy for you. I'm going to spoil the shit out of that little one."

Our laughs echo across the pasture.

"So now what?" John tucks his hands into his pockets and starts walking toward his truck as I follow him.

"She's moving here. We're gonna raise us a Bishop, *together*. Here. The best place in the entire world for a kid to grow up, honestly." As the words leave my tongue, pure happiness covers me. Never in my life would I have expected this, but River makes me want to go from zero to fifty in a heartbeat. I'm just happy I'll be holding her hand on our next adventure.

"Better tell Mama," he warns. "I'll pretend like I don't know."

"Good." I give him one last smile before I walk to my truck, but once I'm inside, I sit there and stare up at the room where River is sleeping. Yesterday, she was a thousand miles away, and today, she's within arm's reach. Dreams do come true and good things happen to good people. With anyone else, it would have been a curse, but for me, having a baby with River is nothing short of a blessing.

I sleep like shit. Tossing and turning knowing my woman who's carrying my baby is at the B&B drives me fucking crazy. I want nothing more than to drive over there, crawl into bed with her, and never let her go. Ever.

But we're taking it slow.

And I'm going to try to hold back the reins as best I can, but fuck, I've missed her so much; it's going to take all the willpower I can muster to be the proper gentleman.

If I continue to lie in bed staring at the ceiling as memories and fears rush through my head, I'll drive myself to drink. And we all know that drinking at four in the morning is a terrible idea. So instead of continuing the insanity, I get up before the roosters crow and get dressed. Considering it's in the mid-twenties this morning, I dress in thick layers. Just as I'm pouring coffee into my thermos, Jackson stumbles in.

"What the holy fuck?" I glare at him. "Where the hell have you been all night?"

His face is full of smeared red lipstick, and his hair is disheveled. What confuses me the most is the hay stuck to his clothes.

"Don't worry about it, little bro," he slurs. Jackson's a hard worker, so I rarely have to get on him for that, but hell if he isn't a hot mess most of the time.

"Please tell me you weren't fucking in the barn again? Romping in the hay like an animal. You do realize it's cold as hell outside right now?" I arch a brow, wondering if he has a death wish or if he's just crazy.

He laughs, plops on the couch, kicks off his boots, and closes his eyes. "Why do you think I came home? Now if you don't mind, I'd like to catch a few z's before I have to be at work in two hours."

"You did it to yourself. Hope she was worth it," I add, knowing his schedule is full of horseback riding today.

"*Totally* worth it," he says, rolling over onto his side, dismissing me with his middle finger.

After I place the lid on my coffee, I grab my cowboy hat and walk out shaking my head, trying to put all the pieces of the puzzle together. River is moving to Texas. She's having my baby and going to be living *here*. Holy shit. I have a lot of things to figure out in just a few weeks.

Cranking the truck, I let it warm up before I drive across the property to go check in with Dad. The man never sleeps, and I'm sure he's up drinking coffee already.

As soon as my parents' house comes into view, my nerves get the best of me. Today, I'm going to have to drop the bomb on them about River and the baby. Dad won't say much—I can read him like a map—but Mama will be a different story. Thinking about her reaction makes my stomach twist because it will either be really good or really bad.

I turn off the engine of the truck, and as I walk to the porch, I look up at the sky and can still see stars. The Milky Way is almost as bright as the moonlight, and I smile thinking about all the stars I wished upon over the past three months. Somehow, I roped the moon and got my girl.

Pulling my keys out of my pocket, I insert the right one into the door and swing it open. Just as I suspected, Dad is already up drinking his morning coffee. As soon as he sees me, he checks his watch, confused to see me at this early hour.

"Mornin', Dad."

He looks up at me. "You're up early today."

"Yes, sir. Couldn't sleep, so thought I'd get started a little earlier than usual if that's okay."

Sipping his coffee, he nods. "It's never too early to work."

Somehow, I knew he'd say that. I grab the keys to the work truck off the hook by the door and give Dad a quick wave. Before I completely walk away, I turn around.

"Dad, can we do lunch today, around twelve?"

Tilting his head, he narrows his eyes at me. I know it's a little out of my norm, but this needs to be talked about today, and I won't be able to relax until they both know what's happening.

"Everything okay?" he asks, curiosity in his tone.

"Life is grand, Dad."

"Sure. Twelve it is. I'll tell your mother to prepare somethin' good considering hell has frozen over outside." I smile, knowing that this weather is definitely something Southerners aren't accustomed to.

After I walk out, I'm able to breathe just a little easier, but I'm still a nervous wreck. Mama's always wanted grandkids, though. Luckily, my sister, Courtney, broke the ice with her pregnancy announcement not too long ago; however, my situation is a little less traditional. Nevertheless, Mama will have to get used to it because what's done is done. I'll need to think and plan what I'm going to tell them exactly; fortunately, I have a few hours to think about it.

To keep my mind busy, I get started with the day. I'd usually wait for Dylan, but I can't today. The busier I stay, the better.

After the animals are fed and before I head back to the barn to meet Dylan, I call the B&B and leave a message for River at the front desk. I'm sure John will guarantee the message is delivered when he arrives.

Lunch is at 12. I'll pick you up.

And I can only hope the next eight hours pass by quickly.

CHAPTER SIXTEEN

RIVER

FOR THE FIRST time in months, I slept like a baby. The temperature was perfect, and the bed was as soft as clouds. Sleeping late isn't something I typically do because of my early work shifts, but it was nice to get a few extra hours, especially after traveling.

I lie in bed, the fluffy quilt surrounding my body, and I can't help but smile. Everything finally feels like it's going to be okay. I felt uneasy during the plane ride over and wondered if Alex had moved on.

What if I would've shown up and he was in a relationship with someone else or was back to his routine of random hookups? Luckily, I had a fallback plan for either scenario. I would've told him out of respect, but then left and carried on to raise the baby on my own, expecting nothing in return. I knew I could do it, albeit hard, but I was a strong, educated woman who was resourceful. I'd be ignorant to come all the way down here without some kind of backup plan, but I didn't need it.

To know Alex waited for me and had been thinking of me as much as I'd been thinking of him, even when we agreed to leave it all in Key West, means more than he'll ever know. We shared something magical and meaningful on that island, something I hope wasn't brought on by bucket lists and beaches, but only time will tell.

Being able to see the reaction on his face and how happiness radiated from him when he found out he would be a father confirmed I did the right thing after all. I'll never forget that moment for the rest of my life—no matter what. He could've pushed me away. He could've argued with me or told me to fuck off. Instead, Alex embraced me like a long-lost lover and looked at me like I was his whole world.

The feelings that swirl through me as I think back on it are so intense my eyes water, and a tear rolls down my cheek. I swipe it away, cursing my damn emotions that have been getting the best of me the past few weeks.

I stand and stretch, adjusting my top that is now tight against my belly, then walk over to the large window and open the sheer curtain that allows the right amount of morning sunlight to leak in. I stare out and take in the beauty that I'm definitely not used to seeing back home. The land goes on for days, and as much as I want to go explore, I remind myself that I'll have plenty of time. The thought excites me while another one catches me off guard. Am I really moving to Texas?

After I shower and get ready for the day, I walk downstairs and see a large buffet area set up with breakfast platters just as Alex mentioned. Before I can even make my way over to the plates, John walks up holding a folded piece of paper.

"Mornin', ma'am," he says with a big grin.

Southerners are so damn polite; I just want to bottle them all up. "Morning."

"Did you sleep okay last night?" he asks. I know he's making small talk, which I actually don't mind. I want to get to know everyone in Alex's family as best as I can.

"I did, thank you. I think that bed is better than the one I have at home." I tuck my hair behind my ears, and when I look over at the buffet table, John realizes he's stalling.

"Oh, sorry. Make sure you try everything on the buffet. It's all delicious and from my mama's recipes."

"I'll do my best." I grin, keeping the thoughts to myself on being nauseous in the mornings and how some of their country style food is foreign to me.

"Well anyway, Alex left a message for you." He hands me the slip of paper.

"Thank you." I smile, and he gives me a head nod before walking away to help a guest check out. The more I look at John, the more I notice how similar their mannerisms are.

I open the note and recognize the Circle B Ranch emblem on top.

Lunch is at 12. I'll pick you up. -Alex

Looking at my watch, I see it's only a little past nine, which means I have a few hours to get my mind right before I meet his parents. My nerves are stretched thin, and I can only hope they like me. Given the circumstances of how Alex and I met and got pregnant, I'm not so sure that's a formula for a great first impression. However, I am having their grandbaby after all, so hopefully, they'll warm up to the idea quickly. I feel like a teenager again, meeting the parents of a boy I like and all that.

I grab a plate and put a few items on it. As I walk down the buffet line, I see stuff that looks a little scary. The woman next to me is pouring white gravy on top of biscuits, and the thought of it grosses me out. I grab some fruit, bacon, a blueberry muffin, and a large cup of orange juice—all of which I recognize and pass all the Southern delicacy like buttermilk pancakes with icing, grits, and cornbread.

There's a lounge chair by a window across the room, and I decide to sit there and eat my breakfast. As I stare out the window, I take a bite of a blueberry muffin, and it's so damn delicious that I'm tempted to snatch up the rest of them and stuff them in my purse so I can eat them throughout the day. However, I find some self-restraint and stop after my second one. I feel the juice in my belly. The sugar always makes the baby toss and turn. It's the weirdest, but coolest feeling ever.

Just as I'm getting ready to place my empty plate in the dishpan, John walks in with a big cheesy smile.

"Howdy," he says.

"You were right. It was delicious." I give him a smile in return, hoping he didn't see I only put fruit and muffins on my plate. He stops in his path and crosses his arms over his chest, then looks me from top to bottom. He narrows his eyes and takes a step forward until he's close.

"Is that right?" He studies me, which is odd because we just spoke not twenty minutes ago. "So, where you from?" he asks with a side grin plastered on his face.

I laugh. "Wisconsin. Is it that obvious I'm an outsider?"

He grins before taking off his cowboy hat and tipping it, keeping his eyes on me. "Welcome to Texas, sweetheart. If you need anything, be sure to let me know. I'd be more than happy to show you 'round."

Before I can respond to his strange comment, I hear shouting coming from behind him.

"Jackson!" When I glance around, I see John walking toward us. My mouth falls open, and I'm so damn confused that I don't even know what to say. That's when I realize they're not even wearing the same damn clothes.

"There's two of you," I finally manage to get out after the initial shock passes. "I forgot. Alex told me once."

John chuckles, smacking a hand on his shoulder. "This is Jackson, my asshole brother. Sorry, it can be kinda confusing when you don't know we're twins. And he's such a dick, he'll pretend he's me, especially around pretty ladies."

"I'm much better looking though, right?" Jackson winks. But honestly, they look identical. There's nothing different about them, so telling them apart is going to be difficult as hell.

"Stop, dickhead. This is *River*," John tells him. Recognition flashes across Jackson's face, and I can tell they have one of those bonds where words aren't needed as they hold a silent conversation.

After a minute, Jackson finally laughs and slaps his leg. "You're a real person. I wasn't convinced." He looks me up and down again. "But *now* I understand."

I playfully roll my eyes. "Well, I hope whatever's been said about me is all good."

"Oh yeah, totally. Just have an obsessed Bishop, which is damn right annoyin' when you're on the other end of that conversation. If I had to hear about that vacation one more time, I was gonna kill Alex."

I laugh, nervously. Slightly weirded out that Alex talked about me so much. "Sorry about that. There's probably a club you could join. My friend back home was front and center for most of it."

"Is that so?" The corner of his lips tilts up. "She single?" He wiggles his brows.

John elbows him in the gut at the same time I laugh. "Sorry, no."

"Damn. Go figure." Jackson shrugs, and the silence between us becomes awkward. "Not to be rude, but why are you here now?" Jackson looks at me somewhat confused.

John clears his throat as if he knows what's going on. "Don't you have work that needs to be done? Actually, I need you to help me with something."

Jackson shakes his head, and somehow, John steers him away. "Nice meeting you, River!" Jackson says as he turns around.

Well, that was...interesting. My heart begins to race as I think about meeting his parents again. Everything's happening so fast that my head is spinning trying to process it all.

I make my way back to my room and try to decide what I'm going to do until lunch. My rental car is still sitting at the cafe so going to town to explore isn't an option. Instead, I grab my Kindle and decide to read and relax. First impressions are so important to me, and even though I'm trying to distract myself and read, I can't comprehend anything I'm reading because I'm overly anxious.

After an hour of fidgeting and not being able to get comfortable, I grab my jacket and decide to go outside and explore the land. I walk through the common room and head toward the backdoor. Everyone is bundled up like it's freezing, and it makes me laugh considering most of them are decked out in scarves and boots. This is considered warm for me, but I feel like a heater now anyway. I know it's common in pregnancy, but I could live without the hot flashes.

As soon as I open the door and stand on the back porch, a smile touches my lips. It's a cool forty-five degrees outside, and I'm actually happy there's no snow and negative temperatures. It's great for around the holidays, but once February hits, I'm over it. Sucks walking and driving in it, so this is definitely a nice change.

The rolling hills are so beautiful as I look out. I allow my feet to guide me as I take the steps down the porch and head toward the stables.

Curiosity gets the best as me as I walk down the path and decide to step in. As soon as I get closer, I can smell the horses and hay. It's not something I'm used to smelling, making me feel like I'm really in the country. Many of the horses are wearing coats, which makes me giggle. As I continue walking through the stable, some of the horses poke their heads over the stall to greet me. I pet a few of their soft noses, and they nip at me, hoping I'll feed them something, I'm sure.

Just as I'm about to make my way through the other side of the stable, I hear my name being called. Turning, I can't help but smile when I see Alex stalking toward me wearing tight pants and boots, a heavy jacket, and black cowboy hat. He's as country as they come, definitely different from what he looked like in Key West. However, it's pretty damn sexy. I take a mental picture of how rugged he looks with the scruff on his jawline and messy hair under his hat. As soon as he's close enough to touch me, he wraps his strong arms around me and kisses my forehead.

"Mornin', beautiful," he says with a sexy gruff in his tone. "Sorry, boundaries. I know. It's going to be hard, though. Just a warning."

"It's okay." The smile on my face might be permanent.

"I couldn't wait to see you. We're not finished for the day yet, but since I started earlier than Dylan, he said he'd cover until after lunch." He loosens his grip on me and swings his arm around my shoulder and leads me toward the other entryway. Once we step outside, I see several trails that lead out in different directions.

"It's so peaceful out here," I say, taking everything in.

"These are the trails we have for horseback riding and for the Ranger side by sides, which are basically beefed-up golf carts. The blue trail goes to a pond. In the summer, it's surrounded by wildflowers and a cute family of ducks. The red trail leads to a beautiful lookout point, and the green trail is for easy riding. It's usually the ones we take the kids on. They're all loops and circle back here. I'd love to take you one day. Have you ever been horseback riding?"

"No, but I've always wanted to, though. Bucket list item," I say with a smirk.

A knowing grin fills Alex's face. "Darlin', start making a Texas bucket list, and we'll check them off one by one."

Hearing him say that sends tingles down my spine. I don't know what it is about this man, but it feels as if no time has separated us at all. We're easily falling back into the same Key West rhythm we were in, but the reality is, it's not just him and me anymore. We're having a baby together, which is a forever commitment, and just thinking about all of that scares the shit out of me. He notices me tense and squeezes my hand but doesn't say anything.

"You know what I *would* like to do?" I smile wide.

Smirking, he lifts his eyebrows. "What's that, sweetheart?"

"I want to take a tour of the ranch. This place is huge. I looked it up on Google, and I just can't imagine what ten thousand acres even looks like."

"Right now?" he asks.

"Whenever you have time. I think it'd be fun."

Alex grabs my hand and leads me back through the stables. We walk past the horse corral to a big red barn that looks like it should be on a movie set. Sliding the large door open, he takes a step to the side and I see 4-wheelers and the beefed-up golf cart things he was talking about.

"I've got all the time in the world for you."

How can he consistently say all the right things at exactly the right time? The past few weeks I've felt horrible, and I've hated the way I've looked, but being around him changes all of that. Alex looks at me with so much fire in his eyes, it almost burns my skin. Just being around him, smelling him, staring into his eyes is making my hormones go haywire. At this point, I might need more self-control than he does because my body remembers every single kiss and touch, and it's been craving him since I left Key West. Pregnancy hormones are way worse than Key West hormones, especially since I already know what I'm missing.

He watches me watch him. As he steps closer, he brushes his fingers across the softness of my cheek before giving me a sweet smile. "A complete tour would take days. We have to be back for lunch in two hours, and Mama doesn't accept tardiness. You'll learn that, though. If you want, we can see a small portion of it right now. We can take the blue trail. They're not going to be riding for a few more hours anyway."

I nod eagerly. "Yes. I'd love that."

Alex grabs a set of keys from the wall and leads me over to the side by side parked in the front. I climb in, and as soon as I sit down next to him, he places his hand on my thigh, and I place my hand on top of his. We both glance at each other and smile.

"Hold on," he says, pressing on the gas, and we zoom out of

the barn, drive around the stables, and make our way down the trail.

"Just remember: baby on board." I nod my head down to my belly. "No major bumps or anything."

"Don't worry. I got you." He winks.

A few minutes into the trail, Alex speaks up again. "I should probably tell you more about my family before lunch. Mama and Dad have been married since they were eighteen. High school sweethearts and all that. Got married young, had babies young. Mama's strict, but she loves with everything she's got. Dad's a tough one to crack, but over time, he'll warm up to you. They're both set in their ways, but with five kids, they've had to juggle a lot. I think I mentioned my siblings before, but just a reminder in case you forgot. I'm the youngest of the boys, so I get shit on a lot for it." He shrugs with a sideways grin. "Then there's John and Jackson, the twins."

I chuckle to myself, thinking that reminder would've been nice a couple hours ago. "Yeah, I met Jackson this morning."

He gives me a sideways glance at the tone of my voice. "Don't worry. John put him in his place." I chuckle.

"Good. So, then there's my sister, Courtney, who ironically is also pregnant. But with triplets."

"Triplets?" I gasp, and my eyes go wide. "I can't even imagine."

"Yep. She and her husband, Drew, tried for a couple of years before seeing some fancy fertility doctor and ending up with three babies. They live in California but come and visit when they can. Oh, speaking of doctor, my oldest brother, Evan, is a doctor."

"A doctor?" I ask, surprised. I really thought they'd all be involved with the ranch in some way, but I know a doctor's busy schedule.

"Yeah. He's a hardass and super smart. He's the only one of us boys who decided he didn't want the rancher life, but Dad makes him come and help on his days off," he explains.

"Sounds like there's never a dull moment with the Bishops." I chuckle. "So thanks for the twin warning ahead of time, by the way. I was really confused this morning when I was talking to John, or I thought I was anyway, and it ended up being Jackson. He had no idea who I was and hit on me until John intervened." I place my free hand in the pocket of my jacket because the wind seems colder now that we're speeding up.

"That motherfucker," he mutters. "Yeah, he does that. *A lot*, actually. Drives John fuckin' nuts, but Jackson lives for a laugh especially when it comes to making any one of us uncomfortable. Sometimes he likes to wear the same clothes as John, and it makes John so mad. But it's pretty funny. Mostly because I get to witness it."

"I don't know if I'll ever be able to tell them apart," I add over the roaring of the engine.

He chuckles. "Most people have that issue. But John is the quiet one. He's more sensible, and Jackson likes being an asshole. John is an introvert whereas Jackson is loud and proud, and overly flirty with every woman he sees. No matter her age. They may look the same, but they're complete opposites in personality. You'll figure it out sooner than later, trust me. Jackson doesn't know how to shut up."

"That's good information, actually." I chuckle. "Jackson definitely gives off the party vibe."

He looks over at me with a knowing look. "You have no idea."

We continue down the trail and begin climbing a large hill. By the time we make it to the top, Alex turns off the engine and gives me time to look out. It's magical how the land goes on as far as the eye can see. It almost seems like a mirage, and the silence is so relaxing. There's no rushing cars or city noise; it's so quiet that I can hear the wind rustling the grass.

"Wow," I whisper.

"You've not seen nothing yet." Alex turns on the Ranger and presses the gas. We roll down the other side of the hill and drive into a valley. Time seems to stand still as we continue forward until a large pond comes into view. Trees surround it, and there are a few picnic tables under the trees; I can imagine people having lunch out here. Once Alex cuts the engine, we get out and walk toward the pond. The blue sky and clouds reflect upon the water, and I feel like I could stare out at this view all day long. I can't wait to see it with wildflowers surrounding it, just like Alex described.

We stand next to each other, and I turn and look at him.

"Are you afraid?"

He licks his lips, and his face distorts. "Not even for a second," he replies, confidently. I wish I felt like that, but nevertheless, I'm relieved by his answer.

"I'm scared, Alex. I'm worried about this pregnancy. I've witnessed so much working at the children's hospital, seeing babies suffer, watching their parents cry and fall to pieces. Hell, I saw it with my own eyes with my sister, Rylie, and what it did to my parents. Everything's going to change, and all I can think about is what if this baby is sick or worse. The thoughts are so overwhelming and now being here with you…" I pause, inhaling a much-needed deep breath. "It's all so much."

Grabbing my hand, Alex turns me toward him and tilts my chin up. Staring into his blue eyes, I notice how they're the same color as the sky above us. "I'm here, darlin'. There are going to be plenty of *what-if* and scary moments, but all you need to know is that I'm here. We'll do this together, and everything's gonna be all right."

He kisses me softly, and I melt into him. My body relaxes, and I believe every word he says. Maybe if we're together, everything really will be okay.

We spent too much time at the pond, so instead of going straight back to the B&B, Alex drives us to his parents' house using a different trail. The property is so large that I'm lost and turned around because all the trails seem to connect to each other. My nerves are on fire again as we drive past another barn and he parks the side by side close to the back steps of a large country home. It's got a wraparound porch just like the B&B. When we walk inside, even though my heart is racing, it feels and smells just like home—a home I always wished I had.

"Mama," Alex yells out as soon as we walk in.

"In the kitchen," she responds. I stop and take a quick breath, preparing myself for the possible outcomes. My stomach starts to twist in knots, and I know it's not from the pregnancy this time.

CHAPTER SEVENTEEN

ALEX

BY THE LOOK on River's face, I can tell she's nervous. Before we walk into the kitchen, I stop and hold her sweet face in my hands.

"You have nothing to worry about." I try to offer her some sort of comfort even though I've been pushing my own nerves below the surface. "Trust me, okay?"

She nods. "I trust you."

I grab her hand and lead her down the hallway toward the kitchen. Mama pulls sugar cookies from the oven and sets the hot baking sheet on top of the stove. She wipes her hands on a dish towel and turns around with a smile on her face that immediately fades when she sees River standing next to me.

Fuck. I know what that look means.

"Hey, Mama." I walk up to her, giving her a kiss on the cheek, then turning to River.

"This is River. River, this is my mama, Rose," I say, introducing them with a big smile on my face, hoping it spreads like wildfire. I almost introduced her as my girlfriend, because it sounds right, but I didn't want to cross the line or make the situation more awkward than it needs to be. Mama's never seen me bring a girl home, and I now realize this is going to be a lot harder than I expected.

"Hello," Mama says, looking her up and down before smiling.

"Hi," River says sweetly. "It's nice to finally meet you."

Mama nods and turns back to her cookies, placing each one on the cooling rack so they don't continue cooking on the tray. Just as I'm about to say something, Dad walks through the back door, placing his cowboy hat on the table.

"I'm starving," he says, pulling out a chair and sitting.

"River, this is my dad, Scott." I grab his attention to us.

"Hi," River says to him.

"Howdy, River." He stands and holds his hand out to shake hers.

"Alex didn't tell us he was bringing a guest, so let me grab you a place setting." Mama gives me a sideways glance, and I know she suspects something.

"Sorry, Mama," I apologize, knowing she doesn't like surprises. Oh well. She'll find out soon enough now.

We take our seats at the table across from my parents, and I try to make small talk, but the tension in the room is steadily growing. Mama serves baked potato soup in big bowls with tons of cheese and bacon on top.

River and I thank her, and once she sits down at the table with us, we hold hands and say grace. I look over at River who flashes a nervous smile, but she has nothing to worry about. I'll be with her through it all.

"This is the best soup I've ever eaten," River compliments after a few bites, and Mama offers a soft thank you.

"So you want to tell us what's goin' on?" Mama directs her question at me, and Dad pops his head up, wanting to know too.

I grab River's hand under the table and interlock my fingers with hers. "Well, turns out you're going to be grandparents to another little bundle."

Mama glares at me. Dad's face stays exactly the same, no reaction surfacing. The silence seems to drown on.

"How did this happen?" Mama asks, looking back and forth

between River and me. I can almost taste the venom in her words even though she tries to cover her disdain with a smile.

"Well, it's kind of a long story. We met in Key West when Dylan and I went last October." I don't want to go into details about our relationship and our vacation hookup agreement. Mama would never approve of my past lifestyle, which is why she isn't privy to that type of information.

"Well, son, I have to say I'm quite shocked right now. I feel blindsided by this whole situation," Mama says to River and me. And I understand. It's a lot to take in. I'm not a child, but Mama has always had high traditional expectations.

"What does this all mean, exactly?" Dad asks.

"I guess it means I'm gonna be a father," I reply.

Dad chuckles softly. "You two raisin' the baby together?"

"Yes, sir."

Mama sets her spoon down in her bowl and pushes it away. After wiping her mouth with the napkin from her lap then setting it on the table, I get the hint that lunch is over. Maybe bringing River here and dropping the bomb this way wasn't the smartest idea. Maybe I should've told Mama alone so I could get her real reaction, and we could talk it through. The whole situation backfired, and I can sense how uneasy River is by the tightness of her grip. Before getting up to leave, I thank Mama for lunch and tell Dad I'll be back to work after dropping River off at the B&B.

As I go to walk out, Mama calls me back. I place a hand on River's shoulder and tell her I'll meet her outside.

"If you weren't a grown man, I'd slap you right now," Mama says with her arms crossed over her chest. Fuck, I haven't seen her this pissed since she caught me stealing the tractor for a joyride when I was ten years old.

"What's your problem? You always said you wanted grandkids. Now you're going to have one close to you, and you're being rude. You didn't treat Courtney this way with her big announcement," I tell her and instantly feel terrible for playing the comparison game.

"Your situation and Courtney's are completely different. Courtney is married and settled. You, on the other hand, decided to knock up a stranger and bring her here, then expect me to welcome the news with open arms. Maybe you should've thought this through. Are you sure it's even yours?"

"Mom!" I scold her quick judgment.

"I'm sorry, but this is going to take me a while to process. Where does she live? Is she moving here? It's obvious the poor girl doesn't know anything about our lifestyle and has a lot of learnin' to do. And that's gonna need to change real quick. You know my motto, son: can't stand the heat, get out of the kitchen."

Good lord. If this is how fast she's blurting words out, I can't imagine how fast her mind is racing.

"Well first, yes, River *is* moving here from Wisconsin because I want to take responsibility for my baby, and we're going to be together. I know this is out of your traditional values, but what's done is done. You can be on board with it or not, but this is happening, and there's nothing you or anyone else can do about it but accept it." I search her face before I walk away, but I don't wait for her response because I'm pissed, and she knows it.

Before I walk outside, I put on a fake smile because I don't want River to be upset. We climb inside the side by side and drive across the pasture.

"She doesn't like me," River says on the way back to the B&B.

"She doesn't *know* you. I'm sure she'll fall in love with you. I have no doubts about it. Just gotta give each other a chance," I say confidently, and I truly believe that. It's just going to take a little adjusting for everyone. "Mama will come around."

"I hope so." She bows her head, chewing on her bottom lip.

I drive us around to the back and pull the side by side in the barn at the B&B. We sit in silence for a moment before I turn and look at her. "I'm sorry for that. I truly expected a different reaction from them both."

Sweetly, she places her hand on top of mine. "It's okay. I honestly didn't know we were telling them about the baby right away. I thought maybe I'd meet them first, and then you'd mention it later when I wasn't around to feel their wrath." She falls silent.

"I'm so sorry. Stupid decision on my part, but I think Mama already had it figured out. She's as smart as a whip, and not much gets past her. Though you're the first girl I've ever brought to lunch, so I should've expected her to suspect something. I was just so excited for them to meet you, I didn't think it through."

"It's fine. At least they know, and we can move on, I guess." River isn't happy, and I hate knowing I disappointed her.

We get out and walk toward the back porch of the B&B, and I don't want to leave her, not in this state, but I have to get back to work, or I'll never hear the end of it. Just as the thought crosses my mind, I get a phone call. I pull my phone from my pocket and see it's Dylan.

"Yes?" I answer.

"Where the fuck are you? I need help getting this hay in the middle barn loft. I can't do this shit alone. I need you to go pick up the trailer and bring it over so we can load this shit and be done with the day."

"I'll be right there," I tell him.

River turns and looks at me. "Is that Dylan?"

I nod.

"Tell him hi for me!" River says, and she's smiling again —thankfully.

"I heard her," he tells me. "Tell her I said hey and that your ass needs to leave right now before I drive over there and drag you back."

All I can do is laugh. "Okay, okay. I'm heading that way. Give me fifteen minutes."

I walk River inside, up the stairs, and to her room. Yawning, she sits on the edge of the bed, kicking off her shoes. There's nothing more I wanna do right now than pull her into my arms and hold her until the sun goes down. It's barely past one, and I'm sure she's exhausted from everything we did today.

"So I guess we have a lot of planning to do. When does your plane leave?" There are so many questions to ask, but I feel like I have zero time to get them all out, especially with Dylan waiting for me.

She lies back on the bed. Her blonde hair surrounds her face, and she looks so damn beautiful. She folds her hands over her belly, and I smile at the small bump forming on her petite frame. I blink hard making sure I'm not imagining any of this because since I saw her at the diner, I've been in a dream state.

"Tomorrow at twelve. I didn't initially plan to stay very long. Get in, get out type of thing because I didn't know what your reaction would be. Plus, I have to be back to work on Wednesday." She props herself up on one elbow and looks at me with so much passion in her eyes I'm forced to hold myself back. She has no clue what she does to me with just one glance. I ball my hands into fists and tell myself I can't do the things I want to do. But if I could, I'd lay her down, make sweet love to her, then fuck her really good for making me wait this long.

"Okay," I say, my eyes wandering up and down her body. "Oh, we're planning a surprise birthday party for Mama next month, so my entire family will be there, and I'd really like you to be there, too."

River sits up straight. "I don't know if that's a good idea, considering she hates me."

I sit next to her, needing to touch her in some way, just to make sure she's really here. I face her and grab her soft hands in mine.

"It's a really big deal. Mama's turning fifty. All my aunts, uncles, and cousins are coming. Even the ones who have to travel from hours away. I'd really love for you to meet everyone, so we can share our news. Don't know the next time we'll all be together again."

She chews her bottom lip, stewing it over. "Well, I can't make any promises, Alex. If I can, I will, but I have to go back to Wisconsin first and make arrangements. Pack up my apartment. Find a moving company. Put in my two weeks' notice and see if a transfer close is even available before coming back here. I don't even know where I'm going to stay or what I'm taking with me. There's so much up in the air right now that I don't feel like I can commit to anything, even if it's a month away. A lot can happen in such a short time, so I just don't want to disappoint you." I can hear the worry in her voice.

"Darlin', don't worry about anything here. I promise I'm going to work on all that and have it settled before you come back. And let me say, the sooner, the better. I honestly wish you didn't have to go back at all."

She nods, her green eyes meeting mine, and I can't stop myself any longer. I pull her to my chest, my mouth magnetized to hers. River sighs against my lips, and her body melts into mine as we kiss slowly and passionately, not rushing. I want to take all the time I can with her because this moment seems too good to be true. When we finally break apart, her chest rises and falls, and I watch as she swallows hard.

"Sorry," I whisper, knowing I've crossed her boundaries once again.

What we had in Key West, that insane connection, is still here and is as strong as ever.

Smirking, I stand. "I have a feeling I'm going to be apologizing for doing things like that a lot."

"We're supposed to be taking it slow, remember?" She chuckles.

I shrug. "I know. But it's hard when I finally have what I've been missing all these months," I admit.

"Yeah, what's that?" River raises an eyebrow and studies me.

"*You.*"

Before we can get too caught up in each other, my phone vibrates in my pocket, and I realize I've lost track of time again. I reject the call. Dylan needs to find a little patience and give me a fucking break.

"Dylan and I will get your car from the diner and park it

downstairs for you, so you don't have to leave any sooner for the airport than you have to."

River stands, digs in her bag, and hands me the keys. "That'd be great considering I have no idea how to get to the diner from here. Since my flight leaves at noon, I should be there around ten."

"I wish you didn't have to go," I tell her and watch her face soften.

"It won't be forever," she reminds me as she hands over the keys. Leaning forward, I kiss her on the cheek before telling her goodbye—something I already hate doing.

"I'll come back after work if that's okay."

"I'd love that," she says, walking back to the bed. "I think I'm going to read for a while and maybe take a nap until you come back."

"Okay, darlin'. Sweet dreams." I smile before walking out. As soon as I'm in the hallway, I send Dylan a text and let him know I'm on my way to get the trailer then I'll meet him. All I get in return is a middle finger emoji.

It takes me no time at all to drive to the middle pasture where the large storage barn is. Bales of hay are plopped on top of each other in the entryway, and I back in the old work truck and trailer. Slamming the door shut, I get out and yell, "I'm back, asshole!"

"'Bout damn time!" he says, throwing another bale of hay from the loft above. It hits the ground with a thud, causing dust to rise. I put on my gloves and begin loading them on the trailer until it's full. It's backbreaking work, but I welcome the distraction.

Once we've got the truck packed down, Dylan climbs down the ladder.

"So, how's Daddy doin'?" he teases. When I told him earlier, he wasn't shocked at all, but it hasn't stopped him from giving me shit and making daddy jokes all damn day. I don't imagine that will stop anytime soon, either.

"Shut the hell up," I tell him as we climb into the truck.

"How'd it go today?" He turns the heater on full blast and places his hands over the vent.

"Mama wasn't happy about it. Shoulda probably told her alone."

"She'll get over it, though. Remember that time Jackson thought he knocked up that preacher's daughter? Remember how angry she was? I thought she was gonna grab a shotgun and hunt Jackson down."

I chuckle, completely forgetting about that. "Yeah. I remember now. But she was pissed because she heard it through the grapevine *at church* and not Jackson's mouth. So it's kinda different."

We drive down the rock road, kicking dust up in our wake, and head over to the B&B to unload the hay into the stables. Considering the group of riders will be back within the hour, Dylan and I make quick work of it and stack hay in the feed room until it's full. After we're done, we drive around the property and drop hay for the horses and cows. It takes more time than I predicted, but that's to be expected when there's so much land to cover.

Before we call it quits for the day, I ask Dylan if he'll ride with me to get River's car. Rolling his eyes, he agrees. We drop the work vehicles back at the barn and take my truck to the diner. The sun is setting in the distance, and I know we don't have much time before darkness falls. Fifteen minutes later, we're pulling into the parking lot. When I see Mrs. Betty inside wiping a table down and getting ready to close, I decide to step in really quick.

"Hey, honey!" she says with a big wide smile.

"Hey, Mrs. Betty." I give her a hug. "Can I order a piece of chocolate cake to go? Actually, make it two."

"Sure thing." She walks around the counter and cuts two huge slices and places them in boxes, then bags it. I hand her a twenty and tell her to keep the change.

"You always spoil me," she tells me. "Is that for your lady?" Her eyebrows raise as she waits for my answer.

"Yes, ma'am. The other piece is for Mama."

"I'm sure there's a story behind that one. You'll have to come see me sometime this week and fill me in," Betty says just as someone walks up to pay their check. I promise her I will and make my way out the door.

"I'm not driving that," Dylan says, pointing to the Prius. "My dick may actually fall off if I even sit in that thing."

I hand him the keys to my truck. "Hopefully your dick will be okay with that."

Unlocking the car, I walk over to it and shake my head, understanding why Dylan was so reluctant. As soon as I open the door and attempt to sit, I search around the seat to slide it back so my legs have more room. Once I've adjusted the seat and mirrors, I press the button to crank it but can't hear the engine. I don't have to search around for the lights because they turn on as soon as the engine roars to life. Seriously, what is this futuristic shit? I put it in reverse and step on the gas, and it moves, but I'm not convinced the damned thing is even on.

The whole way back to the ranch, I can smell her shampoo, and it causes my mind to wander back to the beach. That really was a trip of a lifetime that changed both our lives forever.

I turn onto the country road that leads to the ranch, and Dylan follows close behind me. Instead of going straight to the B&B, I turn on the long driveway that leads to my parents' house where Dylan's truck is parked. When I get out with a to-go box and plastic fork in my hand, he looks at me confused.

"I'm gonna be a while. I have to talk to my Mama before going to see River. I have an apology to make for being disrespectful."

Dylan hands me my keys and walks toward his truck. "You better apologize then. Mama can make your life heaven or hell, and you ought to know by now you get more bees with honey than vinegar."

"Story of my life. See you tomorrow!" I tell him as I walk up the sidewalk that leads to the front door. Before stepping in, I inhale a deep breath, say a little prayer, and hope I can smooth this over. Pushing my ego to the side, I turn the doorknob and enter.

Mama is sitting on the couch with a blanket on her lap watching one of those cheesy movies on the Hallmark Channel that always fades to black.

She glances at me then focuses on the TV.

"Hey, Mama," I say sweetly, sitting next to her on the couch.

"Hey, baby." She speaks, but she doesn't look back at me. The tension in the room is so thick, I could cut it with a knife.

"I'm sorry for being short earlier. You raised me better than that." I hand her the piece of cake and fork.

She opens the box and immediately smiles. "Trying to sweeten me up with Betty's cake? Your father taught you right."

Before she even asks, I walk to the kitchen, pour a big glass of cold milk, and return to the living room. "I just want us to be okay. That's all. I don't like going to bed angry. Something you taught me a long time ago."

"Sit," she demands, taking the milk willingly. "Listen to me, son. I love you no matter what. Okay? I'll always love you and your brothers and sister. Knowing that you're all going to start having kids of your own makes me realize that you're no longer my babies, that you're growing up, and moving on."

I open my mouth to speak, and she lifts her mighty finger to stop me.

"I always wanted you all to have a better life than I had. Than your father had. I wanted you to experience everything you possibly could, but most of all, I want you to be happy."

"Mama, I'm so happy. I'm the happiest I've ever been in my life right now. And that's why it's so important to have your acceptance. I want Dad's approval, too. It hurts me to know that you're disappointed in me or in the situation or that you don't like the woman who's carrying your grandbaby."

She takes a bite of cake and closes her eyes as she chews. Betty's cake is the best in six counties; even Mama knows it.

"Honey, I don't know her. How can I not like someone I don't know? I just thought you'd settle with some sweet Southern girl who has the same values as us, not someone from a different world. But I've had to realize that's not my choice, that's *yours*. However, I was shocked today. It took me by surprise that's all. Out of all my sons, I didn't think you'd be the one to be in this situation right now. If anyone, I thought it'd be Jackson, honestly."

That makes me laugh because she really has no idea. Jackson talks a big talk, but he doesn't walk the walk. He's a loose cannon on most days.

"I know, Mama. But I thought you'd be happy to hear I'm doing the right thing. We're going to do this together and be a family, which strangely enough, is all I want. She came here to tell me she was pregnant and keeping the baby but didn't expect anything from me, just thought I deserved to know. I begged her to move here so I could be involved. She's leaving the only life she's ever known to be with me because that's the best chance we have of having something real."

She blinks, taking in everything I've just said, and her shoulders visibly relax. "Do you love her?" she asks.

It takes me less than a second to respond. "Yes, Mama. I think I do." Memories of us together flash through my mind. The way River's face looks when she laughs and how pretty she is when she's sleeping are all I can think about. I try to imagine my life without her in it, and it's just not possible. "I've never felt this way about anyone in my life."

The corner of her lips tilts up. "That's good enough for me, son. Come here," Mama says, setting the cake on the coffee table. She opens her arms, and I fall into them.

"I love you, Alex."

"I love you, too, Mama. I always will."

CHAPTER EIGHTEEN

RIVER

INSTEAD OF TAKING A NAP, I sit on the back porch and read for hours. In Texas, they seem to eat before five o'clock, and I hadn't realized I was hungry until someone mentioned dinner was being served. Somehow, I clear a plate of pot roast and mashed potatoes like I haven't eaten in weeks.

After dinner, I read until dark. I had to know what happened at the end of my book regardless of my eyes being tired. Not knowing what time Alex would return, I decide to crawl into bed for the night because I'm exhausted. I don't know how long I've been sleeping when I wake to the door of my room slowly being cracked open. The moonlight streams through the window, and I'm groggy as I turn to see Alex walking inside.

"Hey, sweetheart," he says, softly.

"Hi." I barely get out. I hadn't realized how damn tired I was till now. He doesn't turn on the lights, but instead, he sets a Styrofoam box and plastic fork down on the small dresser next to the bed. As he steps closer, I can smell him. He smells like hay and leather all mixed with sweat, and it's a scent I'd like to bottle up and bring back to Wisconsin with me.

"I'm going to take a shower if that's okay," he whispers close to my face, brushing the hair off my forehead and pressing a soft kiss there.

I nod, closing my eyes, and drift in and out of sleep as I hear the water run in the bathroom.

Just as I'm falling deeper into sleep, I feel him crawl into bed next to me. The warmth of his body from the shower feels good against my skin as our bodies mold together. He holds me like he's never letting me go, and when his hand brushes against my stomach, I smile, then tense up when all the memories of us in bed flood in.

"I just want to hold you," he says against the softness of my neck, and it feels like home. For the first time in months, I feel complete with Alex next to me, and that thought scares me. Whatever's going on between us has to work. I want it to work, but the possibility of it not is still there. I push the thoughts out of my head, and when I hear the low sound of his heavy breathing, I know he's asleep. It doesn't take long for me to follow him to dreamland.

I wake up in the early morning and wonder if last night was all a dream because Alex is nowhere to be found. The Styrofoam box is still in place, so I know it wasn't.

Checking the time, I realize breakfast is still being served and take the opportunity to go downstairs to get more of those delicious blueberry muffins. As soon as I see them, my mouth instantly waters. I grab two and sit in my favorite chair by the window.

Just as I'm stuffing my mouth, a man walks in wearing dark blue scrubs with an ID badge pinned to his top. He must be the older brother, Evan—the doctor. I watch him as he walks to the counter and speaks with John. He shares similarities to Alex with the same dark blond hair and build, and those same bright blue Bishop eyes. However, Evan's face is more aged, and I can tell he's the oldest of the brothers. His jawline is cut with darker scruff, and the stress from his job is evident in his features.

I don't realize I'm staring until John points over at me. Lifting my hand, I wave and try to swallow down the huge bite of muffin I took. Evan makes eye contact with me then walks over. The way he's looking at me like he knows all my secrets makes me nervous as hell. Cocky confidence must be a Bishop thing because they've all got it.

Evan doesn't ask before he sits in the chair across from me.

"I'm Evan. Alex's older brother," he says, formally introducing himself.

"Hi, I'm River. Nice to officially meet you," I tell him, wondering if he's an asshole doctor because if I had to judge him by his looks and the way he carries himself, I'd say he was. He has that brooding and serious look down.

"I'm just going to cut to the chase." He looks at his watch then back at me. "I know about you and Alex. I also know you're a pediatric nurse. You know I'm a doctor. See what I'm getting at?"

I continue eating my muffins because I have no clue what he's insinuating but pretend like I do.

"If you're really moving here and need a job, I can put in a good word for you, if you're interested. Alex said you were worried about finding work here, but we're always looking. We can use all the help we can get at the hospital, especially on the children's floor. Not many people with your experience move to Nowhere, Texas, so we're always shorthanded."

Well, these Bishops just get straight to the point, don't they?

I swallow down the muffin. "You're offering me a job?"

"Well, I don't do the official hiring, but one phone call and you'd have an interview within an hour. Mostly just to make sure your references pan out and that you are who you say you are. Then there'd be official paperwork for you to fill out and all of that, but if you want it, then yes, I could help make it happen." His words make my head spin because I hadn't decided what I'd do for work yet or if I'd wait till after the baby was born.

"Wow…I don't know what to say."

"Think about it and get back to me. No pressure. Just wanted you to know the option is there."

"I will, thank you." I smile, feeling the stress melt away. I love my job and working with kids, and knowing I'd be leaving it behind is a hard reality to swallow. However, if I could continue some of that work here, I wouldn't feel so useless and dependent on Alex.

"Get settled and learn the area and people, and if you want to wait till after the baby, the job will still be here for you."

I'm shocked to the point of almost being speechless.

"Working with kids was a dream, so I really can't imagine doing anything else."

"We don't have a pediatric hospital—just a ward—so it's not as large as you're probably used to, but they could use a nurse with your experience. In fact, they *need* someone like you. It's a nice community, and even though you're not one of us, you'd eventually fit right in," he teases.

I smile, chuckling. Evan isn't anything like I'd expected, but that could change. The last three minutes have been strange, to say the least.

"I don't know what to say…" My mind is racing from information overload on top of everything else.

"No worries. Just think about it. I don't need an answer now."

"Okay, well thank you. I certainly appreciate it."

He winks and checks his watch. "Sorry, I'm going to be late for my shift if I don't get going," he says, standing. Before he walks away, he turns and looks straight at me. "Oh, nice meeting you and congrats."

All my words have vanished. I remember Alex saying his brother was a doctor, but I didn't realize he had so much pull at the hospital. His words keep replaying in my mind. The hospital needs *me*. That's all I needed to hear to help me solidify my decision. Sure, the children's hospital in Milwaukee needs me too, but it's not dire. There are handfuls of other nurses who are just as well versed as I am. But moving here would be different. It'd be more intimate at a smaller hospital. And I don't think he'd lie about needing my experience. After I finish eating, I go upstairs, grab my cell phone, and call Natalie. I have to talk to her now. Considering she's off today, I know she's awake and probably doing nothing.

"Nat!" I say as soon as she answers, my excitement building.

"What? Is everything okay?" she asks, and I can tell she's walking.

"Yes, it's great. I have so much to tell you." I sit on the edge of the bed. "Alex wants me to move to Texas."

"Oh, my fucking gosh! That's so great, River! See, I told you! Sorry if I'm breathing heavily; I'm climbing the stairs to my apartment because the elevator line was too long."

"So his brother is a doctor…" I add.

"No fucking way. A *hot* doctor?" she asks, her tone rising in pitch.

"I am *not* answering that, soon-to-be Mrs. Adam Mathews. Anyway, he says he can help get me a job at the hospital on their children's ward. This shouldn't be this easy, right? Like I'm starting to second-guess everything."

She laughs. "I was wondering if old skeptical River was going to come out and play."

"Ha-ha." I roll my eyes even though she can't see me. "Actually, it's not been that easy. I met his mother yesterday, and I don't think she's too fond of me. She was nice, but the way she looked at me, I just got the feeling she wouldn't blink twice if I caught on fire."

I hear Natalie unlock a door then I hear it click closed. "Mothers don't like *any* girlfriends. Do you think Adam's mother loved me when we first met? Hell no, she didn't. She thought I was the devil who was taking away her only son. Just gotta kill her with kindness, and you'll grow on her. Remember you're always the second woman. *Trust* me on that." Natalie laughs, and I remember some of the stories she'd told me when they first started dating, and it helps me relax slightly about my situation. It's been so long since I've been in any sort of real relationship that I forget these types of things are normal.

"Thanks, Nat. Oh, don't forget to pick me up from the airport around five tonight."

"Yeah, babe. I know. I'll be there. Just hope you don't get delayed. The snow won't fucking stop. I feel like I'm in a frozen winter hell."

I can't help but smile. "Don't jinx me, dammit! I'll text you as soon as the plane lands or if I get delayed beforehand. I'd better go pack because I have to get going soon if I'm going to make it there on time." I look at the clock and realize I have to leave in an hour.

Natalie squeals. "Can't wait to see you!"

We say our goodbyes, and I start packing my suitcase. I grab all my toiletries from the bathroom and make sure I don't leave anything behind, even though I'll be back soon. Just as I glance over, I see the Styrofoam box that Alex set on the dresser last night. My keys are sitting right next to the fork. I open the box and see it's a giant piece of chocolate cake. Smiling, I decide I'm taking it to the airport with me and eating it while I wait for my plane.

After everything is packed, I roll my suitcase down to the car. The airport is a little over an hour away, and I should leave soon, but this time, I'm not going anywhere without telling Alex goodbye. Once my foot hits the bottom step, I see John rushing toward me. He grabs my suitcase and carries it to the car for me like a perfect gentleman.

"You coulda called me. I would've been happy to help you with this."

"I know, I know. I'm just used to doing most things by myself and forget to ask. Thank you so much, though," I tell him as he loads the suitcase in the trunk before shutting it.

Just as I turn around, I see Alex walking and looking straight at me.

"Safe travels, River. We'll see you real soon," John says then walks back inside, giving Alex and me some privacy.

"Hey you," Alex says. His clothes are dirty, and he even has dirt on his face and hat.

"What the hell?" I look him up and down, lingering a little too long on his *package*. Those tight pants are giving away his secrets, and I can't help but glance down.

He lifts his hat and scrubs a hand over his face and hair. "The cowboy life is rough." A sexy smirk plays on his lips as he notices where I was looking. His hair is disheveled, and he looks so damn sexy as he stands in front of me.

"I knew you'd be leaving soon, so I wanted to give you a proper goodbye and get your number; something I shoulda done a long ass time ago," he says, pulling out his phone and unlocking it. I grab it and program my number into his contacts, then text myself so I've got his too.

I can't help but think how ironic and strange it is that we're just now exchanging numbers.

"Please text me when you land so I know you made it back okay. And call me when you get home so I can at least rest easy tonight knowing you're safe," he says softly as I hand him his phone.

I smile. "I will." And this time, I mean it. "Promise."

Even though he's dirty, he wraps his arms around me tightly, not wanting to let go, and it's something I welcome. "Bye, River. Come back to me soon."

"I will. I'll keep you updated on everything, too. I'll give you a timeline as soon as I get my life situated," I tell him as he loosens his embrace.

"If you need any help with *anything*, just let me know." Alex leans in, pulling my bottom lip into his mouth, and sucks on it. He runs his fingers through my hair and kisses me, and my hormones go haywire as I taste him. When we break apart, I realize that's the goodbye we should've had in Key West.

A week has passed since I've been home and taking care of business. I'm nervous and have asked myself at least a thousand times if this is the right decision, but each time I speak with Alex on the phone, my heart reminds me it is.

After doing some research and pricing moving companies, which was way out of my budget, I decide to list all my furniture online instead. Then I'll pack and ship a few boxes of things I want to keep, then donate the rest. Luckily, I don't really have that much, considering I didn't spend a lot of time in my apartment except to sleep and eat.

Once I returned from Key West, I kicked out my roommate because she kept bringing Asshole around, and I didn't want that kind of negativity in my life anymore. I planned to move into a one-bedroom apartment, then found out I was pregnant. Now, I'm grateful I'd been downsizing.

There are only two things left to do before everything is

wrapped up in Wisconsin: give my parents the news and say goodbye to Natalie.

My parents live up north, so I call them and ask if they can drive down to meet me after lunch. Even though they're divorced, I want to tell them together in person.

I'm almost ready to start a new chapter in my life, as odd as it feels. Everything's happening so quickly, which might be the norm when it comes to Alex Bishop, but that's yet to be determined.

My job was very understanding and allowed me to take the rest of my vacation days instead of working the final two weeks. Leaving was hard, but I took my time saying goodbye to my patients. It was bittersweet.

After I eat a quick bite, I take a bus across town to a coffee shop where I asked my mother and father to meet me. I'm nervous, but I don't expect either of them to beg me to stay or anything. Since Rylie's death and their divorce, they haven't been the same. Even when I was around, they acted like I was invisible.

It's been years since the three of us have been together, and for once, this is a good reason. Or at least I hope that's what they'll think.

When I walk in, they're sitting at a table, pretending the other isn't there. They're not holding a conversation or even looking in the same direction, which kind of hurts my heart.

"Hey, you two!" I say, trying to lighten the mood.

"Hey, River. How've you been doing?" Dad asks, standing up to greet me with a hug.

"Good. Really good," I tell him, giving Mom a hug next before I sit down.

"That's great, River," Mom adds.

"How was the drive? Traffic okay?"

Dad purses his lips. Mom narrows her eyes.

"Traffic was fine," Mom finally answers. Geez, you'd think I asked them to perform a rain dance ritual or something. I know their marriage ended badly, but it's been years. You'd think that hostility would've diminished by now.

"Well, I'll just cut to the chase since you both have to drive back tonight. I'm sure you're wondering what's going on," I say, inhaling a deep breath.

My heart begins to race, and I know I need to spit this out, but it seems like I'm walking through thick honey and can barely move.

"I've decided to move to Texas in a few weeks."

They both stay quiet for a moment until finally, my father speaks. "What prompted this decision?"

"Well…" I pause, wishing I would've bought a bottle of water because my throat is as dry as the Sahara. "I recently found out I was pregnant, and the father lives in Texas. We're going to see where things go between us, but I also want the baby to have him in his or her life."

Tears of happiness stream down my mother's face. "River," she says in a hushed tone. "We're going to be grandparents." She looks at my father, and his eyes meet hers as if he's seeing her for the first time in a decade.

"Hell, had I known getting pregnant was the trick, I would've tried it back in high school," I tease.

"That's not even funny," Mom scolds, but I laugh anyway.

"I wish you weren't moving so far away," Dad adds. "We'd like to be involved too."

Guilt washes over me because I didn't think they'd care that much, considering they haven't wanted to be involved in my life in a long time.

"You can always come visit. We can text and FaceTime too. I'm sure you'd love it there. No snow. Horseback riding. All the typical Texas stuff: cowboys, cacti, and horses." I smile, knowing their love for winter sports trumps anything Texas could offer.

Dad lets out a sigh.

"As long as you're happy, sweetie. That's all that matters. If moving to Texas to be with this man is what you want, I fully support your decision."

"I do, too, baby," Dad confirms. My shoulders relax, and it feels so good to get it all out.

"Does he treat you right?" Mom asks.

I grab her hand with a lopsided grin. "Yes, Mom." I sigh. "He treats me like a queen."

"You deserve to be," she says with a smile on her face.

"You really do," Dad adds.

For a moment, I feel my emotions bubble over. I'm halfway shocked when tears stream down my face because their reactions shined light to a dark corner of my heart. After the conversation is over, we exchange hugs and goodbyes, then Dad leaves, and Mom follows behind him. I take the bus to Natalie's apartment and try to replay everything that happened today.

As soon as she opens the door, she pulls me into a big hug. Out of everything that's here, Natalie is who I'm going to miss the most. She's my best friend and has been for as long as I can remember. I hope and pray distance doesn't affect our friendship.

"Come in," she tells me as she releases our embrace. I don't hesitate before stepping inside.

I walk in and smell cookies baking, and I know she made them just for me. Sitting in the recliner, I prop up my feet and lean back. "You're making chocolate chip oatmeal cookies again, aren't you?"

"Of course, I am, Mama. They're your favorite." She smiles and sits on the couch. "How'd your parents take the news?"

"Surprisingly well," I admit, and I'm still kind of shocked by their response.

"That's great, River. They don't really have a choice other than to accept what's going on, you know?" The oven beeps, and Natalie quickly gets up and takes them out. She grabs a spatula, places a few on a plate, and pours two large glasses of milk. She spoils me. Before Adam gets home, we talk about everything— about me moving, her coming to visit, keeping in touch,

FaceTiming, and how I have to keep her involved in every aspect of the pregnancy. We lose complete track of time reminiscing, and when I realize hours have passed, I decide it's time for me to go.

Natalie pulls me into a big hug, and we squeeze each other so tight it almost hurts.

"I'm going to try not to cry," she says.

"No tears. This isn't goodbye forever. We're going to chat all the time," I remind her.

She chokes back tears, and I do too. Sucking in a deep breath, I somehow find the strength to walk away.

"Text me when you get home," she says as I step onto the elevator.

"I will!"

She waves goodbye just before the doors close, and I wipe the tears away.

I guess it's really all settled now. There's nothing else holding me here.

CHAPTER NINETEEN

ALEX

"SHUT THE HELL UP!" I yell at Jackson as he irritates me from his bedroom.

"You're the one who's forcing me to move out," he retorts as he carries boxes outside to his truck.

I laugh when he walks back in and flips me off with both hands.

"I'm paying thousands of dollars for you to leave. You've wanted your own place for a while anyway. It's not going to take that long to finish that house. Dad already told you that."

Since River will be here tomorrow, I've been trying to get everything settled, and Jackson's deadline to get all his shit out was yesterday. Being the asshole procrastinator he is, he waited until the very last minute to pick up the remaining boxes. This whole process hasn't been the easiest, considering Jackson and I split the cost to have this house remodeled. So, to be fair, I paid him his half, which will help him fix up an old farmhouse on the other side of the property.

Unfortunately, he's been giving me shit ever since Mama suggested it. I was surprised when she did, but luckily it was her idea, so Jackson caved and did what she wanted. But until the house is fixed up and remodeled, Jackson's staying with John, who isn't happy about the whole idea.

After a few more trips to his truck, Jackson comes back in breathing heavily. "That's all of it."

"Thank God." I sigh, relieved.

He takes a few steps forward, and at first, I think he's going to punch me, but instead, he gives me a big brotherly hug. "Better be glad I love you."

"Don't get all mushy on me," I tell him, and he laughs.

He looks down at his watch. "Gotta go. John's gonna be home, and I want to meet him at the door wearing the same clothes."

"You're such a prick."

He laughs and gives me a sarcastic thumbs up. "Not many people have a twin they can fuck with. Gotta take advantage of it every chance I get."

I shake my head, and when I hear the rumble of his truck in the distance, I let out a deep breath. The house almost looks empty without his shit all over the place, but that'll give River a blank space to make this place her own. I just hope she accepts living with me since I haven't officially asked her yet. I wanted to make sure she was standing in front of me when I did. If she refuses, there are a few more options, but I don't even think about that. I promised her I'd have everything worked out by the time she returned, but this is a big step, even for me.

Not wanting to push her limits, I had an extra bedroom set from the B&B moved and set up in Jackson's room since River decided to sell her furniture. I wish I could sleep next to her instead, but I'm not rushing things, just as she wanted. The more I thought about us while she was in Wisconsin, the more I realized she was right about taking it slow. I plan to spend all the time I can getting to know every little thing about her. I want our relationship to have a solid foundation, considering she already has my heart.

It's almost been two weeks since River left, and today, she's finally coming back to me for good. I wake up, feed the animals, finish my day, and clean up before heading to the airport to pick her up. It's close to five p.m., and I'm exhausted, but just knowing she's on her way gives me an energy boost. During the hour it takes me to drive there, I do nothing but think about her and our future. It's all still hard for me to believe.

I sit in the chairs that line the wall and wait for her plane to land. The airport is tiny, so when I finally see a small plane slow and stop, I know she's here. My heart pounds with happiness, and I can't wait to hold her in my arms again. As soon as I see her, looking as pretty as ever in a pair of black leggings, a sweater, and snow boots, I stand to greet her. Almost immediately, she spots me, and a smile fills her gorgeous face.

Walking over to her, I can't help but smile too. I'm tempted to pull her into my arms, but I remind myself of those boundaries she asked for previously. It was impossible the last time she was here, repeatedly crossing those lines, but I'm making a solid effort now. If I want us to have a chance at making this work, I know I need to keep my distance, so we *can* start fresh.

She wraps an arm around me for a side hug, which I gladly accept. Whatever pace she leads, I'll follow from now on. Grabbing the carry-on bag from her hand, I walk beside her to the truck, making small talk.

"Nice boots," I say with a laugh, buckling up. Once we're both settled in our seats, I back out of the small parking lot.

"They're not shit slingers, but they made sure I didn't fall on black ice. I'm so happy to see sunshine. You have no idea."

"Sunshine? Is that my new nickname?" I tease, and she gives me a sideways glance with a grin.

As I drive us back to the ranch, I'm able to breathe a little easier knowing she's finally here—*home*.

"How was the flight?" I ask as we turn onto the old dirt road.

"Sucked. I hate those little planes. They're horrible. Thought I would need the barf bag, but I saved myself from the embarrassment and held it back," she admits. "Perks of being pregnant!"

"I can only imagine." I grab her hand as I park the truck in front of my house. She turns and looks at me with wide eyes.

"Where are we?" she asks.

I look at her and kiss her knuckles before I speak. "We're home."

River's mouth falls open, and I smile. She gets out of the truck, and I interlock my fingers with hers as we walk up the steps that lead to the modest farmhouse. Before we walk in, I stop her at the door.

"You can say no, but first let me just say this. I thought maybe living together would make the most sense for us, seeing that you're having a baby and all. That way we can raise him or her together and see where things go between us. If that's moving too fast, just let me know. But I did kick Jackson out, so you can have his room."

"Seriously?" she asks.

I nod and open the door, hoping that's a good reaction. She walks in and looks around, the smile on her face not faltering.

"Give me the grand tour, please," she says, reaching for my hand. I take it and never want to let it go. Her skin brushing against mine feels like home as we walk through the house.

"This is my bedroom." I open the door, and she steps inside, sucking in a deep breath.

"So this is where the magic happens?" She turns and looks at me with an arched brow.

"Only if you want it to."

She licks her lips as I eye her. I notice her breathing harder but decide to just tease her until she can't handle it anymore. Pulling her out of the room, I walk her around the rest of the house. "Here's the kitchen, a bathroom…"

When I open the door to Jackson's old room, her eyes light up. All the bedroom furniture is set up how I imagined she'd want it. "And here's your room."

She walks to the bed and her hand smooths the handmade quilt my grandmother made. "I can't believe you did all this for me."

"I'd do anything for you, River."

She bites her bottom lip, and I'm so tempted to lay her down on that bed and break it in properly. She doesn't even know how beautiful she is right now, and I want nothing more than to tell her as she looks up at me with seduction in her eyes. I remember that look in Key West and know it oh so damn well.

"There's more," I say, breaking the silence before I strip her clothes off and make sweet love to her. She follows me as I take her to the room where we kept our pool table, but now it's empty except for an old rocking chair. "This is the baby's room. I didn't paint or anything because I thought maybe we could do it together."

"Wow." Her eyes light up. "It's perfect," she whispers, walking around the empty space. "Thank you for doing this. I honestly didn't expect any of it."

Once River explores the space, she comes back to me and wraps her arms around my waist, pulling me close to her. I inhale the scent of her hair, and I want her so damn bad it almost hurts. Eventually, she takes a step back, creating space between us.

"So, you're okay with this arrangement?" I finally ask. "Sharing a house and setting up a nursery together?"

"Yeah, definitely." She nods, taking it all in. "It'll be like we're…roommates," she adds with a grin. "However, the last roommate I had slept with my ex-boyfriend, so hopefully you'll be better than her," she teases.

"I can promise you I won't be sleeping with anyone's boyfriend," I joke with her. "But don't walk around nude because I don't know if I'll be able to hold myself back. And if you'd like to save a horse and ride a cowboy instead, you just let me know," I tell her with a wink.

Her breath hitches and blush hits her cheeks. It's so damn cute when I catch her off guard. After shaking off my words, she finally speaks and changes the subject.

"You have a really nice house."

"It's *our* house now."

"Why are you so perfect?" she asks.

"Trust me, I'm not." I shrug. "But you make me want to be."

"See, that's what I'm talking about. You always have something sweet to say."

I chuckle, giving her a smirk. "Do I?"

"You know you do!" She laughs and playfully slaps my chest. "You've got this charm thing down to a science."

I can tell she's happy being here. All the stress from traveling has already melted away, and it's easy being here with her like this.

We're still standing in the baby's room, and she takes a step back and looks it over again. "We should paint it a neutral color like yellow. When the sun rises and sets, it will make the room glow even more when the windows are open."

"Whatever you want, sweetheart," I say, placing my hand on her shoulder. Right now, I know what true happiness is. There's no other place in the world I'd rather be than with River, and when she turns and looks at me with a sweet smile on her face, I know she feels the same way.

"Are you hungry?" I ask, knowing she's bound to be after traveling. It's nearly six thirty.

"Did you hear my stomach roar?" She giggles.

"Nope. But come on, we'll go to Mama's."

When her eyes meet mine, my heart does a flip-flop in my chest. I'm constantly at war with myself, telling the devil on my shoulder that I can't kiss her or make love to her, and bending her over the couch and fucking her senseless ain't gonna happen anytime soon. My body remembers Key West like it was yesterday, and I wish we could fall into the same step we were in before we left. I want to go from zero to sixty in five seconds with River, and just being around her for this short amount of time is a constant reminder of where we are right now—taking it slow. This is already proving to be harder than I ever imagined, but Mama raised a perfect gentleman, and when she wants me, she'll let me know—hopefully.

We walk to the truck and drive down the old country road until my parents' house is in view. Once I've parked and we get out, I lead her up the porch, but she stops me before we walk inside.

"I'm nervous," River says.

"Don't be, darlin'. Mama's expecting us." I open the door for her. As soon as River walks in, my cousin Benita jumps out of her chair and says hello. Her face lights up when she sees me following behind. She runs up to River and gives her a big hug like they're longtime friends.

"I'm Benita! It's so nice to finally meet the pretty lady who's been stealing my cousin's heart. I'm so excited for you guys! I heard the news last week." Benita glances over at me as she hugs River. I relax because when Benita is around, everyone seems to be in a good mood. Her energy is always high, and she's loud and doesn't give a shit about anything. I seriously love her like my sister.

"I didn't know you were gonna be here," I whisper, giving her a hug.

"Well, my mama wanted me to drop off some dishes that were left at church last Sunday when they had their ladies luncheon. Also, I came to sneak some pictures from your dad for the party this weekend. Mama put me up to it by saying I was Aunt Rose's favorite, so she'd never suspect anything. She still has no idea about the party," Benita whispers, pulling a handful of pictures from her coat pocket.

River turns and looks at me, giving me a big smile when Mama yells for Benita and pulls her away from the conversation. We walk toward the kitchen, and I lean forward and whisper loud enough for her to hear. "You're beautiful."

She turns, and I can see how nervous she is.

"Everything is going to be okay," I tell her, placing my hand on the small of her back, trying to give her a dash of confidence considering our last visit didn't go over so well.

When we enter, I see Mama already set the table and has burgers cooking on the stove.

"Hey, son," Mama says to me, then smiles at River. "How was your flight, dear?"

Mama's in an extra good mood tonight, but I think that's because Benita's here sprinkling her happiness everywhere.

"It was fine, minus the fact that I nearly take up two seats now. Glad to be back in Texas, though, with no snow," River says, real friendly like.

Mama pulls french fries from the pan and places them on a plate with a paper towel to soak up the excess grease. She adds cheese to the burgers, sets out buns, and works around the kitchen like a natural.

"Hi, Mr. Bishop," River says to my father as he sits at the table.

"Hey there, River. How are you?"

"Great, thank you," River tells him as she sits across from him at the table. Benita begins to talk River's head off about the area and how she wished she could make snow angels at least once in her life. She has us all rolling with laughter because the way she words stuff sometimes is so over the top. Benita's busy talking about babies and everything else when John, Jackson, and Evan all come rushing in one after another.

"You're late!" Mama scolds. They all sit down, and Jackson starts blaming John.

Dad whistles real loud, stopping everyone from talking over each other, and all I can do is laugh. It's always like this when we get together and has been for as long as I can remember.

I look over at River, giving her a look that says *welcome to being a Bishop!*

"So, River," Evan speaks up first, "I heard you saved Dylan's life in Key West." I swear to God I'm going to punch Dylan in the mouth for telling Evan anything about Key West.

Mama's eyes dart toward River, and I can tell she's curious and even a little impressed.

"Yeah, I guess so," River says quietly, and I know she doesn't want the attention. "He nearly drowned. Apparently, he wasn't a good swimmer, so when I saw Alex pull him out of the water, I knew something was wrong."

"Why in the hell was he in the water?" Jackson asks.

"Because he's an idiot," John tells him.

"We were paddleboarding," I clarify. "He just went too far and fell off."

"Oh, so you were both being idiots." Jackson laughs, and I roll my eyes at him.

"Well, he would've drowned if River wouldn't have been there to give him CPR. I think it was the moment I fell in love with her." I grab her hand, and she tenses but continues to smile. Maybe I shouldn't have said that in front of everyone, but it slipped out, and it's the truth. It was the moment that I knew she was unselfish, caring, and an angel. It was the first real moment that brought us together.

Benita lets out a big *awwww,* and the room fills with conversation again. After we're finished with dinner, Benita and River help Mama pick up all the plates and wash them. I can already tell they're going to be friends, which makes me so damn happy because Benita lives close and can relate to the mom stuff.

"You didn't bring the twins tonight?" I ask Benita about her toddler boys, Reagan and Beau. "Haven't seen them in a while."

"Nah, left them home with Aaron for a bit. It was his turn to chase them around the house." She laughs.

"Twins?" River gasps, glancing at me. "And you said Courtney's having triplets, right?"

"Yep."

"You sure you're only having one?" Benita teases. "Multiples run in the family."

River's eyes go wide, and even though Benita's joking around, it's always a possibility that one of us Bishop boys could have twins. My money's on Jackson, though. After the shit he puts us through, he deserves five sets of twins.

When River starts yawning, I know it's time to go. She's had an emotional jam-packed day, and I'm sure she's exhausted. Just as I stand to tell everyone we're leaving, Benita stands and says she better get home and rescue Aaron before he loses his mind. Taking it as our cue to leave, we all split at the same time, exchanging hugs and goodbyes.

Once outside, the cool air touches my cheeks, and River turns to me. "Is that really when you fell in love with me?"

I lick my lower lip, thinking back to our time together. "There's a handful of moments when I knew I was falling for you. Moments I didn't want to admit to myself at first."

She smiles as I lead her back to the truck. "Is this real life?" she finally whispers as I open the door for her. She climbs in and buckles up.

"As real as it'll ever be," I tell her, backing out of the driveway.

As we drive home, I remind River about the details of Mama's birthday. "You came back just in time. It's this Saturday. Benita and Mama's sisters planned the whole thing, but everyone's coming since it's a big one. Benita's a sweetheart and would do anything for anyone, but party planning is right up her alley. The twins slowed her down, but now that they're older, she's back at it."

"I honestly can't imagine carrying two babies."

I nod and laugh. "We're lucky, considering everyone's popping out multiples in the family."

Pretending to wipe sweat from her forehead, she giggles. "Dodged a bullet there."

"Well, there's always next time." I wink.

"Funny," she deadpans.

"You sure we're only having one baby though, right?" I ask because stranger things have happened.

"I'm positive. I *think*. Now you've got me stressed that there could be two babies in the oven."

I chuckle loudly. "Guess we should book an appointment with the doctor soon."

"Shut up." She laughs. "Seriously."

"Okay, okay." I grin.

"That reminds me, though. I'll need to find a doctor here."

"Shouldn't be too hard considering there are only two baby doctors at the hospital. I can ask Evan for a referral."

"That's okay. I can call. Or give me Evan's number and I can talk to him myself. I'm sure the last thing you want to discuss is mucus plugs and stretch marks."

I glance at her and see her biting down on her lip to prevent a laugh from escaping.

"I bet Benita would love to have you around as she decorates the church for the party." I slyly change the subject. "I can text her and ask if you'd like."

"That actually sounds like a lot of fun. I really like her already. She's nice, and I can tell she's got a kind heart. I really like everyone, actually. I don't know how your parents handled all you boys, though."

I can barely contain my smile. "We were a handful; that's for sure. You'll have a good time tomorrow, and I'm sure Benita will enjoy hanging out with someone who's under fifty." I laugh.

We park and walk inside, and I notice she's yawning more frequently.

"You should go to bed," I suggest, sweetly.

"You're right. I'm exhausted." She smiles with a cute, sleepy look on her face. "Come tuck me in, cowboy."

She walks to her room, and I follow behind her. I watch her hips sway, and all the things I want to do hit me with full force. I want her so badly, I have to adjust myself and force my eyes to the ceiling instead. When she turns around, I pretend I'm just fine. I lean against the doorway and watch as she climbs into bed.

"Alex," she says, "thank you again for everything."

Walking toward her, I brush my fingers across her cheek, stopping myself before my lips meet hers. "Thank *you* for everything. Good night, darlin'."

After I turn off the light, it takes everything I have to walk to my room. All I want to do is crawl into bed with her and hold her.

As I lie in bed, the only thing on my mind is River and how even after three months of being apart, she consumes my mind as if no time had passed at all. Even after everything we've been through, she still has no idea what she continues to do to me. That's going to have to change, but after I get rid of these boundaries.

"Yeah, I go a little extra on parties. Something you'll have to get used to." She winks.

I narrow my eyes, curious to what that means. "Don't think you're having that baby without a proper baby shower." She points a finger at my belly with determination.

A baby shower? I hadn't even thought about that.

"I-I don't know." I wrinkle my nose. Honestly, I'd feel guilty taking anything from Alex's family. I just met them, and I don't want it to seem like I'm taking advantage.

"Oh, it's not optional." She grins.

I can't help but laugh. Shrugging, I change the conversation. "Okay, so tablecloths and centerpieces, I can figure out, but where do you want the balloons and streamers to go?"

For the next hour, we work together on decorating the tables and setting up the buffet line with the plates and plasticware. Centerpieces and confetti are sprinkled down the middle of the tables. Next, we work on the streamers. Benita stands on a ladder and attaches them to the middle of the ceiling until three blue and three red pieces are hanging down to the floor.

"Aaron will be here soon, so he can help us twist these and stretch them across the room. It'll look awesome once all six are spread along the ceiling," she explains, stepping down. I can envision it already and know it'll look great.

"I love it." I smile. "What about the balloons?"

"Hmm…" She thinks for a moment before her eyes light up. "What if we blew them all up and found a way to attach them to the ceiling, like with a net or something? Then when she walks in, we pull a string that releases them at the same time!" The excitement in her tone is short-lived when Aaron comes strolling in with their twin boys.

"That'll never work," Aaron says, setting the boys down so they can run over to Benita. She wraps her arms around them and smiles.

"Don't underestimate me," Benita warns without taking her eyes off the twins. I love how they cling to her as if she's their whole world. When they finally turn around, I see the resemblance of Benita and Aaron in both of their features. "Daddy has a fishin' net I'm sure I can borrow. Tack it up and attach it to a string so once it's pulled, the balloons all come down."

Aaron keeps his stance, crossing his arms over his chest and pouting. "There's no way that's going to stay, babe. Trust me."

She narrows her eyes and scowls. "Nope. I'm callin' Daddy." She reaches for her phone before looking up at me. "Oh, River, this is my stubborn ass husband, Aaron. Stubborn Ass, this is River, Alex's…lady friend."

I snort, shaking my head at her description. Though she's not really wrong either. We aren't putting labels on our relationship at this point since we're taking things slow, but I'm definitely more than just his *friend*.

"It's nice to meet you," I say, wondering if he's the shaking hands or hugging kind. He steps toward me and takes my hand.

"You too. I've heard a lot about you."

I blush. "It's all probably only half true," I joke, and Aaron laughs.

A few moments later, Benita is off the phone and smiling wide. "Daddy's comin' to help. You and the boys can go play out back since you don't believe in me."

Aaron groans as if he's been through conversations like this before. "C'mon, boys. Let's leave Mommy to drive other people crazy for once."

"Okay, you two are kinda made for each other," I tell her once they're out of earshot.

"I know." She beams. "Though he drives me up a wall, I love him so much."

"All good men do, honey," one of the ladies I met earlier says from behind us.

We continue decorating, and twenty minutes later, Benita's dad arrives with all the supplies we'll need to make a balloon dropper. After she introduces us, he puts us both to work. I take the opportunity to sit and start blowing up the red and blue balloons. We also picked up a few that had "50" scattered over them. I'm nearly out of breath when Benita announces the net is ready.

"Oh my God!" She claps her hands. "It's going to be epic."

"Should we try it out first? Put a few in there and test the string?" I ask.

Benita's dad releases a loud humph. "This ain't my first rodeo, darlin'."

"Oh." I feel bad for doubting him now.

"That's not what she meant, Daddy." Benita comes to my rescue. "Better be sure than find out tomorrow." She grabs a few of the balloons and climbs back up the ladder to stick them inside. "Want to pull the string, River?"

"Sure." I walk toward her, and just for fun, start counting down from three.

"Three…two…"

"One!" Benita yells, and I pull the string. "Yes!" she instantly cheers when the net releases and all three balloons fall.

"Told ya." Her dad snickers, and I chuckle.

"You did great, Daddy. Thank you!" Benita sets it back up, so I can start tossing the balloons up to her. Takes us a good five minutes to get all the balloons packed, but once it's done, it looks awesome.

"That was a great idea," I tell her, looking around the dining hall and seeing how amazing everything turned out. The buffet table is set up minus the food. All the round tables are decorated. The streamers are twisted and hung up, and so is the balloon drop. "Well, you weren't lying," I say after giving the room another once-over. "You're definitely extra."

Shortly after, Alex surprises me when he walks in with a bag from the Main Street Diner.

"I thought Benita might be working you to death and you'd be hungry." He smiles before kissing the top of my head and sitting down next to me at one of the tables.

"Oh, you're a smart man." I smile, reaching for the bag, and moan when I see a juicy cheeseburger inside.

"Hey, where's mine?" Benita teases, peeking inside the bag.

"You're not eating for two," he retorts.

"Oh, so only when I'm pregnant you'll get me food?" I look at him, sucking in my lower lip to hide the smile.

"Dug yourself that one," Aaron blurts.

I chuckle, taking the burger out and taking a bite.

"Everything looks great in here." Alex looks around. "A bit much for a spaghetti dinner though." He laughs.

Benita reaches over the table and whacks him one. "We worked hard, thank you very much. Aunt Rose is gonna love it."

"She is," Alex confirms, narrowing his eyes on the balloon dropper.

"Benita risked her life for that," I joke.

"Well, Daddy helped." She grins.

I continue stuffing my face when everyone stops and stares at me. "What?" I ask around a mouthful of food. Once I swallow, I look at Alex. "Do I have something on my face or something?"

"Nope."

Turning my head toward Benita, I ask, "What? Do you not eat burgers down here or something?"

"No, you're just eating like you haven't eaten in a week," she teases. "It's cute. You're pregnant."

"I'm just worried I didn't bring you enough," Alex jokes, and I scowl at him.

"You both suck. Picking on a pregnant woman. Shame on you."

They laugh, and I finish my burger in two more bites.

"My sister wants me to FaceTime her, so I can show her the hall and meet you."

"Now?" My eyes widen. I'm hot and sweaty.

"Yeah, that okay?"

I wipe my mouth and feel around my head for how messy my

hair is right now. "Sure, if she doesn't mind that I look like a hot mess right now."

"She's almost seven months pregnant with triplets; I can guarantee you she feels more of a hot mess than you do," Benita says.

"Okay, well that makes me feel better."

I know I'm not meeting Courtney face to face, but I'm nervous. I want Alex's family to like me, and since he only has one sister, I'd really love if we could have some kind of relationship, too. Especially since our kids will be cousins.

"Hey!" she shouts, waving. Alex has his phone aimed at both of us when he makes the call.

"Hi," we both say in unison.

"This is River." Alex points the phone directly at me. "And this is my annoying little sister, Courtney."

"Hey!" she scowls. "I don't know how you put up with my brother, but bless your soul for doin' so."

I laugh, already loving her personality. "Yes, please pray for me."

"I got your back." She winks.

"So how are you feeling?"

"Um, pretty much like I'm carrying triplets." She half-laughs, half-sobs.

"I can only imagine. Geez, makes me feel bad for complaining about the heartburn."

"Yeah, let's talk when you can't see your feet or vagina anymore."

I nearly choke and die laughing, especially when Alex's face turns red and Benita chuckles.

"I like her," I tell Alex.

"Yeah, I had a feeling you two would hit it off."

"You break her heart, Alex Bishop, I'm taking her side," Courtney warns.

He rolls his eyes, adjusting the baseball cap on his head. God, I love when he wears that hat. It's the one he wore in Key West, too.

It's dark gray and worn to shit, but there's just something about how it looks on him that makes me want to jump his bones.

Oh God. I need to get those images out of my head. We're not having sex, at least not for a long time, even if my hormones are going wild for him.

"It was great to finally meet you, River. Tell Alex to give you my number so we can text, okay?"

"Definitely! It'd be nice to chat with a girl Bishop for once." I grin. "Bummer you can't be here."

"I tried to talk Drew into flying there first class, but it was a hard no." She pretends to pout.

"Well, as a nurse, I'd have to agree with your husband on that one." I smile.

"I know." She sighs. "All right, now give me the grand tour of Mama's party," she tells Alex.

He takes his phone and walks around the hall, showing her the decorations, the buffet table, the balloon drop, and the centerpieces. I hear her aahing and oohing, and it makes me feel good about helping Benita get things done today. I'm slowly getting closer to his family, which makes me feel better about uprooting my life and moving down here.

"Well, the boys are getting into everything, so we better get going," Benita says. I stand up, and she wraps her arms around me—always the hugging down here. "Thanks again for your help."

"No problem, but it doesn't feel like I helped that much."

"You did great. My mama ran out to pick up more food from the grocery store. If she asks, we went to get the boys ready for bed."

"Sounds good."

"We're heading out too," Alex interrupts. "Haven't seen my girl all day."

My heart beats a little harder.

We exchange goodbyes, and when Alex and I walk out to his truck, he grabs my hand and leads me to the passenger side.

"I was thinking we could take a little detour before going home. Whaddya think?"

"I think I'm okay with that." I grin as we get in and buckle.

He drives us down a country road that takes us out of town. I love watching out the window because everything is so open, and the land goes on for miles. It's easy to see why Alex and his brothers love it out here so much. A rush of emotions overcomes me as I think about raising our baby in the same small town community where Alex was raised. The baby will be cared for and watched over by so many who love him or her. A warm feeling rushes through me.

"You okay?" Alex reaches for my hand and squeezes it three times.

Turning to look at him, I can't contain my smile. "I'm great." I squeeze his hand back.

Several minutes pass when Alex drives the truck off road and parks at a lookout area that gives the most breathtaking view of an ongoing prairie and rolling hills.

"Where are we?" I ask.

"Found it four-wheeling one day. It's a great place to view wildlife. Just far enough from the road, so they don't get spooked. Sunset is the best time to come up here."

I check the clock and see it's at least another two hours till then.

"It's so peaceful," I say, sinking into my seat as I stare out at the vastness. "Makes me think about how busy city life is, speeding along, always having somewhere to go. There's no time to stop and take in the fresh air and just breathe. So much is taken for granted rushing through it."

"I couldn't agree more."

We sit in silence, and it's not even awkward anymore. Being comfortable with Alex has never been an issue, but the sexual tension in the air is always lurking between us. Not that it isn't now, but both knowing that we're taking things slowly takes away that pressure.

"A deer," Alex whispers, pointing to the right.

"Wow." I smile. "The only deer I've seen in Milwaukee were on the side of the highway."

"That's morbid." He laughs. "What about where you grew up?"

"Eagle River," I say. "I lived in town, so I never saw any close up like this."

"Weird," he murmurs.

"What?"

"That some people don't see wildlife like this. There's turkeys 'round here sometimes too."

"Well, there's petting zoos, but I don't know if you can really call that wildlife anymore."

"Yeah, don't get me started on those."

I chuckle.

"Told you. It's a different world down here." The closest town barely has a population of two thousand people. There's a church, grocery store, Dollar General, small health clinic, feed mill, gas station, diner, and school. Everyone knows everyone, and the old ladies who sing at church run the rumor mill. It's absolutely nothing like home, which terrifies yet comforts me. It's the ultimate fresh start.

He turns his body and faces me, reaching for my hand again. "Do you think you'll miss it?"

"Wisconsin?"

"Yeah. Where you grew up. Your home? I don't want you to resent moving here for me even though I'm really, really happy you're here." He flashes a small smile.

I contemplate how to answer. "Well, there is something about city life. It's definitely not for everyone, but it's exciting. It's always busy, something to do, and someone to talk to. There are touristy parts of Milwaukee, but not where I worked and lived. I guess if I wasn't used to it, I'd hate it. I moved there for college first from a small, boring town, so the city life was exciting at first. However, it's hard to compare to a place like Texas."

"That's because Texas fuckin' rocks." He smirks.

"I made a lot of great memories there, but I know I'll make great ones here, too."

"Good, I hope so." He brings my hand to his lips and places a soft kiss. "I'd really like that, too."

"Can I tell you a secret?" I ask, swallowing hard at what I'm about to admit.

"You can tell me anything."

It takes me a moment to collect my thoughts, but I know I'll feel better once I get this off my chest.

"I know I've told you about my sister, Rylie, and how having a baby scares me because of the what-ifs and complications than can arise."

He nods, keeping his eyes planted on mine.

"On top of those fears, I'm terrified I'll be one of those parents with no maternal instincts. I know my mom did the best she could, given the circumstances, but between my dad's distant attitude and their divorce, I didn't have the best example. I know the basics of parenting, but that's all textbook stuff. I love working with kids and helping them through their illnesses, but in an effort to avoid getting too attached, I've always blocked a part of that getting too close connection out of my brain. It's like they drill it into your head in nursing school. Learn the facts, don't get too close, do what you need to do to diagnose and treat your patient. It's why so many of our doctors are great. They keep a healthy distance because if you got emotionally invested in every child you lost, you'd be an emotional wreck."

I finally take a breath, letting Alex catch up on my rambling. He's listening so intently, which I absolutely adore about him, but now I'm afraid I've scared him.

"I'm an emotional dud," I add.

"You are *not*," he finally says. "Keeping an emotional distance so you can do your job right and loving your child are going to be two completely different things."

"How do you know?"

"Because I've seen how you've opened up to me in the short amount of time we've known each other. I've seen the effort you put in to get to know Mama and my dumbass brothers." He grins. "I've seen your friendship with Natalie. You're not giving yourself enough credit."

His words sink in, and I hope he's right. I know I'll love this baby no matter what, but the insecurities continue to weigh on me. I think about the times Rylie looked so helpless, and how badly I wanted to fix it all for her but couldn't.

"After Rylie passed, I shut down. For a long time. I think part of that still haunts me. Then when I started nursing school and my clinicals, I dug back to that time and shut down that part of my brain, so I could emotionally separate myself from getting too close. Focusing on the facts and patient treatments was my way of keeping those feelings at bay. My professors would praise me for how well I handled certain situations, and the more I heard it, the more I kept it below the surface. I don't know. Now that I'm saying it aloud, it all sounds so stupid."

Before I can drop my head, Alex catches my chin and tilts it toward him. "It's not stupid, River. Nothing you feel is stupid. I'd be lying if I said I didn't carry my own burden of insecurities. I'm scared shitless to be a father. I still can't believe it, but I know when the time comes, as long as you're by my side, there's nothing we won't be able to figure out."

"You really think so?"

"I do."

"This kid is going to have the most obnoxious uncles." I laugh.

"They really are." He chuckles, and soon we're both laughing hysterically.

"It's hard not to think about Rylie at times like this because I want nothing more than to be able to talk to her about everything. About you. About her being an aunt. I know she was sick, but she had so much life in her. Had so much life to live that she was robbed of. It's not fair." I close my eyes when the tears start to surface. I hate crying in general but even more now that I'm pregnant. The emotions are ten times more intense.

Alex doesn't speak. Instead, he crawls over the center console and wraps me up in his arms. While he holds me, I cry against his chest until the tears dry out.

CHAPTER TWENTY-ONE

ALEX

I NEVER WANT to let River go, not when she's giving me her heart and opening herself up to me. The emotions she shared were raw and deep, and I knew she'd been harboring those feelings for a while. After we drove home, I thanked her for sharing herself with me and reassured her I'd always be there for her, no matter what. That's one promise I intend to keep.

The next morning, Benita picks up River, and they head straight to the dining hall to make sure everything and everyone are in place. Considering most of my family can't keep a secret to save their lives, I'm more than shocked when I pick up Mama, and she has containers of muffins packed and ready to go.

"What's this for?" I ask as she hands them over to me to carry.

"I made dessert for the spaghetti benefit. No one even mentioned that, so I thought I'd surprise everyone and bring my famous muffins." She smiles, actin' real proud of herself.

I try hard to hold my poker face because the moment she realizes she baked muffins for her own party, she might die laughing or at least everyone else will.

"Where's River?" Mama asks politely.

"Benita asked her if she'd help, and she agreed." I smile, actually telling the truth.

Mama's pleased with that answer. "That's real sweet of her."

After I place the muffins in the backseat of Mama's Cadillac, I open the door for her.

"Patsy told me a ton of tickets were sold for the benefit. That makes me so happy," Mama says with a big smile, climbing in. On the drive over, I play along, and she doesn't suspect a thing, chatting about how much money they're gonna raise. The story Aunt Patsy and Aunt Charlotte came up with is flawless, and I can't wait to see the look on Mama's face when she realizes everyone's really there to celebrate her birthday.

As we pull into the parking lot, Mama smiles big, excited to see it jam-packed with cars. People are parked on the grass, and some are lined on the street, and I'm almost shocked by how many people showed up. But it's a small town, and there's not too much more for people to be doing on a Saturday afternoon.

She looks over at me as we unbuckle. "I don't think I made enough muffins."

"Mama, they aren't even expectin' dessert. I'm sure it'll be fine."

She nods. "You're right. I just don't like people goin' without."

We get out of the car, and I grab the muffins then follow behind her. The temperature is perfect, and the sky is blue without a cloud in sight as we walk across the parking lot toward the entrance. Making sure to be a gentleman, I open the door for her, and she walks in. The room is packed full, and people yell, "*Surprise,*" just as balloons fall from the ceiling. At first, Mama is confused because she really believed the lie, then she immediately puts the pieces together. She never really makes a big deal about her birthday, and over the years we haven't either, so it's bound to be a shock to her for so many people to care. Covering her mouth with her hands, her emotions take hold, and she holds back tears of joy as Benita, Patsy, and Charlotte all walk up and tell her happy birthday.

"I shoulda known you three were up to somethin'," Mama tells them with hugs. "But I have to admit, you got me. I even made muffins!" She turns and points at the containers I'm holding. I smile, and Benita takes them from my hands and carries them to the kitchen.

Across the room, I see River is laughin' to the point of tears and sitting next to her is Jackson who's obviously running his mouth. Whatever he's saying to her is probably about me and embarrassing as fuck. By how John keeps rolling his eyes, I know it is.

I walk toward them, trying to break up whatever is goin' on, but it doesn't really work. As soon as I make it to the table, River swallows down her laughter, but the big smile on her face doesn't falter. Honestly, Jackson can keep talking, especially if whatever he said makes her this happy.

"What's so funny?" I lift an eyebrow at her, and she snorts.

"Nothing, *cow patty*," Jackson says with a smirk. Now I know why John had that reaction. It's the story that'll never die, apparently.

"And he walked around with cow shit on his ass all day and had no idea. He looked like he shit himself. Even went to town like that." Jackson pats his leg, overly amused with himself.

"River, if you keep encouraging him, he'll *never* stop talking!"

"There was another time Alex decided he was gonna be a big rodeo star," he continues.

I walk over to River, grab her hand, and pull her away.

"Wait, I wanted to hear that story," she says with a grin.

Mama walks up to us, and I give her a big hug. "Love you, Mama. Happy Birthday!"

"Happy Birthday, Mrs. Rose," River says.

Unexpectedly, Mama pulls her into a hug. "Thank you, hon. Thanks for helping set up too. Benita told me. It's beautiful. The decorations. Everything."

"You're welcome." River hugs her back while looking at me over Mama's shoulder with wide eyes. I give her a wink and a grin. It may have taken a little while for Mama to start coming around to the idea of us being together and River having my baby, but I think everything's gonna be just fine.

Soon Aunt Patsy announces it's time to eat and everyone starts lining up and grabbing plates. I take it as my opportunity to introduce River to aunts and uncles, cousins, and family friends. Considering there are so many people here, and our family is so large, I don't imagine she'll be remembering anyone's names, which is okay. We fill our plates with food and grab big glasses of sweet tea, then sit with Benita, Aaron, and Dylan.

River instantly starts chatting with Dylan like they're old friends. "Not been in any large bodies of water lately, right?" River kids.

"No, ma'am. I'm staying away from all beaches and lakes unless I'm in a boat." Dylan laughs, continuing to make small talk.

Just as Dylan starts talking about Key West to Benita, River takes a huge gulp of sweet tea and starts coughing. "What the hell!"

"What?" I ask, sipping my tea.

"How do you drink that? It tastes like overly sweetened toilet water."

The three of us burst into laughter. "No, it doesn't. It tastes like a delicious honey drink." I clink my glass with Dylan's, and we drink it down like it's the sweetest nectar in the south. She pretends to throw up in her mouth a little.

"You better get used to it, River. Us Southerners drink sweet tea by the gallons," Dylan tells her.

"I'd throw up because apparently, I don't have the taste buds for it. Can you get me a bottle of water, pretty please?" River turns and asks me sweetly.

Dylan looks at me like I'm whipped, and maybe I am, but I don't hesitate to get up and grab a bottle of water. When I sit back down, River's laughing at Benita's twins who are too busy playing with their food instead of eating it.

"They're so cute," River says.

Benita winks, then fixes Beau's hair that's sticking up in all different places. "You'll have one of these in about four months. You're going to have the most beautiful baby; I know it. It's fun to imagine what he or she will look like. Do you want a boy or a girl?" She tilts her head and looks at River and me.

"Maybe we'll just have one of each," I joke, but River doesn't laugh.

"I swear, I'm going to hurt you if you keep joking about us having twins."

Benita chuckles. "You're not big enough for twins. No way, especially not Bishop twins. You'd be twice as big and twice as miserable. Aunt Rose talks about how they all weighed ten pounds each, like big ass turkeys."

River stops eating and glares at me. "You were an eleven-pound monster baby? Oh my God."

"Oh yeah. Mama's been taking it out on us ever since. Ask Evan," I tell her.

"Twins. Giant babies. Anything else I need to know?" Her eyes meet mine, and she laughs nervously.

"Nothing I can discuss in front of our current company."

Benita rolls her eyes. "Thanks for sparing me."

As soon as Mama's finished eating, Patsy carries in one of Mrs. Betty's famous chocolate cakes from the kitchen with candles lit. Everyone starts singing "Happy Birthday" just as the cake is placed down in front of her. Mama looks around the room at all the family members and friends, and I can see tears on the brims of her eyes ready to spill over. Dad places his hand on her shoulder with a big grin. She's so damn happy that it's contagious, and there's not a face without a smile in the entire room.

"Make a wish!" I hear Jackson yell from the back of the room, causing everyone to laugh just as Mama leans over to blow out the candles. As soon as she does, we start clapping and hooting and hollering.

"Real quick," Mama says, holding up her hand getting

everyone's attention. The room quiets, and she stands and speaks. There's a softness in her tone as she makes eye contact with each person in the room. "I just want to thank every single one of you for comin' out to celebrate my birthday. This is a day I'll never forget for the rest of my life. Thank you from the bottom of my heart."

Chatter fills the room, and Aunt Patsy immediately leans over and cuts the cake then slaps it on plates and hands them out. River and I take a slice and walk to a table that has pictures of Mama from over the years spread around.

"Wow, your mom is beautiful," River whispers then looks at a photo of her and my father together in high school. "They were so young. Wow! You look just like your dad."

I place my hand on the small of her back. "A lot of people say that. Especially the older ladies that thought my dad was a looker back in the day."

She snickers. "I can't imagine growing up here. Reminds me of a movie. Cowboy hats, horses, ranch life, and your parents are a real-life Southern love story."

I burst into big, hearty laughter, and all I want to do is pull her into my arms and kiss the fuck out of her. "You're too cute."

Tucking hair behind her ears, she looks up at me. The constant pull between us is becoming too much. When her eyes meet mine, everything that surrounds us disappears. In a room full of people, it's just her and me, and I know she feels it too. With one single look, River causes my heart to race, my head to spin, and my body to react.

"You two are plain ol' disgustin'," Jackson says, walking between us and breaking our trance to look at the photos on the table. He's eating his cake real loud with his mouth open like a savage.

"Do you always just appear at the exact wrong time?" I ask, slightly annoyed by him.

"I try my damnedest!" He chuckles, and somehow River and I escape his presence without him noticing too much.

Just as we're about to walk back over to Mama, my phone vibrates in my pocket, and I see it's Courtney trying to FaceTime me. I instantly answer it, and it's so loud in the building that I can barely hear a word she's saying, so I walk her over to Mama and hand over the phone. They exchange I love yous and I miss yous then she hands the phone back.

"Tell River I said hi!" Courtney shouts, and River pops her head into view.

"Hey, Court!"

I have no doubt that if Courtney lived closer, the two of them would be the best of friends. So far, everyone in my family seems to adore River and especially now that Mama seems on board.

"Take care of my dumb brother," Courtney teases with a laugh.

"I'm the smartest brother you have," I tell her defensively, and she just giggles.

"I'd say you're the biggest pain in my ass. Always annoyin' the hell out of me when we were kids."

I narrow my eyes at her. "You're right. I can't even argue about that one."

After we end the call, I pull River close, just needing to be by her. John and Evan walk up to say their goodbyes, and I can tell the party is coming to an end because the room isn't as loud.

"Are you ready to go?" I ask River quietly.

"I thought I'd help Benita clean up," she says, looking around at the mess that's left over.

Confetti is sprinkled everywhere, and it looks like a party train wreck happened with all the streamers and decorations. It'd take Benita a good hour to clean this up alone.

"That's a good idea, and she'd probably appreciate it."

After we help Benita clean the dining hall and all the tables are put back in the storage room, River and I make our way home. It's barely after five in the evening, but we're both exhausted. As soon as we walk through the front door, we both plop on the couch and let out a sigh of relief. The day was busy and full of fun, but it's good to sit in quiet for a minute and decompress after being around so many people.

"I think I need a shower," River finally says. "I just feel…sticky."

"Welcome to Texas, darlin'." I smirk.

River stands, and I can't help but look at her cute little tummy. She notices and gives me a smirk with a quick little eyebrow raise. "Do you want to see?" she asks.

Her question takes me off guard for a moment, but I look back and forth from her belly to her eyes and nod. "Yeah."

Slowly, she lifts her shirt and reveals the cutest little bump. "It almost doesn't look real."

"Trust me, it's real." She chuckles. "The skin is stretching and itching like hell though. Not to mention all the stretch marks that are starting to form." She sighs, curling her lip in disapproval.

I reach for her hand and pull her between my legs. I place a palm on her tummy and press a soft kiss on top. "Stretch marks or not, you're the most beautiful woman I've ever laid eyes on." I wink, meaning every word.

Biting her lip, she pulls her shirt down before she walks to the bathroom.

Damn, she's so sexy. I close my eyes and imagine her straddling me on the couch. Just the fantasy of her has me adjusting myself. It's to the point where being with her is no longer a want. It's a burning need that's poisoning my mind with dirty thoughts.

As the door to the bathroom opens, I turn my head, and soon she's stepping out with a towel wrapped around her petite body. My mouth slightly falls open, and I have to force myself to close it. My eyes don't leave her until she walks into her bedroom.

After she's dressed, we warm up leftovers and eat in front of the TV like an old married couple. Once we're finished eating, River lets out a big yawn.

"I think I'm going to lie down and read my book," she says

with excitement in her tone. "I left off on this one chapter, and now I have to know what happens next."

"Oh, what kind of book?"

Her eyebrow ticks up. "Romance."

"Dirty romance?" I tease.

"Let your imagination wander then go ten steps past that."

"Oh, that's *real* dirty," I tell her as she walks to her room.

Taking off my boots, I place my feet on the couch and flip through the channels, not able to focus on anything until I hear River calling my name.

"Yeah?" I instantly stand and go to her, not even waiting for a reply.

When I walk into her room, she's lying there with a sweet smile on her face. Her blonde hair surrounds her head, and she looks so damn sweet.

"Everything all right?" I ask.

"Yes, come here. Hurry. I think I felt our little peanut flutter," she says, waving me over.

"Really? Will I be able to feel it too?" I sit on the edge of the bed, and the heat of her skin touches mine.

"Oh, I felt it again." River places my hand on her belly, and I almost feel the air still around us as my hand feels her soft skin. We both sit in silence, waiting.

"I don't feel anything," I tell her in a hushed voice.

"Keep talking. It happens every time you say something like he or she's excited to hear your voice!"

I smile at how happy she is. "Okay. So once upon a time, there was a Bishop kid."

"There it is again! Keep going," she encourages, but I don't know what to say.

My eyes flicker to her Kindle, and I pick it up and begin reading out loud.

"I love it when you're a greedy whore, sugar lips. Your cunt is so tight and wet and tastes so fucking good. Your body just aches for my

cock." I gasp, laughing. "River! What the hell is this book you're reading?"

She begins laughing as a hint of blush hits her cheeks, and I continue because I love hearing the sound of her laugh.

"*He rubs his thumb down my pussy and back up again before circling my rosebud between his fingers. He knows it drives me wild, and he won't stop until he feels me come once again.*" I cough, needing to breathe a moment. "Woman. This is some kinky shit. But I kinda like it."

I take a deep breath, and as I get ready to continue, she stops me.

"Okay, okay. Don't read that anymore. It's not appropriate for the little one. But every time you talk, I feel movement. I think he or she likes the sound of your voice. It's good for the baby to hear you talk because then he or she will recognize it after their born."

I grab her hand in mine and squeeze. "I can start reading your books to you every night if you want me to."

"Oh my gosh, no. But then again, it did sound pretty sexy in that accent of yours. Especially when you say 'sweetheart'."

"What was that, *sweetheart*?" I lick my lips, wanting, no —*needing* to taste her.

"Oh, there it is again!" She presses my hand harder on her stomach.

"I can't feel anything yet. But wow. Just knowing there's a life growing inside you right now is making me feel… I can't explain it. It's indescribable. Grateful? Excited? Whatever it is, I'm just so fucking happy I get to experience it with you."

Her green eyes meet mine as we share this special moment together.

We're going to be parents, and every single day it becomes more real.

CHAPTER TWENTY-TWO

RIVER

As ALEX and I walk outside hand in hand, I inhale the fresh, crisp air while it's still breathable in the morning. Early May temps in Texas feel like August in Wisconsin. Hot as hell. And it's only going to get worse.

It's been over two months since I moved, and although there have been many perks to being here during the Wisconsin winters, I'm starting to think I won't survive the Texas summers. My body isn't used to this heat so early in the year, and I've debated stuffing bags of frozen peas in my shirt and shorts.

"Are you excited?" I'm nearly bouncing to the truck. "I can't wait for you to see the baby on the 3D ultrasound."

"Explain to me what that means again?" He opens the door for me and helps me inside. Now that I'm over six months pregnant, and my growing belly is much more noticeable, Alex has definitely been extra protective. A quality I definitely like in him.

Once he rounds the front of the truck and hops inside, I explain. "Well, it provides three-dimensional views of the baby, and you can see all their little features in great detail. A regular ultrasound you can see the outline and sometimes the small facial features, but with a 3D ultrasound, it's like seeing the baby right in front of you. It also provides better analysis of the assessment."

"Oh, I think I've seen one of those before. Makes the baby look like an alien," he cracks, starting the engine. Immediately, I crank on the air because being pregnant is a self-heating oven as it is.

"It does not." I slap his shoulder and scowl.

He looks over at me and winks. "I'm just kiddin', babe." He shifts his baseball cap around and leans over the center console for a kiss. "It'll be the cutest alien baby there ever was."

"Stop it." I crack up laughing at his cuteness but lean in for a kiss anyway.

"So, are we going to find out the sex? Everyone keeps asking me, and I just keep saying it's a boy."

"You're telling people it's a boy?" I chuckle. "What if it's a girl?"

He shrugs, keeping one hand on the steering wheel while he holds my hand in the other. This is as much as we touch, but my body begs for more. I keep holding back, trying to remind myself that we can't rush this like we did the first time. Even though he's been a complete gentleman, it's getting harder and harder to deny the fact that I need him.

I want to strip off his clothes and ride him like a mechanical bull.

Oh God. Now I'm starting to sound like Natalie.

"If it's a girl, I guess she'll be wearing a lot of blue," he teases.

"No way. Pink and purple."

He snorts. "Yeah."

"Then I guess we better settle it today and find out."

"Fine by me." He shoots me a wide smile.

We could've found out when I was twenty weeks, but with the hospital being an hour away and a severe case of morning sickness that day, I ended up canceling my appointment. Since there's only one radiologist available, I had to wait for the next opening, which is today.

"Have you thought of any names?" I ask him when we finally hit the highway.

"Not really. Unless you like Bruno?"

I furrow my brows at him and curl my lip in response.

"That's what I figured. Then nope. Have you?"

"A few, but nothing that's really stuck."

"Well, we have some time to figure it out."

"I guess, but it's going to fly by quick. We have less than three months left. But knowing the gender will help. Then we only have to brainstorm for one gender."

"My money's on it being a boy." He looks over at me and grins.

"Well, knowing my luck, and the fact you have three brothers, I wouldn't take that bet." I chuckle. "Probably is another wild Bishop boy."

"Yee-haw!" Alex shouts.

We arrive at my appointment with five minutes to spare and end up getting in right away. I'm so anxious I can barely contain myself. I've also had to pee for the last half hour, but having a full bladder helps get the best images.

"Doctor Granger asked for some measuring stats, and once I get those, we'll take some pictures of your baby, okay?" the tech tells us as I settle into the seat.

Alex sits next to me, holding my hand and eagerly watching the screen that's hung on the wall across from us.

"The detail is unreal," he whispers. I smile and nod. It really is.

"That's definitely a Bishop nose," I say, laughing.

The tech continues measuring the head, heart, and length of the body. When an ultrasound is performed at twenty weeks, it's a little easier to measure everything, but itching close to seven months means the baby has less room to stretch.

"I think I see it," Alex announces, narrowing his eyes on the screen. "Yup, it's definitely a boy!"

The ultrasound tech pulls her lips in to hide a smile, but I can't.

"That's a leg, you fool!" I laugh so hard, the tech has to stop the wand until my stomach stops moving.

"Oh, come on," he groans. "Here I thought I produced a legend."

I snort and take a deep breath, so the tech can continue.

"This is why I can't take you places," I tease.

He smirks and flashes another wink. Hell. Doesn't he know what those do to me? Or shit, maybe he does, and that's his plan.

After another five minutes, the tech tells us she's finished measuring everything. I see the heart beating rapidly and smile. "Everything looks okay?"

I know she's technically not supposed to say anything since the doctor has to look at the scans first, but she flashes me a grin that reveals what I need to know.

"Everything looked really great."

"So what's the gender?" Alex asks, looking back and forth between me and the screen.

"You really wanna find out? Are you sure?"

"I do, but only if you want to."

I bite down on my lip, contemplating, but decide I do want to know. "Yeah, let's find out!"

The tech moves the wand around until we can see between the legs, and as soon as the baby shifts a little, I see it.

"You see the baby's two legs moving right there?" I point to one side of the screen as we get a view from behind the baby.

"Yeah?" He tilts his head.

"See that thing between it?"

The tech snaps a pic and freezes the frame.

"Wait…" Alex says, narrowing his eyes. "Is that a—"

"That's a penis!" the tech blurts out.

"It's a boy? It's a boy!" Alex jumps out of his seat still holding my hand. My head falls back, laughing at how excited he is right now. "I knew it!"

"Yes, you did." I smile.

He leans down and cups my face before pressing his lips to mine. It's not a quick kiss like we've been sticking to, but one that lingers. It's sweet and passionate, and if we didn't have an audience right now, I'd be tempted to deepen the kiss.

Once we break apart, the tech prints out the pictures and tells us congratulations.

"Thank you," I say before she walks out of the room to give us privacy.

"I can't believe it." Alex sighs.

I grab my clothes so I can change.

"Okay, but we aren't naming him Bruno," I warn.

He snorts, giving me one of his irresistible looks. "We'll see."

Once we're back in the truck, I snap pictures of the ultrasound photos with my phone so I can send them to Natalie and my mom. I add the words "I'm a boy!" to the message and hit send. I promised to keep them updated as much as I can, but there's always so much going on, I often forget. I want to surprise Alex's family and tell them in person.

"Before we go to the mall, I need to find some food," I tell Alex as he pulls out of the parking lot. Since my appointment was this morning, we planned a whole day while we're in the city. I need a few things for the nursery yet, and now that we know it's a boy, we can start gathering more stuff.

He looks at the clock and then back up at me.

"Yes, I know I just ate before we left, but I'm hungry again." I grimace.

He lifts a hand up. "I didn't say a thing."

I throw him a faux scowl. "You didn't have to. I can read your body language pretty well, cowboy."

He smirks, keeping quiet.

"We need to find a gift to send to Courtney and Drew, too. I feel awful they're up there all by themselves now. I wish we could've flown up there with your mom and Benita last week to visit them in the NICU." They could only stay a few days to meet the babies and visit. Since the babies are preemies, they'll be in the hospital at least for a couple months, which I know is hard.

Courtney went into labor ten days ago and had a C-section. Two boys and a girl. All three are in incubators and breathing machines until they gain more weight. I've seen a lot of babies in the PICU and NICU, and it was always devastating to watch the parents cry and beg to hold them. It brings me to tears just thinking about it.

"Babe, what's the matter?" Alex notices the shift in my mood and grabs my hand. "Why're ya cryin'?"

"I'm fine." I swipe the tears away. "Hormones make me way more emotional than I should be."

"We can FaceTime Courtney later if you want? Check on them."

I nod. "Yeah, if she's up for it, I'd love that."

I know Courtney and Drew have friends in California, but there's just something about being stuck in a hospital for hours and days at a time that can drive a person mad. I've seen it too many times to count.

"We should get Courtney and Drew a gift for just them and then something for each of the babies for when they come home."

"Sounds good, sweetheart."

Courtney and I grew pretty close over the past several weeks. Ever since Mama's surprise party, we've texted and FaceTimed to chat about our pregnancies and all the cute baby clothes they were stocking up on. They decided to wait on having a baby shower until the babies were born and back home, so I hope Alex and I will be able to visit when that time comes.

After we stopped to refuel the truck, we stop for food to refuel my belly.

"What are we looking for exactly?" Alex asks when he drives around for a parking spot at the mall.

"Well, we need a crib for starters. A changing table. Dresser and nightstand. Some kind of bassinet. Clothes. Diapers. Humidifier—"

"River," Alex blurts, grabbing my hand to stop my rambling. "If you'd just let Benita and my mom throw you a shower like they want, we could get everything we need and more."

I give him a look; the same one he gets every time it's brought up. "You know how I feel about that."

"About them wanting to shower you with gifts?"

"About taking advantage of their generosity. I barely let Natalie take me out for my birthdays. I just don't feel right taking gifts from people."

"Think of it as them showering the baby with gifts instead."

I flash him another look when he finally finds a parking spot.

"Hey, it's what Southerners do. We throw parties and give gifts. Sometimes all at the same time. Hell, sometimes for no reason at all. Not accepting it is an insult."

"So, you're saying if I don't let them throw me a party, they're going to be insulted?"

"Yes. They enjoy that kind of stuff. They *live* for that kind of stuff. Plus, it'll give you and Mama more time to bond."

I keep my lips tight and force out a smile. "Fine." I grit my teeth.

"That's my girl." He winks. "So we can head back home then?"

I scowl, tightening my grip on his hand. "No. We need a gift for Courtney and the babies, plus something blue so we can tell your family it's a boy. And maybe some new yoga pants because my ass is falling out of these."

He starts to snicker.

"Don't you dare laugh at me. Your huge baby is doing this to me."

"Considering all of us boys are well over six feet tall, my guess is he's going to be big too."

I sigh. "Might as well skip the newborn clothes and go straight to the twelve-month clothing."

"Let's find him a little cowboy hat, too." He grins. I say something smart but just seeing him all excited melts my heart.

We browse the mall for hours until my lower back starts to tighten. Looking down, I see my ankles are starting to swell, too, and that's when I know it's time to sit. We ended up finding matching green onesies for the triplets that read *I'm new here* on the front. Even though we got the zero to three month size, they won't be able to wear them for a while.

I found Courtney a baby journal so she can document everything that happens while they're in the NICU. I've always found that journaling helps me cope with stress and figured she could write in it while she's recovering from her C-section.

Then we found a blue onesie with a matching bib set that reads *I get my looks from my daddy* and plan to show it off to everyone to announce we're having a boy.

Alex was such a champ shopping with me today. He didn't complain once and even pointed out stuff that we should put on our baby registry. Sometimes I'd just stare at him and wonder how I got so lucky to be with a man who's this excited about becoming a father. Not that I wouldn't expect him to be in normal circumstances, but given our situation, I truly had no idea how he'd react to all of this. Considering I barely knew him, there were a handful of reactions I was anticipating, but none like this.

"You're really great, you know that?" I tell him when we're both standing in the nearly empty nursery.

He arches a brow. "You're just now figuring that out?" The corner of his lips tilts up, grinning.

I teasingly roll my eyes and move close. "Are you always this humble?"

"Very."

When I step into his space, he takes advantage and wraps his arms around my waist to pull me even closer.

"Pretty soon, my belly is going to be so big, your arms won't be able to fit."

"Nah. I have long arms." He flashes me a wink and tightens his grip.

I gaze up at him, my eyes telling him everything my mouth doesn't. He leans down and presses his lips to mine. They feel so good; I don't stop or push him away. Hell, I welcome them. I reach my arms around him, fisting my fingers in his shirt. My breath hitches when his lips move down my jawline and suck on my neck. My head falls back, encouraging him, and when he moans against my flesh, I nearly lose it right then.

His lips make their way back to mine, and as he cups my face, I feel the hardness under his jeans rub against me. It's been so long that I'm desperate to touch and taste him again, but I don't want things to change between us. The moment sex is back on the table, I know there will be that shift. Once those boundaries have been crossed, we can't ever go back. We're waiting, building our relationship from the ground up, and making sure what we have is something that can last. Jumping back into bed together can create a whole other set of problems that we don't need.

At this moment, though, I don't let those thoughts stop me from kissing him. His hand roams down my side and grips my ass, pushing my hips harder into his erection. Fuck, it feels so damn good. It makes me want him even more, and I'm ready to throw all our rules out the window because feeling him inside me again is the only thing I can think about.

My fingers cling to him as if my life depends on it. He reaches under my shirt and cups my breast, squeezing. A moan releases from my lips, and just as I grab for his jeans, his phone rings and interrupts our moment.

We break apart, both panting. Alex curses and pulls his cell from his pocket.

"Yeah?" he answers, annoyed.

I try catching my breath, adjusting my bra and shirt. Oh my God. That got out of hand way too fast.

"Fuck. Okay, I'll be right there."

He hangs up the call and looks at me with dreamy eyes.

"Sorry, that was John. He needs help with the horses quick. Apparently, a gate was left open, and they're roaming freely around the B&B."

I lick my lips and nod. "Okay. I'm going to get ready for bed."

He steps forward, closing the gap between us. "I'll be back as soon as I can." He kisses my forehead before walking out of the nursery.

Once I hear his truck rumble to life, I lean against the wall and slide down it. Shit, that was intense. And close. I was nearly ready to rip off his jeans and ask him to fuck me six ways to Sunday.

I'm not sure if Alex and I can ever recreate the intensity we had in Key West, but I know being around him always ignites a fire inside me. Anytime he's near, I can't deny it. One thing I know for sure—if his phone hadn't rung, the small shred of willpower that's been stretched to the max would've finally snapped.

CHAPTER TWENTY-THREE

ALEX

THE DINING HALL is covered in blue from top to bottom. I never knew so much blue existed. Between the tablecloths, decorations, balloons, and streamers, it looks like Cookie Monster exploded in here. Considering it's a baby shower planned by the Bishop family, I'm not even a little bit surprised.

"I'm so excited y'all are having a boy. The twins will have someone else to play with besides each other." I overhear Benita talking to River who's sitting on a chair in the middle of the room. She's smiling, but I know she secretly hates all the attention.

After talking her into letting Benita and Mama host her a baby shower, those two wasted no time in planning. Even after I told them to take it easy, Mama scoffed and told me since she wasn't able to plan Courtney's baby shower, this was her chance to do one right for her grandbaby. Of course, Benita didn't listen to me either. In the center of the room above where River is sitting are large alphabet balloons that read B-A-B-Y with blue streamers twisting along the ceiling.

As if that wasn't enough, Mama called River's mom, their official "meeting," and asked her to send some baby pictures of River. So there are framed baby pictures of River and me scattered all over the hall.

The buffet table is decorated with bright blue bottle-shaped confetti. Mama made her famous shredded beef sandwiches. Aunt Patsy made the potato salad, and Benita brought fruit. There's no such thing as a Bishop gathering without everyone bringing a side dish, so the table is jam-packed. And of course, sweet tea in a big ol' punch bowl. Fortunately, Benita snuck in a bottle of juice for River, so she doesn't have to pretend to like it for fear of being ostracized.

Everything looks way over the top, but what do I know? River's eyes lit up like the Fourth of July when she walked in; whether or not that was a genuine expression is yet to be determined.

Standing in the back with the other husbands, Dylan, and my three brothers, we watch as they pass River presents and squeal at everything she opens. River is wearing one of those sashes that reads *Mom-to-be* as well as a corsage with blue flowers and baby's breath. I had no idea what all the fuss was about until Benita schooled me.

Hell, I'm not even sure what half those items are she's opening.

"What is that?" Jackson leans over and whispers.

Dylan and I narrow our eyes, trying to figure out what the bag and tubes are. "It looks like some kind of bottle," I say with uncertainty.

"It's a backpack of bottles," Dylan adds.

"But the bottles have tubes on them." Jackson folds his arms over his chest as we all stand and analyze the mystery contraption.

"You idiots," Evan mutters.

Aaron snorts, shaking his head at us.

The three of us turn and look at them. "What?" I shrug.

"It's a breast pump," Evan tells us.

"Oh!" we say, accidentally grabbing the girls' attention.

"Everything all right back there, boys?"

"Just fine, Aunt Charlotte," I answer with a smile.

"Why don't one of you boys grab the cake from the fridge so we can serve that next?"

"I'll do it," John says, already walking toward the kitchen.

River continues opening each gift, and every time a new piece of clothing is revealed, they make her hold it up against her stomach oohing and ahhing as she forces out a smile. I can tell she's out of her comfort zone right now, but she's a real trooper about it all.

John brings the cake out, and Aunt Charlotte rushes over to check it.

"Well, what do you think, Daddy-to-be?" She smirks up at me.

"Looks great." I smile, looking at the blue-frosted cake she and Benita made.

Evan comes from behind with a cake server set. "Want me to cut it?"

"No!" Aunt Charlotte blurts out. "River and Alex need to stand behind it so we can take some pictures for the baby book."

"No one said there were going to be pictures," I groan.

"What are you, new? Of course, we're taking pictures."

River walks over after all the gifts are opened looking exhausted.

"Looks like we'll be set for a while." I chuckle at all the gifts sprawled out on the tables. Mama invited the entire family and most of the town. It was also her idea to make it a co-ed party, but I think that was just so she'd have us here to do the heavy lifting.

"I can't imagine one little baby needs all of that."

"Oh, that's because we know there'll be more babies coming down the road." Mama winks, intruding in on our conversation and then leaving like it's nothing.

"What did she just say?" River whispers, panic evident in her tone.

I shake my head at Mama as she watches me from the other side of the table. "She's still holding out hope we have more than one."

"Those Bishops do love to multiply," Mrs. Betty adds, who's

been quiet all day, but the moment more babies come up into the conversation, she's all attentive.

"Well, let's see if I can even survive this Bishop." She points at me and everyone laughs.

Jackson walks toward me and pats me on the shoulder. "It's funny because it's true."

"If anyone's having multiples, it's you," I retort, shrugging his hand off me.

"Nope. I'm always packing."

River snorts and giggles. "So did Alex."

"Okay, well let's take those pictures so we can cut the cake," Mama interrupts flawlessly as she tends to.

We finish up the party with lots of photos and cake. As the guests eat, my brothers and Aaron and I load up all the gifts. Bags of diapers, clothes, and toys take over my back seat, then we put the bigger pieces in the bed of the truck. My parents bought the crib that River picked out as well as various other things but mostly just clothes that say *I love Grandma.* Aunt Patsy gifted us a swing and bouncy seat. Benita stocked us up on baby toys, diapers, and wipes, and told us she'd have lots of boy clothes to pass down to us as well. Between all that and all the other random gifts, there's no way we're going to need anything else for a while.

"Are you ready?" I ask River as she stands around and chats with the guests who haven't left yet. "Truck is locked and loaded." I flash her a wink.

"Yes! I need a nap." She chuckles. "You can put all the furniture together while I sleep."

"Or we could both nap?" I tease.

"Funny. Take me home, cowboy."

I love hearing her say that. *Home.*

"Yes, ma'am." I tilt my cowboy hat at her.

"Oh wait," she squeals, holding her belly. Benita, Mama, and Aunt Charlotte all freeze in place. "He just kicked really hard."

The three of them crowd around River in seconds, placing their hands all over her stomach.

"Where?" Benita asks.

"Over here by my ribs," she says, placing Benita's hand over the area. We wait for a few minutes, and when no more movement happens, they give up. "Maybe next time."

"All right, you kids." Mama walks over. "Get on goin' so we can clean up."

I thank her and kiss her cheek. She swarms River and hugs her. "Take care of my grandbaby in there."

"I will, ma'am." River smiles.

Grabbing her hand, I lead her out to the truck, and before opening the door for her, I push her up against it and kiss her deeply. One of those soul-crushing kisses I know she likes.

"What was that for?" she asks, catching her breath.

"Thank you for today. It meant a lot to my family. And to me."

She tilts her head. "You don't need to thank me. I should be thanking you and your entire family. I wished my mom had been able to come."

"Me too." I brush a piece of blonde hair behind her ear. "Hopefully, she can fly down once the baby's born."

"I hope so."

River and her mom have a complicated relationship, and I'm doing my best to tread lightly when it comes to it and how disappointed River gets anytime she brings it up. I understand that she's the one who moved away, but I wish her parents would make an effort to come and visit her at least.

I drive us home, and River nearly falls asleep before we make it there.

"I'm going to take a nap. Do you mind?"

"Not at all." I kiss the top of her head. "I'll bring everything in."

"Okay." She smiles before walking down to her room.

I jog back outside and grab as many of the gift bags in my hands as I can and carry them to the nursery. Just as I'm hauling one of the larger boxes in, I hear River calling out my name.

"Alex, hurry!"

I set the box down and rush down the hall until I'm in her room. "What is it? Are you okay?"

She's lying on her side with a hand resting on her belly. "Hurry, come here."

Walking over, she pulls up her shirt and reveals her stomach.

"He's kicking."

She grabs my hand and places it near her ribs. "Say something," she tells me.

"Like what?"

"Anything."

"Should I read another one of your romance novels?" I tease, but before she can respond, I feel a big kick against my palm. "Whoa!"

"You felt it!" Her eyes light up. "Keep talking."

"Uh…okay." I kneel on the floor next to the bed and place both palms on her belly. "Maybe I should tell him about the first time I saw you." I grin and shoot her a wink.

"He's a little young to be hearing about the birds and the bees, don't ya think?" She crooks a brow.

"Not the first time we did it. The first time I *saw* you," I clarify. "It was the morning we were both at the continental breakfast, and when you looked over at me and saw that I was already sizing you up, you blushed and looked away like I had creepy-crawlies all over my skin or something."

She chuckles, keeping her hand on top of mine. "That's not true. Don't be telling our son lies now."

"You said *our son*."

"Well, he is."

I can't stop the smile that spreads across my face. "I know. I've just never heard you say it aloud before."

Another hard kick.

"Dang, the little guy is strong."

"I told you. It's your voice."

"Yeah, he likes it." I wink.

"Must be that Southern drawl," she teases. "It's what got me."

My head falls back as I laugh. "Don't lie."

She shrugs. "Okay, you're right. It was the alcohol and the way your tight jeans hugged your ass." Grinning, she moves my hand up a bit farther, just under her breast.

"Well, I was drawn in the moment I saw your mama," I tell the baby, though I keep my eyes on her. She sucks in her lower lip as I continue. "She was wearing tiny little jean shorts and a tight top, so it was hard not to notice her. Then once I heard her speak and put me in my place, I knew I had to have her."

She chuckles, licking her lips. "You and I seem to remember the story differently."

"What?" I shriek, pretending to be offended.

"You were hitting on me with the cheesiest pickup line in the book. Then when that didn't work, you threw your friend into the water as a stunt to get my attention."

I know she's teasing, but I narrow my eyes at her anyway. "Don't believe her, son. The only reason she was on the beach that morning was because she was looking for me."

"Oh my God." She bursts out laughing. "Not true! Natalie and I were drinking and beachin'."

"Right. Just happened to be the exact same beach we were on."

She sinks her teeth into her lower lip, hiding the smile that hasn't faded since I walked in.

"But the moment I knew I really liked your mama," I speak to her belly again, "was the time I had her bent over, and she spread her thighs so wide…"

"Oh my God, Alex!" She smacks my shoulder, but for shits and giggles—and because I love getting a rise out of her—I continue.

"She was nearly begging for it, demanding I get inside her right then or else." I lick my lips and watch her blush, loving the way it's affecting her the same way it's affecting me. Hell, I'm going to need a cold shower after this. "So I spanked her ass hard and slid right in to home base."

"You're terrible," she says, shaking her head. "He's going to be scarred for the rest of his life now."

"Doubtful." I smirk. "He'll be watching way worse by the time he's ten."

"That's gross." She wrinkles her nose.

I wink at her before directing my words back to her stomach. "Then she came on my cock so damn hard, I felt her trembling from the inside. It was the hottest fucking thing."

Her breath hitches, and when I look up at her, I see desire in her eyes. Fuck, I should've thought this through, but seeing her lust after me the same way tells me she's close to cracking.

She swallows hard as she shifts her body. I stand up and lean down, tempted to kiss the fuck out of her like I want. Instead, I press my lips to her forehead.

"Enjoy your nap." I turn and walk out before I change my mind. "Gonna go take a cold shower," I mutter, adjusting my jeans because my cock is so goddamn hard right now.

After bringing in the rest of the boxes, I start working on the crib. I know River's dying to get the nursery set up, and since I'm home today, it's the only time I'll have since I'll be working in the pastures all week.

After two hours of cursing, the crib, changing table, and one dresser are all set up. All that's left is the nightstand and the swing. I decide to take a break and finish the rest after I get something to eat and shower.

I peek inside River's room and see she's sleeping peacefully. As I look at her belly, it still boggles my mind she's carrying our baby. Our son. There are days I'm overwhelmed with emotion that she's really here and that we're going to be a family of three.

Thinking back to those early days in Key West, I was a different man. I'd gone there ready to party and hook up with as many girls as I possibly could. Hell, I was sure I wouldn't be sober till the plane landed back in Texas, but one look at her, and everything changed. I don't know how or why, but they just did.

Something brought us together in Key West at the same time, and I'll never question that fate. She's here, and she's mine.

As I step into the shower, visions of our time together haunt my mind. The words I said to her belly echo in my ear, and I can't help as I replay every instance we were together. Her plump ass, her tits bouncing, her pussy wet. Fuck. It's hard not to get worked up thinking about her.

My cock's hard and every muscle in my body is tense. I haven't fucked anyone since the day I met River, and this waiting game has been sexually frustrating, to say the least. I have no doubt in my mind that'll it be worth it, but that doesn't ease the need.

I palm my shaft and stroke it a few times, fantasizing about River being in here with me. Memories flood in from all the intimate moments we shared, and I'm desperate to feel those again, more than anything, but I know waiting is what's best. But fuck, being around her every day hasn't made that easy.

Tightening my grip, I pump myself faster as I place my free hand on the wall for support. Her gorgeous face, her sweet voice, her stunning eyes. Everything about her flashes through my mind as I envision making sweet love to her again. Those memories of us haunt me, fueling every stroke I make harder and harder until I have nothing left.

CHAPTER TWENTY-FOUR

RIVER

"I miss you so much," I tell Natalie, standing in front of my phone so she can see how big my belly is getting. I've been trying to FaceTime with her as much as possible, so she can be involved, too. When we chat like this, it's almost as if she's here with me, which helps comfort the anxiety that creeps up every once in a while.

"You're the cutest pregnant woman I've ever seen! Nothing but belly. I'm not even kidding. I hope to look half as good as you when I start popping out Adam's spawns." Natalie's been gushing about how great I look during the entire call, and I find it quite comforting considering I feel like a blimp these days.

"You're just saying that because you're my best friend," I quip with a big smile, turning to the side. "Tell me about the wedding details. Did you set a date yet?" I lower my shirt over my belly and walk closer to the phone.

Her face lights up, and her tone goes up in pitch. "We're planning something for the fall, but no exact date yet. As soon as we set it in stone, you'll be the first to know. I can't walk down that aisle without you up there next to me."

"You know I wouldn't miss it for the world. When do you plan to go dress shopping? Anytime soon?"

"Nope, not yet. You know how I am though." Natalie chuckles.

"Procrastination station."

We continue our conversation until I hear a horn honking outside.

"Shit. I gotta go, Nat. Benita is here to pick me up for lunch."

She waves her hand. "Already replacing me, huh?"

"Trust me when I say no one could *ever* replace your obnoxious loud mouth."

Placing her hand over her heart, she lets out an *aww*. We say our goodbyes, and I grab my purse, lock the door, and walk to the car. Benita is singing at the top of her lungs to Taylor Swift, and she's so into her vocal performance, she doesn't hear me knocking on the window to unlock the door.

"Shit," she says when she realizes and turns down the music.

"There's something about T. Swift that gets me all pumped up," she admits.

"Really? I'd think you'd be into that old-time country music," I say as I reach for my seat belt and buckle.

Benita playfully rolls her eyes with a smile. "I'm not a Southern cliché, River!"

I arch a brow, challenging her statement.

"Okay, maybe a little." She shrugs, and I chuckle.

On the way over to the diner, my stomach starts growling, and that's when I realize how hungry I am. By the time we park, I'm ready to eat a damn horse—the whole thing, by myself.

As soon as we walk in, Betty gives us a big wave from across the small dining area and walks over to us with menus.

"Hey, Mama," she says to me, patting my back. "You've been doing okay?"

"Yes, ma'am. I've been really great," I tell her.

She takes our drink order, and as soon as she comes back with them, we order our food. As Betty walks off, Benita excuses herself to call Aaron about the boys. I pull out my phone and take a photo of the diner and shoot it over to Natalie, so she can see how country it is with the western décor randomly placed on the wall.

Just as I get a text from her, Benita returns.

"Took you long enough," I joke, but she doesn't say anything.

I'm so into my phone, that when I look up, I don't see Benita sitting across from me. My smile instantly fades as the blonde woman glares at me with her fingers interlocked together on the table. She's staring, studying, and judging me. Her dark eyes scrutinize me as she narrows them.

"Can I help you?" I ask, returning the daggers she's shooting at me.

A fake smile touches her lips, but it never meets her cold eyes. "You must be the girl who snagged *him*."

My heart races, and I arch a thin brow at her. "What are you talking about?"

"Oh, let me formally introduce myself. I'm Carly." She holds her hand out, but I just look at it as if it's covered in mold, then back at her. I refuse to pretend to be polite, especially when I'm hormonal and hungry. After she realizes I don't have anything to say to her, she lowers her hand and continues.

"Pity you haven't heard about me. By our intense sexual relationship, I really thought I meant more to him. Who knew snagging Alex was as easy as getting knocked up? I might've purposely forgotten to take my birth control and actually had a chance. Nothing like an *accident* to help you rope someone for life. Amiright?" Her smile is more like a sneer, and the shade she's throwing at me isn't lost.

"Carly, is it?" I throw attitude right back at her. "You're probably too dense to understand this, but I'll talk slowly for you. Your words have no impact on my life, and the fact you have to spew hate to a pregnant woman you don't even know shows the type of person you actually are—not me. So if you're done, you can help yourself out." I shouldn't have fed her the attention she's obviously seeking, but she severely underestimated my tolerance for catty bullshit. The rage is building in her eyes, but before she can respond, Betty walks over and places extra napkins on the table. She looks over at Carly and then at me, feeling the tension in the air. "Is everything okay over here?"

"Perfectly fine," I tell Betty, and she searches my face, trying to read me. Unfortunately for Carly, I'm not easily intimidated because of all the shit I've dealt with over the years, and the longer she sits here in front of me, the more pissed off I become. Betty walks away, but I see the skepticism on her face.

"Well, sweetie. You see, I was on my way out when I saw you sittin' here and just had to meet the talk of the town. The Northerner who's been able to tame the untamable guy who's broken more hearts than even he can count. But let me fill you in on a little secret," she hisses, leaning across the table and her voice drops even lower. "It's not just me who doesn't like you, honey. And trust me when I say there's a line of women ready to rip Alex's balls straight off for what he did to them. So the next time you're in the grocery store and a woman's giving you the side-eye, more than likely her heart was destroyed by Alex Bishop, too. It's how he is—the Bishop curse. He'll treat you real good, make you feel like you actually mean something to him, then when he's bored of you, he'll drop you like a bad habit. I'm sure it's just a matter of time until your time is up, too. Bet you'll find out soon enough since his commitment issues run deep. But maybe not, considering your *situation*. It's a small town, and he got around, just like the news of you, if you know what I mean." She gives me a fake ass smile just as Benita walks up fuming. I've never seen her this mad, ever.

"What the fuck is this?" Benita asks between gritted teeth.

"*Benita*," Carly says as she slides out of the booth and walks out of the diner.

I don't realize my hands were balled into fists until I feel my nails digging into my palm. It's been years since I've been this mad. I shake my head, not wanting to believe everything I just heard, but it's hard not to because he's told me from the beginning he doesn't do relationships.

"What the hell did she say?" Benita is so mad her hand is trembling.

I shake my head, but Benita encourages me to tell her.

"She basically said Alex is known for sleeping around, and he'll probably get sick of me, just like all of them. The line of them." My voice sounds weak.

Betty sets our food in front of us, and unfortunately, my appetite vanished the moment Carly sat down and opened her big mouth. Benita doesn't touch her food either.

"Is it true? Am I the town joke right now because I'm with Alex?"

Letting out a long sigh, Benita gives me a soft smile. "You are *not* the town joke. If she said that, she's a liar. They're all just jealous, River. And yeah, maybe Alex is known for his history with women, but that's because no one was ever good enough to steal his heart the way you did, and they resent you for that."

I take a bite of mashed potatoes, and they taste so damn good I can't ignore my food regardless of not feeling like eating.

"Do you think he's with me just because I'm pregnant, and he's the perfect gentleman, so he's forcing himself to do the right thing?" I know it's crazy to even think that considering how close we've grown these past few months, but I can't help thinking that maybe it's been too good to be true.

Benita gives me a look that tells me I'm crazy. "*Hell no*. Before you came here, you're all he talked about. He stopped dating. He stopped going out. He worked, slept, and refused to move on. It was River this, and River that. Key West this, and Key West that. It was sickening how obsessed he was with you and really annoying because it was *all the time*. He's not the man Carly knows. Alex has changed for the better, and it's all because of you. I know my cousin, and I know what love looks like. Trust me when I say there's a happy ending to all this that starts with a beautiful couple who is starting a beautiful family together." Benita grabs my hand and squeezes. I give her a small smile in return.

"Thank you. I really hope you're right." I let out a breath.

We continue with the small talk as we finish eating, but the mood is sour, and we both can feel it. Benita tries to make me laugh and smile, and she wins sometimes, but it doesn't stop the insecurities from bubbling inside me. Mrs. Betty knows something happened, too, and after we pay, she hands me a to-go box with a big slice of her famous chocolate cake because cake makes everything better. She gives me a big hug, rubs my belly, then sends me on my way.

On the drive home, I stare out the window, and Carly's words play on repeat in my head.

"Don't let it get to you," Benita says as she parks in front of my house. "If you do, she wins. She's a drama queen and attention whore who's just trying to get a rise out of you. Why do you think they call her Crazy Carly?"

I snort at that.

"Promise me you'll stop thinking about it," she pleads.

I give her a smile, not willing to make a promise I can't keep. "I'll try," I tell her because that's the best I can do in my current state. We exchange a hug goodbye, and I go inside and try to busy myself until Alex comes home.

ALEX

As soon as I walk in, I can tell there's something wrong. The look in River's eyes is unsettled, and I don't like it one bit. I'm exhausted from herding cattle all day, but nothing can stop me from figuring out what's going on.

"Hey, Darlin'. Everything okay?"

She swallows hard as she sits on the couch and looks up at me. I stalk toward her and wrap my arm around her shoulders, but she doesn't lean into my touch the way she usually does.

"What is it?" I ask, concerned.

"Well, I met Carly today," she finally says.

That's all I need to know to understand the issue.

"*Crazy* Carly?" I ask.

"Apparently."

"You know we call her that for a reason, right? Because she's a psychopath. Ask Dylan if you don't believe me."

"Well, she told me things about you that have made me feel uneasy all day. Things that are true. About your past. How you couldn't settle down with anyone, basically. Everything she said played on all my insecurities, and it makes me afraid that you're not capable of settling down long-term. That you're going to get bored of the baby and me and want out because when all of this isn't new anymore, you'll realize it was a big mistake. It's nothing you've done, Alex, but I'm terrified you'll go back to your old ways."

I hold her cheeks in my hands and force her to look into my eyes. "No fucking way. *Never.* You'll be by my side as long as there's breath in my lungs and a beat in my heart. Do you even understand what you mean to me, River? What our unborn child means to me? I may've been like that in the past; I won't deny it. I have no reason to. I've been straightforward with you since day one and will continue to always be. I did some bad shit, I know, but I'm not that man anymore. Before Key West, I couldn't see a future with anyone—mostly because no one made me feel the way you did—but now I don't see a future without you in it. You and our baby are everything to me. If anything, you're gonna have to get rid of me, River, because I'm not going anywhere unless you want me to. Simple as that. Darlin', you've tamed me more than any woman ever could. You're the stars of my night, the love of my life, and the only person who has ever been able to steal my heart. I'll spend every day proving that to you. And you know what, sweetheart. It's yours. You can keep it. Because I love you, River Lancaster. I love you so damn much."

Her face softens right before my lips crash into hers with so much fervor that I'm blinded by the emotion in our kiss. I can't get enough of the way she smells and tastes or the soft moans that escape her lips as our tongues intertwine. As I consume her, everything she is, I'm greedy and need more. I want to go to the next level, but somehow, I find the strength to pull away. Our lips are swollen, and bodies are full of want and desire, but it's best if we don't go too far off the ledge because together we'll fall and destroy the boundaries we've worked so hard to keep. Just because I said those three words doesn't mean we fall into bed together. I respect her more than that.

By the time we catch our breath, she leans over and places her hand on my cheek, pulling me back to her greedy lips. "I love you too, Alex. I always have. I'm sorry I ever doubted you."

Her words rush through me in full force, and I've never experienced happiness on this level. To have the woman I love with every fiber of my being love me in return is the greatest high in the world. River leans forward and paints her lips with mine in slow, precise movements. With every breath, she encompasses and captures me, and I hope she never lets me go.

CHAPTER TWENTY-FIVE

RIVER

"I SWEAR TO GOD, Natalie. I'm going to be pregnant forever." I groan, placing a bag of frozen peas on my neck. "And it's so fucking hot. Texas is hell. That's what it is. This ninety-something degree weather is for the damn birds." I'm going off, I know, but I'm so damn miserable.

"So I guess you're adapting to the heat," she teases.

"I hate you so much right now." I narrow my eyes at her, but my cell service sucks out here and keeps freezing during our FaceTiming.

"I know, babe. You hate everyone." She chuckles, clearly amused by my misery.

"How can I have another six weeks of this? That feels impossible. This baby is going to pop out of my belly button."

I hear Adam snort in the background, and just then Alex walks into the living room.

"Is it safe to come in? It doesn't sound very safe."

"Run, Alex! Run!" Natalie shouts when she hears his voice.

Alex laughs from behind me as he wraps his arms around my waist and kisses my cheek.

"Oh my God," I nearly scream, pushing Alex away. "What is that ungodly smell?

"Crap, sorry. Yeah, that's cow shit."

I look back at my phone and Natalie is losing her damn mind, laughing so hard I'm worried she'll pee herself. I pretend to sob and press my face up to my phone screen. "Help me. *Please*."

"You made your bed, girl. Now lie in it. Or rather, lie in shit."

"You're the worst best friend in the world," I deadpan.

Alex chuckles, kicking his shoes off and unbuttoning his jeans.

"What are you doing? Natalie can see you," I remind him.

"Shh, don't stop him," she whispers before Alex can respond. "I wouldn't turn that away if his hair was on fire."

"You know I'm right here," Adam interrupts.

"Like she cares?" I joke. "Should've seen her at the beach googly-eyeing all the man meat."

I turn around and see Alex has tossed his jeans. Then he wraps his arm around his neck to pull his shirt off. Oh God, help me. I love it when he does that. The way he fists the fabric and shreds it off his back. I feel my ovaries combusting all over again.

"Sweet baby Jesus." Natalie's words interrupt my dirty thoughts.

My eyes widen, and that's when I take the phone and end the call.

"That wasn't very nice," Alex says with a sexy smirk on his face.

"You were two steps away from giving her the full strip show."

"Well, I didn't want to walk through the house with shit on my clothes. I was going to jump in the shower."

"You couldn't have done that in the kitchen?" I scold.

"I could've, but then I would've missed how flush you get when I take off my clothes." He winks, and I swallow hard to contain myself.

He walks out in only his boxers, giving me a perfect view of his ass. Damn him. He's doing this on purpose.

Later that night, we snuggle on the couch and watch a movie after dinner. I'm starting to really get used to this lifestyle of ours.

Alex works a lot and sometimes really long days, but I love the feeling knowing he's coming home to me. He's always close by if I need him, and that security reassures me that everything is going to work out the way it's supposed to.

Ever since Alex told me he loved me two weeks ago, I can't get enough of it. We're continuing the no-sex part of our relationship, which is fine by me considering I look and feel like a whale. But our heated kisses tell me everything I need to know.

He's not going anywhere.

Crazy Carly and Jealous Jenna and Petty Penelope—or whoever was his past—no longer matter. I won't let his past come between our future.

I end up falling asleep on the couch and vaguely remember Alex carrying me to my room and tucking me into bed. His lips brushed along my cheek before I fell deeper into sleep.

"Holy fuck," I shout, sitting up in bed. A sharp pain stabs me in the back, waking me up from a dead sleep. Pressing my hand against my lower back, I trying adding pressure to where the pain is, but it doesn't let up.

"Shit," I mutter, shifting my body to see if that works. I've never felt this kind of pain before, and it feels much worse than just a regular back spasm.

I sit on the edge of the bed and try taking a few deep breaths. The stabs keep coming, stronger now, and I'm worrying it might be the start of labor.

"Alex!" I shout through the pain. I'm not sure he can hear me, so I say his name again. When I get no response, I reach for my phone and call him. I don't hear his phone ringing in the next room or him, so I somehow manage to get up and walk into the hallway. "Alex! I think the baby's coming!"

I thought for sure that'd wake him up, but since it's two in the morning, he's probably in a dead sleep. I knock on his door before walking in, another sharp stab riveting down my spine. "Fuck!"

Flicking the light on, I look around and see he's not in bed. The sheets are pulled back, but he's not here. "What the hell?"

I search the bathroom next, and it's empty. Then I walk into the living room and kitchen—nothing! Where the hell could he be in the middle of the night?

"Ah! Oh my God!" I lean over the kitchen table, panting and trying to breathe through the pain. About thirty seconds go by, then I'm able to walk back to my room and grab my phone. I call him again with no answer, then text him. My entire back feels like it's contracting, and I'm so goddamn pissed that Alex isn't here.

Why the hell would he leave in the middle of the night and not tell me when he knows I'm eight months pregnant?

I decide to call John next just in case there was another cattle emergency. When he doesn't answer, I call Jackson. "Fuck," I shout. Evan's phone is always on, but I hate to call him since he lives a half hour away. He probably works in a few hours, too, but after calling Dylan and not getting a response, I have no choice but to call him.

"River?" he answers, picking up right away. "Everything okay?"

"No," I whimper. "I think I'm going into labor, and Alex isn't home. He's not picking up my calls."

"What's wrong? Did your water break?"

"No, but I woke up with these really sharp stabbing pains in my back, and they last for about thirty seconds, but they take my breath away. They just came out of nowhere."

"How much time between when they stop and start up again?"

"Um…I don't know. A few minutes, maybe?"

"Okay, hang tight. I'm on my way."

I feel so unprepared even though I've been reading *What to Expect When You're Expecting* with Alex for the last couple of months. He surprised me one day when he came home and said he'd ordered it for me. I started reading it while he was at work all day, then when he'd get home, I'd recap all the highlights, so he knew some of the basics, too. I've worked with kids and babies for years, but it just feels so different when you know it's going to be yours, and you have to take this baby home and raise it.

Another sharp pain rips through me, and I swear they're getting more and more intense. I text Alex three more times before calling again and leaving another voice message. Finally, as my last resort, I call Mrs. Bishop.

"Hello?" she answers, sleep evident in her voice.

"Hi, I'm so sorry to wake you, but I can't find Alex. He's not answering his phone, and neither are Jackson and John. Do you know if there was an emergency or anything that he would've needed to leave for?" I ramble on as quickly as I can, then wonder if she caught any of that.

"River, darlin' is that you?"

"Yes, ma'am. I'm in a lot of pain, and Alex isn't home. Do you have any idea where he could be?"

She curses under her breath, and I hear her muttering her husband's name. "Scott, wake up. Did you send the boys out recently?"

A few silent moments pass until I finally hear his mumbled response. "No, why?"

"River's on the phone looking for Alex."

"No idea."

"Sorry, dear." Her voice is louder as she speaks directly into the phone. "Are you okay? Do you want me to come over?"

"Evan's on his way. He was the only one who answered."

"Okay, well you call back if you need anything or have any updates, all right? If I hear from Alex, I'll tell him you're looking for him."

I thank her before hanging up, and another sharp stab jerks my body off the bed.

"Holy fuck. This is intense." I lean over the bed, my palms flat and my legs straight as I breathe through it. Once it slows to an annoying, dull ache, I sit back down. I'm so goddamn mad at Alex right now. Where the fuck is he?

Anger boils through me as I think about his past and if I can really depend on him during times I need him the most. He promised me. Said he'd always be here for the baby and me.

Then where the hell is he?

I'm lying on the bed for twenty minutes trying to breathe through the pain when I hear someone walk in.

"Alex?" I sit up, but I'm disappointed when I hear Evan.

"No, it's me." Evan steps into my room, wearing his dark blue scrubs and carrying a bag. I wonder if he sleeps in those damn things, considering it's all I see him in.

"How'd you get here so fast?"

"Went eighty the entire way."

"You trying to kill yourself?"

"No, but I'm going to kill my brother. I called him ten times."

I groan. "Join the club."

"Show me where it hurts."

I point to my lower back and wince. "Radiates all the way up my spine."

"How have they been since you called me?"

"They've been feeling more intense, but that's probably because my blood pressure is skyrocketed with anger."

"That tends to happen when you're in pain, too. I'm going to find you a heating pad and see if that helps the pain. You're about thirty weeks?"

"Thirty-four," I clarify.

"Still too early," he states. "As long as your water doesn't break, you can stay here and wait to see if the contractions slow down. Once they're five minutes apart consistently for an hour, then it'll be time to get you to the hospital."

"You really think I could be in labor?"

"I don't know. Early labor signs are common, but you can't ever be too careful. My guess is Braxton Hicks, but I don't want to rule out early labor just yet."

Evan tells me to get comfortable in bed as best as I can and searches for the heating pad. Once he returns, he helps me adjust my body, so it rests on my lower back.

"How's that?" he asks after a few minutes.

"Good, the heat seems to be helping."

"I'm going to set my stopwatch and keep a timer on my phone. Tell me when you feel another contraction coming, and I'll keep track. If they don't let up, I'm calling your doctor."

I swallow. "Okay." As mad as I am at Alex right now, I just want him here. I don't want him to miss this. Though considering no one seems to know where he is right now, I can't help but worry about him too.

Fifteen minutes go by when Evan's phone rings. "It's John."

He picks up and answers. "Hey." Pause. "He did what? Oh, for fuck's sake." Another pause. "I'm with River right now. She was having contractions and couldn't get ahold of Alex." Another brief pause. "I'm going to kick his ass."

He hangs up, and I can tell it's not good news.

"Dylan's driving him back here right now. Jackson threw a party, and John called him to come handle it since he was out, then when John got back home, they were all drinking. Dylan, too, but he's sobered up enough to bring Alex back."

"Wait, what? They were drinking?"

"I guess." He shrugs.

Grinding my teeth, I bite my lip. So many questions swirl around in my mind, and the anger that formed earlier is now in full force. I can understand him doing John a favor and making sure the party doesn't get out of hand, but why the hell would he then drink himself knowing I'm home. He couldn't even consider sending me a text, so I knew where he was. He didn't even bother to check his phone to see that we've all been calling him! God. I'm so pissed.

"Another one," I tell Evan so he can start his timer again. Luckily, the gap between them has slowed down, but they're intense. He's been so nice to sit with me and talk me through all of this. He explained back labor and how some women get it worse than others, whereas some don't get it at all and suffer from cramps in their abdomen.

"Twenty seconds," Evan tells me once I motion that it's done. "They're not lasting as long, so that's a good sign."

"The heating pad really helps," I say, lying on my side with pillows surrounding me. "I think I'm going to be sleeping with this for the rest of my life."

He chuckles. "As long as you don't keep it on too long at one stretch."

"I won't."

Ten minutes later, we both hear a commotion coming from the side door. I hear Dylan mumbling as shit is being knocked over.

"For Christ's sake," Evan mutters, stalking out of my room and stomping down the hallway. Shit, he's just as pissed as I am.

"Are you fucking kiddin' me?" I hear Evan roar.

"Evan?" Alex asks, and I can tell he's wasted by the high pitch of his tone. His voice slurs, and he's chuckling at nothing. "What're ya doin' here?"

"Alex, I told you," Dylan pipes in. "Evan's helping River."

"Oh right," he says, lazily. "Is she okay?"

"IS SHE OKAY?" Evan shouts, making me jump. Holy fuck. "She's been in excruciating pain while wondering where the fuck you are. You know how to answer a goddamn phone?"

"Dude, chill," Alex snaps, and then I hear some stumbling.

"Are you fuckin' serious?" Evan growls. "Don't push me, Alex. I know you're wasted off your ass right now, but you fucked up, man."

"Let's just get him into bed, so he can sleep it off," Dylan suggests. I'm tempted to walk out there and give Alex a piece of my mind, but I doubt it'd make any difference right now.

"Yeah, get his ass to bed."

"Whatever," I hear Alex mutter.

"Don't come crying to me when River leaves your ass again. You did this to yourself." Evan's voice is harsh, and I wonder how things are going to change between us now. The pain shifts from my back directly to my heart. How could Alex do this to me?

"Shut the hell up," Dylan shouts. "Both of you."

I hear footsteps as Dylan walks Alex to his room next to mine. "I'm not undressing you," he says. "But I'll take off your damn shoes."

"Don't touch me. I'm fine," Alex slurs. "Let me talk to River."

"I don't think that's a good idea."

"She's my woman, Dylan. Get the fuck out of my way."

Evan's standing in my room, arms crossed and shaking his head. I hadn't even realized I was crying until tears start falling from my cheeks.

This is what I've been afraid of since the start. Completely heartbroken.

"River!"

He walks down the hall and stumbles into my room. Evan holds an arm out to keep him from falling. "She's resting," he tells him in a lower voice.

"What happened?"

"She's been having Braxton Hicks contractions. It's where the body starts practicing for labor—"

"Yeah, I know," Alex interrupts. "So she's not in active labor?"

"I don't think so. They've slowed down, and the heating pad seems to be helping for pain."

Alex walks toward me and drops to his knees so our faces align. He looks like absolute hell. He can barely keep his eyes open, and his face is pale. There's no doubt in my mind he's going to be sick as hell tomorrow.

"I'm really sorry, sweetheart." His voice is so low, it's almost torture to hear.

I inhale deeply as another jab comes, but I do my best to push the pain away.

"I could've been in labor, and you would've missed it," I say, softly. "I really needed you tonight."

He grabs my hand and hangs his head. "I let you down. I'm so, so sorry."

I squeeze his hand three times, but I don't plan to let him off that easy. "Why don't you go to bed and sleep it off?"

"No, I'm not leaving you again. I want to help."

"You're drunk," I remind him. "And Evan's here, so I won't be alone."

I feel his body tense up at the mention of his brother's name. Evan's a professional, and I trust him, but that's all this is. I've done my best to get close to Alex's family, but Evan isn't around as much as the others. However, after tonight I feel like I'm getting closer to him now, too.

"You sleeping this off is the only way you're going to help her," Evan interrupts. "I'll stay with her till the contractions stop."

Alex swallows, keeping his lips tight. "Wake me if anything else happens," he tells Evan when he helps him off the floor.

"Yeah, I will." Evan pats Alex on the back.

"I love you." Alex bends and kisses my forehead.

Another hour passes, and the contractions have dulled to almost nothing. "You can leave," I tell Evan. It's almost eight in the morning, and I doubt he slept much before I called him.

"I don't mind. I'll stay for another hour, then I have to leave for my shift."

"Evan…" My voice lingers, but exhaustion is starting to take over. "How are you going to work after being up all night?"

The corner of his lips curls up, amused by my question. He's leaning on the wall closest to my bed and has been for most of the night.

"What? You think you're the first girl to keep me up all night before a long day at work?" He winks, and I can't help but laugh at that.

"That's the most Bishop thing I've ever heard you say."

CHAPTER TWENTY-SIX

ALEX

I'VE NEVER SOBERED up so fast in my life. The moment I saw River in pain lying in bed, it was like the whiskey never happened. God, I felt like the biggest piece of shit as soon as I heard she was having labor pains. Had I known, I would've never gone over to John's house to check on things like he'd asked. I should've known better though. Jackson has a way of encouraging me to drink, and before I knew it, I was six shots and several beers in.

It's noon before I wake up, and I immediately feel everything I ate yesterday start to come up. Rushing out of bed, I whip open my bedroom door and make it to the bathroom just in time. I empty my stomach contents but still don't feel any better.

Fuck! Today's gonna suck.

I hear the door creak and footsteps walk in, and when I peek up, it's not River I see.

"Alexander Scott Bishop."

Mama.

She's pissed, to say the least. She taps her foot and crosses her arms over her chest. Her lips are in a firm line, and I know I'm about to get an earful.

I stand and grab the towel to wipe my face.

"What are you doing?" I ask, treading carefully.

291

"Came to see if my youngest son hit his head and suffered a concussion because that'd be the only excuse for your behavior last night."

Partying with Jackson and nursing a hangover isn't something new, but Mama hadn't known about that side of me. At least not the extent of it, so I know she's about to give me a lecture.

"I drank too much. I know, Mama. You don't need to scold me." I walk past her toward River's room. When I peek inside, I see she isn't in there. Mama follows as I walk to the living room then the kitchen next. "Where's River?" I start to panic, and when I look at Mama's face, I see disappointment all over her features.

"Benita drove her into the city, so she could get checked out by Dr. Granger."

"Fuck." I scrub my hands over my face and inhale deeply. I reach for a glass and fill it with water.

"She could have the baby any day now, Alex," she warns me, even though I already know this. "You need to be here. No excuses."

"Mama," I say, setting my glass down harder on the counter than I mean to. "I know. I fucked up, and I plan to make it up to her."

"Listen to me, son." She grits through her teeth, her tone grabbing my attention to her face. "First, you will watch your language around a woman, do ya hear me? Next, you'll be doing a lot more than making it up to her. You make things right, you get me?"

I furrow my brows, tilting my head. "Make things right?"

She nods, curtly.

"You want me to marry her," I confirm, exhaling. "Mama, it's not about me not wanting to marry *her*. It's about if she wants to marry *me*. I love River more than anything in this world, and I'd gladly spend the rest of my life proving that to her."

She flashes a relieved smile. "Good."

"But just because she's pregnant doesn't mean it's the right time to get married."

"Fine, but you apologize to her for your behavior last night and vow to never do it again. She'll forgive you. I see the love she has for you in her eyes. Your daddy has done countless things to piss me off, but I always forgive him. We're human, after all."

"I will, Mama. I promise. Last night was the first time in nine months that I drank like that. It's never gonna happen again." Nothing is worth losing River over.

She pats my cheek, a little too roughly, though, and smacks it. "Good boy. That's what I like to hear."

"Do you know when she'll be back?"

"I imagine in a couple of hours. So take a shower and get cleaned up. You have some groveling to do."

Three weeks have passed since River's Braxton Hicks started, and even though I royally fucked up that night, she's forgiven me. I've apologized countless times, but it's more than just telling her. I'll show her until the day I die.

I'm so grateful she's given me a second chance because I don't plan to leave her side ever again, and I'll do whatever it takes to prove that to her.

"So how're things going?" Dylan asks as we wrap up for the day. I'm covered in mud from working with the horses. It rained last night, and water pooled in the fields.

"Good, I think. River's miserable, though."

"Yeah, this summer's been a bitch. Especially this month," Dylan says.

"July is brutal. I feel bad she wasn't able to watch the fireworks last week." The central air has been cranked for weeks, and even though I offered to drive her out for the fireworks show and stay in the car with her, she was persistent on staying home.

"She's gonna go stir-crazy if she stays holed up all day and night," he tells me.

"Yeah, I know. On top of being hot as fuck, she can't get comfortable sitting or lying down, so she's not sleeping much. I read to the baby in hopes it'll help her relax enough to fall asleep, but she always wakes up a couple of hours later with back pain."

"That means it's gonna be soon." He pats me on the back.

"Doctor said she measured at three centimeters already, but that means it could be now or another two weeks. Honestly, though, I don't think River has another two weeks in her."

Dylan chuckles. "He'll come when he's ready."

I snort. "Don't say that 'round River. Natalie told her the same thing the other day, and she *growled* back at her."

"Good to know." He laughs. "Did you guys pick a name yet?"

"I think so, but we aren't revealing it till he's here." I smile, thinking of our talk a few nights ago. River had a list of names she liked and asked for my approval on which ones I liked best.

"Well, good luck." He gets into his truck, and I follow suit getting into mine. I need to shower badly. Once I'm cleaned up and eat, I plan to rub River's back and feet and anything else she needs. She's texted me about fifty times today, and even though the heating pad helps, it's not enough. I feel awful.

"River?" I call out as soon as my shoes hit the floor of the kitchen.

"In here," she shouts from her bedroom.

I quickly strip down to my boxers to avoid getting mud on the carpet. Setting my hat down, I brush a hand through my hair to remove the dust. When I round the corner and see her lying in bed, my shoulders fall.

"How ya doin', sweetheart?" I walk over and kneel beside her.

"I went walking today."

"In this heat?" My eyes widen.

"No, Benita picked me up, and we walked around the dining hall."

"Why?"

"It's supposed to help jump-start labor. Then I did squats and bounced on a big ball."

"Oh man." I suck in my lower lip to hide my smile. "Didn't work, huh?"

She groans. "Well, do you see a baby?"

I bite the inside of my cheek and shake my head. "Sorry, darlin'. He's just not ready yet."

"I'm thirty-seven weeks. That's technically full-term. He can come any day now," she whines.

"I know, but according to the book, you could go as long as two weeks over your due date."

She tightens her lips and scowls at me. "Fuck that book. I am *not* going another five weeks. I will pull this baby out myself if I have to."

Swallowing hard, I realize there's no reasoning with her right now. I know not to take it personally when she snaps at me like this. *Hormones*, I remind myself.

"I'm going to take a shower quickly, then how about I rub your feet for a bit?"

Her shoulders relax, and as she nods, she starts crying.

"River?" I hold her face in my hands and kiss the top of her nose. "Baby, it's gonna be fine. We'll get through this, okay?"

"Whoever said pregnancy was beautiful is a liar," she grumbles.

"If I remember correctly, you said those exact words last month."

She blinks and looks up at me, her scowl on point as she groans. Okay, probably not the best thing to say.

"Do you need anything before I hop in the shower? I'll be ten minutes tops otherwise."

"Could you get me some of that Butterfinger ice cream in the freezer?" she asks, wiping her eyes.

"Oh, um…I think you finished that off last night after dinner." I cringe, regretting not buying another pint when I was at the grocery store.

Her head falls back on the pillow as she mutters, "*Fuck*." I'd offer to run into town and buy her more, but I have a feeling she'd change her mind by the time I returned and want something else.

I quickly shower and scrub all the dirt off my skin. Being outside all day has me covered in sweat. I try to dry off throughout the day, but it's not easy keeping up with the heat.

Once I'm washed and dried, I walk back to my room and grab a pair of gray sweats and a dark blue T-shirt. I shake out my hair, and when I walk back to River's room, I see she's finally fallen asleep.

Oh, thank God.

I know she probably won't sleep for long, but she needs it.

Stepping into the nursery, I look around and smile. River's been working hard on getting it ready. All the baby clothes are washed and hung. The diapers and wipes are both stocked. She picked out the cutest crib bedding set with a ranch theme. Cows, horseshoes, and cowboy boots are displayed on the quilt. The sheet has cowboy boots and stars on it—perfect for our little guy.

Mama, Aunt Charlotte, and Aunt Patsy have all made us blankets. Benita made a special blanket, too, with *Bishop* crocheted on it. This baby is definitely going to have everything he needs and more. As the days tick by, I find myself more and more excited, but I'm nervous too. I haven't been around babies like River, but I like to think I'll catch on and already plan to be up with River when he wakes up for feedings or changings.

The rocking chair is in the corner next to the nightstand and lamp. I made some floating shelves for all the books we received and are displayed next to the chair as well. Everything's in place and perfect. I can't wait to hold him for the first time and bring him home *finally*.

After I grab myself something to eat, I peek in on River once more and am relieved when she's still asleep. I head to my room and decide to watch some TV and relax.

I'm dozing in and out, my head bobbing up and down when I hear footsteps in the hallway. My door slams open, and River walks in like she's on a mission. Her long, blonde hair is pulled up, and she's breathing heavy.

"What's wrong?" I pop up, looking at her. "You okay?"

"Take off your clothes," she demands as she starts pulling down her shorts.

"Wait. What?" I ask, jumping up.

"You heard me, cowboy." She kicks her shorts off and flings them across the room.

"River, what are you doing?" I tread carefully, making sure I'm reading the situation correctly.

"I want to have sex."

"Now?" I arch a brow. "I thought we were waiting, taking things slow and all that."

"Slow ended weeks ago. Any slower and my vagina is going to fall off." She's completely serious, but I'm certain this is the hormones talking again.

"Sweetheart…" I walk toward her, closing the gap between us and cup her face in my hands. "Don't take this the wrong way, because I absolutely want to make love to you, but I want to respect your wishes. Building our relationship from the ground up, starting fresh, and having a solid foundation. We don't have to have sex to prove our love to each other. I'm not going anywhere, I promise."

"It's time," she says softly.

"Darlin'…"

"Hey, you owe me."

"Huh?

"You said you'd do anything to make it up to me when you went out and got drunk that night."

I try to hide my laughter but fail. "River, you're acting like making love to you would be a chore. Trust me when I say I've had to pray for some serious willpower to stop myself around you. I've dreamed of making love to you again, so believe me, I fucking want to—desperately. But I want to make sure it's what you *really* want and not just because you're hoping it induces labor."

Her shoulders drop, and she pouts. "Damn, I forgot you read that book cover to cover."

I smirk. "Twice."

"Okay."

I bring our mouths together and tangle our tongues as we kiss deeply. She fists her hands in my T-shirt and pulls us closer. Fuck, she tastes good. I feel the way she arches her hips against me, and that willpower I was just talking about is diminishing by the second.

"River, stop." I pant against her lips.

"No." She wraps her hands around my waist, pushing my erection into her stomach. "Please, Alex."

Goddamn, is she *begging*? Fuck me.

"I want to make you feel good, sweetheart, I do. But I'm afraid after all this time waiting, I'm going to end up hurting you. Or the baby."

"You won't, I promise."

She reaches for my cock and begins rubbing it. Considering I'm wearing sweatpants, there's not much fabric between us.

"I'm so damn horny, Alex. My hormones are going insane."

I snort, pressing our foreheads together and moaning when she increases her pace.

"So take off your damn pants."

"River." I plead with my voice, though I don't want her to stop. Fuck, it's been way too goddamn long.

"TAKE. OFF. YOUR. PANTS," she demands slowly. Her eyes shift, and I watch the rise and fall of her chest. She's as worked up as I am, and I'm not sure I can deny her much longer.

"You tell me if I'm hurting you?" I look in her eyes and demand.

"I will," she vows.

"And darlin'?"

"Yes?" She swallows, her breaths growing shallower.

"As mad as I was that first time I saw you at the diner, I still wanted to fuck you so goddamn bad."

She licks her lips as she looks at me with hooded eyes. "Then what are you waiting for, cowboy?"

Wrapping a firm hand around her neck, our mouths crash together, and I carefully guide her to my bed. The only way this is going to work right now is if she's bent over the bed.

My lips trail along her jawline before lingering to her ear and pulling the lobe in between my teeth. "Turn around and bend over," I order.

She happily spins around and digs her elbows into the mattress, spreading her thighs wide for me. I slide a hand down her spine and carefully lower her as much as she's able without putting any weight on her stomach. She's hanging off the edge of the bed with her fingers gripping the sheets. Once I make sure she's comfortable in this position, I graze my hand down to her ass and pull her panties to the side until I can press a finger along her slit.

"Fuck, baby," I growl as soon as her wetness coats the tip. I rub along her pussy and find her clit. The pad of my finger circles it, and she immediately starts trembling. "You okay?"

"Yes," she pants. "I'm overly sensitive down there."

"I can tell."

My cock is rock hard and throbbing that it's becoming painful. I slide her panties down her legs before spreading them wide again. Once I remove my pants and shirt, I align my cock with her entrance and grip her hips, slowly guiding myself inside.

"Oh my God," River moans.

"Relax, sweetheart."

She does, and when her hips arch, I thrust in farther. "Christ,"

I hiss, grinding my teeth down. Her pussy feels like a vise grip as she clenches down on me, and I know it's not going to take long to get either of us off.

"That feels so good. Shit, really good." She rests her cheek on the bed, and her eyes roll to the back of her head.

Once I'm all the way in, I pull out and in again. Keeping my grip on her hips, I make sure to keep my stance and not lean over her like I usually would. Smacking of skin against skin fills the room along with our heated moans, but I can feel the orgasm building inside her. I squeeze her ass cheeks and spread them wide.

"Holy fuck," I growl, keeping up with her pace as she rocks her hips back and forth against me.

"Right there," she says. "Don't stop."

I thrust harder, chasing the release I know she's desperate for. My cock gives her what she's begging for, and when I wrap a hand around to her pussy and rub her clit, her entire body shakes as she screams moments later.

"Fuck." That was so damn hot. "*Goddammit*," I curse between my teeth as she tightens her pussy around my cock, and I can no longer hold back my own release.

My entire body jerks as I come inside her. I feel her muscles relax as we both come down from the high. Once I slide out, I help her stand up and turn her to face me.

She's flushed, and I love that I made her feel that way. Wrapping my hand around her neck, I bend down and kiss her lips. She moans softly, and I can tell she's relaxed and sated.

"Darlin', you're sleeping in my bed tonight," I say against her mouth, and she nods, happily. "In fact, you're sleeping in my bed every damn night."

CHAPTER TWENTY-SEVEN

RIVER

THE FINAL TWO weeks of my pregnancy have been both heaven and hell.

Hell, because I feel like a beached whale, and I'm sweating in places I never knew existed. It's the end of July in Texas, and I'm ready to claw my skin off.

Heaven, because being back in Alex's arms every night has been the only thing keeping me going with a semi-positive attitude.

He's kept his word and hasn't left my side, even though, at times, I enjoy the quiet time to myself. I know he still feels guilty about that night he went out and got drunk, but I'm over it now. He made a mistake, and he's more than learned his lesson. I believe him when he says it'll never happen again, and the fact that he'd given me a second chance without much thought after how things ended in Key West tells me the kind of person he truly is.

But that doesn't mean I can't enjoy the make-up sex in the meantime.

"River," Alex whispers against my hair. We're lying in bed together after a restless night. It's Saturday, so he doesn't have to rush off to work since he's off this weekend. I'd been up at least once every hour. Either because I had to pee or couldn't get comfortable.

"Mmm?" I murmur.

Before he can respond, his stomach releases a wicked howling sound. I chuckle, knowing exactly what he's going to say.

"Hungry?"

"*Starving*," he confirms. "What about you?"

I look up at him from the crook of his arm. "Do you even have to ask?"

He smiles, kissing the top of my head. "I'll go see what we have. Otherwise, we'll drive into town and go visit Betty."

"Sounds good to me. Except it might take me until lunch to roll off this bed."

"Let me help." He chuckles, standing up and reaching his hands out for me to grab them. He pulls me into a sitting position to the edge of the bed, and when I look down, all I can see is my huge belly.

"Thank God it's flip-flop season," I mutter, annoyed with how co-dependent I'm becoming. I hate asking him for help even though he reassures me he doesn't mind.

He tilts my head and presses a soft kiss to my lips. "You look beautiful, so stop whining."

I wrinkle my nose at him and scowl. "We'll see when I'm sweating and screaming through ten hours of childbirth."

"And you'll still be the most beautiful woman in the world." He winks.

"How do you always manage to do that?"

"What?" he asks, grabbing one of his shirts from the closet.

"Give me flutters every time you say something sweet and charming. Like you don't even have to try. The words just naturally fly out of your mouth."

He chuckles, pulling his shirt on before grabbing a pair of jeans from his dresser. "It's the Bishop way, darlin'. Just accept it."

I sigh, relaxing my shoulders as I feel anything but beautiful right now.

"I'm going to check the fridge, but I'm almost certain we only have a gallon of milk and a jar of Aunt Patsy's homemade jam." He heads out and walks down the hallway toward the kitchen.

"Okay, I'm going to attempt to get dressed. See ya in an hour." I groan.

Placing my palm down on the bed behind me, I start pushing myself up. After some twisting and shifting, I finally manage to stand. I really underestimated what carrying a Bishop baby would feel like. I'm convinced all those pictures of those cute pregnant women in their last month on the internet are Photoshopped.

I wobble down the hallway to where my clothes are stored in my room. We haven't made the final transition of making Alex's room *our* room yet, but as soon as the baby's out and we're back home, I plan to turn it into a guest room of sorts. I want my parents, and eventually, Natalie and Adam, to come visit.

"Oh my God," I screech as I reach in my closet for one of my maternity shirts. "Dammit." I groan and let out a growl. I'm pretty sure I just peed myself.

Why does no one tell you this happens during pregnancy? I'm going to write one of those truths about pregnancy books because that sugarcoated shit they fed me was a lie.

I step back and decide I'm going to need a shower, but that's when I realize the liquid is continuing to run down my legs.

Wait.

My abdomen tightens as another gush of liquid lands at my feet. *Holy shit*. Oh my God. My water just broke.

I'd had some Braxton Hicks contractions over the last week, but nothing that was consistent. Now I'm sure this is the real deal.

"Alex!" I shout, stepping aside from the mess.

He doesn't respond, and I stand in complete shock. It's finally time!

"Babe, where are you?" I hear him in the other room.

"Down here, hurry!"

His feet rush down the hallway, and when he swings the door open, he spots my wide eyes and immediately comes toward me.

Before I can warn him, he steps in the mess on the floor and cringes.

"What the…?"

"I think my water broke," I finally tell him, blinking and meeting his eyes. "First, I thought I had peed myself, but then it just kept coming."

"Oh my God…" He steps in front of me, holding my face. "Does this mean it's time? It's *really* time?"

Nodding, tears surface, and my lip trembles. Now that the reality of having this baby is happening, I can't help feeling scared out of my damn mind.

"Sweetheart, don't cry." He wipes his thumbs under my eyes before pressing a sweet kiss to my lips.

"I'm nervous," I admit. "What if this baby is like…fifteen pounds and ruins my vagina for life?" I blurt out, and I can tell he wasn't expecting that by the way he chokes on his laughter.

"I will love our fifteen-pound monster and your vagina no matter what, okay?"

I smile and nod, though I'm not convinced about how my body is going to handle labor.

"Let's go have a baby."

We're packed and on the road in less than thirty minutes. I text Natalie, my mother, and Benita to let them know we're heading to the hospital. Alex calls Evan and says he'll let them know to be expecting us since he's already on shift. I doubt we'll see him till after the birth, though, since he works in the ER. Between calling his parents and his brothers, I've barely come to terms with the fact that I'm really in labor this time.

"How are you feeling?" Alex asks me, reaching for my hand and squeezing three times.

"The contractions are getting more intense. Worse than the Braxton Hicks because I feel it in my back and my stomach."

"Well, maybe that means he'll be here sooner than later."

"God, I hope so. I like to think I have a high pain tolerance, but then again, I've never pushed anything the size of a watermelon out of my vagina, so I guess we'll both find out."

He coughs to hide his smile, though I know he's trying to be supportive.

"Well, I'll be by your side the whole time."

"And I'm sorry if you were hoping I'd be one of those girls who wanted to have an all-natural birth, but I'm not. I plan to go as long as I can without any meds, but when it makes me want to cut off your balls, I'm getting the epidural," I inform him, wincing from another discomforting jab. God, it feels like my menstrual cramps are on steroids.

He shifts his body as if to guard his balls. "I'm on board for anything that saves my junk."

"Don't make me laugh," I beg, choking on my own laughter. "How much longer till we're there?" My head falls back on the seat, and as I hold my belly with one hand, Alex squeezes my other hand three times.

"Not too much longer. As long as there isn't traffic."

I groan, praying that I can breathe through this pain long enough to get into a room.

Within the hour, we're at the hospital and in the delivery unit. They set me up in a room with monitors and fluids. The contractions are intense, and when my doctor finally comes in to check me, I've only progressed to five centimeters, even though I've been at a three for weeks.

Natalie asks if she can FaceTime me and since I'm bored, I let her.

"Oh my God! I can't believe it's time!" she squeals as soon as I accept her call.

"He's already being stubborn," I groan.

"Just like his Mama," Alex blurts out, and I turn and scowl at him.

"Well, he's not wrong." She laughs.

"You're supposed to be cheering me up," I remind her. "Distract me. Talk to me about something else."

"Okay, well hmm…" She twists her lips, thinking. "Adam and I found a few houses we really like, so we're doing another private showing on one of them next week."

"Oh, that's exciting! Are you leaning toward one more than the others or is it a tie?"

"Well, the two we were looking at are one-bedrooms with a big kitchen. Then one we looked at yesterday is a two-bedroom, and though the kitchen isn't as big, the yard is really nice."

"Hmm…well are they priced around the same?"

"Yeah, pretty close, so we've been writing down pros and cons of each, but I think we're already leaning toward one." There's a hint of amusement in her voice, but I shrug it off as pure excitement. Now that she and Adam are engaged, they're finally settling down and buying a house in the suburbs of Milwaukee. Close enough so Natalie didn't have to drive far for work, yet not too close they had to deal with city noise.

I squeeze my eyes tight as a contraction comes to light, and Alex grabs my hand and rubs circles over my knuckles. "Breathe, baby," he reminds me.

Thirty seconds later, it passes, and I can breathe normally.

"You okay?" Natalie asks.

"Yeah, keep talking," I say as I grab the cup of ice chunks on the table next to me.

"Okay, so the pro is the extra bedroom, and the con is that it's an HOA neighborhood."

"Oh." I don't hide my disapproval. "You hate being told what to do, so maybe not." I chuckle.

"Oh, I know. But I think we could really use the extra bedroom, and it has everything else we need. So as Adam says, I need to put on my big girl undies and follow the rules."

I snort laugh.

"Wait. Why could you use the extra bedroom? You hate company." I narrow my eyes, confused.

"Well I mean, eventually we'll need it." She tries to cover her tracks, but I don't buy it.

"You're lying."

"Just tell her, babe!" I hear Adam shout in the background.

"Shut up!" she hisses.

"Tell me what?"

"It's nothing. I can tell you later. Today's your day." She smiles, guilt all over her face.

"Natalie…" I warn. "Shit." I wince again, feeling the next contraction rip through me. Once it's over, I go back to my phone. "You better tell me, or I'll withhold baby pictures from you!"

"You wouldn't!" She gasps.

Alex is next to me shaking his head.

"What?" I ask him.

"You really don't know what she's trying to say?" He raises his brows, and I follow his eyes down to my belly.

"What?" I screech, looking back at Natalie. "You're pregnant?" I sit up straighter. Her expression tells me everything I need to know. "Oh my God!"

"Yep, you're going to be an auntie!"

Tears start flowing down my cheeks before I can stop them, and I know I'm a hot mess right now. "Our kids are going to be close in age, and you're all the way up there."

"But we'll visit and vice versa. There's no crying during labor," she teases.

I chuckle, wiping my face. "When did you find out?" I ask, but before she can answer, a harsh contraction begins.

"They're getting closer together," Natalie states. "Are you getting the epidural?"

"Alex, press the call button. It's time." I squeeze my eyes shut and try to inhale and exhale slowly.

"Good luck, sweetie! Alex, FaceTime me when she starts pushing so I can watch!"

"Ew, no," Alex responds. "I'm staying above the waist."

"You better not!" she scolds. "You get down there and watch your son being born!"

"Okay, I'm hanging up now! Bye!" Alex presses the button before Natalie can retaliate.

"Do you two have any boundaries at all?" he mutters, but I can barely breathe to respond. "Okay, I'm paging the nurse right now."

Another thirty minutes go by, and I finally have an epidural and some relief. It felt like a couple of boxers were punching me down there, and now I feel happy as ever.

"I can't believe Natalie and Adam are going to be parents," I say, dreamily.

"I see the meds are working." He grins.

"Yeah, they are..." I rest my eyes and enjoy the comfort.

ALEX

I sit next to River's bed and hold her hand as she falls in and out of sleep. I'm so relieved she doesn't have to feel her contractions anymore, but I know this is just the beginning.

Hours go by, and when the doctor checks River's progress again, she's only dilated to six centimeters.

"All of that, and I'm only at a six?" she whines to the nurse. She looks to be in her mid-thirties, and when I look down at her ID tag, it says Amelia.

"I'd suggest walking around, but you can't once you've had the epidural."

"I know," River says. "I used to work as a nurse up in Milwaukee," she adds.

"Oh, how cool. They have great hospitals up there. What brings you all the way down here?"

River points at her belly and then at me. Amelia chuckles.

"Well, then you probably know that these things take time. Rest as much as you can now because once you're at a ten, the doctor's gonna want you to start pushing."

"Great." She moans, her head falling back against the pillow. "Pushing alone can take a while."

"Up to two hours sometimes for a first pregnancy."

"Two hours? I don't think I even have twenty minutes in me."

Amelia pats her hand and smiles. "Let me know if you need anything, okay?" She directs her question at me.

"Will do, ma'am."

My phone is blowing up, so I start texting my brothers and Dylan back. I tell John to call our folks to give them an update before tending back to River.

"You want a foot rub?" I ask.

"Have sex with me," she blurts.

"River," I scold.

"It'll help me dilate. C'mon."

I laugh, knowing she's desperate to progress naturally and have the baby.

"I'm serious." She pulls on my hand, pouting.

"You can beg all you want, but there is no possible circumstance that will make me say yes to that right now. Also, I'm pretty sure that puts you at risk for infection since your water already broke."

"Argh," she groans. "That stupid book."

"Want me to read to you to distract you and pass some time?"

"Ooh yes. No, wait. That'll just make me want sex more. You'll have to find a thriller or something to read instead."

I click open my phone and begin searching. Once I find something she agrees to, I start reading aloud. She eventually falls asleep, and I step out momentarily when Evan knocks on the door just as Amelia comes back in with River's chart.

"How's it goin'?" he asks.

"Fine, I guess. Slow. River's getting anxious."

He pats me on the shoulder and pulls me in for an unexpected hug. "Proud of you."

"Thanks, but I'm not the one pushing out a Bishop."

He chuckles then makes a wincing face. "Well, text me if you need anything, okay? If you get hungry, I can bring you somethin'."

"Will do, thanks."

An alarm going off behind me grabs my attention and both of us come rushing in.

"What is it?"

Evan searches the monitors and answers. "The baby's heartbeat monitor. The heart rate is dropping."

"What? Why? What's that mean?"

Amelia clicks the button and mutes the sound. She's looking it over and tells us she's going to page the doctor.

"Is he okay?" River asks, panicked.

"River, let's move you to your side. Sometimes that helps."

Evan steps in and helps Amelia shift River till she's lying on her side. Amelia adjusts the monitor and continues watching it for several minutes until the doctor finally arrives.

"His heart rate went back up a tad, but it's not staying steady," I overhear Amelia say.

"River, I want to check you again and make sure everything's okay. The nurse is going to help you roll back over so I can take a look."

I squeeze River's hand three times once she's rolled onto her back. The doctor checks her progress, but this time her face drops when she looks back up at us.

"You haven't dilated anymore. I could give you a dose of Pitocin to help speed it up, but with his heart rate being inconsistent, I don't want to risk it."

"Why isn't she dilating?" I ask.

"The baby's not dropping, which makes me believe the cord could be wrapped around his neck."

"Oh my God," River screeches.

"Or his shoulders are too wide," the doctor adds. "He could be stuck."

"What does that mean? Now what?" I ask, trying to keep my voice steady for River's sake even though I'm panicking inside.

"I think the safest option right now is to start prepping you for an emergency C-section. If the cord is wrapped around his neck, it puts both you and the baby at risk," the doctor explains.

River and I both look up at Evan for confirmation. I trust the doctor, but getting my brother's advice is just as important to me. Evan nods and says he agrees it's the safest option right now.

The next ten minutes flash by in a blur. I didn't read much up on C-sections, stupidly assuming River wouldn't need to go this route, so I'm hanging onto every word the nurse tells us.

Before they roll River's bed out, I cup her face and kiss her. "I'll be right there next to you, okay?"

Tears fill her eyes, and I swipe them away. "I love you."

"I love you too," she chokes back. "Hurry up and meet me in there."

"I will." I wink before pressing my lips to hers once again.

Once she's rolled out of the room, I'm instructed to put a pair of scrubs over my clothes along with a scrub cap. Having Evan here is helping me stay calm, but inside, I'm freaking out. River's about to have emergency surgery to get our baby out, and I've never felt this terrified in my entire life.

"She's gonna be okay," Evan reassures me. "Doctor Granger is very skilled at what she does. River's in good hands."

"She fucking better be," I mutter under my breath. He leads me down the hall, and when Amelia steps out, she waves me inside.

"Good luck. I'll be out here waiting," Evan calls out.

I rush over to River who's spread out on a surgical bed with her arms out. "Hey, baby," I say softly, rubbing my hand on her head and dipping to kiss her forehead.

"I can't believe this is happening," she whispers. The doctor and nurses are already working on her, but there's a small sheet hanging above River's chest so we can't see anything. "I know this is a routine surgery, but I'm scared."

I want to comfort her, but at the same time, I'm as scared as she is right now. Regardless, I'll always put her needs before mine no matter what.

"Do you remember that first song we slowed danced to in that bar?" I ask, that night feeling like it was a lifetime ago already, yet I remember it so vividly.

She wrinkles her nose, then nods. "'Slow Dancing in a Burning Room'?"

"Do you remember what we said about the lyrics?"

"They were sad and tragic," she says.

"Yeah, and that was the night I made you mine. I knew the meaning behind that song, yet I wasn't willing to accept it was about us. A relationship ending that hadn't even started, yet we took the risk. And look where it's brought us now."

She smiles up at me, an oxygen tube running under her nose and still looking cute as hell.

"I always think of that night when I hear it," she admits.

"It's a night I'll never forget." I rub my nose along her hairline, desperate to kiss her.

"To think it was only nine months ago." Her eyes widen. "So weird."

I chuckle. "Crazy what can change in just nine short months." I wink.

"River," Dr. Granger calls out. "You're going to start feeling some pressure now, okay? I'll have him out in the next sixty seconds."

Holy shit. Sixty seconds.

"You're doing so good, sweetheart," I tell her, reaching for her hand closest to me.

"I hope he's okay." Fear evident in her voice.

I can tell she's starting to tear up, so I rub my finger along her cheek.

"Everything's going to be perfect," I promise, squeezing her hand.

"Okay," she says, barely above a whisper.

I can see the doctor's movement as the nurses all shuffle around, passing Dr. Granger objects and removing them from her hands. They're moving so fast, by the time I look down at River and back up again, she looks like she's elbow deep inside her stomach.

"A little more pressure, River," the doctor warns.

I give her hand three squeezes, and when I lean forward a bit, I see Dr. Granger removing some filmy stuff from the baby's face. I notice his face is blue, and that's when I see the cord is, in fact, wrapped around his neck.

My face drops, and River takes notice.

"Is he okay?" she asks nervously.

I watch the doctor wedge her finger between the cord and his neck. A nurse hands her a clamp, and within seconds, the cord is cut.

"Oh my God." I smile, relieved when I see his little mouth move. "You're doing great, sweetheart. He's almost out," I explain.

Within ten seconds, Dr. Granger pulls him the rest of the way out and is holding him up for me to see.

"It's a boy!" the doctor announces, giving me a wink. "Do you want to come cut the umbilical cord, Dad?" she asks me.

"Absolutely."

I take a few steps forward, and when the nurse hands me the tool, I grab it and cut where they tell me to.

The doctor holds him up higher over the sheet so River can see him. It's not for long though. Soon she passes the baby off to one of the nurses who starts cleaning him up right away.

Loud screams erupt from his little body, and it's the most perfect sound I've ever heard.

RIVER

Watching Alex hold our baby is the most beautiful thing I've ever seen. He looks even smaller in Alex's big arms, but he came out at ten pounds, eight ounces and twenty-one inches long. So suffice it to say he wasn't a small baby.

"He looks so peaceful," I say, watching Alex rock back and forth on his feet. He's cradling him in his little security blanket while the baby sleeps soundly.

"I can't believe we made this." He looks up at me with pure happiness on his face.

"He definitely looks like a Bishop," I say. "Blond hair, square jaw, build like he's been ranching since conception."

Alex laughs, agreeing. I love how he can't take his eyes off him, watching him so proudly.

"He has your features, too," he tells me, though I'm not convinced. The baby looks like a Bishop from head to toe.

"Fatherhood already looks good on you. Go figure." I chuckle. "You've got that sexy dad look goin' on."

The corner of his lips tilts up as he shakes his head at me. "I think he's ready to eat." He walks over and brings him back in my arms. His little mouth is twitching, searching.

It's been two hours since they rushed me into surgery, and between stitching me up and cleaning him, it's the first intimate moment we've all had together as a family of three.

I slide my gown down and bring him to my chest. "I wish I'd been able to hold him right away."

Alex steps toward me and flashes me a sad look. "I know, darlin', but I'd rather have both of you alive and healthy."

"You're right." I look down at him and smile. "He's here now and healthy."

I FaceTime Natalie and then my mom and dad to introduce

them to the newest member of the family. Later that night, Alex's family all come up and visit us. Mama is over-the-moon excited and can barely contain herself as she looks over my shoulder and stares dreamily at him.

"Are you excited to meet your uncles?" I coo, rubbing my finger along the softness of his cheek. "They're a crazy bunch."

"And it's about to get even crazier," Evan chimes in.

"Is Benita coming too?" I ask, wondering if we should wait to announce the baby's name or if she's coming later.

"She had to get the boys to bed, but she said she'd be coming first thing tomorrow," John tells me. Though it's disappointing she can't be here tonight, it's kind of nice just having Alex's parents and brothers here.

"So be honest," Jackson begins. "You named him after me, right?"

I snort, chuckling. Alex rolls his eyes.

"You want to tell them, darlin'?" Alex asks with an encouraging smile.

Everyone's standing around my bed, watching as I lay the baby on my lap, so they can all see him. "Okay, y'all," I start, purposely dragging out my Southern drawl. "Meet Riley Alexander Bishop."

CHAPTER TWENTY-EIGHT

ALEX

THREE MONTHS LATER

Becoming a dad has been one of the greatest moments of my life. Just when I think I've got it all figured out, Riley surprises me, and I'm forced to adjust again. He's already smart as a whip and funny, like a true Bishop, and makes me so damn proud to be his dad every day. The amount of love everyone has for him is almost unfathomable, and with a single look, he had all the Bishops wrapped around his little pinky. Mama and Dad spoil him and demand to see Riley every single day, no excuses. Jackson, John, and even Evan become big ol' softies anytime Riley is around. They always fight over who gets to hold him first, but as soon as he shits, they can't pass him off to someone else soon enough.

The day Riley was born, I made a pact with myself that I'd always provide, protect, give love and advice, while being firm but fair, just like my father. Though only a short amount of time has passed since he entered this world, he's given me a new meaning to life. A once-selfish man has been transformed into a selfless one because of him, and for that, I will forever be grateful.

It took months, but we're finally on a somewhat normal sleeping schedule. Good news is Riley's already on a rancher's schedule, up before the sun and snoozing right after dark. After he's tended to each morning, it gives River and me a chance to drink coffee on the back porch before I leave for work. It's those quiet moments together that I've learned to treasure the most.

After returning from Natalie's wedding last month, I've had a lot on my mind. Mainly *forever* and what that really means. I met River's parents, and they were more than kind. However, everything River had told me about her past finally made sense. I understood why she was so apprehensive about us and not wanting to follow in her parents' footsteps of a failed relationship.

"Are you almost ready to go?" River asks, rushing around our room, completely distressed as she tries to finish getting ready. We're supposed to all be meeting at my parents' house for lunch.

"I'm ready," I tell her as I put on my boots. She walks from the bathroom, putting her hair into a tight ponytail, and no matter how much time has passed, I still find myself mesmerized by her beauty. I'm so fucking lucky to have her as mine.

Stalking forward in long strides, I pull River into my arms and kiss the fuck out of her. She smells like flowers and summer breeze, and I just want to strip her of her clothes and lie naked for the rest of the afternoon.

"If we weren't running late, I'd bend you over that bed," I growl in her ear.

She playfully slaps at my chest. "Mama doesn't like tardiness. Something you told me the first day I met your parents."

"You're right." I wink. "Let's go."

We drive over to my parents', and as soon as we walk in, Mama goes straight to Riley and pulls him into her arms and kisses his little cheeks. Evan and John walk in laughing about something and sit at the table. Soon, Jackson is rushing in—late, as always. We have lunch and talk about everything and nothing all at the same time. I look around, see everyone's smiles, and just know how lucky I am to have a family like this, a beautiful woman by my side, and a life worth living.

After we're finished eating, River helps clean up and chats with Mama. Soon Jackson is pulling River by the arm. "Time to go, sweetheart."

"Go where?" She looks at him like he's lost his fucking mind, which is a normal reaction considering. I stand in the doorway and watch as she glances at me with questioning eyes.

"Go on," I tell her with a smirk.

"Uhhh." She nervously laughs as Jackson tugs at her by the arm. At first, River is super confused and almost protests until Mama shoos her out the door and turns and gives me a wink.

RIVER

"You are as stubborn as a damn horse. Come on, now. Do I have to coax you with a carrot?" Jackson jokes.

I narrow my eyes at him. "What are you up to?"

"Don't worry your pretty little face about it."

We walk down the steps of the back porch, and there's a side by side waiting with an envelope tied to the steering wheel. Confused, I untie it, open it, and pull out a piece of paper.

It's been exactly one year since Key West.
That vacation was the best.
Hills, trails, and prairies galore.
A body of water, flowers, and more.
Keep your eyes open, good luck navigating.

This is where the next clue is waiting.

I look over at Jackson who's smiling and shrugging his shoulders. The ranch is huge, and there are tons of picnic tables under trees, but I can only recall one body of water. Jackson jumps in the other side and allows me to drive.

"I might need oh-shit handles," he kids when I press on the gas, and we take off faster than I expected toward the blue trail. The cool breeze blows across my skin as we take hill after hill toward the pond Alex and I once visited. I'll never forget that day. I remember how the clouds reflected off the water of the pond and how he told me about the flowers that grew along the banks in the summer. At that point in my life, I was nervous as to what would happen between us, becoming a mom, and moving away from everything I ever knew. It feels like a lifetime ago, but then again, so does Key West. Jackson keeps talking shit about my driving the whole way over and has me laughing so hard that I purposely drive bad and run into every pothole I see.

We round the bend and drive into the prairie until the pond comes into view. I drive across the way until I see the picnic tables under the tree, but then I notice two horses tied to a post. Glancing over at Jackson, he laughs.

"Giddyup," he says.

I park the side by side and walk up to the horses where another envelope is tied to the saddle. I can't open it fast enough.

I never forgot about your bucket list.
To ride a horse is pure bliss.
Giddyup, sweetheart, let's get going.
From this location, you'll feel the sun glowing.
Stand at the top, and you can see it too
That's where the next clue is waiting for you.

There's a map of the property that's hand drawn with different points on it. There's a little X by the pond that says *YOU ARE HERE.*

"Wait," I say, reading the note again. "I have to ride a horse?"

"Why do you think I was volun-told to come along?" He bursts into laughter. "Mainly to make sure you don't hurt yourself or get lost."

I look at the large, intimidating horse and saddle. "I don't even know what to do."

Jackson walks over and explains the details of riding. "This thing around her head is a halter, and this rope is called a lead rope. I'll make sure to hold her steady for you just in case she wants to move as you're trying to get on. This is the stirrup. You'll stick your foot in here and hold on to the horn and pull yourself up. You'll fully swing your leg over the saddle then place it in the other stirrup. Once you're on, you'll grab these reins, and then it's as easy as driving a car. Move the reins left, the horse goes left, right she goes right, pull back and she stops. Her name is Willow. I know she's a big ol' girl, but she's gentle and one of the horses we put the kids on. So there's really nothing to be afraid of."

I'm pretty sure he could see the worry in my eyes. I look over at Jackson's horse, jet black, pawing at the ground with his hoof. "And I guess yours is the one the headless horseman rides? He looks like the devil," I say with a laugh.

"He's feisty, just like me. So we get along good. Better get going." Jackson holds Willow steady, and I stick my foot in the stirrup like he instructed. At first, I struggled, then was able to finally pull myself up on the saddle. I look down at him and can't believe I'm actually on a horse. "This is weird. I can't explain it."

"You get used to it. Hold the horn and the reins." Jackson unclips the lead rope and walks over to his horse and hops on like it's nothing. He looks over at me. "Come on. You're leading."

I reread the note again, trying to get comfortable on Willow and look at the map. There are several different places that could give me a view, but I have a feeling about this one. "The red trail to the lookout point. That's where we should go."

Jackson doesn't give me any clues, as I turn the horse and head toward the post that's painted red. Horseback riding is so different. This giant animal and I are as one as we continue slowly down the trail. I can't stop smiling and looking at my surroundings. This place is beautiful, and the sun is shining on my shoulders. It's so warm and covers me like a blanket. As I take it all in, I'm so grateful to be able to call this home and be able to raise our baby here.

"Ready to gallop?" Jackson asks, clicking his mouth and passing me up. "Just hold on real tight with your legs and keep your arms down, so you don't look like you're flying away. Willow is a sprinter, and she's as fast as the wind," he says before going into a full run ahead.

I suck in a deep breath and barely kick, and Willow takes off. At first, I feel like I might bounce right off until she goes faster and we're moving in a smooth rhythm together, racing down the trail following Jackson's dust. I'm absolutely fucking elated as I hold on to the horn for dear life. This is freedom as the cool October breeze hits my face. At the end of the trail, where it splits into two, Jackson is stopped and waiting for me with a huge smile on his face.

"Now I know why you want to do this every day." I'm breathing hard, adrenaline rushing.

He gives me a quick head nod. "So which way now?"

I point. "Over there. At the top of that hill, where the lookout is."

"After you," he says, and I guide Willow down the trail, and Jackson follows. As we climb up a hill, I can see Mr. Bishop driving a tractor with a trailer full of hay bales. Once at the top, I pull the reins back, and Willow stops.

"Now, be careful getting off. Hold on to the horn, swing your leg over and touch the other side of the ground. She won't move on you, but make sure you don't stumble and bust your ass," Jackson tells me. He rides past me, grabs the reins, and I somehow manage to dismount without falling.

"Alex may have gotten himself a little cowgirl after all." He chuckles.

I flip him off where only he can see it, and he pats his leg, finding it overly hilarious.

My hair is windblown, and as I walk over to Mr. Bishop, he hands me another envelope with a big smile. I take a moment to fully take in the view. The land goes on for as far as my eyes can see, and it's so calm and beautiful out here.

> *How's the view, you'll have to let me know.*
> *Take a good look before you go.*
> *The leaves are changing,*
> *the grass is turning brown.*
> *Your next clue is in town.*
> *Chocolate cake and pecan pie.*
> *While you're there, tell Mrs. Betty hi!*

I can't stop smiling. I'm pretty sure it may be permanent after this. Once I climb onto the trailer and sit on a bale of hay, I see Jackson lead Willow back down the trail we came from. The hay smells dry and sweet, and it reminds me of the first time I visited Texas.

We take an unrecognizable path, and I see parts of the property I've never seen. As we continue forward, I try to take it all in: the sunshine, the brown grasses, and the rumble of the tractor engine. I can't believe Alex would go through such a big effort to celebrate our one year of meeting. It was a moment that changed the entire course of our lives, monumental even. This is all completely unforgettable, just like him.

Soaking in the scene, I can't help but think about everything that's happened over the last year. Though I was scared to death to become a mother, it all feels like second nature now. That unconditional love consumes me, and I never thought my heart could be so full. Between the love of my life and our baby, I'm living my greatest life possible.

I used to think love like that only exists in fairy tales, but every time I hear Riley's little coos, I know that's not true. Now, I can't help thinking back at my apprehension of being a mother, because it's one of the greatest joys of my life. Considering Natalie is pregnant, I've been helping her work through the mind fuck the hormones create too. Admittedly, I might not have it all figured out, but thanks to Google and all the mamas I'm surrounded by constantly, I can get answers quick. Alex was right; everything did work out just fine.

As I study my surroundings, I'm pretty sure we're on the other side of the property by the ranch hand quarters. Moving closer, I see several bunkhouses and vehicles parked around, so my suspicion is confirmed. The gate is open, and Mr. Bishop rolls through it then stops by a Jeep, with the top off, waiting for me. I get off the trailer and wave bye to Mr. Bishop. He gives me a head nod and a quick wave and a smile before he pulls away.

The Jeep is still running, and I climb inside and take my phone from my pocket to navigate toward the diner since I have no clue where I am. Once the quickest route loads, I select it, then shift the Jeep into gear. I smile the entire drive over to the diner. Just as I put the Jeep into park, I see Evan standing by the door.

"I guess all the Bishops are involved in this little celebration," I say with a chuckle.

"Of course. A year is a big deal for any Bishop boy." He hands me an envelope, and I practically rip it open.

> *Think back to coming to Texas, the very first day*
> *Where was it that you booked to stay?*
> *Go to the counter and grab the clue.*
> *There's a special surprise, waiting for you.*

I look at Evan, and he's all smiles. "You better tell Mrs. Betty hello before you hightail it on outta here."

"Shit," I say, not even thinking about it. As soon as I walk in, Betty comes to me and gives me a big hug. "Happy one year!"

323

"Thank you! I was told to tell you hi! But I really gotta go."

She hands me a piece of chocolate cake in a to-go box, and I smile, but I have a feeling it was all to stall me. By the time I walk outside, Evan is already gone. I climb into the Jeep and head straight to the B&B. My heart is racing, and I'm so fucking excited that I'm smiling like a crazy person as I turn down the gravel road. The B&B comes into sight, and I can't get there fast enough but force myself to drive slowly. Once I park, I get out and run to the front door, open it up, and go straight to John. There are a dozen roses on the counter waiting for me with another envelope. I take a quick moment to stop and smell the flowers.

"Go ahead, River. Open it up," John encourages.

I swallow hard and do exactly what he says.

> *This is the last and final clue*
> *You know what you have to do*
> *Meet me at Mama's in the backyard*
> *Finding me won't be too hard.*
> *I've got a surprise you'll never guess*
> *I love you darlin'; you're the best.*

All I can do is laugh. Happiness like this should be illegal. I have no words as I tell my heart to stay calm because it's about ready to flutter out of my chest. There's too much excitement bubbling inside me as I grab the flowers and turn around.

"Wait up, I'm riding with you," John stops me before I make it to the door. I wave him on because I'm so damn impatient right now, I can barely contain myself.

We get in the Jeep, and I carefully place the roses in the back seat. It takes no time at all to arrive at his parents' house. As soon as I park and shut the door to the Jeep, my adrenaline spikes. John is nothing but smiles as we walk around the house. It takes everything I have not to run to the back like a kid.

Once we're in the backyard, I look everywhere for Alex but

don't see him. At a closer look, I see a group of family members under the old oak tree and can hear them chatting and cutting up.

John and I move closer, and I can't see Alex, but I see Benita and Aaron, the boys, Mr. Bishop, Mama, Patsy, Charlotte, Evan, Jackson, Dylan, and John goes to join them. When I get about twenty feet away, everyone who's standing close together, moves out of the way, and that's when I finally see Alex. He's standing in a black tux and tie with messy hair and a sexy smile on his face. He's holding Riley in his arms who's also dressed in a little tux. When our eyes meet, the world around me fades away. My breath catches, and I feel like I can't take a step forward.

I glance around at everyone, forcing myself to walk toward him, wondering what the hell is going on. Just as I open my mouth to say something, Alex drops to his knee, holding Riley close to his chest. My hands fly to my mouth when I realize what's going on. Mama takes Riley from Alex's arms, and he waves me closer with a smirk.

"River," Alex says, digging inside his suit jacket. When he pulls out a black velvet box and opens it to show me the most beautiful ring I've ever seen, I don't feel like I can keep standing because my knees go completely weak.

"Meeting you a year ago has changed my outlook on everything. A life without you in it is no life at all, and every night, I thank God for you and Riley. I can't imagine a day without the two of you, and I never want to. You're the absolute best thing that's ever happened to me, and I'm so happy to call you mine."

Before he can even finish the rest of his speech, I fall to the ground and swing my arms around his neck, not able to hold back the tears that stream down my face. I have to kiss him, taste him, touch him.

"I love you, River."

"I love you so much," I say, my voice barely working. I don't want this moment to end.

"Please spend the rest of your life with me," Alex whispers across my mouth.

My eyes flutter closed, and it all seems like a dream. "Yes, yes. Forever."

For a moment, I forgot everyone was standing around watching us until Jackson yells out, "*GET A ROOM*!" We start laughing and pull away, and he wipes the tears from my cheek with his thumb before he slides the ring on my finger.

We all exchange hugs and congratulations, and I'm so overwhelmed, so damn happy, and completely ecstatic that I'll be a Bishop too. Today is the anniversary of our beginning, and it also marks the start of our forever. The excitement doesn't wear off, and then Mama tells me she's keeping Riley overnight. At first, I hesitate, but when Alex squeezes my hand three times, I agree.

"I want to be alone with you. I brought everything she could ever need for him while you were on your little treasure hunt," he whispers in my ear as we walk hand in hand toward the house. Benita is chatting about bridal parties and wedding showers, and when she asks me if she can start planning them, I tell her yes, because it makes her happy, and I know she'll go above and beyond because she's a party planning extraordinaire. She hugs me tight, and Aaron pulls her away with a chuckle.

"Welcome to the family. So excited I get to keep my honey bun overnight," Mama says, giving me a big hug. As soon as Riley was born, they turned Alex's old bedroom in the house into a nursery. It was a sweet gesture that warmed my heart, and I'm happy his parents want to be involved. She's a wonderful grandma and proves that every single day with her love.

After we say our goodbyes, I can't stop glancing over at Alex in a full tuxedo and tie as he drives us home.

"What?" He smirks.

"Nothing," I say with a smile, and he grabs my hand, looks at the ring that fits perfectly on my finger, and kisses my knuckles.

Once we park, and we're inside, nothing in the world can keep us apart. Our mouths gravitate together as waves of need wash over my body.

"God, I need you so fucking bad," he growls against my neck as his lips drag across my skin. Tracing the shell of my ear with his warm mouth, I lose myself in his gentle touch as his hand runs under my shirt and cups my breast. My head falls back on my shoulders, and I lose myself in his kisses.

ALEX

Her skin tastes sweet, and I want to kiss every inch of her body, and tonight, I just might. To know River is going to be my wife, be my *forever*, makes me so fucking happy. I'm the luckiest man in the world, and each time I look at her, it's confirmed.

As I try to take off my suit jacket, she grabs my hands to stop me.

"Keep it on, just a little longer."

I smirk. "So you like this look?"

She wraps the tie around her fist and pulls my face closer to hers. "Sure do, cowboy."

Taking my time, I unbutton her shirt, watching her breasts rise and fall as I remove it from her body. Gently, I run my fingers across the tops of her breasts and reach behind and undo her bra. She watches me intently as I touch her, and it's so fucking intense. As the bra hits the floor, I dip down, taking her taut nipple into my mouth, swirling my tongue around the tall peak. River's eyes flutter closed when my hands slip lower, snapping open her jeans. I slide my hands into her panties and can already feel her arousal. Her breath hitches when I hook my fingers in her panties, and I slide them down along with her pants. Kicking off her shoes, she steps out of her clothes and stands before me naked. Stepping back, I take my time admiring every curve of her sun kissed body.

"Damn," I whisper, meeting her eyes, going all the way down to her cute toes and back up again. I take a mental snapshot of this woman who agreed to be my wife, my everything. "You're so fucking beautiful," I tell her, and she's all smiles.

"You are too." River stalks toward me, shaking her hips. Taking control, she takes her time removing my tuxedo jacket and tie and unbuttons my shirt. Her soft hands trace down my abs, and my breath increases. Not able to wait any longer, my greedy mouth is on hers. My hands are in her hair, and soon her legs are wrapped around my waist. Holding her ass tight as she straddles and kisses me, I walk us toward the bedroom. After I set her on the bed, she continues to watch me as I remove the rest of my clothes.

"I have to taste you first. Edge of the bed," I demand once I'm fully naked, and she smirks.

She doesn't hesitate, but I grab her ankles and quickly move her closer before dropping to my knees and placing her legs on my shoulders. As I dip my tongue into her sweetness, she lets out a long sigh, running her fingers through my already messy hair. I move my tongue up and down her slit, teasing her as much as I can. Immediately, her body responds, and I gently place a finger inside. As she moans, I watch as she grabs her nipples between her fingers and pinches. It's such a fucking turn on to see. I slip in another finger, giving her exactly what she desires. She's so fucking wet as I slide my fingers in and out in a slow rhythm while I apply pressure to her hard nub. River arches her back, writhing, as I apply more pressure and increase the pace. With white knuckles, she fists the comforter, pushing her body harder against me. Placing my hands under her ass, I pull her to me and drive my tongue deeper inside.

"Fuck," she pants, practically begging for release. "I'm so close."

Though I slow down, wanting the orgasm to teeter on the edge as long as possible, it doesn't take long before she's buckling beneath me. Her breath quickens, and her mouth falls open while she loses all control of her senses. As she rides the wave of her orgasm on my mouth, her moans are like sweet music to my ears.

A crescendo of emotion as her body eventually goes still. I stand, and she moves her body up the bed until her head rests on the pillow. With a smile, she curls her finger, demanding I go to her, which I happily do. Kissing up her stomach, her breasts, her neck, I place flutters of kisses across her jawline until my mouth finally meets hers.

With hooded eyes, she looks up at me. "I love you, Alex."

"You have no idea how much I love you."

She grabs my face with her hands and searches my eyes. "I do."

Taking my time, I tease her opening with the tip of my cock. She opens her legs wide, begging to feel me, and I can't hold back any longer. In one long stroke, I fill her with my length. She's so fucking wet, so fucking beautiful, and it makes me hard as steel. Her fingernails scratch down my back, and she holds me tight as if she's never letting me go as we rock together in slow motion. Her soft pants against my skin cause emotions to swirl through me as I pump in and out of her.

"I want it harder, Alex. I need more."

"Mmm, whatever you want, darlin'." I grab her earlobe in my mouth and suck.

I don't make her beg, and I give her exactly what she wants. She screams out my name as I slam my cock into her, over and over again. I don't want this moment to end, but I know if I keep at this pace, I'll be crumbling to pieces soon. The orgasm quickly builds, and I force myself to slow so I can enjoy her as long as possible. As we continue to make sweet love, our hearts and bodies mend together as one. The emotions I'm feeling are almost too much as the orgasms sneak up. Another thrust, and I almost feel blinded by the orgasm. The intensity practically takes my breath away as I lose myself inside her. River is my everything, and without her there's nothing.

My heart is so full as she looks at me, her green eyes glimmering, completely satisfied, and I smile back. After we clean up, she crawls back into bed, and I pull her close, needing her skin against mine. As I hold her tight, she draws circles on my chest and listens to my heartbeat then wraps her leg around mine. We're a tangled mess, and I never want this to end.

"I can never get enough of you, River."

She props herself up on one elbow and smiles sweetly.

"Well luckily, we have forever," she says, glancing down at her ring before leaning over and tugging my bottom lip into her mouth.

EPILOGUE
RIVER

SIX MONTHS LATER

EACH DAY, Riley grows up more and more. He definitely has a strong personality but is an all-around happy baby. In nine short months, Alex and I have already watched him crawl for the first time, and even heard him say his first word, which happened to be "horse." I know once Riley starts walking, we'll be in trouble because he's already so independent, super curious, and wanting to do everything himself. We're raising our own little cowboy and couldn't be prouder.

With the exception of the day Riley was born, my wedding was the second most beautiful day of my life. Natalie and Adam flew down, and so did my parents. They all stayed in the B&B for almost a week, and I had a hell of a time showing them around the ranch and teaching them how we do things in Texas. I may be an implant, but I consider this home now.

After the proposal, we wasted no time on planning. The wedding was more than I could've ever imagined. The weather was perfect, which was needed considering it was outside. Since Alex's sister was married a few years prior on the ranch, the boys had plenty of practice with setting up giant tents and dance floors in the backyard. When the sun set, that's when the dancing and drinking really started. There were so many family members and friends in attendance, it felt like the whole town was there. All I have to say is the Bishops really know how to throw an epic party.

Looking back a few years ago, I never would've imagined this would be my life—a happy little family living on a ranch in West Texas. I didn't know what truly living was until I met Alex Bishop. My household is so full of laughter and love that it makes my heart burst with emotion. Though we didn't all get off on the right foot, Alex's family is everything I could've ever wished for and more. I'm the luckiest woman in the world, and each day that I hear my little boy giggle and feel my husband's touch, I know that's true.

Six months after having Riley, I decided to take Evan's offer and put my application in at the hospital. I was offered a position the following day and was happy to get back to a job I knew I loved, even though I knew I'd miss Riley tons. Mama Rose begged to watch him during my shifts, but she didn't need to beg hard because I know how much she loves and adores him. Riley loves his grandma so much and instantly smiles every time he sees her. They keep each other company while all the boys are out working too.

Alex and I decided to postpone our honeymoon because of our work schedules. However, we're planning to visit Key West again, and I can't wait to check things off the new bucket list we made. After the wedding on Friday, we said goodbye to our guests, then spent Saturday and Sunday alone at home as husband and wife.

Monday morning comes quick, and Alex and I rush around. After I feed and change the baby, I kiss Alex goodbye then take Riley over to Mama's house. She greets me with a smile at the door in her robe. I pass him off with a quick smooch, give her a big hug and thank you, then head to work.

While I drive to the hospital, all I can think of is how quickly the weekend went by. How everything these past six months have gone by so fast. The wedding events happened too quickly, and my head is still spinning at how magical and unreal it feels. As soon as the hospital comes into view, I let out a laugh when I think about Evan. A little birdy told me a rumor about him, and I can't wait to call him out on it because I'm pretty sure it's true.

I park and walk in, taking in the familiar smell of the hospital. No matter the location, they all seem to smell exactly the same—sterile, clean, and oddly enough, it brings me back to my childhood when we'd be in and out of the hospitals for Rylie. As I ride the elevator, I think about my baby sister. Though she's not physically here with me, I'll always carry a piece of her in my heart.

A smile touches my lips, but when I step off the elevator and see Evan, it grows into a shit-eating grin. My timing couldn't have been more perfect. He looks up from the chart in his hand and sees me walking toward him. Pretending to groan, he goes back to his paperwork.

"So…how was your weekend?" I keep the right amount of sweetness in my tone.

Evan glares at me. "How do you think it was?"

"If the rumors are true, I'd say it started off at a ten and dropped down to a one really quick." I chuckle.

Amelia, my labor and delivery nurse with Riley and who also became my partner in crime after I started working here, walks up smacking her gum with her eyebrow popped. "Rumors?"

Evan's uncomfortable with the conversation, but it's good for him to squirm every once in a while, and now that I'm family, he can't be rude. Mama's rule, not mine.

"Oh yeah. Juicy rumors, too. Apparently, Evan hooked up with some random chick the night of my wedding. Some friend of a friend and no one knows who this mystery woman is other than her name. Stellllllllllaaaaaaaaaaaaa."

I watch as he takes a deep, annoyed breath and releases it slowly. I bet he's hoping I don't know the end of the story too, but he's not that lucky. There are no secrets when Jackson is around, and even he knows that.

"And apparently the morning after, he woke up and she was gone, along with every piece of the tux he rented. Underwear and all." I chuckle, biting down on my lip to keep my laughter under control. " Had to call every single one of his brothers to bring him a set of spare clothes." I'm laughing so hard, I can barely get the words out. "And the only person who answered his call was John. Apparently, there were some *pretty* desperate voicemails left." I glance at Evan who's wearing a scowl.

"Damn," Amelia says, her eyes wide. "Who does that?" She chuckles.

"Stella! He would've been better off wrapping a sheet around his waist and making a run for it. Because they're never going to let him live it down," I tell her. We're both bent over laughing, and Evan isn't amused, but we continue talking about it like he's not there.

"Don't you think I've gotten enough shit from my brothers about this weekend? Just *had* to bring it to work too. Go ahead, laugh it up. I'm glad I could amuse you both." Evan shakes his head before handing the file to a passing nurse.

Amelia and I continue poking fun when we hear Evan suck in a deep breath. I look up and realize the new doctor is stepping off the elevator with a lost look in her eye. Trying to make a good example, Amelia and I straighten up but continue giggling at Evan's expense.

"Who's that?" Amelia asks, looking back and forth between us.

"I'm pretty sure that's the new ER doctor they told us about last month. Dr. Emily Bell. She just finished her residency and has to work under Evan."

I look over at Evan who'll be training her considering he's the attending supervisor. Evan's been working as a emergency medicine doctor for several years and when Dr. Lockhart retired recently the hospital had to find a replacement.

Evan becomes stiff as a board, and I elbow him. "Lighten up before you scare the poor girl away."

He stifles a sarcastic laugh, and his entire demeanor changes as she stops at the nurses' station. I hear her ask for Dr. Bishop, and he rolls his eyes with a deep groan.

"What's wrong with you?" I ask him.

His jaw tightens. "That's *her*. That's the woman who stole my goddamn clothes," he says under his breath, shaking his head and scrubbing a hand over his scruffy jawline.

Amelia and I both turn our heads and get a good look at her. She's gorgeous, stunning actually. Her chestnut brown hair is pulled back into a long, sleek ponytail, and she's wearing a black pencil skirt so tight it could be painted on. Her cream blouse is tucked into her skirt, revealing a small waist. Her slender legs are accompanied by red heels at least three inches high. Black glasses frame her dark eyes and the deep red lipstick she's wearing says she doesn't take anyone's shit—the ultimate man eater.

As I glance back at Evan, I'm dying inside trying to hold it together. *What are the odds?*

"It was her?" I ask, confused. "Emily?" My jaw drops. "I thought mystery girl's name was Stella?"

"So did I," he says between gritted teeth, and now it all makes sense. Ultimate man eater confirmed, except she chews them up and spits them out.

Evan shakes his head and crosses his arms over his broad chest. The air in the room seems to dissipate and is replaced with thick awkwardness. Someone points out Evan, and she smiles then walks toward us. Once closer, recognition and maybe a hint of regret flash across Emily's face before she pushes the emotions away and continues forward.

Before she can even open her mouth, Evan speaks. "Emily? That's *real cute*." Evan throws shade her way.

She sucks in a deep breath and releases it. "And you're *Dr. Bishop*, aren't you?"

Going to work just got *way* more interesting.

AVAILABLE NOW

Continue the Bishop Brothers series with Evan Bishop in *Needing Him*

Evan Bishop is your typical hotshot doctor.
Hardass, brooding, and all business.

Instead of working on the family ranch, Evan broke the mold and became an ER doctor. He's good with his hands—in more ways than one—smart as a whip and is the definition of God's gift to women. Being a gentleman is in his Southern roots, but that doesn't mean he isn't flawed. Exclusive dating has never been a top priority and his tragic past makes him stay at arm's length. Deciding to let loose for a wild night, he takes a page from the Bishop brother's relationship book and hooks up with a mysterious girl he'll never have to see again, which is perfect for this self-proclaimed bachelor.

Emily Bell is a city girl through and through but is determined to get away from her family and past. All she wants is a fresh start and to make a name for herself in the medical field. No random hookups and no dating coworkers—that's her new motto after being burned time and again. When she agrees to attend a wedding as a plus-one, she's soon ditched and left to drink solo—but not for long. Mr. Suit is the ultimate temptation with his Southern charm, messy blond hair, and irresistible sex appeal. Everything about him screams bad news, but he makes her reconsider her rules just for one night.

After all, some rules are made to be broken.

They want the same thing—one night of passion then they'll go their separate ways. No cuddling afterward. No next day phone calls. No awkward goodbyes. Too bad the universe has other plans—one that'll be obvious when they report to work on Monday morning.

ABOUT THE AUTHOR

Brooke Cumberland and Lyra Parish are a duo of romance authors who teamed up under the *USA Today* pseudonym, Kennedy Fox. They share a love of Hallmark movies, overpriced coffee, and making TikToks. When they aren't bonding over romantic comedies, they like to brainstorm new book ideas. One day in 2016, they decided to collaborate under a pseudonym and have some fun creating new characters that'll make you blush and your heart melt. Happily ever afters guaranteed!

CONNECT WITH US

Find us on our website:
kennedyfoxbooks.com

Subscribe to our newsletter:
kennedyfoxbooks.com/newsletter

facebook.com/kennedyfoxbooks

twitter.com/kennedyfoxbooks

instagram.com/kennedyfoxbooks

amazon.com/author/kennedyfoxbooks

goodreads.com/kennedyfox

bookbub.com/authors/kennedy-fox

BOOKS BY
KENNEDY FOX

DUET SERIES (BEST READ IN ORDER)

CHECKMATE DUET SERIES

ROOMMATE DUET SERIES

LAWTON RIDGE DUET SERIES

INTERCONNECTED STAND-ALONES

MAKE ME SERIES

BISHOP BROTHERS SERIES

CIRCLE B RANCH SERIES

LOVE IN ISOLATION SERIES

Find the entire Kennedy Fox reading order at
Kennedyfoxbooks.com/reading-order

Find all of our current freebies at
Kennedyfoxbooks.com/freeromance

Printed in Great Britain
by Amazon

81593792R00202